Love in the A Shau

A Novel by

Denis J. LaComb

Love in the A Shau

This is a work of fiction. The characters depicted herein are products of the author's imagination. Any resemblance to actual persons, living or dead, is purely coincidental.

Some of the locations depicted in this book are real, but the characters and incidents are imaginary.

Published by BAMs² Publishing

A division of Sharden LLC

Credits:

Book cover design by Vida Raine

ISBN: 0988420341

ISBN-13: 978-0-9884203-4-2

This story is dedicated to Sharon, my wife, friend and life-long partner. To my children, Brian and Melanie, who have always been supportive of my ideas and endeavors - although they certainly questioned some of them … a lot of the time.

To Michelle for all her help with book design, editing, site development, and numerous other publishing endeavors. To Deb for creating such a fantastic song for my book trailer. To Vida who was so helpful with web development, editing and guiding my first excursion into blogging.

To my sister Marlene, and her friends Judy and Connie, for their honest and insightful comments on my first draft. To Denise and Ruth for their constructive criticism. The women's comments were monumental in keeping this project going.

CONTENTS

"In war, there are no
unwounded soldiers."

- José Narosky

Summer after High School: 1966

Blue-Eyed Beauty Queen

The Italian boy was sure he'd get into Colleen's dress before the night was over. After an evening of strolling through the piazzas and other landmarks of Rome's finest attractions, Roberto made his move. He'd performed his amorous maneuvers many times before. This time would be no different. He casually walked the beautiful young woman back to his favorite hunting ground…the Spanish Steps.

There, along with other lovers, foreign and domestic, the twenty-something bon vivant began to work his magic. Unlike many of the other hustlers on the steps, Roberto had refined his seductive techniques until they worked like clockwork. He found a spot on the steps far enough away from the others that they wouldn't be noticed. They sat down and he wrapped his arm around her shoulder.

"Your dress is so beautiful."

While still being stylish, Colleen wasn't a slave to fashion. Her new dress, a Valentino signature piece, was obscenely expensive. Colleen's mother had insisted that she must have it for her time spent touring Italy.

The wine had begun to take effect on Colleen. She was happy and giggling and blissfully unaware of Roberto's casual arm on her shoulder. Smiling smugly to himself, the dark-skinned lover felt halfway home even before he began to slide his hand down toward his date's firm breasts.

Colleen leaned back against her date and laughed at the other couples. Roberto lowered his hand as he whispered in Colleen's ear. He spoke just softly enough to make her lean back even closer against him. He blew softly into the auburn hair that rested on her shoulders. Casually, he ran his hand up and down her arm and caressed her neck with his soothing touch. Colleen was practically purring when his hand slid gracefully to rest on her breast. He squeezed the firmness in his hand.

"Di neutralità!" Colleen snapped as she pushed her date away, "Oh, no you don't, buster!"

Roberto caught himself before falling backwards and steadied his hands on the steps. The Italian had been there before. He wasn't about to be dissuaded by this initial rebuff. Roberto leaned in again, whispering "Colleen, darling," bringing his hand back up to Colleen's chest.

"No, dico sul serio," Colleen slapped his hand away for a second time.

This time her reaction was stronger and unmistakable. She meant business and fondling wasn't in the cards for that night. "No, I mean it, Roberto!"

"I am so sorry! You misunderstand me. I like you." The hustler flashed his trusty pearly whites framed by light olive skin. "I like you a lot. I want to be your friend. Will you be my friend?" He moved in for a third attempt.

Colleen laughed, this time completely in control. She may have been lightheaded from the wine, but not enough to make a fool out of herself. It didn't matter that most of the other women around them were either making out or allowing their dates to round bases like major leaguers. Colleen wasn't about to be felt up by some gigolo she'd just met.

The redhead elegantly sprang to her feet and put her hands on her hips. "I have to return to my hotel. My parents expected me back by now. Thank you for the dinner and the wine and the fractured conversation. If you're ever in the states, don't bother to look me up." She took a step closer to the Italian leaning against the stone railing, nursing his pride. "Don't worry about escorting me home. I can get my own cab. Arrivederci!"

She left her date to stifle his arousal with cupped hands.

Upon arriving at the Plaza Pierzio, Colleen breezed through the lobby ignoring the calls of several other tour members who had spotted her from the bar. She was angry and embarrassed at the same time. She had no idea why she had put herself in such an uncomfortable situation. The arranged date was a disaster waiting to happen and Colleen had the fingerprints on her dress to prove it. She slipped into the elevator, narrowly avoiding a boy from the group that had been following her like a lost puppy the entire holiday.

Her parents were on the sofa watching television when she entered. "They don't have anything worth watching," her father announced as Colleen walked in. "And most of it is in Italian," her mother added.

"Did you have a nice time?" Mary Rose asked her daughter.

"Yes, Mom, he was very nice … until he turned Italian!"

Completely missing her daughter's comment, Mrs. Fitzpatrick smiled and said "See, my cousin was right. She said you and her nephew would hit it off. Was his English good enough to understand?"

"Oh, yes, Mother, his English was just fine. I understood him all too well.

I knew just what was going on in his mind … and elsewhere."

"Will you be seeing him again?"

"Probably not. He's got a lot of school work to finish before he can go out again. Besides, I think he has a stiff muscle to deal with."

"I don't understand."

"That's too bad," Colleen's father interrupted. "He seemed like such a nice young man."

"I'd say he was probably your typical Roman male. He certainly fit the description of most Italian males I've seen in the movies."

"I don't understand, dear, what are you saying?"

"Nothing; he was fine." Colleen grabbed a Vogue, Rome Edition, off the coffee table and began flipping through it for ideas of other Roman adventures - preferably not involving anyone of the opposite sex.

Colleen kicked off her shoes and snuggled into the corner of the long sofa. She leaned toward her Dad and whispered in his ear. "Thanks so much for this trip, Daddy. It's been wonderful and such a nice way to spend our summer vacation before I go off to college."

Roberto wasn't the first man who wanted to score with the beautiful and classy Colleen Catherine Fitzpatrick. Her vibrant personality, charm and quick wit had attracted more than her fair share of young suitors. Most settled for being her friend. A few had aspired to go further; their goal being the Promised Land - but none had gotten there.

Deep inside, Colleen knew the right thing to do. Going diamond for a high school flame wasn't it, even if she liked him a lot.

It all fit a very consistent pattern for Colleen. She was practical, smart, and sensible. She was too leery of lingering high school romances to be distracted from the opportunities that would unfold once she began college in the fall.

This European trip was the perfect break between Rochester Senior High School and the collegiate adventures that awaited her in the Twin Cities. A little distraction like the roaming fingers of Roberto was only a minor bump in the proverbial road ahead.

Colleen Fitzpatrick was born upper crust and she knew it. Her father was a noted surgeon at the Mayo Clinic. She was raised on what they called 'Pill Hill'; the new development outside of Rochester proper where most doctors, lawyers and CEOs made their home. Her mother came from old East Coast money.

Her strata of society held its wealth in high regard but never in a manner considered too ostentatious. Understatement was the overriding principle adhered to and embraced among her kind. The homes, the cars, and the clothes spoke only of fine taste and refinement. It was all second nature for Colleen. She had the self-confidence and knowledge to carry herself as she was expected to - and feel comfortable in the process.

She knew the kind of young men her parents would approve of and those they would turn a cold eye toward. Arthur and Mary Rose were both confident they had nothing to worry about. Colleen was a good girl that would not disappoint. They knew it and Colleen knew it.

Great Expectations

The Time magazine, dated April 15th 1966, lay tossed aside on the ground. Across its bright red cover, a banner touted the hottest city in existence - London, England. They subtitled it 'the swinging city'. Inside, articles went on about happenings on Carnaby Street, the latest English fashions, the glorious bands, and other wondrous things happening in swinging London. It was the place to be and to be seen.

No one was reading the magazine at the moment. It lay crushed under the thick thigh of Summer Blaze as she thrust her hips up against her boyfriend. Over and over again, she ground her round middle up to meet Daniels penetrating push. She moaned and groaned and rolled her eyes back in her head. Daniel ogled his rotund girlfriend in bewilderment. If she wasn't dying, she was certainly in a world of sexual bliss.

They were having sex for the first time and it wasn't going well. After months of persuasion, Samantha Berkowitz (aka Summer Blaze) had convinced Daniel to consummate their friendship the only way she knew how.

It was over before Daniel started to feel any build up inside. Summer was a pro. A quick roll in the grass after the last day of school might be adventurous work for an amateur like Daniel. For Summer, it was just confirmation of their casual fondness for one another.

She had Daniel on his knees, out and ready for penetration, before he realized what he was supposed to be doing. She quickly moved under him and guided the projectile on its flight path and scored a direct hit on target. Summer controlled the thrust of the missile until it exploded as intended.

Daniel was left breathing heavily and peering down at his shrinking member as Summer simply shifted out from under him; adjusting her skirt to cover her private parts. She grabbed the Time Magazine from beneath her bottom and briefly skimmed the pages. Tossing it aside, she reached into her rainbow colored sack and pulled out an old copy of the New Musical Express, a British pop music weekly.

"Lay next to me Daniel. I want to see what they say about the Beatles … I want to go there so badly Daniel. You should come with me!"

"Sure, Summer." Daniel moved over to lean against a tree nearby.

"Don't you want to sit by me?"

"Just keep reading and I'll watch for anyone passing by. Tell me all about this London town of yours." Daniel barely concealed his amusement at Summer's fascination with that foreign city.

"It says that the pirate radio station called Swinging Radio England coined the term 'Swinging London'. Did you know that?"

"No, Summer, I didn't know that. So where did they get the name swinging?"

Summer frowned. "Daniel, don't you know anything? Swinging means hip, with it, you know…very fashionable. Vogue Magazine called it the most swinging city in the world last year."

"*Vogue*? You read *Vogue*?"

"Oh, stuff it, Daniel."

"So, what else does it say about London?"

Summer glanced up at Daniel to gauge his interest. "'The edgy cults of James Dean and the Angry Young Men are done. Skiffle and coffee bars have passed their time. Bill Haley and his version of rock and roll are over. Now it's the Beatles and Rolling Stones that are on the vanguard of a new age of British rock music.'"

Daniel was tickled by Summer's enthusiastic read of the magazine. She was a true hippie at heart as well as in dress. In addition to being far more advanced in sexual ventures; Summer had done some drug taking and explored a lot more far-out, esoteric ideas than Daniel. She relished discovering new trends, new music and what the hip kids were doing after school.

They both came from similar dysfunctional backgrounds and shared a longing for something better in their lives. They were just going about it in two very different ways.

"Sounds like your kind of place, flower child. No place for a badass greaser like me." They both laughed. Daniel stared out at the river boulevard that ran by the woods. Like a black gash among the swath of green trees and bushes, the pathway wound its way past the open field of grass and toward the college that Daniel planned to attend in the fall.

The College of St. Paul was one of the oldest colleges in the state, and only one of three in the state that admitted just men. It attracted a wide variety of students including the wealthy from out East who were attracted to its Midwestern business and medical connections.

Aside from the elite of local high schools, there was also a small minority who were admitted only because of the school's strong religious conviction that the poor and undereducated needed a chance to succeed as well. Daniel fit into the latter category. He was just plain lucky to have gotten in.

This summer would be the culmination of four years of struggle in high school and the dissolution of his past life. Daniel was moving on. Many of his old high school friends weren't.

Daniel would be entering college without Summer as his sidekick and sometime companion. She would be gone to someplace within a month or so; never to return to the Twin Cities, she claimed. This was their last summer together and probably their last time as soulful intimates whose relics of a past life left little to encourage them on into the future.

The grassy knoll where they had chosen to slap bellies was a known hangout for drinking, pot smoking, and the occasional sexual encounter; but Daniel didn't personally know anyone that had actually done it so close to the river boulevard.

Summer grabbed her panties and nonchalantly stuffed them in her bag.

"Come on, Droopy, you got what you wanted; just sit next to me while I read about my next destination - Swinging London."

Daniel looked over at his short, overweight girlfriend and shook his head. Summer had beautiful brown eyes even though she wasn't very pretty. But she was a confidant who would listen to all his stupid dreams and not go apeshit in the process. She encouraged him even when she wasn't sure what he was rambling on about.

"I really want to go there, Daniel!" She pointed at the picture of two women in their mini-skirts outside of a Carnaby Shop. "I want to hop a plane and *just go* to London!"

"Summer, you don't have any money. You don't have a job. Your parents would never let you go."

"Then I'll go to New York."

"New York? You don't know how to drive. How would you even get to the coast?... Hitchhike, alone?!"

"Yes, or San Francisco. They've got an art school in Frisco! I did well in art class and they'll let almost anyone in."

"What about Swinging London?"

"It can wait until I've got the money to fly first class - or maybe I'll take a tramp steamer like Jack London did."

"Now you're talking nonsense, Summer. You'll probably get a job at Burnick's Department Store downtown and end up a senior clerk or something like that." Daniel wrapped his arm around her. "But keep dreaming big, girl. That's what I love about you."

"And what'll you do after you graduate from that snobbish college of yours?" Summer pushed Daniel's arm away, laughed, and grabbed her crotch. "Maybe you'll marry some rich virgin from that girl's school and have tons of perfect little stuck-up babies."

"You're something else, Berkowitz."

"*Blaze*, dipshit! Call me *Summer Blaze*. That's my name now. Berkowitz is my parents' name!"

"Pulling a Bob Dylan, are you?"

They both laughed and Daniel put his arm back around her. He looked out at the people meandering down the pathway; some lost in their own thoughts - others going someplace in a hurry. "It was good, Summer, while it lasted. I'm glad we became friends in high school. You made the time go a lot easier. We're two of a kind, you know. I'll be sorry to see you go, but when you do go out West or East, I think you'll do just fine … love beads and all."

"It was good, wasn't it, Daniel?" They both went back to watching the people streaming by.

Who are these people? Daniel wondered. *Are they students, executives ... or just working stiffs like me?* He wanted to share his thoughts with Summer like old times; about college and what might lie beyond, but he knew that would be a waste of time. They were on two different paths now.

"Summer, we'll stay in touch," Daniel lied. "Two outlaws like us gotta stick together."

"Wanna try it again? I think I can make you hard."

"No … I've got to start the evening shift at old man Dryer's grocery store. Gotta break in the new high schoolers tonight. Being a shift manager is a lot of responsibility."

"I'm gonna stay here for awhile and read more about my future hometown." Summer waved Daniel off.

Summer was still engrossed in the Time Magazine as Daniel hopped on his bike. As he rode away, he replayed his first sexual encounter and smiled to himself. Awkward though it was, he enjoyed having sex with Summer. It was hardly the kind of experience to brag about, but he liked being that close to a woman.

Freshmen Year: 1966-1967

Beanies & Dingbats

Orientation Week at Mother of the Lake College followed an age old pattern; trying to distinguish itself from other colleges in the Twin Cities. The week was meant to introduce freshmen to their esteemed school with an emphasis on its rich history and many traditions.

It began with a Freshman Tea on Sunday right after noon mass. By that evening all the parents were gone and the young women were on their own. The rest of the week brought placement tests, dormitory assignments, and purchasing books at the student bookstore. There were orientation classes covering everything from extracurricular activities to volunteer opportunities. And of course, time for a mixer or two with those fellows down the road, the College of St. Paul boys.

Colleen met her new roommate, Peggy Scranton, the first day on campus. They had a mutual admiration for one another with a stubborn competitive streak between them from the start. They were both eager to make their respective marks academically and socially - with a greater emphasis on social for Peggy and academic for Colleen.

Like Colleen, Peggy came from a very well-to-do family in the Twin Cities. She'd gone to Blake School, an Ivy League prep school for the affluent and entitled. Her family lived in Edina, a decidedly upscale neighborhood just southwest of downtown Minneapolis. Her father was a business executive and her mother, a stay at home mom. Peggy had all the energy and charm of Colleen but with a bit more spunk that Colleen hadn't quite mastered. Together they made a very formidable pair. Their shared laughter at some of the silly formalities of Orientation Week reverberated down the hallway of their dorm.

One evening during that first week, Colleen and Peggy were sequestered in their dorm room, pouring over class assignments and perusing the pile of books that towered over their small study desks.

"Can you believe the number of books we have to read this first year?" Peggy asked.

"Hold on, it only gets more complicated as the year goes on. I've heard that by the second semester, the number of books we have to read doubles or triples for most classes."

"Speaking of the challenges ahead, are you going to the mixer this Friday?"

"I guess, are you?"

"Absolutely. We're supposed to get involved in extracurricular activities, aren't we? Going to the mixer is a great way to meet new friends from down the road and perhaps a future lifemate."

"Lifemate? Is that what we're calling them now?"

"Oh, Colleen, you know what I mean."

"Yeah right, Peggy."

"Anyway, let's plan on it. I've got a darling red dress that will catch everyone's attention, and French cut undies to go with it. What do you have to wear? If you don't have anything, I've got a ton of clothes you can choose from."

"Peggy, what I wear to the mixer is the least of my concerns right now. Journalism 101 is my top priority, followed by Chemistry and Algebra. After that, I can worry about what to wear."

"Suit yourself, Miss Academic. We all have our priorities."

They laughed and went back to studying.

Colleen kept leafing through the pile of reading material in front of her until she came to a colored flyer. "Oh my God!"

"What? What is it?"

"I can't believe it!"

"What, Colleen?"

"Nancy. She's going to be *here*. She's the guest speaker during Founder's Day. I can't believe it."

"Nancy who?"

"Are you kidding, Peggy? Nancy Dickerson, the news correspondent. I've been following her career since high school. She's exactly who I want to be. She's a brilliant journalist. She's thorough in her research. She cuts to the chase in her interviews and she writes wonderful articles. She's even been on television. She is everything I love in a journalist. I can't believe she's going to be *here*."

"I assume that means you're going to Founder's Day?"

"Peggy, I wouldn't miss it for the world. It's being held at the St. Paul

Hilton. Want to come with me? You'll love her, believe me, she's great."

"Sure, Colleen, count me in. I've always wanted to get the inside scoop on Washington and what goes on inside the beltway."

The first freshmen mixer was quaint, and very boring. It was more like a high school sock hop rather than the elevated collegiate affair promised on the flyers. The boys from St. Paul College lined one side of the gym and the girls from Mother of the Lake, the other. Even Peggy's bright red dress didn't bring on the boys.

The second mixer was a little better attended, but neither Colleen nor Peggy made any headway in meeting new boys. The more sophisticated men could pick out the more experienced girls in a second. They made haste connecting and securing those eager women for the evening. The rest of the girls, Colleen and Peggy included, were left to dance with each other or line the walls and sit in chairs for most of the evening. It was another bust.

Peggy told Colleen about the first officially sanctioned dance of the school year to be held next. It was not just for freshmen this time. All students from both colleges would be welcome to attend, and it would be at the College of St. Paul gymnasium. There would be decorations, refreshments, and a really good band.

"It can't hurt to try again," Peggy urged Colleen who by then had little interest in trying for a third time to meet some of St. Paul's finest. Colleen shrugged her shoulders. "You're too desperate, Peggy. Boys can sense that a mile away. Why don't we just skip the dance and focus on our studies?"

"Colleen Catherine, I am not desperate and I do intend to give it a try - with or without you." Peggy gave her roommate a broad bright smile. "So won't you come along with me? Please!"

Colleen put her book down and let the pages flip over her hand. She flicked her finger from under the cover then slid the book across her desk. "Yes, my desperate friend, I will go to the dance just to make sure you don't offer yourself to the first male specimen that comes along. But I'm not staying if it's like the first two."

"This time will be different, just you wait and see. Let's see what you have to wear." She walked over to Colleen's closet and opened the door. "You didn't tell me you've got a closet full of designer outfits!" She began leafing through a stack of Colleen's sweaters. "Oh, and *look* at your *brassieres*!"

"Peggy!"

"Well, not everyone gets sent off to college with outfits from Mary Quant."

"My mother insisted on buying those at Bazaar, Mary's store in London," She got up and reluctantly walked over to Peggy. "And remember what I said, Peggy. If it's a bust, we leave."

"Now wear something cute, but not white," Peggy cautioned Colleen.

"Not white?"

"Your underwear, silly. If you wear white they can see your underwear."

"Desperate!" Colleen shook her head and went back to her studies.

College of St. Paul, Fall Semester

Freshmen orientation on the College of St. Paul campus mimicked Mother of the Lake very closely. There were the mandatory classes on academic life, study habits, social events and faculty expectations that far exceeded those of high school. In short, it was a fast-paced introduction to the wild, wonderful, wacky world of higher education; sans the lecture on sex, alcohol and recreational drugs.

Pep rallies were designed to instill in the malleable freshman brains the rich tradition of the school's sporting history. Clubs, social activities and fraternity pledging would come later in the week.

Registration Week proved to be Daniel's first collegiate test filled with card table stations for class assignments, dorm selection and extracurricular activities. There were notices to pick up and stuff in his backpack, cards to sign and bills to be paid on the spot. There was even a table to sign up for lectures from visiting professors on Saturday and Sunday mornings. *Amazing*, Daniel thought, *college goes on seven days a week around here.*

After traversing the minefield of table stations and overzealous sophomores eager to help, Daniel found himself alone in the campus quadrangle, trying to catch his breath. He grabbed a corner bench and watched the other freshmen, most with their parents in tow, passing by him. He should have been so lucky.

Daniel felt alone among the milling crowds of confused, scattered freshmen and TA's answering their multitude of questions. Daniel had pretty much stumbled through, faked and barely passed the academic requirements to be accepted to college. He'd missed academic probation by only a few points and knew he was on notice to improve his grades or seek an education elsewhere.

Daniel got up and headed for the bookstore. It was certain to be another onslaught of pushing and jockeying for position as he tried to buy his schoolbooks for the year.

St. Paul's bookstore turned out to be the challenge Daniel had expected. As Daniel jostled his way through the crowd he couldn't help but be amazed at the tenacity shown by his opposition to find books and other classroom materials.

To identify and humiliate the freshmen, the upperclassmen had a longstanding tradition of making all freshmen wear multi-colored (in the school colors) beanies for the first two weeks of the fall semester. In addition to the beanies, all freshmen were to be addressed as 'Dingbats'. Daniel took it all in stride. If this was the price to be paid for being a part of this world, he would gladly accept the silliness of it all.

There was only one other freshman that Daniel knew from high school. Michael was more gifted academically than Daniel, but sorely lacked the same desire that fueled Daniel's presence on campus. Short and rotund, Michael was labeled a slacker by his friends and enemies alike. It was a moniker he wore with pride.

As they had planned, Daniel met up with Michael in the campus coffee shop after his foray through the bookstore. Michael, ever the old kindred spirit, had two cups of coffee waiting as Daniel walked in. He was holding something in his lap.

"What's that?"

"Jack Daniels for the soul, my friend. Want something to lighten up your coffee?"

"What? Are you frickin' nuts, man? Stuff it. Jeez, if they see us with that booze, they'll kick us both outta here for sure."

Michael frowned and pushed the flask back into his pocket. Daniel leaned in close to his friend. "You are a putz, Michael. I mean *certifiable*."

"Well, BFD! How'd you do at the bookstore?"

"Got screwed."

"Typical, they screw everybody. I heard the only ones who don't get screwed are the seniors."

"Why's that?"

"Because by the time they become seniors, they've learned how to play the game and get their books during their junior summer. They have the pick of the crop. So they come to campus locked and loaded, ready for class."

Michael proved to be a good counterbalance for Daniel. He was bright while Daniel certainly didn't see himself that way. He was an extrovert, while Daniel was more reserved. Michael was sarcastic and rude at times. Daniel was the peacemaker. Daniel worked on his friend's social skills and Michael educated Daniel on ways to survive his first year in college. Daniel had to study long and hard to grasp his coursework and Michael hardly ever opened a book, but he was always there for Daniel to clarify a point or help with his homework.

"So what the hell are two losers like us doing here?" Michael asked Daniel as he sucked in his gut and tried to get comfortable in their narrow booth. "Did you see all those jerks by the Student Union just snapping at us tadpoles this morning?"

"Dingbats."

"Whatever we're supposed to be called."

"Oh, Michael, it's just part of the pecking order. We'll probably be just as obnoxious when it's our turn"

"Not me! Most of these freshmen are just ankle biters, hardly been off their Mama's tit. You and I aren't like them. We've been in the real world."

"Unfortunately."

"What do you mean?"

"Michael, it doesn't matter. Nobody is admiring the notches on your belt. Or how much hooch you consumed last night. They're looking for academic excellence. Remember what their brochure said? It's not your experiences with the opposite sex that counts here."

"I've got as much smarts as any other slug here, but I don't intend to spend all my time in the library with my nose buried in some book. I mean college is supposed to be a blast, man. I intend to soak up as much of the culture as I can."

"Culture - you?"

"Ah, shit twice and die. You've seen those Playboy articles about college campuses. I mean, the women over at Mother of the Lake are just *waiting* for it."

"It?"

"Those girls are looking for a real man to show them the ropes. You know what I mean."

"You are a troubled person, Michael. Focus on getting an education and if you score with the ladies that'll just be an added benefit."

"Let's split and get some brew, man"

"At ten in the morning, are you nuts? Come on, Michael, you've got to cut that shit out. You're drinking far too much. Besides, I don't have any bread. Old man Dryer hasn't paid me yet."

"So, are you going to the dance in a couple of weeks?"

"What dance?"

"Oh man, the first official dance of the semester. It's not just for freshmen like the first two stupid mixers. There'll be sophomores and juniors there. Fresh meat! Let's go to that one."

"Calm down, boy. Yes, I'll go with you. But right now I've got a three o'clock and some other stuff to get done before tonight. If we go to that thing and there's not some quality chicks, I'll be ditching you to hit the books."

Michael put his hand on Daniel's shoulder. "Don't take this college stuff so seriously, Daniel, my boy. I don't and look where it's gotten me so far. Booze and snatch, man, booze and snatch."

Daniel shook his head as he thought about the free and easy approach Michael was taking toward his classes. It wasn't smart academically but Michael didn't seem to care. His grades weren't a concern to him. Having as much fun as possible was his priority. That wasn't Daniel's cup of tea but nor was it his business either. If Michael didn't change his ways, Daniel was convinced he would never last his freshman year.

Footprints of Birds in the Sky

One benefit of attending the first official dance was the freedom to officially ditch their beanies and wear some real clothes. Colleen and Peggy couldn't wait to dress like mature women without the yellow-striped bowls on their heads.

After an initial attempt to circumvent the dress code, Colleen settled on a muted knit skirt and a soft blue sweater. A unique brown belt, a gift from her grandmother, tied the two pieces together. Her crisp white blouse beneath the sweater was open at the collar. She had a simple silver chain around her neck and her auburn hair had been slightly curled at the ends. Just to satisfy Peggy she even dabbled a tiny bit of perfume around her neck.

For her part Peggy was dressed to the nines and on the hunt. She wore a simple black dress that she'd had altered to be shorter than normal. Her black stockings had done a good job of hiding the shortness of the dress from the prying eyes of the nuns. She had a gold belt around her waist and she wore her hair plain and straight. She almost looked like Mary Travers from the folk trio, Peter, Paul, and Mary, who had played at the college just the week before.

They could hear the dance music half a block away. As they approached the gymnasium, they saw a large crowd milling outside the main entrance.

“Are you sure you want to do this?” Colleen asked Peggy.

“Absolutely, I wouldn’t miss this dance for anything.” Colleen shrugged her shoulders and followed Peggy into the strobe lights and thundering maelstrom of noise.

The gymnasium floor was crowded with freshmen, men and women. There were a few sophomore and junior men circling the crowd like sharks trying to pick out the most attractive women. Only the refreshment stand was packed with young men eager to impress their dates with a coke. Colleen was amused by the maneuverings going on around her.

“I thought college dances were supposed to be different!” she yelled at Peggy.

Peggy tilted her head, cupped her ear and shouted back, “What?”

Colleen shrugged her shoulders and gave a dismissive wave. She motioned for Peggy to follow her as she began weaving her way through the crowds toward the bleachers across the room.

Seeking some refuge from the huge standup speakers that were blanketing the gym floor with waves of rolling decibels, the pair found a less-loud spot along the back wall bleachers. They settled in to watch the theatrics around them.

Initially, it seemed like the dance would end up a disaster like the first two mixers; a lot of the underclassmen followed their past performances by hugging the walls and bleachers. Collectively they were envying the students on the dance floor but weren’t about to venture out by themselves. It didn’t take long for both Colleen and Peggy to find a couple of kindred souls among their large freshman class of women. Several girls joined them on the dance floor and together they danced through several numbers with glee and laughter.

If the boys didn’t want to join in, Colleen didn’t care. She and Peggy were having a good time and enjoying themselves. After one long and ruckus rock and roll number, the two girls collapsed on the front bleacher laughing at their own gyrating antics.

“Great dancing,” a voice said directly behind Colleen. She turned to see two young men sitting several rows up, looking down at her and Peggy.

One was overweight and dressed like a slob. He was grinning ear-to-ear and seemed a bit out of sorts.

The other young man was strikingly handsome. He wore his hair a bit too long and over his ears. His clothes were neither preppy nor casual but rather more work-orientated. Yet his jeans were pressed with a crease and his penny loafers appeared to shine in the gym light. He had on a dark brown sports coat and a white shirt underneath. Colleen could tell by its cut and the way it fit his torso that he was muscular and well built. He looked a little out of place at a college dance but it was his eyes that caught Colleen's attention and held it.

His eyes were deep brown and penetrating. They spoke of interest and sincerity and curiosity. Colleen doubted he was a student from St. Paul College and had probably snuck into the dance. *He isn't hard on the eyes,* she thought.

"Thanks," Colleen answered with a quick smile and turned back to Peggy. They smiled at one another.

"No, I mean it! You two were really good," the voice spoke up again.

Colleen looked at Peggy then back up at the two young men. "Again, thanks," she said, allowing no expression to escape her face.

"Mind if we join you?"

"Suit yourself," Peggy answered. A lip curl told Colleen of Peggy's true intent.

The two young men arose in unison and stepped down the bleachers. They seated themselves one row up from the girls. Michael was first, plopping himself down right across from Peggy. Daniel followed suit but ended up further away from Colleen.

"Hi, my name's Michael," he said to Peggy, "Edina, I'm guessing?" He wore a deadpan expression on his face. He tilted his head as if to ask the same question again.

"How did you know?"

"Do you know what Edina stands for?" Without waiting for Peggy's response, he answered, "Every Day I Need Attention!"

The joke was met with stone cold silence from both girls. Undeterred, Michael turned toward Colleen. "And where are you from?"

"Rochester, do you have a joke about that too?"

"Pill Hill … and do you know what they call people from Lake Minnetonka?"

"That's enough, Michael," Daniel said, embarrassed by his companion's antics. Michael ignored him and turned back to Colleen and Peggy.

"Other than that, Mrs. Lincoln, how was the play?" he asked in a bellowing voice and then burst into laughter.

"Enough already, Michael. I have to apologize for my so-called friend. Michael's normally semi-polite, but he's been toking again."

Michael smacked his fist against Daniel's shoulder and kept laughing.

"What does that mean?" Peggy asked in a serious tone of voice.

Colleen started to laugh. "Oh come on, Peggy, you have to admit that was pretty funny. Sick humor, but funny - I've never heard that definition of Edina before."

"No, I mean … well, what about Pill Hill?"

"Doesn't bother me. That's what they call our neighborhood anyway. So what?"

"I'm Daniel," Daniel interrupted. "What are your names?"

Peggy gave Colleen a quick glance and then turned to Daniel, ignoring Michael. "I'm Peggy and this is Colleen. Do you go to St. Paul College?"

"Yeah, we're both freshmen here. You?"

"Colleen and I are too. At Mother of the Lake, I mean. Did you go to the first two mixers?"

"No," Michael answered. "We wanted to see if we could mix it up with some upperclass gals so we came to this one instead."

"Well, have you?" asked Colleen.

"No, that was Michael's idea. I just came to make new friends."

"Any new friends then?" Colleen asked.

"Not yet, but I'm feeling good about this encounter so far."

Colleen wrinkled her eyebrows at Daniel. "You make it sound like you're looking for a conquest!"

"Colleen!" Peggy said.

Colleen laughed and turned back to Daniel.

"Well?"

"Just looking to make friends," Daniel said, locking eyes with Colleen.

Before her clothes, before her stylish hair, before her firm and trim body, it was Colleen's expressive eyes that had grabbed Daniel's attention. Now he and the beautiful redhead were exploring each other's eyes, oblivious to everything around them. Daniel could feel his heart racing and tiny beads of perspiration begin to form.

The music started up again and Michael stood up. "Want to dance?" he asked Peggy.

“Sure, I guess.” Leaving Colleen and Daniel alone, they made their way to the dance floor.

“Would you like to dance?” Daniel asked as he stepped down to her row and sat down next to her.

“No, I wore myself out on that last one. I just want to sit for a while.”

Daniel surveyed the dance floor as it filled with students, some of whom were dancing and others who were just faking it. He turned to Colleen who hadn’t given him eye contact since he sat down next to her.

“I like your outfit. It compliments your hair color and your complexion.”

Colleen turned to Daniel with a surprised look on her face. “That’s a strange thing to say to a girl you’ve just met. Are you a clothing designer or artist? Or just on the hunt?”

“Colleen,” Daniel said with mock seriousness. “I told you I’m just here to make friends. I’m not on the hunt. Jeez.”

“Daniel, I’m kidding! Relax. Don’t take what I say so seriously.” Colleen laughed and her reddish auburn hair swirled around her smiling face. “OK,” she said suddenly, “I’m ready to dance.”

Daniel was up and extending his hand to Colleen in an instant. He led her out to the dance floor and quickly put his arm around her waist. At first They expertly avoided the interest of the strict chaperones, dancing not too close and yet without a yawning gap between their bodies. Soon, however, Colleen began scanning the room distractedly.

“What are you looking for?”

“The nuns. They caught me leaving the dorm and said my skirt was too short. I had to go back and change clothes just for them.”

“Your skirt is just fine.”

Colleen leaned in close to Daniel. “I rolled it up a couple of inches after Peggy and I left campus. I could get in trouble if they catch me a second time.”

The next hour went by in a whirl with several fast dances that Daniel faked and a couple of slow ones that he worked on with limited success. Michael and Peggy had disappeared in the crowd of dancers and didn’t reappear until some time later.

“Let’s go outside,” Peggy said. “It’s getting too hot in here.”

“Suits me,” Daniel agreed. “Colleen, do you want to go outside?”

“That’s fine. I can use some quiet time after all this loud music.”

The four of them made their way to the exit. As they entered the hallway outside the main entrance, Michael announced that he had to take a leak. Daniel gave him a frown but then followed him into the men's bathroom. Colleen and Peggy stood outside.

"What do you think of Daniel?" Peggy asked Colleen.

"He's nice. I mean he dances pretty well. I'm not sure if he's my type but I didn't see anyone else here tonight giving me the eye. I don't know. What about you?"

Peggy shook her head. "Well, Michael is definitely not my type. He's a little weird. I mean he goes on and on about the government, the war in Vietnam and strange things like that. He's OK for tonight but I definitely will not be seeing him again in the future … I don't think either one of them is our type, Colleen. They're more like rough-cut lumberjacks, not college freshmen. I thought their school had higher admission standards than that."

"Oh, come on, Peggy. They're not that bad. Certainly not like the Edina crowd or the Ivy leaguers you're used to, but they're sincere. Just pretend you're out slumming for the evening."

"Col-*leen*! We're here to meet our future husbands or at least a proper companion for the next four years. The lumberjacks can stay home for all I care."

Colleen wrinkled her brow.

Daniel and Michael came out of the men's room and the four of them wandered over to the quadrangle in the middle of campus. A few other pairings had the same idea. Some couples were sitting on the grass and talking, others were smoking and laughing off to one corner.

"Where do you want to sit?" Daniel asked Colleen.

"I don't care. I just don't want to get any grass stains on my skirt."

"Colleen!" Peggy interjected.

"What?... Oh, Peggy, get your mind out of the gutter!"

They all laughed and walked toward a slope that crested up toward the campus library. Before she could sit down, Daniel whipped off his coat and laid it down for Colleen to sit on. She gave him a warm smile.

The library building was dark. It blocked out a good part of the night sky. The dark canopy above them was pinpointed with bright speckles of light. Michael plopped himself down on the grass and Peggy sat down next to him.

Colleen lay back on the grass and carefully tucked her skirt under her legs. Daniel lay down beside her. They stared up at the stars for a long time.

Michael rambled on about something and Peggy gave him lip service in return. The air was cool and still with just a hint of fall weather in the forecast.

Daniel looked up at the darkened building. "That's my Rock of Gibraltar," he said.

"What do you mean?"

"Well, I go there every day and try to conquer my studies. Seven days a week."

Colleen wasn't sure how to respond. "I just love to look at the stars and envision all kinds of figures and symbols and signs up there."

"I think I can see the footprints of birds," Daniel said.

Colleen tried to remember what footprints of birds looked like, and then briefly searched the stars for which ones Daniel was referring to.

"...Or more like the sound of fish playing."

Colleen looked over at Daniel, "That makes no sense whatsoever."

"I know, I just made it up."

Colleen laughed and threw another look Daniel's way.

He smiled back at her then said, "That pattern of stars does remind me of a dress I saw in some Vogue magazine my friend had. It was about the fashion industry in England. You know swinging London and all that."

"Are you serious now?"

"Yes."

"I was just there this summer," Colleen said. "London, Paris, and Rome - for starters."

Daniel arose on one elbow. He looked down at Colleen who was still mesmerized by the stars overhead. "You were there!" he said excitedly. "Did you go to Carnaby Street? By Oxford Circus? My friend wants desperately to go there, but I don't think she ever will."

"Yes, my parents took me to Europe as a reward for doing so well in high school. We went to England, France and Italy. I think I had the most fun in London, but France was a close second."

Daniel's enthusiasm was contagious. "Oh, that's so cool! Is it true what they say about Carnaby Street? Do the girls really wear their skirts that short over there? The ones they call the dolly birds?"

Colleen ignored the question, "I even got a couple of dresses that were designed by Mary Quant. One of them is the same dress that Patti Boyd and Jane Asher wore to some of those Beatles concerts. There were some highlighted in Sixteen Magazine but they were too juvenile. I wanted something more sophisticated."

"My friend knows all the shops over there; Foale & Tuffin, Lord John, TreCamp and Kleptomania. She can just go on and on."

"She must be quite a shopper."

"No, she just talks a lot," Daniel answered. "Sometimes I think she could get lost inside a paper bag. She can be a bit ditzy at times. But it's her world and I just let her talk."

"Like a true friend."

"Summer said this new fashion thing started in the borough of Hammersmith by the mods; that's slang for modernists."

"As opposed to the trads or traditionalists!" Colleen threw back with a smile, "I read an article about it in an old copy of Town Magazine when I was in London."

"Cool," was all Daniel could say in response. He'd never met a girl like Colleen before and it was beginning to scare him a bit. He collected his thoughts and tried again.

"Last summer the two of us hung out in Dinkytown a lot. They had some great folk singers at the Ten o'clock Scholar and the Purple Onion. Summer told me about this place near Harvard called the Club 47 on Mount Auburn Street. They're supposed to have great folkies there too."

Colleen smiled.

The group grew silent and took in their final moments of stargazing.

"It's getting late. I've still got a lot of homework to do," Colleen announced.

"Hey, bro!" Michael said, suddenly sitting up. "I've got an idea. I know where there's a happening. A real hippie party over on West Bank. You guys want to go?"

"No," Colleen answered. "I've got homework."

"Oh, come on, Colleen," Peggy interjected. "You can let that go for one night. You've got all day Sunday to get it done. Come on. I want to go see what hippies do at one of their own parties."

"Are you sure we can get in?" Daniel asked Michael.

"Yeah, I can get in. All we have to do is bring some booze and they'll let us in."

"Where do we get some booze?" Peggy asked.

"In the trunk of my car," Michael answered flatly

They all laughed and got up.

Daniel looked over at Colleen but couldn't read her face. "We don't have to go if you don't want to," he said to her softly.

"I know," she answered. "It might be interesting. Besides, if I want to be a journalist I need to explore that slice of life, don't I?"

"I guess."

"Right," she replied. "So let's do it."

"To the hippie party it is," Peggy announced and quickly fell into step behind Michael who was already walking toward the student parking lot. Daniel looked over at Colleen and shrugged his shoulders.

"Come on, it might be interesting," Colleen said and picked up the pace behind her roommate. Daniel smiled at her and caught up with the three of them.

In A Gadda Da Vida

The West Bank of the University of Minnesota sits on the high bluffs above the Mississippi River. During the Depression and long afterwards, it was home to a motley collection of tarpaper shacks and flimsy structures of wood and cardboard called the Bohemian Flats.

The Flats had been an enclave of radical bohemians, working class poor, and students exploring the flip side of academic life. Each spring, the Flats would flood out and then be rebuilt by its occupants. In the late 1940's, Hennepin County and the Federal government kicked them all out and leveled the river bank for good.

In the mid-sixties a new kind of resident started moving back into the area, easily mixing in with the poor and underclass of humanity. Young radicals and followers of the beat culture mixed with hippies who were trying to create a new community based on love and sharing.

The hippie population managed to eke out their existence amid the hodgepodge of dilapidated dwellings and storefronts.

Michael's hippie party was in a rundown house hidden behind several low income apartment buildings. The location was far enough away to seldom command the attention of patrol cars that cruised the neighborhood. Coffee houses, dive bars, and some rundown storefronts lined the dirty thoroughfare nearby.

Michael drove through the neighborhood for several minutes before pulling up in front of a ramshackle house. An old car, wheel-less and up on blocks, was in the front yard along with a baby crib and assorted gardening junk.

"Are you sure this place is safe?" Peggy asked. Colleen nudged her but she persisted. "I mean it doesn't look like a very safe neighborhood."

"Trust me, it's OK," Michael said as he got out of the car and went toward the trunk. Daniel quickly got out and held the door open for the two girls. "It really is safe here," he whispered to Colleen with a quick smile. Colleen's look told him she wasn't so sure about that, but she followed him anyway.

Michael led the way through the maze of debris in the front yard and up the rickety steps to the front door. Colleen and Peggy held back, standing at the bottom of the steps. "Are you coming up?" Daniel asked.

"Let's see just who or what answers the door first," Colleen answered. Peggy nodded in agreement.

Michael knocked several times then resorted to pounding on the door. They could hear loud music with a heavy bass reverberating off the walls. Mixed with the music was the sound of laughing voices. No one answered the door. Michael continued pounding in a rhythmic pattern.

"He's got the beat!" Daniel announced. Michael laughed and the girls kept staring at the door that wasn't moving.

"Hey, it's 'Iron Butterfly,'" Michael said, recognizing the tune coming from inside.

"What's that?" asked Peggy.

"Oh, man," Michael said. "Don't you know 'In A Gadda Da Vida'? It's a great song." Peggy still looked a perplexed.

Daniel looked down at Colleen and smiled sheepishly. She looked back up at him and returned his smile with only a partial smile. *She's too hard to read*, Daniel thought.

The door opened with a loud groan and a bearded man wearing torn jeans and a tie-dye shirt stood there. He was stoned and feeling no pain. He looked out at the four newcomers with glassy, vacant eyes. Wavering on his feet, he seemed poised to tumble down the front steps. He caught himself on the doorframe and tried to focus on his visitors.

"Do you know the password, man?" he asked Michael with a slur.

Michael thrust a six pack of Schlitz Malt Liquor into his face. The hippie's eyes lit up and he grabbed the beer. "Yeah, that's it. Come on in!"

“We’re here for the party,” Michael said to the man as he followed him inside. “A crazy man told us all about it. Got any stash?”

The hippie smiled, prominently displaying several missing teeth. “If you got the cash, we got the stash. We also got some fine uppers and some mean juice if you’re interested. Some Acapulco Gold too.”

Michael signaled the girls to follow him. Daniel stood and waited for Colleen and Peggy to come up the stairs.

“Are you sure this is safe?” Colleen asked as she reached the landing.

“It should be fine, but if you’re uncomfortable we can leave whenever you want.”

“Like now!” Peggy said.

“We’ll give it a chance,” Colleen answered as she turned to Peggy, “We can leave whenever you want. Is that OK?”

Peggy reluctantly nodded and followed Daniel and Colleen inside. Michael had already disappeared into the milling crowd.

“What’s that smell?” Peggy asked immediately.

Daniel and Colleen laughed.

“What?”

“Peggy, I’m guessing its marijuana or some other noxious weed they’re all smoking in here,” Colleen said.

Peggy’s wide eyes betrayed her amazement at the activities all around her.

The party was in full swing in the tattered living room. The room was pitch black except for strobe lights flashing everywhere and a reflective metallic globe twirling on the ceiling. Flickering, flashing lights cast an eerie, almost sinister feel to the room. The noise was deafening, a thunderous, numbing assault to the auditory senses. The record player was playing ‘Pictures of Matchstick Men’ by the Status Quo.

“Oh, man, I love this song!” Daniel shouted above the roar. Colleen shot him with a strange look and then smiled as he began to undulate with the music as if he were in a trance.

Daniel quickly regained his composure and looked around. The crowd was so thick in the living room Daniel knew he’d never be able to talk to Colleen there. “Come on, let’s find some place a little quieter.”

No one noticed the three newcomers wander through the room of twisting bodies and into the back kitchen.

Although the kitchen offered little respite from the noise, there were far fewer people there. Daniel saw that a back door was wide open and several hippies were sitting on the back stoop passing a joint. A tub of beer piled high with ice was by the back door.

Michael reappeared for a moment, pulled two bottles out of the tub, and then disappeared back into the living room leaving the other three standing in the kitchen.

"This place is so filthy," Peggy commented as she looked around. "I don't want to touch anything, much less a glass."

Daniel reached into the tub of ice and drew out three beers. He fished out a bottle opener from a kitchen drawer and opened the bottles. They stood by the beer tub for some time watching the hippies in the living room smoking, laughing and dancing.

There was one couple in particular that caught the trio's attention. Both hippies were in the final stages of serious lovemaking. His shirt was off and her dress was riding up over her hips. She was wearing tiny white panties and rubbing her leg against his thighs. Their lips were locked and rubbing furiously against one another.

"Do you think they're going to…?" Peggy asked.

"If they are, I'm leaving," Colleen answered Peggy, giving Daniel a strong look of disapproval.

"I said anytime you want, we can leave."

"But Michael has the car!" Peggy said.

"And I have his car keys," Daniel answered with a smile as he patted his pants pocket. "I've done this before."

"Let's just go out back," Colleen offered. "It's too hot in here. I need some fresh air." Peggy looked back at the chaotic living room.

"You two go. I want to see if those two are really going to consummate their curiosity."

"You aren't serious." Colleen admonished.

Peggy gave Colleen a mischievous wink. "You guys go out back. I just want to stick around here. It's kind of exciting, don't you think?"

"Come on, Daniel. I think my roommate has gone bonkers."

Daniel followed Colleen out back and over to a small bench in the corner of the dirty grass-patched backyard. They sat down and began to drink their beer. Daniel quickly downed his. Colleen sipped hers.

"Michael's not always like this. I'm sorry if he embarrassed you."

"Like what?"

"His stupid comments at the dance. His drinking. I mean he's a good guy. He's actually quite smart. A lot smarter than I am. If he'd just learn to focus…"

"Is that why you're his friend?"

"We go way back. Even before high school. He was always there for me when no one else was. Before my friend Summer, he was the only friend I ever had. Michael usually doesn't drink so much but I think college has got him a little spooked. He's got the brainpower. He's just not applying himself."

"So you're gonna show him he can?"

"I guess. Moral support, maybe. And grab his car keys on a night like tonight. I hope he didn't give you a bad impression of us."

Colleen took another small sip of beer and set it on the ground, "I'm here, aren't I?" She smiled "No, I think I could see through your friend's wisecracks pretty quickly. Peggy, not so much. I guess she's more cautious than I am … but, I must tell you Daniel, Michael does seem quite different from you."

Daniel searched for the right words. "Well, we come from the same place. I mean our upbringing. But I think we're on two different tracks now. I hope he can get his act together. I guess I feel the need to be here to help him if I can."

"You're a good man, Charlie Brown," Colleen said whimsically, "I like that."

Daniel could catch the occasional whiff of Colleen's perfume as a slight breeze moved through the backyard. It was an intoxicating smell that made him want to move even closer to her and perhaps even touch her. He did neither and just sat quietly next to her, enjoying her company.

"I'm envious of your travels to Europe. I've never been out of the Twin Cities. I'd love to be able to walk down Carnaby Street and go to the theaters. There's so much going on with the British music industry, the film industry and so many great artists like the Beatles."

"It was interesting. I took a lot of notes. I want to be a reporter someday. Are you a musician?" she asked, her curiosity aroused.

Daniel noticed that she was tilting her head ever so slightly. He read it as a sign that she was really interested and not just being polite. "No, not at all. I don't have any musical talent. But the whole creativity thing with the hippies fascinates me - and the beats before them. Their clothes, for example."

"What do you mean?"

"It's no accident that the beats loved to dress in black; somber, serious, devoid of any color. Like most of their poetry. Then you've got the hippies with very colorful clothes and flowers in their hair. Bellbottom jeans, sandals, bare feet… Free as the wind. Their look just shouts of individuality."

"But they're always talking about sex;" Colleen protested, "the Beatniks in their poetry and the hippies in their music and posters. I think they can be kind of weird at times. I'm more interested in mainstream media. Nancy Dickerson is one of my favorite journalists."

"I guess my perspective is different than yours," he said, shrugging his shoulders. *Now this is getting deep,* he thought, *watch your words.*

"What do you mean your perspective is different?" Colleen asked.

"My friends think some of my ideas are strange - out of the mainstream. But like I tell them, I'm always searching. It's like a vision quest or a journey of self discovery. The Chinese call it Tao."

"For what? I mean, what are they searching for? Or more specifically, what are you searching for? I don't get it."

"The same thing you're looking for here in school," Daniel replied.

"Meaning?"

"Freedom, creativity, and for you, learning the craft of writing and reporting. We're all on a journey of self discovery. Or we can be if we open ourselves up to the possibilities that life presents us."

Colleen gave Daniel a puzzled look. "I guess I'm far too practical for all that. I just want to be a reporter or a journalist. I want to write for a living and maybe have a career in the newspaper industry; digging for the facts and reporting the truth without embellishment. Or maybe I'll become an editor for some famous magazine in New York City. I might even write a book; some great American novel like…" she laughed and shrugged her shoulders, "or just write."

Daniel studied Colleen as she elaborated. He couldn't help but reflect on the differences between the two of them. Academically it sounded as if they were polar opposites. She obviously came from money. She had her whole career pretty well figured out.

His mind drifted back to Colleen's voice. "…so they think they've got my whole life planned out for me - and they probably do to a great degree."

"They?"

"My parents! Haven't you been listening?"

"Of course, I have," Daniel lied. "So what if you can't find a job that you like? What then?"

"According to my parents, I should get married and settle down and have kids."

"And instead you want to…?"

"I told you, I want to write."

Daniel tried to change the subject, "Peggy seems nice."

"Oh, she's wonderful," Colleen answered, her irritation dissipating. "I couldn't have picked a nicer person for a roommate. She is a little different from me, but that's what makes her so interesting."

"So how is she different?"

"Staying in the kitchen to watch those two going at it, for example."

Daniel laughed. "Not your cup of tea?"

"Fornicating in public? No, I don't think so!"

Just then they saw Michael stumbling onto the back porch. He had a bottle of beer in one hand and a joint in the other. He was in a daze and looked around without really seeing anything.

"Guess you're driving home tonight, Daniel," Colleen said, standing up. "Come on, let's find Peggy and go home. I've still got a ton of homework waiting for me tomorrow morning."

"Can I see you again?" Daniel asked suddenly as they made their way back to the house.

"I'm sure I'll see you around your campus," Colleen said, offering no more commitment than that. She stopped in mid-track and turned back to Daniel. "If I don't see you, I'm in Frazer Hall. We've got a phone at the end of the hall - but I don't know what that number is."

"So if I do some investigative journalism, I can probably find out what that number is."

"Exactly!"

"I'll be giving you a call."

"OK," Colleen answered with a smile.

Daniel followed the three of them out the front door. *Damn!* he thought, *College is gonna be all right.*

Classy Women don't Advertise

Daniel drove Colleen and Peggy back to campus, racing to meet their curfew. It was well past midnight as he snaked through the darkened neighborhood, taking every shortcut he could think of. Michael dozed on and off in the back seat, snoring up a storm. Daniel swung the car up to the dorm building and hurriedly got out to open the girls' door. As they climbed out of the car, a shrill voice pierced the air.

"Child of God, you owe that man nothing!"

Daniel and the girls looked up to see a frail old nun hanging out of a second floor window. She was waving her arm down at them.

"What the…" Daniel was stunned.

"Don't worry, Daniel," Colleen said. "It's just crazy old Sister Agnes. She does that to all the boys when they come back with their dates. We love it. She's great entertainment and it really scares some of the boys. You aren't scared, are you Daniel?"

Daniel laughed, "Even old Sister Agnes won't keep me away if you'll let me come back."

Colleen smiled. "Got to go," she said, grabbing Peggy's hand and rushing the two of them up the dormitory steps. Before entering the quiet building, Colleen flashed a quick wave back toward Daniel. Then she was gone.

Michael was babbling loudly in and out of consciousness by the time Daniel got to their dormitory. He dragged Michael out of the car and propped him up as they stumbled toward their building. "Shut up, Michael," Daniel warned his roommate. "You'll wake the front desk and we'll both be in deep shit."

The Proctor was fast asleep as they slipped through the front door. Daniel clamped his hand over Michael's mouth and maneuvered past the front desk. "Did you get any snatch tonight?" Michael whispered in Daniel's ear as they and started down the hallway.

"Hardly." Daniel opened their dorm room and let his roommate fall into his small bed. Michael let out a loud fart and rolled over to his side.

"But I really like her," Daniel said as he stood over Michael's prone body. He walked over to his own bed, kicked off his shoes, and threw his sport coat aside.

"Like her? Hell, you just met her."

"Yeah, but she's beautiful and smart and has a neat personality. I think we really hit it off tonight." Daniel plopped down on his bed and pulled off his shirt. He got lost in sweet thoughts of the night just spent with that beautiful red head. "That's the kind of chick I could see spending the rest of my life with."

"You're talking about getting married? Hell, you haven't gotten laid yet. Ten to one she's still a cherry. Probably tighter than bark on a tree. See the way she was all decked out. Just a cover if you ask me."

"Listen dickhead, that was a woman of substance. Besides, classy women don't advertise. They don't have to."

"Yeah, Miss Goodie Two Shoes who follows all the rules. Probably a brainiac besides. Now her roommate, she may carry some slack … if you know what I mean."

"Colleen's not like anyone else I've ever met before. I think she's a class act. I felt really good just being around her."

"Come on, man. You like the folk mass at Newman Center. She's probably still into the Latin mass in the campus chapel. I'll bet she still listens to 'Hobb's House' on CCO radio. And you like the Beatles and Bob Dylan. Man, it'll never work out."

"It could."

"Well, forget it. People like that don't hang out with people like us. Tonight was just a fluke. When we're around people like her, you and I are just background. It's called class in America. Class discrimination is very much alive and well, despite what all those crazy hippie socialists say about equality for the masses." He let out a loud fart, "Face it my friend; if you were to marry her, you'd really be marrying up."

"Probably."

"No, listen man. What a woman, any woman, really wants is soft fingers and an educated tongue."

"You are demented!"

"No, I'm serious, man."

"So am I!"

"So, tell me Daniel, if this broad is so smart and intelligent and classy, why in the hell would she want to spend time with the likes of us? Doesn't make sense. Take my advice. Get what you can because sooner or later she'll wise up and dump your sorry ass. Boost that notch count on your belt while you can."

"You are an asshole, Michael. Funny at times, but still a certifiable asshole."

"Yeah, probably. But I've had more experience with the ladies than you have. So stick with the foxes and forget the squares!" Michael rolled over and was soon snoring loudly in his sleep.

Daniel was too charged up by the night's events to sleep. He ambled back out into the hallway and stood there for a long time. The building was quiet except for an occasional loud snoring that bounced off the linoleum floors. He and Michael had just beat the curfew by minutes and saved their ass from either detention or a call-up before the Dean of Students.

Daniel could only hope to monitor his roommate's behavior and call it to his attention if it got out of control. But with a screwed up family life like his own, Daniel wasn't about to abandon his friend just because he drank too much at times.

Dealing with Colleen was a whole different story. This woman who had just come into his life presented a confusing and yet a compelling and exciting next stage. That is, a next stage if she would have him in her life.

Despite Michael's harsh assessment of their compatibility, Daniel knew he was smitten with Colleen. She was unlike anyone he'd ever met before. If she would have him, he intended to continue their relationship. No matter where it might take him.

When Colleen and Peggy got back to their dorm room, neither one of them was ready for bed. They were still pumped up by the excitement of the hippie party they'd just experienced.

After waving goodbye to the boys, Colleen and Peggy opened the front lobby door and stepped inside. There was one senior at the front desk, engaged in a heated discussion with her boyfriend about something. Mrs. O'Reilly, the dormitory mother, was slumped back in a large oversized lounge chair, a Bible spread open on her lap. She was snoring loudly.

They snuck past the distracted senior and snoring dorm matron then gingerly edged up the circular stairway leading to the second floor. As they unlocked their dorm room door and slipped inside, their giggles could be heard wafting down the empty hallway.

"That was fun," Peggy exclaimed as she threw herself backwards onto her small bed, shifting it until it was up against the wall. She kicked off her shoes.

"More strange than fun, I'd say, but definitely interesting. I certainly didn't expect to spend tonight with a bunch of stoned-out-of-their-mind hippies. I don't think I'll be telling my parents about this."

"What did you think of the two of them?" Peggy asked as she rolled her nylons down her thighs.

"Daniel's cute. Michael is a little strange - definitely not my cup of tea. But Daniel … I could see myself going out with him again … perhaps. Once in a while … maybe … oh, I don't know, Peggy. I mean I did have fun tonight. Granted, it was a little strange. But it was fun nevertheless."

"So you like Daniel?" Peggy asked.

Colleen thought for a moment. "He's definitely a free spirit…"

"Which you're not!"

"He's curious about everything around him. I've never met anyone who has so many interests in such a variety of subjects. And he seems so determined … I mean it's obvious that he's already struggling in school but he seems resolved to make a go of it."

"How do you know that?"

"I just do."

"How?"

"I've seen that same kind of intensity in my father, that's how!"

"So he's unfocused, not that mature and borders on being a hippie. I mean look at his clothes. And the way he speaks. There's no panache. No class." Peggy laughed, "Oh, and he might be a college dropout before you finish your first finals. Is that what you're saying?"

"He's cute!" Colleen threw back, "How's that? Reason enough for you?"

"Perhaps. So you think you'd actually go out with him again?"

"Yes, I think I'd go out with Daniel again, Peggy."

"He's a little like James Dean, don't you think? A real JD."

"He's not a juvenile delinquent," Colleen answered with a frown. "He's not preppy, I'll give you that. But he's no JD either."

Peggy wasn't buying it. "Don't forget where you come from, Colleen."

"Meaning?"

"Oh, come on!"

"Daniel comes from a different cut of cloth, I'll grant you that. He may be going to St. Paul's but he doesn't come from money. Not by the way he acts … or dresses!"

"But he's sincere," Colleen countered, "and nice. No chance of hubris on his part."

"Well, I certainly wouldn't go out with Michael ever again," Peggy exclaimed. "And I don't see you dating Daniel in the future. I'm sure he's nothing like your old boyfriends back in high school. Or what you envision your future husband to be like. He's nothing like any of them."

Colleen started to protest but Peggy cut her off. "…and don't forget your parents. If they're anything like mine, there is no way they'd approve of someone like Daniel. No way!"

"Peggy, for God's sake. I'm just saying I might see him again - not marry him. Just date him once in a while … if he asks me."

"Well it was obvious you liked his company tonight. But mark my words; it will go no place in a very short while. No place good, that is."

"Why? Because we've got such different backgrounds? He seems ambitious, I like that. My dad would like that in him too. Not my mother, she's the snob in the family."

"I'm just saying…"

By now Colleen was getting exasperated with her roommate. "Enough already with the talk about Daniel and Michael. I'm going to bed. If you're going to stay up, just keep quiet, OK?"

Peggy wandered into the bathroom, mumbling under her breath.

"I know what you're mumbling, Peggy Jean," Colleen said. "And I don't appreciate it."

Peggy stopped by the bathroom doorway. "Listen, roommate … we're here for four years. That's four years to get a good education. Maybe a career if that's what you want. And, don't forget, this is the best opportunity you will ever have to find the right man. Between the pickings at the College of St. Paul, the U and some of the other private colleges, you've got a lot to choose from. All of them could be a ticket to future happiness and kids, if they're part of your equation too."

"You are nothing short of unbelievable, Peggy."

"Why? Because I intend to get my M.R.S. in addition to my bachelor's degree? Nothing wrong with that, Colleen Catherine." Peggy closed the bathroom door.

Colleen stared at the closed door for a long time. Was that true? Was Colleen going to find her future husband during the next four years? Her mother would have been delighted with that prospect. Her father would be fine; whatever his little girl wanted is what he wanted.

Teenage Elixir

Despite Michael's prediction to the contrary, Colleen and Daniel managed to find time to go out for Cokes at the corner drugstore, take long walks along the River Boulevard and chat for hours by the pond on Mother of the Lake campus. They pretended they weren't dates, just excuses to get together and talk.

As the months went by, their time together gradually expanded to include movies, pizza nights and more long walks along the River Boulevard. The two of them were doing something almost every weekend. In the evolution of their dating cycle, it soon became a curious 'you show me and I'll show you' kind of game.

Colleen introduced Daniel to the Walker Art Center, the Minneapolis Institute of Arts, the Bell Museum of Natural History and the Science Museum of Minnesota. She also insisted that they catch a play once in a while at the Edith Bush Little Theater not far from her campus.

Daniel enjoyed introducing Colleen to his side of the world; the unwashed, rougher, opposite side of life. He took her to Ralph's Diner in downtown St. Paul where drunks, dealers, cops, politicians and everyday workers all mingled and managed to ignore one another. The food was mediocre but the atmosphere was electric; nothing short of eye-opening for an aspiring writer like Colleen.

He took her to the best small movie theaters in town. The Grandview in St. Paul for foreign films. The Heights and Riverview for old reruns of the classics from the 30's and the 40's. The Oak Street Cinema and the Lagoon Cinema for largely unknown films from Europe. They even took Michael's car to the Drive-in in Cottage Grove once.

Colleen drew the line when Daniel suggested they go slumming on Hennepin Avenue in downtown Minneapolis. Colleen insisted she wasn't prejudiced but she had no desire to see those people caught up on the backside of life. When Michael joined them on their outings, the discussions could range from serious to raucous to just plain silly. Occasionally the trio would be asked to leave the library or campus cafe when their laughter became too obnoxious.

Daniel found in Colleen someone he was completely comfortable around. He could be himself totally and without apology. Colleen was a bright, beautiful woman who was also strong-minded, independent and focused. He didn't mind her strength of character. In fact, he found it refreshing to find a woman so sure of herself and so focused on her career in journalism.

Colleen found in Daniel a puzzling study in ambition, stumbling self-discovery, a surprising litany of curious facts, and a young man still searching for his own identity.

While their off campus activities offered a refreshing break from studying, both were facing heavier workloads and more homework as each week passed.

Not surprisingly, Daniel was struggling with his class load while Colleen was cruising through without a lot of effort. Daniel took to complaining about his classes and the heavy work schedule he faced every day. To change the subject, Colleen would talk about the hippie party and the crazy antics of those stoned out characters there.

He would forget about his classes and begin talking enthusiastically about the amount of creativity that this whole new Hippie Nation thing was showing in so many ways; in the arts, in music, in the environment and in politics. He talked about their disdain for politics as usual. Daniel began rattling off the names of Peter Max, the illustrator, and the artists who were creating artwork in San Francisco. He even mentioned his friend, Summer Blaze, and her letters talking about the craziness of Haight-Ashbury.

Daniel had begun to read a lot of books by writers like Jack Kerouac, Michael Burroughs, Allen Ginsberg and Lawrence Ferlinghetti. Many of those names came at the recommendation of Summer, whose friends had discovered them in North Beach.

While Colleen appreciated from afar Daniel's newfound enthusiasm for such creative endeavors, she reminded him of his first priority while in college; to pass his classes so he could come back the next year. In short, she dismissed most of his ramblings into that literary wilderness as a waste of time.

Daniel acknowledged that his interest in creativity had gotten the best of him, but he insisted that he could manage his class load and still explore different avenues of creativity for himself. He even stopped shaving and began wearing jeans like Bob Dylan - for all of one week.

His newfound interest in all things hippie came to a crashing halt one afternoon when the Dean of Students caught him. Daniel was just crossing the quadrangle on his way to class when a booming voice cut him short.

Father Robert James Rollins was not a man to be trifled with in terms of student behavior and dress. As an ex-Army Chaplain, Rollins had served time in Korea before joining the College of St Paul as campus chaplain and Dean of Students. He was tough on student behavior and fastidious when it came to student dress and appearance.

"Hey, you!" Father Rollins shouted as he exited the library and saw Daniel crossing the quadrangle in front of him.

Daniel stopped and looked around. He spotted the Dean walking quickly toward him. Daniel stood his ground, not sure what to expect next, but he was certain it wasn't going to be a pleasant conversation.

"Forget to shave this morning?" Rollins said, stepping up to the freshman. He planted his feet directly in front of Daniel.

Other students quickly the Dean and Daniel a wide berth and looked away as they passed by.

"Dean Rollins."

"Well, young man? Did you forget to shave this morning?"

"No, sir, I didn't."

"You know the rules for facial hair on campus - or you should. Freshman, I assume?"

"Yes, sir, I am."

"Shave! By tonight. I don't want to see you on campus again with facial hair. No ifs, ands, or buts. No haircut and you'll be looking at time in front of the Disciplinary Council. Is that understood, young man?"

Daniel was taken aback. What was he waiting for? The Dean of Students had him dead to rights and he had no excuse for violating college policy, as stupid as he thought it was. He wanted to say something about how dumb that policy was. He was in college not high school. He had a right to express himself, to *be* himself.

"Yes, sir, I understand," Daniel answered reluctantly. The chips were all on the Reverend's side. *No sense in fighting him on this one,* Daniel thought. Better to capitulate than face more problems on top of the academic challenges he was already facing.

"Good, see to it that you do. And get some proper clothes, for God's sake. You look like a bum."

When Daniel relayed to Colleen what had happened to him with the Dean, she just laughed. "So there goes everything hippie in your life," she said, "Just as well. You were going down the wrong side of the tracks on that one. Dress for success. Play the role and it will become natural to you."

Daniel let it go. If that was the price he'd have to pay to continue at St. Paul's and not threaten his relationship with Colleen, then he'd play the game. The stakes were too high not to.

Daniel and Colleen's relationship was gradually growing into something more than just casual dating. The rest of the fall semester was a whirlwind of mixers, football games on Saturday afternoons, late night dessert in the student grill, and afternoon study sessions that usually ended up with a little cuddling in a corner of Colleen's student lounge.

The relationship evolved into something that was very comfortable for both of them. Colleen found she could talk to Daniel about practically anything and he wasn't judgmental like her parents or discouraging like some of her classmates. Neither of them was looking for anyone else. Despite Peggy's warning about Daniel's social status, Colleen found herself not wanting to expand her cadre of male companions. She was happy where she was - for the time being.

Daniel was supremely happy with their arrangement just as it was. He'd found in Colleen a kindred soul. One who understood his anxiety about his classes, his continuing although curtailed interest in creativity and some things hippie. And his endless pondering of what might lie ahead for the both of them.

They found camaraderie in their adventures with each other, which usually found the three of them down by the campus pond at day's end. Michael would inevitably bring out a flask and Colleen would politely decline, as would Daniel. Michael would drink and get sillier by the minute; until all three of them were laughing and rolling on the grass at his stories and assorted antics. It was fun. It was comfortable. And it was a good way to ease the stress of tests, class assignments and Daniel's continuing uncertainty about his future on campus.

A World Outside of Her Own

The early months on campus went by quickly and soon the harsh winds of winter began sweeping through both campuses. The trees had been shorn of their leaves and the grounds were turning into a quilt of muted browns.

Coursework for both Colleen and Daniel was growing exponentially and both were finding it harder and harder to break away for a real date or even an occasional Coke. This separation brought with it new challenges and opportunities for both of them.

Most campus activities had been moved indoors. With that, the chances of meeting other young men began to grow for the women of Mother of the Lake College. On more than one occasion, Colleen and Peggy found themselves engaged in casual conversations with men from the other nearby colleges. Colleen soon found herself looking forward to such encounters. Their conversations were remarkably different from those with Daniel - neither better nor worse, just different. A new world of social interaction was opening up for Colleen. And she found herself looking forward to these new encounters with the opposite sex.

Over time, Colleen could feel that something was amiss in her personal life. It wasn't just Peggy's occasional innocuous comment about Colleen only dating Daniel that was beginning to bother her, nor her parent's innocent inquiries into her dating life. Something else was beginning to gnaw at Colleen's comfort level around Daniel. It wasn't anything substantial that she could put a label on, but she was becoming aware that dating only Daniel carried with it certain liabilities.

Daniel was caring, thoughtful and attentive. Sometimes too attentive. He would ask her about her weekends when they weren't together. He would wonder where she was if he called and she wasn't in the dorm. He'd dropped by her dorm room unannounced on several occasions. It was almost as if he was checking up on her to see if someone else was in the room with her.

As much as she enjoyed Daniel's company, Colleen began to want for more freedom in her life. She began to yearn to go out with whomever she wanted to. A plain and simple 'let's go to a movie' date with someone new, someone different perhaps. Maybe even someone more like herself. The stark differences between her and Daniel were beginning to crack the foundation of their once solid relationship.

Peggy assured her it was a reasonable request. She encouraged Colleen to talk to Daniel about her feelings and ask for his understanding. But Daniel's heavy course load and continuing struggles with his classes made Colleen reticent to bring up the topic. Hedging her bets and wanting to avoid a confrontation with Daniel, Colleen decided her best course of action was to subtly begin making herself available for class excursions and other off-campus activities that involved men. It would be all class related, she assured herself, and therefore not cheating on Daniel in any way.

"So why are you feeling guilty?" Peggy asked Colleen one day over coffee.

"I think Daniel will be very upset if he finds out that I'm seeing other guys. I know we're not an item like some other couples on campus, but I just don't think he'd be very understanding."

"He doesn't own you, Colleen Catherine. Heck, he hasn't given you any reason to believe that he's going to be around at the end of four years. You don't want to tie yourself up freshman year and then watch him struggle for the next three years, do you?"

"No, of course not, but I like him - a lot. I just don't like his being so possessive of me. He gets very defensive when I try to bring up the subject of dating other people."

"So what you're telling me is that he isn't giving you any choice but to take action yourself. I like what you said about meeting new guys through your classes or campus activities. That seems safe and Daniel can't get on your case for doing that."

"Watch him," Colleen answered.

"Then he's out of luck as far as I'm concerned,"

"I just don't want him to think I've gone behind his back."

"Look, girlfriend; you tried to talk to him about it and he won't talk to you. So go ahead and put yourself in situations where you're bound to meet new guys. Let nature take its course. If none of those guys measure up to Daniel, you haven't wasted your time and you know you've got the right guy in the first place."

"Sounds plausible, I guess."

"Pass me the sugar and stop worrying about Daniel's response to this."

"I need to be true to myself, don't I?" Colleen's tone of voice betrayed her own uncertainty of the situation.

"The sugar, please!"

Shadowy Truths

Neither Daniel nor Colleen brought up the subject of spending the holidays together. They both sensed that meeting the family was far too premature for their relationship. Daniel didn't even know if Colleen's parents knew of his existence.

Daniel went home to stay with his mother for the holidays. He managed to grab a couple of days working at the grocery store for the quick cash. Michael disappeared, rumored to have gone to Chicago with some buddies for the heavy drinking and night life.

Colleen spent the holidays in Rochester with her family and local relatives. There was a quick trip to Chicago for shopping and visiting more long distance relatives. Colleen was back on campus in early January.

It seemed like an eternity since Daniel had seen Colleen. Several weeks before the holiday break, Colleen had casually mentioned to Daniel that she would be gone for the weekend. She was heading up north to visit her uncle who lived in Duluth and to work on a class assignment at the same time. Daniel accepted her absence as unfamiliar family duty and thought nothing of it.

The day before classes resumed, Daniel met Colleen in front of her dorm. They were going to the movies and a long overdue make-out session. It ended abruptly when his fingers managed to slip down her slacks. Colleen practically jumped out of her seat and yanked Daniel's hand out of her pants.

“Don’t!” she snapped at Daniel. “Not here where someone can see us.”

“Then where?”

“Well, not here! Just watch the movie. Or take a cold shower.”

Daniel looked into her eyes and smiled. Colleen smiled back and kissed him on his cheek. “We can’t let anyone catch us doing this in public.”

“I’ve got a dorm room.”

“Can you take a cold shower first?”

“I don’t get it.”

“More popcorn, please.” Colleen pushed Daniel back into his seat. “I need more popcorn.”

“Then can we….?” Daniel asked teasingly.

“Fine!” Colleen said, suddenly standing up. “I’ll get it myself.” She moved along the row of chairs and bolted for the lobby. Daniel moved quickly behind her, catching her at the doorway.

“Colleen, I was kidding. Come on. It was a joke.”

Before Colleen could answer a voice called out, “Colleen, is that you?”

They turned to see a preppy looking young man dressed in boat shoes, corduroy pants, knit sweater and leather jacket walking toward them. He extended his hand to Colleen who hesitated at first and then reluctantly shook it. The man then turned to Daniel and extended his hand.

“Hi,” he said. “My name is Justin DeRosha.”

“So did you ever recover from our quickie up north?” he laughed as he turned back to Colleen.. “Just kidding,” he added quickly. “I mean our quick weekend trip to God’s country. I still don’t think Professor Anderson believed we did all that research in Duluth in such a short amount of time. It amazes me too, when you consider all the time we spent in that bar.” He turned to Daniel, “She tell you about the incident when the waiter came over to our table and…?”

“Justin,” Colleen interrupted, “we were just leaving. Sorry but we’ve both got early morning classes. It was great to see you again, but we really do have to go.” She grabbed Daniel by the arm and pushed him toward the front entrance. She turned back to Justin once and waved as she rushed them out the front door into the cold January night.

“I can explain,” Colleen said before Daniel had a chance to say a word. “Don’t get mad until I tell you just what happened that weekend. It wasn’t anything like he said. Justin has a tendency to exaggerate things - a lot!”

"You lied, Colleen. You lied to me."

"I didn't lie to you Daniel." Colleen shot back as she got into Michael's car. "I did see my uncle that weekend - briefly. But, yes, I did go up with a group of students from St. Paul and Mother of the Lake. It was a research trip, just like Justin said, and yes, we did spend some time in a bar. But that was only after spending most of the day combing the shoreline of Lake Superior for rocks and agates for our Geology class. I didn't tell you about it because I thought you'd get jealous and make a scene. That's why I didn't tell you."

"If we're going to be friends, we have to be completely honest with one another. You could have just told me that you were going up as part of a class assignment and I..."

"Oh, right!" Colleen interrupted. "And you would have been OK with that? You wouldn't have asked me a million questions and wanted to go along yourself. Tell me you would have been perfectly comfortable with my going off for the weekend with a bunch of guys."

"I thought you said there were girls from Mother of the Lake there too?"

"There were!"

"How many?"

"Does it matter?"

"How many?"

"One other girl. OK, a senior was there too."

"How many guys?"

"That's it!" Colleen snarled and slammed her hand on the front seat. "Either this is not an issue or else I get out and walk the rest of the way home. And you can consider this relationship over."

Daniel grew quiet. His anger quickly dissipated at the mere thought of Colleen walking out of his life.

"Don't get so worked up," he said backtracking. "I just think I have a right to know the truth and not some half truth about that weekend."

"Nothing happened!"

"I didn't say it did. Did I?"

"You implied it. Just by the way you're reacting right now."

"I did not!"

Colleen caught her breath. She settled back into the car seat and stared out the window. The silence was building between them. Neither one wanted to risk the next statement or question. Colleen turned to Daniel and put her hand on his knee.

"Listen," she said softly. "Daniel, I don't want to fight and I don't want to end our friendship over that weekend. Nothing happened. I'm sorry I didn't tell you about it. If I ever have another research trip like that again, I promise I will tell you all about it. Is that fair?"

Sensing a compromise, Daniel let a weak smile escape his lips and nodded. "Sorry I raised my voice," he said, offering a white flag. Colleen leaned over and gave him a kiss on his cheek. The rest of the trip home was quiet and subdued. Daniel gave Colleen a long kiss in front of her dorm. She responded by pressing her body tightly against his and wrapping her arms around his neck.

She looked up into his eyes and said "Sorry." Daniel pressed her even tighter against his chest and answered, "That's OK."

In Love with Love

Daniel and Colleen only stopped by his house once during freshmen year. They'd been out on a date and Daniel needed to pick up some more clothes for school. Daniel's mother and boyfriend met them at the door. After an awkward introduction in the entry way, Daniel ran upstairs to get his clothes.

Daniel's mother invited Colleen into the living room and offered her a seat. They chatted briefly about nothing in particular until Daniel came bounding back down the stairs.

Colleen didn't say much as they drove back to school other than to inquire about his mother's boyfriend and how long his father had been gone. It was brief and inconsequential. They didn't really talk about the meeting again.

But Daniel's mother had other ideas. During his next visit home, she ushered him into the kitchen and asked him to sit at the table. She poured a cup of coffee and sat down across from him. She had a serious look on her face.

"So how long have you known that girl?"

"Not long. I just met her at the beginning of the semester."

"Are you two serious about each other?"

"Mother!"

"I'm just asking!"

"Asking what?" Daniel asked, already aware of the undercurrent building. His mother had never mentioned Daniel's girlfriends before. She'd met Summer Blaze and had no comments about her other than the fact that she seemed a bit lost to the world. *Why would she care about Colleen?*

"She said she's from Rochester. That her father is a physician at the Mayo Clinic."

"So?"

"She's obviously rich, Daniel. I could tell that right away by the clothes she was wearing. They were tailored. Not off the rack."

"What's your point? That she dresses well?"

"My point is that if you date a girl like that she will eventually dump you. I don't want to see you get hurt, that's all."

"And where the heck did that come from?" Daniel's voice raised in anger. "You met her for all of five minutes, if that. How the hell do you know she's going to break up with me?"

"Trust me, I know these things. I've seen those kinds of girls before. They're rich and spoiled and only think of themselves. When she finds out you're poor, that you have no future, she'll drop you like a hot potato."

"What do you mean, I don't have a future? I sure as hell have a future."

"Oh, don't get all worked up."

"What do you mean I don't have a future? I'm going to college, aren't I?"

"Son, you know as well as I do that you don't have the grades or the intelli … the skill to become a doctor or a lawyer. You'll do just fine in a job. But it won't be the high paying kind of job a girl like that would expect you to have. When she finds out that you can't give her what she wants out of life, she'll dump you. I'm just telling you that now for your own good."

Daniel stood up and angrily pushed his chair back. "I'm outta here. I have to get back to campus."

"Daniel, that girl is in love with love."

It stopped Daniel in his tracks. "What? What does that mean?"

"It's an old phrase I heard a long time ago, but it fits her. She has been so spoiled that she just expects to have men fall for her. She's attractive so she probably has already had a lot of men in her life."

"That's got to be the dumbest thing I've ever heard," Daniel shouted back.

"Maybe she doesn't even know it, but that's what those kinds of girls do.

They fall for someone, get all caught up in the throes of love, but it isn't genuine. It's all surface and physical and not real at all. It's being in love just for the sake of being in love."

"What do you know about love?" Daniel shot back.

His mother looked at him with a snarl developing on her lips. "I loved your father at one time - before he left us. Don't tell me I don't know about love, young man. I damn well know what love is all about."

"How about loving me? Was that something you sort of forgot about while you were raising me?"

"Damn you, Daniel, how dare you talk to me that way?"

"I'm out of here," Daniel shot back as he stormed out the back door.

Unintended Consequences

By the end of freshman year, both Daniel and Colleen were beginning to realize the true extent of their involvement. It was like fuel for Daniel's ambition, but it was fast becoming a source of gnawing guilt to Colleen. A crazy quilt of mixed emotions was tugging at her heart while all the while nagging at her conscience.

They'd spent hours and hours just talking to one another about their hopes and dreams, but Daniel was still floundering at school. His grades were barely passing and he still hadn't chosen a major. He was as academically challenged as Colleen was gifted. The differences were beginning to weigh heavily on Colleen.

One night while making out, Daniel had put his hand down Colleen's pants but stopped when he felt her turn stiff and unresponsive. It was obvious she didn't want to go any further.

"What are we doing?" Colleen asked after Daniel removed his hand and she buttoned up her pants. She sounded frustrated.

"What do you mean?"

"I'm serious now, Daniel!"

"Colleen, so am I! What do you mean? What's wrong? I don't get it."

"Where are we going? I mean what's going to happen to us in the future? Do you envision us doing this for the next three years?"

"This?" Daniel asked, glancing down at Colleen's lap.

"No, not that! Our relationship! Where is it going? I like you Daniel, a lot. But we're still so different. I don't understand why we're still together. I mean if I told my parents about you, they'd freak. They assume I'm dating some guy from Edina or North Oaks."

"Not some hillbilly from the cities?" Daniel said mockingly.

"Don't!"

"Don't what?"

"Don't talk stupid, Daniel. You're not stupid. So don't talk that way."

"Colleen, sweetheart. You aren't making any sense. What's wrong with our relationship just as it is?"

"I simply don't understand where this is all going, that's all. You're the only person I've met that I feel I can tell anything to. I've never felt that way about anyone else except my dad some of the time, and certainly not my mother. But I don't know if that's enough, Daniel, I really don't. There's just so much more I want to experience in life. Places I want to go. Things I want to do."

"Nobody is stopping you, Colleen. Certainly not me!"

"I care too much about you to let you get hurt."

"I don't understand."

"Daniel, I need to find out who I am. Sometimes I feel like an imposter. Like someone who is doing all the right things because that's what is expected of me. But maybe it's not who I really am - or who I really want to be."

"You can be whoever you want to be. You can do whatever you want to do. I love you just as you are. If you change, that's great too."

"The only time I went away you went ballistic."

"I did not."

"Don't kid yourself, Daniel. You found out I went up north with a couple of guys and you freaked. You practically accused me of sleeping with them."

"Now that is an exaggeration!"

"OK, but you got mad, just the same. I want to take trips without wondering if you're going to get mad. I want to go out and do things with other people."

"Date other men?"

"No … I mean … I don't know. Yes, I want to go out on dates. But that doesn't mean we can't still be together. I'm not talking about romantic dates. I'm talking about going to movies with friends - my new roommates, for instance."

The conversation abruptly stopped. Daniel couldn't believe what he was hearing.

"I was going to tell you once we signed the lease but I might as well tell you now."

"Tell me what?"

"I've got an apartment not far from here on Grand Avenue. It's a three bedroom unit we are going to rent for the summer. I'll be back on campus next fall."

"I thought you were going back to Rochester to work in the Mayo PR Department."

"No, that never came through. But my dad talked to someone at the Saint Paul Pioneer Press and I interviewed for a summer internship there and got it. Isn't that great?"

"That is great, Colleen, but why didn't you tell me what you were planning to do?"

"Because, until yesterday, I wasn't sure if I'd gotten the job. Then Peggy told me about this apartment and I talked to the girls and we hit it off and they're going to let me stay with them for the summer. So I've got a summer job, a place to stay in town, and we can still see each other all summer." Colleen took a deep breath. "So what's not to like about that?"

Colleen took Daniels hands and placed them in her lap. She leaned forward and kissed him. Their lips held for a long time until she backed off. "Daniel, I don't want to stop seeing you. I really don't. But I want to go out with other people too. It will be healthy for our relationship in the long run."

"But your parents would never approve of me?" Daniel asked, removing Colleen's hands from his lap.

"Is that a surprise considering my background? But who cares - I'm still with you. We're still more than friends. Don't misunderstand me, I won't do anything to embarrass or shame my parents. But I'm going to live my own life the way I want to, at the same time."

"I know what you're saying about your parents. I knew it right from the start." He put his hands on her shoulders and drew her in closer. "But, as you said, we get along. We love … like one another - a lot! I do understand that you want to go out with other people. I understand it and I respect it. I don't have to like it…"

"Daniel, I'm not breaking up with you…".

"No, Colleen, hear me out." He took a deep breath. "I understand … I know our relationship is strong enough that we can still go out with other people and I realize what we have something special. I'm willing to give it a try. I really am."

The music of a song was drifting down the hallway. It was 'When a Man Loves a Woman' by Percy Sledge. "Listen," Daniel said, "I love this song. It says it all."

Colleen listened for a moment then smiled at Daniel. She leaned forward and kissed him again. She wrapped her arms around him and drew him in tighter against her body. She let her body go limp and fell backwards so that Daniel was lying on top of her on the bed. His leg rested between her legs and up against her crotch. Colleen began to gyrate her hips and slide back and forth against his leg. They embraced and moved together in fluid motion with the music until she stiffened and a shudder ran through her body.

They lay still, nestled together, legs intertwined. Even as she lie there completely satisfied physically, Colleen's doubts began to creep back into her mind.

Summer of 1967

Summer of Love

School was over and summer had begun, but the problems kept mounting for Daniel. While freshman year had been a breeze for Colleen, it had become one arduous academic journey for Daniel. His grades put him dangerously close to the cut off point for academic probation. His cash reserves were nearly depleted. Even the promised overtime at Dryer's grocery store wouldn't be enough to cover tuition for his sophomore year.

Daniel saw Colleen off at the bus depot in downtown St. Paul after her last exam. They promised to write one another while she was in Rochester but neither was sure if that would really happen. They exchanged a few kisses outside the idling bus but Colleen was anxious to get home. She waved Daniel off before he had a chance to talk about his hopes for the summer beyond boring and time-consuming work at Dryer's grocery store.

Colleen waved once more before the bus pulled out then went back to her magazine. Daniel was left alone in the parking lot as the Greyhound disappeared around the block. He could feel a knot beginning to grow in his stomach. Intellectually, he knew Colleen would be coming back in a couple of weeks. But somehow Daniel could feel that it would not be the same next time around. Their relationship was going to be different that summer.

If Daniel's first year in college was a challenge, Michael's had been a complete disaster. Between partying every weekend and missing far too many classes, Daniel's friend had been asked to leave school at the end of the second semester.

Within a week of dropping out of college, Michael got his draft notice. Several valiant attempts to enroll at other colleges brought only frustration and failure. No other school in the Twin Cities would admit him. So Michael resigned himself to the fact that he would soon be wearing olive drab.

He and Daniel had a long talk the night before Michael shipped out for boot camp. His next address would be Fort Leonard Wood, Missouri.

"How are you going to hack it, man?" Daniel asked. "You aren't in the best of shape."

"I can always get some shit if I need it, either from someone on base or a supplier off-base. I can always get some pick-me-up. That'll keep me going. Maybe this whole Army thing won't be so bad. You know, I'm kinda getting stoked about playing John Wayne and wasting some of the bad guys." He looked over at Daniel who was just shaking his head. "And you watch your ass, my brother, or you'll find yourself sporting khaki too."

They laughed at the idea of the two of them stuck in South Vietnam. Too preposterous to consider, they agreed.

"So what's happening with you and the redhead?"

"I don't really know. She wants us to go out with other people."

"Ah, that's not good, dude. She's breaking up with you."

"No, no, nothing like that. Besides she's gonna be working like crazy at a job she really loves and she's got that new apartment and…"

"I get the picture, pal. I get it. Well, good luck to the two of you. I think there's something there. I really do. It surprised the hell out of me, but you two seem to really get along."

"Thanks, Michael, I'll tell her you said so," Daniel said, throwing his friend a weak smile.

"Before we get back to my place, we need to stop for some beer or whiskey." Daniel just wrinkled his lips and said nothing.

Early the next morning, Daniel drove Michael to the Department of Transportation building in downtown St. Paul. The green Army bus was waiting at the curb for the new recruits.

"Take care of my car 'til I get back," Michael said as he threw the keys at Daniel.

"Got it!"

Daniel hugged Michael and wished him well. Michael shrugged off the gesture and punched his friend in the shoulder. He pursed his lips as if he wanted to say something more to Daniel, but then he just laughed and patted his pants pocket. "A little something for the road," he said. Then he was onboard the bus and waving as the bus pulled away.

Later that same afternoon, Daniel got a letter from Summer Blaze, postmarked San Francisco. His old girlfriend went on and on about the pending summer in San Francisco. They were calling it 'The Summer of Love', and expected thousands of young people to congregate in the city, specifically around the Haight-Ashbury neighborhood.

Summer had gotten a job at the San Francisco Oracle, the well-respected Haight-Ashbury psychedelic newspaper. She was a stringer and was paid, poorly, for leads and stories about her fellow street people and other newbies to the community. After a scare with an STD, she began to offer her help at the Haight-Ashbury free clinic.

She said there were all kinds of new things going on. There were acid tests every night in someone's pad. The Family Dog was holding dances at the Avalon Ballroom and the Fillmore was competing with great bands every weekend. A new drug was on the streets called LSD. Summer had only taken it once and had experienced the most wonderful dreamlike state that no amount of alcohol or weed would ever come close to producing.

She urged Daniel to come out. Summer said she was going to start school that fall and Daniel could easily transfer into the California system. The University of San Francisco might be a bit too rich for him but overall the UC system was affordable and Summer was sure he could get in. He could crash with her and make some bread by panhandling in the streets like she did every day. Summer ended her letter with the phrase written in bright red ink: 'Turn on, Tune in and Drop out! Love, Summer'.

For a brief moment, Daniel was sorely tempted to throw some clothes in a satchel and head toward the interstate pointing west. He could hitchhike to the West Coast, crash with his old girlfriend for the summer and then decide next fall if he wanted to come back or not. It was tempting but it would mean leaving Colleen and he wasn't about to do that. Not when their relationship needed all the attention he could give it.

Golden Legacy

Right after school let out and before her summer job began, Colleen went back to Rochester. Doctor Fitzpatrick used the visit to take her to the Rochester Country Club for one of his infrequent heart-to-hearts.

As they drove past the manicured greens and onto the paved entrance to the clubhouse, Colleen's father kept up a steady stream of praise for her academic accomplishments. Colleen could tell he was hinting at something broader but she couldn't quite put her finger on it. So even before they were ushered to her father's favorite corner table overlooking the first tee, Colleen thought she'd get the ball rolling.

"OK, Dad, what now? What pearls of wisdom do you have for me?"

"Are we being sarcastic, young lady?" Arthur asked with a smile.

"No, Dad, not at all! But, come on, I've had a great first year. I've got a job for the summer..."

"Your mother is not too happy about that, you know."

"But you got me the interview..."

"I know, but your mother was hoping you'd be home for the summer so the two of you could travel, and shop - and whatever else she thinks a mother and daughter should be doing together.

"Dad, if the truth be known, it was really Daniel who pushed me into taking that job. Not directly but indirectly by harassing me about having money and all the pitfalls that money can bring. He used to call it the residue of wealth. I'm not sure if I would have gone after that job as hard as I did if he hadn't gotten to be such a pain about it - that's just being honest. I didn't want to give you the wrong idea."

"Colleen, you still did it! You went after a job that was relevant to your career and you got it. I don't care if Daniel harangued you until you acted. You did it on your own. I'm very proud of you for that."

"So what is it you want to tell me now?" Colleen asked.

Arthur smiled.

"In the world of philanthropy there is a phrase used to describe how children carry out the continuation of family wealth accumulation. There is the bronze legacy of money, which means the children pretty much do what their parents direct them to do. There is the golden legacy of money, which means the children do it their way. They learn to distinguish the right way for them to accumulate wealth no matter how their parents might have done it in the past."

"Now that's a mouthful, Dad. I didn't expect to be talking money so soon. So you want me to follow the golden route of continuing our family wealth?"

"No," Arthur answered, surprising her. "I want you to find the golden route to your own happiness. Forget the money. It can't buy you a thing except material goods. Net worth doesn't mean a darn thing in the long run if you aren't happy. No, dear, I want you to find your own way in life - to blaze your own trail and leave your mark on the world."

"I want to be like you, Dad," Colleen said with a smile. She meant it.

Colleen admired and respected her father for his hard work and dedication to his profession. He was a self-made man and her mother's money had little to no bearing on his success as a physician.

"You have to find a purpose for being - a reason for living. Something beyond just finishing school, getting married, and having kids. You know Pastor Roberts would ask, 'Are you a human being seeking a spiritual experience or a spiritual being seeking a human experience?'"

"Pretty deep, Dad. Seriously, I know what you're saying and I agree with it. I've already thought a lot about those things. I really have. I want to be successful. But I want to do it according to my standards and not have to compromise my values. You and Mom raised me right. I also want you and Mom to be proud of me."

"You know we will be. No matter what direction you take or what you decide to do with your life. We'll always be behind you one hundred percent."

Colleen returned from Rochester after a week but could not get a hold of Daniel. His mother took the call and did not tell Daniel. When Colleen called a second time, it was only to inform Daniel that her job had begun and they would have to work hard to find time to get together.

He went over to her apartment later that evening when her roommates were gone. They watched TV, made out a little then Colleen begged off with a headache and an early morning reporters meeting. As he left her apartment, Daniel feared that was just a preview of what his summer was going to be like.

Triangle Bar

Daniel had originally discovered the Triangle Bar on the West Bank one night after finals. The well known hippie establishment was near the campus of the University of Minnesota.

The Triangle Bar had a storied history. It was built in the early Forties primarily for the Irish and Eastern European families who had taken over from the squatters and poor families of the bohemian flats. For a brief period of time, gays and lesbians hung out there. Now the crowds were, as Michael had promised, an eclectic collection of students, hippies, young business executives on the prowl and even the occasional slumming Lake Minnetonka crowd.

By his third visit to the Triangle Bar that summer, Daniel had become very comfortable among the colorful, often times stoned-out-of-their-minds hippies and artists who gathered there every night. He'd sit and listen to their stories of travel, drug culture and wild lovemaking. Most of it made up or imagined with the help of their psychedelic drugs.

On that particular night, Daniel and a stranger occupied bar stools on the fringe of the dance floor. They were rocking with the blasting ceiling speakers and drinking their 25 cent schooners of beer. The older man leaned over toward Daniel and commented about one hippie in particular.

"Careful of that one," the stranger said. "He's a pusher. Probably selling some high grade shit that will put you under or fry your brains 'til they're crisp."

"How do you know that?" Daniel asked the man.

"He's older than the rest. He's got more money by the looks of his clothes. And he's smooth. A real drugged up hippie isn't going to be that much in control." The stranger inched his stool closer to Daniel. "Trust me. I know these things, I've seen my share of pushers and dealers like him."

Daniel looked over at the hippie with new eyes. He studied the man's clothes and his demeanor. He guessed the stranger might be on to something. "My name's Daniel," he said to the stranger, extending his hand.

The stranger grabbed hold and shook Daniel's hand firmly. He had surprising strength for an older man.

"Stanislaus Zakeritur. But you can call me Zack or Zackery if you want to be formal."

"By your accent, I'm guessing you're not from here?" Daniel said.

"No, I'm from Eastern Europe originally. When the communists took over, we moved to Prague, then France, and finally Brooklyn, U.S. of A."

"So how did you end up here?"

"At the Triangle Bar, you mean? I just live a couple of blocks away."

Daniel laughed, "No, I mean how did you end up in Minnesota?"

Zack smiled and shrugged his shoulders. "Work brought me here at first. Then a woman kept me here. Now house payments won't let me leave. Except for the winters this is a pretty cool place. Not New York or San Francisco but it could rival Chicago or Denver. So I guess I'll stay."

"Where do you work?"

"Around… I usually have friends come over to my place. It's kind of a salon."

"A salon?"

"Oh, sorry. It's a place for folks to gather and talk and drink a little wine. Maybe smoke a little weed and share information. If you want, you can come over anytime."

"Thanks for the offer. Tell me where you live and I'll try to drop by sometime."

By the end of the evening, Daniel had found out that Zack had originally come from Czechoslovakia. He'd escaped the Communist rule in the 50s and came to the East Coast to stay with his sister. After she died, he stayed in New York City for a while and then migrated to the Twin Cities to stay with a cousin who had come there after World War II.

Zack came from a long line of Eastern European Bohemians and intellectuals. He'd had part-time teaching jobs at the University of Minnesota and several private colleges in the area. But his main love and passion was the 'salon' on his front porch. It was there that Zack exercised his passion for intellectual discourse and debate. The hippies in the area and especially those who congregated at the Triangle Bar were his favorite audience. He simply saw Daniel as a newfound convert to his flock.

As he drove Michael's car home that evening, Daniel felt strangely alive and excited at the prospect of engaging in discussions with Zack's group. He had no illusions that he could hold a conversation or debate with those types, but Daniel knew he could learn if he tried. It would be an education outside the confines of his college environment. It might be his window into a whole new world that excited and scared him at the same time. It could be an opportunity to explore deep within that well of desire to expand his horizons.

If Colleen became a part of my personal journey, that would be wonderful, Daniel thought. But he wasn't counting on it, or in reality, even expecting it from her. Colleen was gradually slipping away. Her new summer job, overtime on some weekends and activities with her roommates were all cutting into the precious little time Daniel already had with her.

Daniel realized that Colleen was discovering her strengths and in the process, finding out more about herself. So in that absence, Daniel decided that this summer would be his own summer of love in the Twin Cities. He would spend more time hanging out at Zack's place and the Triangle Bar. He also meant to stay in touch with Summer and learn more about her experiences in the Haight and he'd try to shore up his relationship with Colleen. At least until such time that he could feel confident enough to try to bring her into this part of his new life.

Boat Shoe Boys

Colleen's summer apartment was just a short bus ride down Grand Avenue into St. Paul. It was one of a dozen or so buildings on that block; red brick nondescript eightplex buildings rented primarily to students from the nearby colleges.

The bus ride gave Colleen a chance to read the newspaper and check out the new shops and stores. Several car dealerships hung bright colorful banners advertising their newest models. Corner grocery stores laid out their fresh produce each day and everywhere there were people filling the streets.

The St. Paul Pioneer Press and St. Paul Dispatch printed newspapers for the morning and evening editions. Hundreds of newsmen and women filled an entire building with an air of excitement that was palatable.

Colleen was assigned to the news desk. Her primary responsibilities included running copy to the print shop, minor editing of news pieces and hanging on the coattails of the news editor to be at his beck and call. Colleen realized immediately that she loved the fast paced hustle of the newsroom. Deadlines were something to be reckoned with, not feared. Colleen very quickly caught on to the routine and the hectic pace. She felt at home at the newspaper. Now she was sure that journalism was the right career choice for her.

Although Colleen's fledgling career as a journalist was starting to take off, her personal life was being sorely tested by Daniel's overt possessiveness. As much as he had promised to accept her dating other men, Daniel still couldn't let go.

One night, after a passionate make-out session, they lay on her bed. Colleen nestled her head on his chest.

"I really am happy for you," Daniel said, running his hand down her back and resting it on her bottom. "I think it's great the way your summer job has turned out… I guess I understand why you want to go out with other guys. But it's painful for me even to think about it."

Colleen leaned up to kiss Daniel tenderly on his lips. She held it there for a long time. She nestled back against his body. "Daniel, you're my best friend. I can tell you anything. It's just that I want to do so much this summer. Dating is only a small part of that. I love my job. My roommates are a little lazy but they are nice enough. It's just so important to me as a journalist that I meet new people and get experiences in the real world. I hope you don't think I'm being selfish. I want you to go out and meet new people too."

"I am."

Colleen nestled her head even tighter against Daniel's chest. "My Dad was right. This is the time for both of us to explore our worlds unencumbered by what other people think we ought to be doing."

"So your dating other men is just an experiment in living … like a journalism assignment?" Daniel laughed.

"Daniel, come on," Colleen responded with mock seriousness in her voice. "There are so many stories out there. That's one of the first things I learned at the newspaper. Stories can come from anywhere. Everyone has a story to tell. A good journalist has to find them and dig for the truth."

As she lay cuddled up next to Daniel, Colleen hadn't mentioned the new men she had met through her roommates or the ones from Lake Minnetonka who had come calling within weeks of her being back on the dating scene.

Colleen convinced herself that it was better that way. Daniel had agreed to let her date other men. She wasn't being secretive about it. She just wasn't advertising it either. What Daniel didn't know wouldn't hurt him. And that, in turn, would make their relationship continue smoother than before. A sin of omission, no, she didn't think so.

As Colleen began dating more, she realized the growing number of young men who could provide a rich variety of experiences for her. She even reluctantly admitted to Peggy that she was open to falling 'in like' and if that evolved into falling in love, she would let nature take its course.

Colleen never wanted to lose Daniel's friendship but their past relationship had grown to become far too restrictive. She was tired of feeling like a trophy or a leaning post. Once freed of Daniel's possessiveness, Colleen had found new wings in which to explore her friendship with other men. Wherever that might lead her, Colleen was willing to follow.

The boat shoe boys of Lake Minnetonka satisfied Colleen's desire for new and exciting things to do that summer. The boat shoe boys turned out to be everything the roommate said they were and more - some of it good and some of it bad.

These were the wealthy, very privileged young men who lived on and around Lake Minnetonka in the western suburbs of the Twin Cities. Their attire seldom strayed from their canvas boat shoes and frayed cargo shorts to Career Club shirts. A few would wear t-shirts but only if the shirts had been purchased abroad and identified the country of origin. While they weren't slaves to fashion, each had a closet full of the latest in menswear for each season. During the day, their beverage of choice was either Schlitz Malt Liquor or Budweiser. At night they would only drink Gordon's Gin. The girls favored Smirnoff vodka.

They knew, although seldom appreciated, their own status in society. The young men came from both old money and newly minted fortunes. They hung out at Excelsior Amusement Park for kicks or the Lafayette Club where most had their own junior membership. The cars they drove but seldom owned ranged from the Oldsmobile Tornado to the Pontiac Bonneville and the sporty Mustang to the speedy Corvette. Some even drove Thunderbirds and GTOs. Their car was always the second or third car in the family stable. A few of the boys rode their Honda Scrambler 160s from party to party or just to tool around the lake.

Most days would find the boat shoe boys on their family yachts or cruisers plying the waters of Lake Minnetonka going from one friend's dock to the next. They occasionally stopped in between for quick skinny dips in secluded bays. The pals who weren't there were either in Europe bumming around or surfing the North Shore in Hawaii. Summers on the lake were fueled by indiscriminate sex, recreational drugs, and lots of alcohol.

With no real reason to work, the boys would find mindless ways of entertaining themselves and their buddies. They liked to go slumming on Lake Street by hanging out at Porky's Drive-In with their very expensive convertibles and sports cars. They would venture down to the Gay 90's bar to try to seduce some of the strippers there. Or over to the West Bank of the University of Minnesota to buy some weed or hash from stoned out hippies.

Colleen made it a point to leave whenever the boy's conversations turned to their most recent sexual conquests. She found it cruel and intolerable and insulting to all women. But it was their tack on Vietnam that irritated Colleen the most.

These privileged sons and daughters of the rich and famous laughed at the poor slobs who got drafted and had to fight in Vietnam. The boys all agreed that they sure as hell weren't about to get their asses shot off for that Texas farmer, LBJ. Each and every one of them had a career ahead of them. They weren't about to lose it for some political cause like Vietnam.

Their stance exposed a true misunderstanding of their own privileged status in life. They assumed Colleen would feel the same. She didn't. It might have been some deep-seated fear that Michael might end up there someday. Or that he could be killed over there. It could have been the fact that her father was a veteran of the Korean War and was proud of his time in the service. No matter the reason, the boy's stance on the war aggravated Colleen to no end.

Colleen had been welcomed into that crowd because she had money and came from the Pill Hill crowd. Her roommates assumed that she, like themselves, would become a welcome addition to the boat shoe boy's circle of friends. But Colleen found she wasn't that impressed with all the glamour and prestige of hanging out with that crowd. It simply wasn't her scene.

While her mother encouraged Colleen to stay with them because she explained, "Those are our kind of people," Colleen saw most of the boating crowd as shallow and arrogant and their parents' marriages often a train wreck. She enjoyed the boat trips with her new friends but their blatant snobbishness rubbed her the wrong way.

During the warm summer months, Colleen divided her time between work during the week and weekends on the lake. Her new friends came and went and eventually Colleen found a cadre of select men and women who shared her sense of decorum that summer. She liked hanging out with them. Romance was seldom hinted at and she was OK with that. She enjoyed their company and the club-like atmosphere of their get-togethers.

Daniel was coming by the apartment less and less often. His absence helped ease the guilt Colleen would sometimes feel.

One night in particular Colleen and Daniel got into a heated argument after she came home late from a day on the lake. Daniel was sure she'd been there with other guys but Colleen insisted it was just a bunch of friends from down the block on Grand Avenue. Yes, there were boys on the boat. But no one she knew or cared to know at the end of the day.

Daniel had to accept what Colleen said. What other choice did he have?

Daniel and Colleen drove down the Mississippi River Boulevard and parked in a lot at the end of Summit Avenue. As they got out of the car, Daniel began to mock the boat shoe boys. He began his lecture about the fallacy of trying to follow fashion trends. Or more correctly, the stupidity of thinking that one could ever keep up with the latest of Paris fashions.

"The only way to stay ahead of fashion is to create your own look and forget what everyone else is wearing," he lectured Colleen.

"Oh, Daniel, come on."

"Chasing the latest in fashion trends is spiritually unrewarding. It's only for status seekers. Those socially obsessed folks are always trying to be numero uno."

"Where did you hear that?" Colleen asked, "from your hippie friends?"

"Yeah, so?"

"Oh, Daniel."

“What?”

Colleen gave Daniel a funny look then said, “I think for my mother it’s a kind of mother-daughter bonding. But along the way, she did teach me all about color coordination and fabric quality. I learned a lot from those shopping trips. Besides, I always want to look nice.”

“All I’m saying is don’t be a slave to someone else’s fashion taste.”

“I agree that you can’t always stay on top of fashion… but I wouldn’t criticize someone who tries. If you have confidence, I think it shows in the way you dress. I want to express my authentic self by dressing for me, the way I want to dress. And if that is wearing a new style, I don’t have a problem with that.”

“You can never get ahead of it,” Daniel repeated. “I mean, look at those girls on your campus, they…”

As he was rambling on, Colleen looked over at his attire again and began to laugh, catching Daniel by surprise. “What are you laughing at?”

“I’m looking at your frayed bell-bottom jeans, scuffed boots, your ratty t-shirt and that stubble on your chin you think is an excuse for a beard. You look like a cross between a beat poet and a homeless squatter from the Bohemian Flats.”

“So? I’m expressing myself.”

“And I’m wondering who made you the expert on fashion and how to dress properly.”

“I don’t get your point, Colleen. What are you trying to say?”

“I take pride in how I dress, and I think you should too.” Colleen stopped to face Daniel, “What I’m trying to say, Daniel, is that dressing like some hippie won’t get you into the Playboy Fall Fashion pictorial. If you want to be taken seriously … and I know you do … then you need to get a real collegiate look. If Playboy isn’t your guide, then choose some other magazine to look at for ideas.’

“I’m just saying…”

“I know you want to be creative, Daniel. And I respect that. I really do. But you have to dress the part too. Dressing like a slob won’t cut it. The Beats dress that way because they’re all just a bunch of depressed old men. Besides, I hate your beard. You know that. Why do you refuse to shave if you know I don’t like it?”

Daniel stopped dead in his tracks. “I’m not doing this to spite you, Colleen. I feel comfortable dressed like this. My friends at the Triangle Bar dress this way. There’s nothing wrong with it.”

“You still don’t get it, Daniel.”

"Forget the fashion questions" Daniel reached out to hold Colleen's hand. "Let's just enjoy this night."

Colleen's hand was limp but Daniel held on, hoping she might respond to his touch. She didn't.

Boone's Farm Bouquet

Colleen's hectic work schedule meant that she never knew when she might be called to put in extra hours in the newsroom or act as a stringer for some event in town. Numerous times Daniel would call or stop by but Colleen was either at work or covering some news story. She continued to ask for Daniel's patience but it wore thin pretty quickly as the days dragged deep into summer. With Colleen only having an intermittent presence in his life, Daniel headed back to the West Bank with greater frequency.

The Triangle Bar became a daily stop for Daniel after work. Even most weekends, he'd stop by just to chill out and listen to the music with the other hangers-on.

Zack, the old Bohemian, was seldom there but when he was present, there was always a large crowd gathered with him. Zack invited Daniel over to his house on several occasions but Daniel was too tired to go or maybe just anxious to see if Colleen was available, so he would decline.

One day the old man came in alone and walked right up to Daniel who was sitting on a stool at the bar. Zack slid into the chair next to Daniel and ordered a beer for himself and another one for Daniel.

"Are you ready to meet my friends tonight?" he asked Daniel.

"I am," Daniel quickly answered.

"No girlfriend tonight?"

"No girlfriend tonight," Daniel shook his head, "hasn't been a girlfriend for a good part of the summer now. She's too busy with work, going back home to Rochester on weekends, and going out on dates."

"Your girlfriend is going out on dates? And you're OK with that?"

"I don't have much choice," Daniel answered. "It's something we … I guess *I,* agreed to. It was either that or I think she would have broken up with me."

"Going out on dates with other guys *is* breaking up with you!"

"No. Not really. We have this understanding. We're going to go out with other people because she thinks it will strengthen our relationship."

One of the older hippies sitting next to the pair looked over Zack's shoulder and commented, "She's probably spanking somebody's monkey right now!" he laughed out loud and went back to his beer.

"I don't get it?" Daniel said.

"Boy, she's pulling your chain," Zack caught himself. "But, it's none of my business. Come on home with me and meet my friends. They'll put you on the straight and narrow about relationships."

Daniel laughed and followed the old man out the door and down the street. Zack's place was an old foursquare house with a large screened in porch in front. The front yard hadn't been cut in some time and there was debris lying all around. It was across from a park and surrounded by old houses just a block away from the Mississippi River. Daniel recognized it as close to the hippie house where he and Colleen had gone that first evening together.

As they walked up the front steps, Daniel could hear a multitude of voices inside the front porch. As he followed Zack inside, Daniel could see two bright multi-colored hammocks hanging there. A small group of hippies were gathered in one corner, smoking and drinking from a large jug of cheap wine. One of the hippies raised his glass and muttered "Boone's Farm." Another hippie joined in, "Bouquet," he said. They both laughed.

The old man swung up into one of the hammocks and motioned for Daniel to do the same to the second one. Zack dug deep into his pocket and drew out a thin white cigarette which he tossed to Daniel, then pointed toward a corner table with a large glass pitcher on it.

"Try some of my stuff. It's pretty good," he said. "And some wine in the corner. It's room temperature but after a couple of glasses you won't particularly care."

The night began innocently enough with a couple of marijuana joints. Several glasses of Boone's Farm later, Daniel was beginning to feel a buzz he hadn't felt in a very long time. More people wandered in and drew up chairs to join in the conversation.

That first evening, they talked about everything from the Beats to new age writers, poets, government conspiracies, self-expression, and travel.

They laughed at the San Francisco hippie scene when someone pointed out that it wasn't a location but rather a state of mind. Zack said that the term "psychedelic" originally referred to ideas or approaches that were somehow outrageous or nonconformist. But after some hippie opened the first Psychedelic Shop on Haight Street, the word became associated with the hallucinatory drugs sold nearby. By then the word had become synonymous with a whole hippie lifestyle.

The conversation droned on but Daniel was having a hard time staying awake. The wine and marijuana plus the warm night air all combined to send him into a constant state of drowsiness.

He awoke the next morning stiff and sore from the hammock and facing an empty porch. He lay there for a long time, savoring the deep satisfaction of listening to all those other men discussing topics he'd never addressed before. Zack came out minutes later with a cup of coffee in his hand.

"Here, drink this," he said, "it's Columbian - strong enough to put hair on your pecker. It'll wake you up too." He sat down on a cushion in one corner and started drinking his own cup of coffee. "Did you survive last night?"

"I loved it! I know I didn't participate very much. But it was just so neat listening to those guys talking about everything. It was like my own education outside of the classroom."

"Well, if you come back, we can get you educated on all sorts of things."

Over the rest of the summer, Daniel returned to Zack's place as often as he could. The conversations on those warm summer nights ranged from sane to insane, from religious to sexual to philosophical to just plain stupid. The juxtaposition of the dialogue was often dictated by the amount of alcohol consumed or drugs ingested. Sometimes it made perfect sense to Daniel. Other times, he made no sense of it even with help from the wine and weed.

Gradually, Daniel found himself drawn more and more into the conversations. When the topic was about bucking status and class in America, Daniel talked about his own upbringing by a single parent and neglectful father. He told the others in the room that he rejected the notion that he was born into a certain class in America and that he had to accept that status for the rest of his life. He said his mother disagreed and they'd often get into heated arguments. She thought he should know his place and not be stupid about trying to become something he wasn't equipped to become. He disagreed and said he could become anything or anyone he wanted to be.

The hippies agreed with Daniel. They assured him that if he wanted status, he could and he should make his own but to remain true to himself in the process. Be honest and true to his own values and principles, they told Daniel. Never sell out to the man. Never!

One of the female hippies named Rita, an outspoken lesbian who flaunted her sexuality to both the men and the women, said that American society had suppressed its own far too long. The blacks and the poor were culturally underclass citizens in this country. The working class fared little better. He could certainly identify with her statement.

As the conversation waned that night from suppression of the underclass to the evils of wealth in this country, Daniel couldn't help but reflect on his conversations with Colleen.

He began to realize that his aversion toward rich people had more to do with his own feelings of financial insecurity than any kind of jealousy of their accumulated wealth. He understood more clearly now the wide chasm between himself and Colleen. Not just her current status but also her life in general. Colleen had been raised with many privileges and he had envied them all - her home life, having two loving parents who cared about her, her travels and her access to life experiences that he could never dream of for himself.

Rita took a liking to Daniel. She shut the others up when they started to give him shit and she offered the boy an ear when he wanted to talk. "About the only thing I like better than a salon like this one would be sweet young camel toe," she said one night.

Daniel didn't get it at first but he smiled and nodded anyway. Rita encouraged him to think for himself and to find his own role in life. She told him he shouldn't let other people define who he was or what kind of man he could become. If he wanted to climb up that social ladder, he'd have to build the damn thing himself.

As Rita resumed her litany of advice on the task of building or rebuilding his life, others started to pipe in with their own two cents. Dead-end jobs were soul-destroying, they said. Daniel should find a job he could control. He should be the master of his own destiny; the architect of his own dreams and his own boss. He should find a job that fit his needs - not the other way around. And by doing that, Daniel would be circumventing the archaic rules and regulations of society. He would be making his own pathway through life and not hindered by the expectations of others. In short, he would become his own man.

The crowd at Zack's place seldom varied. It was an odd assortment of hippies, dropouts, a couple of college professors and several strange people who didn't fit any of those descriptions. Wild Man was one of the odd-man-out types.

Wild Man was a middle-aged relic with a tie-dye t-shirt and wild hair that looked as if he had just stuck his finger into a light socket. As he stumbled in one night, a few of the regulars called out his name and he acknowledged them with a wave of his cigarette. He perused the crowd, recognized most of the regulars and then spotted Daniel in one corner.

"What's your name?" he asked as he approached Daniel. He stopped just long enough to scoop up a bottle of beer before stepping in front of the kid.

Before Daniel could answer, Zack called out from across the room. "He goes by the name of Gypsy Boy."

"I do?" Daniel asked, looking over at Zack. This was the first time he'd heard himself referred to by that name.

Zack stood up and started to move toward Wild Man. He pointed at Daniel as he approached the two of them. "I give all my friends names and he looks like some kind of gypsy. And he's still a little wet behind the ears, so I call him gypsy boy." He turned to Daniel who was looking up at the two of them. "That suit you?" he asked Daniel.

Daniel beamed in response. A nickname meant he had an identity within the group. It was a moniker Daniel could hold on to with pride. It was acceptance by this group of intellectual explorers that Daniel admired and wanted so much to be like. "Suits me just fine, Zack," he answered. The smile on his face extended from check to check.

Wild Man sat down next to Daniel. "So, G.B.," he asked, "what are you drinking?"

"I've got a Bud."

"That's shit beer, man," Wild Man said. "You should be drinking some real beer."

"Like what?"

"I got me a Kingfisher here from India," Wild Man answered as he upended the bottle. "It's a good pale ale. You could also try a Myanmar Lager from Burma or Angkor from Cambodia, but stay the hell away from Bia Hoi. Thirty-Three is worse. That shit tastes like formaldehyde. In fact, stay away from the whole damn country. That's Gook beer and it's no good."

"Gook, meaning Vietnamese?"

"Exactly," Wild Man replied. "They're killing white folks there now. It's not like before. It used to be easy duty - after the French and before JFK got us involved. You'd get foreign country pay, hazardous duty pay, and maybe a stipend if you could work it right. Shit, you could make some good money over there. Not anymore!"

Zack sat down on the floor by the other two men. "Wild Man here was a CIA operative throughout Southeast Asia," he said. "The man got into a lot of shit over there. Clandestine operations, cross border intrusions, assassin…"

"But if I told you about it," Wild Man interrupted, "then I'd have to kill you."

Daniel couldn't tell if Wild Man was serious or not.

"Are you in college, G.B.?" Wild man asked, changing the subject.

"Yeah, College of St. Paul over in..."

"What's your major?"

"I haven't declared it yet. But I'm leaning toward business … or art."

"Could you be a little more across the board?" Zack asked. Wild Man laughed.

"What do you mean?"

"Business and art don't mix. They're two entirely different disciplines. One you can make some serious money. The other one will leave you starving most of the time."

"I disagree," Daniel said, surprising himself as the words came out of his mouth. "I think I can get a degree in either business or art and use the discipline I learn to both further my career and make money."

"Then buy houses cheap, fix them up and resell them. Or become a developer," Zack said. "You can always make money in real estate if you know what you're doing and are willing to take risks."

"Is that what you did, Zack?" Daniel asked.

"Before I developed a taste for the finer things in life."

"Like women and wine," Wild Man interjected, "any kind of women and any kind of booze."

"Not quite, Wild Man, but close," Zack said.

Daniel looked at the two and said, "I sometimes imagine what it would be like to go back and…"

"You can't go back, kid," Wild Man interrupted. "Remember that, you can never go back!"

"Wild Man is right," Zack interjected. "I remember the time I was in Brussels at a hostel. I met this beautiful Canadian girl. We were having breakfast together. She had on this pure white turtleneck sweater. Man, she had big tits. I mean she was stacked. She was smart and kind and just plain stunning."

"And?" both Daniel and Wild Man inquired at the same time.

"I kept that memory with me all summer as I traveled throughout Europe. I kept imagining what it would be like to see her again - to be with her again at that hostel. So I made a special trip to go back there. Not really to see her again. She was long gone. But just to relive those feelings I had when I first met her there."

"And everything had changed," Wild Man said as he reached for another bottle of beer.

"Exactly!" Zack answered. "The hostel was still there. But there was a different staff. They were attracting a different kind of traveler. It was a whole different kind of atmosphere. Nothing like before when I was there. Turned my dreams into shit right there at the same breakfast nook where I first met her. Memories were all I had left. Everything else was gone."

"So, G.B., whatever you think you might want to revisit or relive, forget it!" Wild Man glanced over at Zack who nodded in agreement. "Ain't gonna happen! What has passed is the past; relegated to the dust bin of your mind."

Zack handed a bottle of Kingfisher over to Daniel. "Son, if school was hard this last year for you, it won't get any better next year. You can't go back and fix what you did or didn't do back then. And if your girlfriend is growing distant from you, there's a good chance that can't be fixed either. You can't go back to what you had freshman year and try to make the present like the past. It just doesn't work. Believe me, I know."

Wild Man piped in, "Old Zack here has had a couple of wives and many girlfriends. Once they're gone, they're ancient history."

"Sorry for the frank talk, kid, but we like you. We want to give it to you straight. You could learn from the mistakes we've all made."

As Daniel stumbled back to Michael's car that night, he felt changed. A huge burden had been lifted off his shoulders. He was no longer beholden to Colleen's work schedule. He was no longer willing to wait at her apartment building into the early morning hours, hoping that she might get off work soon. If Colleen wanted to date other guys, he'd let her.

For reasons even he couldn't comprehend or explain, Daniel was no longer afraid of dropping out of school, nor of being drafted. If he got his notice, Daniel could decide to go fight or head north to Canada. But whatever he did, Daniel would decide that for himself. And not let Uncle Sam do it for him.

Rainy Day Monday

One cold and overcast Monday morning as late summer slowly dissolved to the subtle changes of fall, Daniel changed his life forever.

He made the decision to drop out of school. He knew he was taking a chance the moment he escaped the crushing confines of collegiate life. But that didn't really matter anymore. Daniel wasn't willing to go back and repeat freshman year. The die was cast. He was moving on with his life.

Matters with Colleen only exasperated the situation. By then, Daniel was questioning everything about their strained relationship. Was it really over? Could he salvage even a part of what they once had; love, friendship, trust and total honesty with one another? The reasons to stay in school were even harder to come by. In the end both seemed hopeless causes.

For her part, Colleen was spending more and more time with her rich and influential friends. Combined with work, the lake, and weekends in Rochester, she was seldom home. When she and Daniel did manage time together, he always brought with him an air of tension and uneasiness. It was nothing like the fun they used to have freshman year.

A light rain was slowly darkening the shoulders of his jean jacket as Daniel trudged over to Zack's place. He was seeking council from his new friends there. Most of them said he should escape to Canada. The only exception was Wild Man who told Daniel to be a man and face his future head on. If Daniel got drafted, Wild Man shouted, he should go into the military and grab all the experiences he could in leadership, skill building, critical thinking, military strategy and self-direction.

"Make the most of it," he chided Daniel. "Don't let these candy-ass pussies tell you what to do."

Daniel smiled at Wild Man's rants, clicked beer bottles with him, and let him go on for another twenty minutes. He thanked his audience, embraced Wild Man in an awkward sign of affection and turned away before anyone could see the tears building.

Now all that was left was breaking the news to Colleen. Daniel knew that she would be crushed and would probably try to talk him out of it. But he'd made up his mind. He was dropping out of school, period.

After calling ahead to make sure Colleen was there, Daniel went to her apartment to tell her the news. It would probably come as a complete surprise to her, he thought. But he would be strong and put on a good front. He would reassure Colleen that it was only two years. And the chances of going to Vietnam, especially since he had a year of college, were miniscule. Daniel was golden. That one year of college had probably upgraded him from meat-shield to stateside duty or the European theater for sure.

As Daniel arrived at Colleen's apartment, he saw her sitting on the front steps. She waved to him as he approached. Good, he thought, she's out front waiting to see me. Now be strong, he reminded himself. Put on a good face.

"I've only got a couple of minutes," Colleen said, "my ride will be here shortly."

"Ride for what?"

"I'm going out with some friends. I told you."

"No, Colleen, you didn't," Daniel answered in a huff. "I wouldn't have come over tonight if I thought you had another date."

"Daniel, come on! It's not a date. It's a couple of friends and we're just going to hang out."

"I wouldn't have come…"

"What did you want to tell me, Daniel?" Colleen said as she looked up and down Grand Avenue. "Come on, I'm listening."

"I'm quitting school, Colleen. I'm dropping out."

"Really?" Colleen asked in an uninterested manner. She kept looking up and down the street.

"You don't seem surprised." Daniel stammered, his heart now suddenly in the pit of his stomach.

"What?"

"I'm quitting school."

Colleen turned to face him. She saw how serious Daniel had become.

"Seriously?" Colleen asked, now focusing her attention on Daniel. "I mean, I knew you had a hard time freshman year and sophomore year was going to be a struggle… What are you going to do?"

"Don't know. Might try to go to New York and work construction."

"What if you're called up?"

"We talked about that at Zack's place. I got advice to run to the border and hide out with the underground, or just enlist instead of waiting for the draft. I think if I get called up, I'll just go."

Colleen was at a loss for words. Gently taking Daniel's hand in her hand, she sat down on the front steps. Suddenly very pensive, she looked up at Daniel and motioned for him to sit next to her. Daniel sat down beside her. "I'll miss you if you go. You know that, don't you?"

"I guess."

"No, guessing. It's true. I will miss you a lot. Who will I have to talk to?"

"Oh come on, face it, Colleen. You and I haven't exactly been burning up the phone lines or spending much time together this summer."

"I know it's been hard for you this summer, Daniel, I really do. But I had to have my space. I needed to get out more and meet new people. And do things I hadn't done when we were together."

"I know that, Colleen. I guess I was just too jealous of anyone else spending time with you… when I couldn't. It was stupid and selfish…"

"Yes, it was!"

"I said it was! I know that now. I know how I feel now and how I felt all summer. I can't change that. I don't want to change that…"

"Who am I going to talk to?" Colleen asked.

"What do you mean?"

"I mean, who can I turn to if I need to confide in someone?"

"Your parents."

"Not all the time. You're the only one that I can trust to be completely honest with me, Daniel. You are brutally frank, even to the point of hurting my feelings…"

"I never intended to…"

"Yes, yes. I know that. I was hoping we could rebuild our friendship next year… Oh, shoot, it's my ride!"

A large soft blue Cadillac convertible pulled up to the curb. Five kids waved at Colleen as she stood up and turned to Daniel. He stood up next to her. She put her hands up, cupping his face close to hers. "I do have to go," she said. "Call me tomorrow and let's get together so we can talk some more … promise?"

"I'm…"

"No, Daniel, promise me you'll call."

"I promise."

But tomorrow never came. Colleen was given a special newspaper assignment the very next morning. She was gone all that day and late into the evening. Her parents insisted she come to Rochester for the next weekend. Her roommates told Daniel they weren't sure when she'd be back. She hadn't left any messages for Daniel.

It was nearly a week before Daniel got a hold of Colleen to set up another meeting. But by then he'd gotten his draft notice and had just two days before his induction.

He went to the Triangle Bar for one last time before shipping out. But it wasn't encouraging.

"She's out of your league," His old cronies reminded him. "She's a player and a prick tease. She will break your heart. Dump her before she dumps you." He listened quietly to all their advice, thanked them and left for Zack's place.

Zack's place was strangely quiet. One hippie, swinging slowly on a hammock, told Daniel that the old man had left town suddenly and wasn't expected back for several weeks. He offered Daniel some weed and Temple wine but Daniel wasn't in the mood. Daniel had hoped to say goodbye to the Zack himself. But instead he just ended up scribbling down a brief message and gave it to the stoned hippie.

He got a call from Colleen the night before he left for boot camp. She apologized profusely for not contacting him sooner but her work, her parents and other obligations were keeping her running around like crazy. She insisted on seeing him and showing him something special. Colleen wanted to be the last person he saw before he went into the service.

When Daniel arrived at Colleen's apartment, he noticed a bright red Mustang convertible parked in front. It was one of the most beautiful cars Daniel had ever seen. It had chrome wheels and tan leather upholstery - a totally bitchin' automobile. Maybe when he got out of the service, Daniel fantasized, maybe then he could have a car like that.

Colleen saw him coming and ran out to meet him. She wrapped her arms around his neck and kissed him on the lips. Startled, Daniel just looked down at her smiling face. Maybe he had been wrong about her. Maybe she really did care.

"Isn't it beautiful?" Colleen said, pointing back toward the car.

"You've got to be kidding. You mean that's yours?"

"My parents gave it to me because I worked so hard this summer. Isn't that great?"

Daniel smiled at the exuberant young woman looking up at him. "It is a nice car, Colleen," he said. "It really is. And I'm sure you deserve it. You did work hard this summer."

"I can't believe you're really leaving tomorrow morning. It just seems like yesterday when we first met at that dance. You and I and Michael and Peggy. That was almost a year ago. Now you're going into the service and I'm about to start my sophomore…"

Daniel forced out a weak smile.

"I'm sorry we never connected after that last time we talked. I mean work got to be so…"

"It's OK, Colleen. I understand. Really, I do."

Colleen began talking again about some of the silly times they'd had together; the loud chatter in the library, getting kicked out of the coffee lounge late at night, their romantic entanglements in the dark confines of the movie theater.

But as Colleen was nervously rambling on, Daniel could feel a terrible sadness descend over him. It wasn't jealousy or envy. He really was glad for Colleen. She did deserve that car. She was a wonderful and beautiful young woman who was blessed with very loving, generous parents.

Instead Daniel felt he'd made a terrible mistake in quitting school. In doing so he'd blown any chance to repair his relationship with this woman he truly loved. He'd dropped out of school without giving it a fighting chance. So while Colleen was charging ahead with her collegiate career, Daniel had effectively derailed his own future.

It was the same overwhelming sense of abandonment that Daniel had felt when his mother wouldn't support his decision to enter college. The same deep internal pain he'd felt when his father had walked out on them, leaving his mother sobbing hysterically in the living room. Now Daniel was abandoning the one thing, the one person who meant the world to him. He was running away. He was abandoning his past for an unknown future.

"I've got to go," Daniel said suddenly. He was desperate to get out of there. He couldn't bear to face Colleen anymore. The pain in his heart was just too intense.

"Can't you stay a little longer, Daniel?"

"No," Daniel lied. "I've still got to see my Mom. I've got to pack and I'm supposed to be in downtown St. Paul at the armory first thing tomorrow morning."

"Well, wait a minute. I have something for you."

She turned and ran back inside the building. Moments later she emerged with a package. She handed it to Daniel.

"Here, open it."

Daniel slowly pulled the paper back and opened the box. It was a metal bird made of polished silver.

"It's supposed to be a phoenix," Colleen said. "I found it in a small shop in Wayzata. I thought about you when I saw it. You can take it with you or leave it at your mom's."

"So you think I'm going to burn myself up and rise from the ashes?" Daniel laughed weakly.

"No. I think the old Daniel is going to come back a new and refreshed person ready to tackle whatever he wants to. That's what it means to me. I hope that's what it will mean to you."

"Well, thank you. It is pretty neat. And yes, I'll leave it at my mother's so it doesn't get lost."

"I can drive you tomorrow morning."

"No, that would hurt too much."

"I don't understand, Daniel. This isn't the end of the world. We can still write to one another. If you're stateside, you can call me." Colleen moved up closer until she was just inches from his face. She put her arms around his waist and drew him in closer. "We're still the best of friends, Daniel. Don't you ever forget that! Life has a strange way of throwing us curves sometimes. But we just have to learn to live with it. Let life take its proper course. It'll all work out in the end. You just wait and see. Seriously, I do believe that. Don't you?"

"I guess."

"Promise me you'll call once you get to camp."

"I don't know if I…"

"No, Daniel, promise me you will call."

"I promise I will try, Colleen, that's all I can promise."

"Good. When will you be back?"

"No idea. Sometimes they give you a break between boot camp and AIT, advanced infantry training. But then sometimes they just ship you from one place to the next. I have no control over that."

"Well, we have to get together when you get back from camp. We can talk more then, when you're not so uptight."

Daniel gave her a hug then a kiss and stepped back. "I'm sorry, Colleen but I really have to go. I'll keep in touch."

"You'd better," was all Daniel heard as he turned and walked away. He dared not look back because he knew if he did, he might be tempted to run back into Colleen's arms. And he couldn't bear the thought of having to leave her a second time.

That evening was the worst night of Daniel's life. He tossed and turned and woke up in a cold sweat. His heart was racing and he felt like a dead man. He'd blown it and he knew it. Everything that had meant something to him was drifting away. Now he had to face an uncertain future and the likelihood that Colleen would be moving on with her life without him.

Sophomore Year: 1967–1968

Stinky Fingers with Sad Faces

The trip to boot camp at Fort Leonard Wood, Missouri started out promisingly enough. Daniel and the other recruits took an overnight bus down through the Iowa heartland. Like Daniel, most of the young men couldn't sleep at all. Instead they just peered out at the blackness surrounding them and focused on the occasional distant farm light. Their chatter was meaningless and just took up the little time they had left as civilians. The bus would pass through small towns illuminated by naked streetlights and an insomniac or two in their living rooms. Eventually it grew deathly quiet on the bus except for the snoring, some muttering and the sound of the bus driver's portable radio playing honky-tonk music.

Daniel was alone with his thoughts of Colleen. She would be sleeping in her single bed by now. He wished he was there sleeping alongside her. He imagined what her flannel nightgown would have felt like, pressed up against his flesh. How her freshly washed beautiful auburn hair would have spilled out across her pillow. He could feel the warmth of her body. He would run his hand alongside her arm, feeling the softness there; then across her belly … lower and lower … until he brushed ever so gently up against her hair. It was coarse but soft. He would press forward until he reached the spot. But he would stop there. She would stir. Did she want him to continue? Did she want to roll over and press her belly against his? Would she spread her legs and invite him in with a deep kiss?

He pushed those thoughts away. Instead he wondered what she was dreaming about. Was she thinking about him? Was she missing him? It was all so very confusing and painful.

That dream and those wonderful images changed in an instant with the harsh grinding of bus brakes and shouts coming from outside the bus. Daniel glanced at his watch. It was four o'clock in the morning. Daniel's life was about to change - and not for the better.

Four drill sergeants, each dressed in identical starched khaki and carrying riding crops, met the recruits outside the reception center. If there was any question in the recruits' minds what boot camp would be like, they had their answer in the first five seconds. The shouts and screams of the drill sergeants assaulted their senses even before the young boys had scrambled out of their seats and off the bus. It only went downhill from there.

They got into formation and were pushed and shoved into proper alignment. The screams maintained as they were jammed into the Induction Center along with other busloads of fresh meat. Clothes were stripped off and drab ugly uniforms were assigned. They had three minutes to get dressed and back into formation. All their hair was shaved off within the first hour.

Housing came next. Each group was broken down into squads of six men and forced to jog two blocks to their assigned barracks. A two-tier bunk was assigned and Daniel found himself on the bottom bunk under an overweight, grumbling black kid from North Minneapolis. He looked as confused and scared as Daniel.

The first week was a blur of screaming drill sergeants, classroom introduction to army life and PT; physical training, five hours a day. The workouts were not as hard on Daniel as it was on so many other recruits. His muscular frame held up well during the rigorous drills and long marches. He didn't like it but he could tolerate it. *If I'm going to be in this man's army, I may as well do it right.*

Boot camp was the place where boys were made mean, then angry at nothing in particular and finally molded into potential killers for their nation. The DIs, drill instructors, started screaming at the recruits at four in the morning and didn't stop their rants until lights out at ten.

Daniel took it all in stride and didn't flinch as most of the other recruits did. He was used to the screaming and shouting and physical abuse. He quickly adapted to the organized chaos and, in a strange sort of way, found it a challenge he was eager to meet and overcome. He did what he was told and he did it better than any recruit in his squad.

The first three weeks consisted of learning the basic skills of a soldier. PT decimated the ranks of the fat, the weak, and the lazy. Those youngsters who couldn't keep up were shoved back to form new squads of losers. They faced the harshest treatment by the drill sergeants whose only intent was to whip those sorry-ass civilians into fighting warriors in as short a time as possible. Fortunately for Daniel, he passed the early physical tests and advanced to the first platoon by the third week.

The recruits were told to write home to assure their parents of their safe arrival. Daniel deferred. His mother would assume he was all right. Colleen was just starting school and Daniel didn't have anything new to tell her anyway. Maybe he'd write to her later on in Boot Camp.

After the physical part of training had divided the recruits into qualified squads and platoons, the fun began. Daniel learned to assemble, disassemble and fire the new M-16 rifle. He also learned to throw a grenade, fire a machine gun, handle a rocket launcher and become an expert in driving an assortment of military vehicles.

Daniel and his squad would do forced bivouacs deep into the hot, dank Missouri forests. There his squad pitched their tents deep in the woods and endured screaming drill sergeants for a good part of the night. It was all part of the routine; each exercise meant to toughen up the recruits and mold them into genuine bad ass soldiers. Under the stern tutelage of the drill instructors, Daniel and his fellow recruits were becoming the killers needed in Vietnam.

Newspaper reports to the contrary, the army instructors told them that the Viet Minh and Viet Cong were not ill-equipped irregulars living on a handful of rice a day. They were, in fact, tightly organized and well-disciplined guerrilla fighters. Their armament came from China and Soviet Russia and was some of the best in the world. The training Daniel and his companions were receiving in basic and then AIT might be their only lifeline should they be shipped off to Vietnam.

Their daily marches kept getting longer and longer. As they marched along, the drill sergeants kept them repeating the same cadence chant over and over. It was an age-old army classic called 'Jody' that went back as far as World War II.

The purpose of the song was simple enough. If any recruit thought his 'girl' was waiting for him back home, the song meant to change his mind. Not only was she no longer waiting for him, she was probably already screwing his best friend. As they marched along, the squads all sang in unison:

Ain't no use in lookin' back
Jody's got your Cadillac
Ain't no use in lookin' back
Jody's got your Cadillac

Ain't no use in lookin' blue
Jody's got your girlfriend too
Ain't no use in lookin' back
Jody's got her in the sack.

The drill sergeants hammered home, every opportunity they could, that the army was the recruit's new home. Most took it to heart. Daniel was caught in between, hoping he could rekindle the love he and Colleen had once shared, but scared to death that it might be over already.

By week seven, Daniel was feeling confident enough to write to Colleen and tell her of his boot camp experiences. It wasn't a long letter but rather sparse on the details and even less on his desire to come home and see her again. He'd said what he had to say before he left. There was no reason to repeat himself.

Daniel called Colleen once near the end of basic training. It was a brief phone call that was safe and pleasant. Colleen was very busy with her classes. She and her new classmates were involved in all kinds of extracurricular activities. Daniel felt a sharp stab to his heart at that comment. He could only imagine what kind of extracurricular activities Colleen was referring to. Had she met someone new? Was she already involved with someone else? His imagination went wild and he had to get drunk just to lessen the pain of thinking about her.

By the end of week eight, the recruits received their next assignments. Daniel was being sent to Fort Benning, Georgia for AIT. He had the option of going there right after graduation or going home first. He thought about it briefly and decided it would be much too painful to go back home and then leave again. He would take the bus directly to Fort Benning. Maybe he'd go home after that.

If Daniel thought Georgia would have a mild climate in the fall, he was sadly mistaken. Heat and humidity dogged his every footstep during training. Three showers a day only lessened his discomfort for a brief time until he was called out again for more training.

It was, Daniel was told repeatedly by the non-coms, good training for Vietnam. The chance that he would be deployed to Southeast Asia was growing more likely by the week.

Daniel became a squad leader. Soon he made PFC, (Private First Class) and then temporary platoon leader. He had a chance to try out for airborne but he declined. Daniel was determined to make the most of his time in the service. But he wasn't about to extend his tour of duty just for the opportunity to jump out of an airplane. He looked into the possibility of correspondence classes, which might transfer back to St. Paul's. There were a number he could take. Once settled in someplace, Daniel decided that was what he would do with his spare time. Daniel was determined to finish college no matter what.

Part of the new soldier's indoctrination to combat training was the acceptance of casualties in war. One of the cadence chants they sang everyday ended with the familiar refrain:

If I die in the combat zone
Box me up and ship me home
If I die in the combat zone
Box me up and ship me home.

Of course, no one believed they would be coming home in the metal box. Even Daniel couldn't bear to think about never seeing Colleen again. By the end of AIT, Daniel was on a leadership track and headed to the Defense Language School in Monterey, California. Next stop after that would be Vietnam.

Once again, Daniel chose to go directly to California instead of heading home.

Daniel was assigned to language school to learn the basics of the Vietnamese language, including the dialect differences. His job would be to act as an interpreter for his combat unit, as yet to be assigned.

After several weeks in school, Daniel called Colleen from a pay phone in the lobby of the Enlisted Men's Club. He was feeling good about himself and his classes were going well. The language school was fast becoming Daniel's graduate school education.

"But why didn't you come home first?" Colleen asked.

"Colleen, it's too hard to explain. There really wasn't enough time if I wanted to get settled in and prep for my classes. Really, it's best it worked out this way."

"Peggy's new boyfriend said that you could have come home if you wanted to. Everyone is automatically given a seven-day pass. You didn't have to go directly to Georgia either. Isn't that true?"

"Colleen, it's like I told you before. It would have been too hard for me to come home for a week of what? You were in school. Michael's gone. There would have been nothing for me to do."

"We could have gone out in the evenings," Colleen offered.

"That's true but…"

"Anyway, how are you?" she asked.

"Well, for better or worse, I'm getting used to this man's army. They've got their own way of doing things here. But if you play the game by their rules, it isn't so bad after all."

"So are you learning their rules?"

"Well enough to get promoted to PFC and made squad leader. I've had a ton of language classes, orientation classes on Vietnam and history lessons on Southeast Asia. They're even talking about teaching us stuff about covert operations if it ever came to that. But mainly, they're grooming me to be an interpreter once I get to Vietnam."

"Vietnam! Are you sure you're going to Vietnam?"

"Sure as shi…" Daniel caught himself. "Yes, Colleen, I am very sure I will be shipping off to Tan Son Nhut in Nam sooner than later. Probably in a month or so."

"Oh shoot! Daniel, I'm sorry. I have to go to practice now. I'm going to be late."

"I understand," Daniel said, not bothering to ask what kind of practice or if it was really that urgent. "I'll call before I leave."

"Do! Promise me you'll call so we can talk longer."

"I promise, Colleen."

"I really do have to go. Sorry," she said and then the phone line went dead.

Daniel stood there for a long time, holding the phone in his limp hand. The veterans were right. It probably would have been smarter and less painful to have not called Colleen in the first place. His phone call had been an exercise in futility. Yes, she was glad to hear from him but hardly ecstatic. She wanted Daniel to call before but it obviously wasn't that big of a deal that he hadn't. The lifers were right. Daniel was stuck in this man's army and his girlfriend had moved on. Army life verses college life; there was no comparison.

Daniel's time at Monterey went very quickly. Language school was two months of intense training with little time off for recreation. After graduation, Daniel's orders came in. He was shipping off in two days for Tan Son Nhut Air Base outside of Saigon. From there, he would be assigned to a combat unit as an interpreter.

At first Daniel was reticent to make another phone call to Colleen. But the thought of not calling and having that question mark on his mind for a full year was too much. Daniel waited until the last night before he was to ship off to make his call.

Daniel found a pay phone in a corner of the dayroom. The room was empty except for a few enlisted men finishing up their game of pool. They left and Daniel was alone in the quiet room. He grabbed a chair and propped it up against the wall and made his last call to Colleen from stateside.

This time Colleen's demeanor was more upbeat and positive. She seemed genuinely happy to hear from Daniel and concerned about the dangers he might face overseas.

"I know it will be difficult but you must write to me, Daniel. I know last summer was tough for you. But maybe you being gone will work out for the best. You know, absence makes the heart grow fonder, they say."

“That is what they say,” Daniel said, mimicking her, and then changing the subject. “I know you’ll do well in school. Are you planning to go back to the newspaper next summer?”

“I may. I’ve got an open invitation to come back. But…”

“But what? That sounds exciting.”

“…I may try something different. Like a smaller city newspaper. Just to try my hand at a different type of journalism. It could be good practice for me. Don’t you think?”

“I think that whatever you try you’ll be very successful, Colleen, that’s what I think.”

Men’s voices could be heard in the background of Colleen’s phone.

“Who’s that?”

“Just some friends. We’re going out later tonight for a movie. That’s all.”

Daniel hesitated. He wanted to ask more questions but he didn’t dare. Why risk getting into a fight with Colleen his last night in the US?

“Well, I’ve got a lot of packing to do so I should be going.”

“Daniel, before you go I need to tell you something,”

“I’m listening.”

“No matter what happens…”

“Oh, that’s off to a good start.”

“No, stop! Seriously, you need to know that you are one of the kindest men I’ve ever known. We had some rough times last summer but we did have some wonderful times too. Freshman year was a blast. I would not have wanted to spend it with anyone else but you. I will truly miss you and your silly antics but also your honesty and candor.”

“Even if you didn’t want to hear it and you got mad at me for telling you?”

“Absolutely!”

“Seriously?”

“Daniel, I told you before, you were the only one who has ever been that candid with me. About everything. And yes, sometimes I didn’t want to hear it. And sometimes I got mad at you. But I never lost track of the fact that you did it because you cared for me.”

“I did care for you.”

“Did?”

“Don’t, Colleen. You know what I mean.”

“I know, and I care for you. Truly I do.”

Daniel could feel his stomach tightening up and his breath getting shorter. "I have to go," he said, trying to hide the catch in his throat. "I'm glad we had this conversation. It'll give me something to remember when I'm over there."

"You will write?"

"It may be difficult. But yes, I will write when I have a chance."

"I guess I have to go too," Colleen said. The voices started getting louder in the background. Colleen put the phone closer and whispered, "I love you, silly boy. Please take care of yourself and I'll see you when you get back. OK?"

"OK," Daniel answered and waited until Colleen hung up the phone.

He sat in the room for a long time. The lights were still on but his world was black. Some Beatles song was playing on the radio. Daniel was alone with his thoughts of Colleen and what she was doing right then with her friends back home. It was too painful to think about so he got up, turned off the lights and left the radio playing.

Most of his bunkmates were playing cards when he got back to his barracks. Daniel sat on his cot, typical army bullshit and young recruit banter filled the room. He was lost in his own thoughts of home and Colleen and Vietnam.

A young man from Tennessee flopped down on the cot next to his, and began talking to Daniel. He was holding a Sergeant Rock comic book in his hand. He started jabbering on about Southeast Asia and the women. Plenty of poontang for the taking, he bragged.

"Yeah," Daniel responded with a deadpan expression on his face, "but watch out for Cathy Rottencrotch."

"What do you mean?" the youngster asked.

"Hanoi Hanna…cock-rot…you haven't heard?"

The young man stared at Daniel who was busy cleaning his fingernails. Daniel looked up and said, "I heard it's so toxic that your pecker will fall off if you get it bad. Just up and rot away."

"No shit?"

"Seriously, man. You better protect your package or you won't get any pussy back here when you're stateside. Or worse."

"What's worse than that?"

"If they can't cure it, they'll quarantine your sorry ass someplace in Southeast Asia so you can't come back to the states at all. You're in army limbo, waiting for a cure. And there isn't any. Totally fucked, my man."

"Seriously?"

"Would I lie to you, Tennessee?"

"Guess not, Daniel. You call your girl tonight?"

"I did. It was good talking to her … Colleen is like that song 'Sunday Morning Sunshine'," he said.

"She's the only woman I've ever met who is so positive, so upbeat, so outgoing. She has this intoxicating personality. It was like an adrenaline rush for me whenever we were together."

"A what?"

"Never mind. Let's just say it was great. Until this summer. That sucked! She got a job and met some guys from the better part of town. Kind of took her mind off simple things."

"Like you Daniel?" a voice called out from down the darkened row of cots.

Daniel smiled and raised his middle finger to salute the voice.

"Don't forget Jody," the same voice called out. "He's already got your girl. Now the only pussy you're going to get for the next six years you're gonna have to pay for. But that's OK cuz I heard Vietnamese pussy is real cheap."

"Two years, wise-ass!" Daniel shouted back with a laugh.

The voice got out of his cot and ambled down the aisle toward Daniel. The young man sat across from Daniel. He jammed a cigarette into the corner of his mouth and lit up.

"Two years. How the hell did you only get two years?" he asked. "I thought they only took regular army for language school?"

"Guess not," Daniel answered with a shrug. "They took me."

"Jesus H. Christ," the man said, "two years. You only got two years in this man's army?"

"That's right. Two years and I'm out of here."

"Well, fuck me, you didn't. You lucky son of a bitch," the man replied. "Hope you don't expect your girl to be there waiting for you when you get back … if you get back.'

"If I get back … I expect my girl will be there … Now whether we still have anything in common … that might be another question."

A crusty old sergeant came out of his room at the far end of the barracks and marched down the row of cots. He was a no bullshit lifer who believed that tough training and even tougher discipline would save lives on the battlefield. A cigar stuck out of the corner of his mouth and he wore a dirty t-shirt. His stance was pure army; straight and erect.

"Son," he said, "I couldn't help but overhear your inane conversation. The best thing you can do to keep your sanity and your hide intact is to forget about that girl. The army is your mother now and your best friend. Not some squeeze stateside."

He turned to the other soldiers who were now watching him intently. "Now you all better get some rest," he growled as he turned away. "No more playing stinky finger with your girlfriends back home. The only nooky you're going to get in the Nam is from fucking your fist. Gentlemen, the Nam is a two-way firing range and those slant-eyed gooks don't much give a flying fuck if you waste every man in their platoon cuz Charlie is still going to try to kill you with his dying breath." The old veteran stopped for a moment and flipped off the overhead lights.

"It's lights out, pecker heads. This will be the last good night's sleep you'll be getting until you're back stateside."

Lying in his cot that night, Daniel was feeling more depressed than he'd ever felt before. He thought momentarily about trying to call Colleen again but realized that was a stupid idea. He'd said what he wanted to say. So had she.

Through an open window, Daniel could hear a new song by Donovan drifting over from another barracks. It was called 'Susan on the West Coast' and it made him think about his old high school girlfriend, Summer Blaze. Right now she was probably getting stoned in some pad in Haight-Ashbury. He thought briefly about writing her but he realized his future lay elsewhere and not with her. The two women in his life were gone, perhaps for forever.

Keeping to Our Own Kind

Colleen ran into Daniel's mother by accident one afternoon in Dryer's grocery store. After several hours of hardcore studying, she and her study mates agreed they were all in desperate need of some Hershey Kisses. Dryer's was the closest spot to satisfy their sweet desires.

She quickly found the Kisses and threw three large packages in her cart then swung around for the checkout lane. As she was about to check out, Colleen noticed a middle-aged woman standing in the center aisle. The woman was fingering her way through several packets of spice. Colleen immediately recognized the woman as Daniel's mother.

The matronly-looking woman was in her late forties, maybe even early fifties. But time had not been kind to her. The stress of her failed marriage and many philandering boyfriends showed itself in her posture and haggard expression.

Now, as the woman in her plain cotton dress began to push her cart away, Colleen pondered her next move. Should she approach her and ask about Daniel? Or should she just let it go and say nothing? Colleen took a deep breath and walked up to the woman.

"Hi, my name is Colleen. I'm a friend of Daniels. You're his mom?"

"Yeah, I am," the woman answered as she glanced over at Colleen briefly then went back to perusing the shelves.

"Have you heard from Daniel?" Colleen asked in a calm tone of voice. "I was wondering how he was doing? It's been quite a while since I've gotten a letter."

"Your guess is as good as mine," the woman answered matter-of-factly. "I don't write to him and he doesn't write to me too much. I've never been good at letter writing." The woman's hands remained on the cart, gripping the handle tightly. *At least she doesn't seem to want to move away*, Colleen thought.

Colleen moved up closer with her own shopping cart, hoping the woman would take the hint and engage in more conversation.

"I know what you mean about letter writing," Colleen said. "Daniel hasn't been good about writing to me either. I think that's because his unit must be on the move a lot. I know it's very difficult sending and receiving letters when they're in the bush like that."

"Are you his old girlfriend, then?"

"Girlfriend … friend … whatever you want to call it," Colleen answered. "Yes, we did a lot together during freshman year. I was so surprised when he dropped out of school and then got drafted. Were you surprised too?"

"Not particularly. Daniel's like his old man. Always wanting to do something about his … place. Never satisfied to be what he was … is. Would never keep with his own kind."

"His own kind? I don't understand."

Daniel's mother looked at Colleen with a mixture of suspicion and distain. "Daniel couldn't stand the idea that he was what he was. Thought he was better than the rest of us by going to a college like that. Hanging out with all those college kids." She looked Colleen up and down and gave her a good once over. "Thought he could just move on up and leave the rest of us behind." The woman pursed her lips, looking directly into Colleen's eyes for the first time. It was almost as if she was looking for a fight. "I probably wasn't the best mother but I did what I could. His father was worthless. It was a blessing when he left."

"I think that's sad," Colleen said without thinking.

"What's sad about it? That's the way I was raised. To know my place. I never wanted Daniel thinking he was better than the rest of us. Never gave him any praise because I didn't want it to go to his head. That's the way I was raised. Nothin' wrong with that!"

"I think he was just trying to better himself. To get an education and a good job."

"There are a lot of good jobs that don't need a college education. His old man had one until he took to the bottle and lost it … then walked out on us." She cleared her throat. "Working class is good class. That's where Daniel came from. That's what he is. And that's never gonna change."

Colleen took a deep breath. She forced out a weak smile. "Well, if I hear anything from Daniel, I could let you know," she offered.

"Don't bother! If he doesn't want to write me, that's his business. He can take care of himself."

"Well, it was nice seeing you again," Colleen offered as she started to step back with her cart. The woman simply turned and walked away.

Colleen walked back to campus and passed out the Hersey Kisses around the study table. She quickly excused herself and walked down to the pond where she and Daniel had spent so many hours talking about nothing in particular. She dropped down on the grass and stared at the cattails waving gently in the soft breeze. Her mind was a tumbling cascade of mixed emotions.

Colleen was beginning to truly realize just how starkly different her upbringing was compared to Daniel's. It was totally opposite in so many different ways. It begged a larger question.

What was it that attracted her to Daniel in the first place? The glaring deprivation of love in his home was even more confusing when Colleen thought back to their first encounter at the dance. She tried to decipher the attraction she had first felt for Daniel. Even during their freshman year together, Daniel had never given any indication of the total lack of support he faced back home.

And yet, there was something remarkable between them. Something unrecognizable and without a label that drew them together. Something made Daniel the perfect sounding board for this rich girl from high society. Something about him made Colleen feel vulnerable and yet very safe in his arms.

Despite a very rough summer with Daniel and his sudden departure for the army, Colleen wasn't about to stop writing to him. She often thought about his unit and what they were doing on a day-to-day basis. That kind of information had to be classified and out of reach for civilians.

Or was it?

An idea began to percolate in Colleen's mind as she walked back to her dorm room. What if she was able to use her journalism skills to track down Daniel's unit in Vietnam? It didn't mean that she necessarily wanted to continue her romance with him, she assured herself. But after meeting Daniel's mother, Colleen found growing sympathy for what Daniel had been through growing up in such a dysfunctional environment. She couldn't help admire even more her old boyfriend's determination to make something of himself.

Indian Country

By the late summer of 1967, Daniel was knee-deep in Southeast Asian muck and army bullshit. Translation: it was SNAFU - Situation normal, all fucked up. And Daniel's adjustment to Vietnam and jungle warfare had only just begun.

Weeks earlier, he had landed at Tan Son Nhut Air Base after a long and grueling nonstop flight from Fort Ord., California. After that it was all Indian country, local translation for hostile territory. Almost immediately Daniel and his unit were flown out to a forward base near the Cambodian border. It was supposed to be a quiet area where they could conduct maneuvers and continue their jungle warfare training. That lasted for all of three days before the Viet Cong, (aka: Charlie), began lobbing mortars and heavier shells into their forward camp.

Veterans told Daniel he'd missed the action of Operation Cedar Falls when army and ARVN (Army of the Republic of Vietnam) troops attacked the VC controlled Iron Triangle region near Saigon, followed by Operation Junction City where they struck at enemy bases north of the city. Now the skirmishes and firefights were getting more frequent and Charlie was probing even closer to their forward camp.

Life at the camp evolved around guard duty, more survival training for jungle warfare and bad food in the mess hall. Normal attire was reduced to fatigue pants and just flak jackets. Daniel wore his steel helmet at all times and like most of the other soldiers, he adorned his iron pot with ink drawings that made no sense to anyone else but himself. Daniel even wrote Colleen next to the outline of a heart. Stupid he thought, but it was his iron pot and he'd decorate it any damn way he wanted to.

Although boot camp and AIT had prepared Daniel for the mechanics of firing his weapon and digging a foxhole, it hadn't prepared him mentally for the rigors of living in the bush where one misstep could mean certain death or injury. His skills as a translator with the local tribes or the occasional captive interrogation began to serve him well. Initially his commander sought him out to fly to nearby camps and bases to interrogate prisoners. Daniel seemed to have a way of drawing out information without antagonizing the captives. It became a routine Daniel quickly adjusted to. Fly in to do the interrogation. Fly back out and rejoin his unit. Fly out again when the calls came in. His absence meant he missed the first of several search and destroy missions and real taste of combat.

Within a couple of months the flights had stopped. Intel from several recon groups had confirmed that Charlie was on the move. Soon Daniel found himself a squad leader commanding other grunts in nightly reconnaissance probes into the surrounding jungle.

There were firefights most evenings. It was like a series of steps and sidesteps both sides performed. First there were flashes of bright gun flares, then screams and grenade explosions that ripped the blackness. That was followed by sudden silence and the occasional moaning off in the distance. Daniel and his fellow soldiers escaped with some light wounds and the nightmares that always followed. If there were casualties on Charlie's part, no bodies were ever found.

It was a routine that became the norm. Light duty during the day. Search and destroy at night - usually with the same results. Charlie was picking the spots where he wanted to fight and would evaporate into the jungle when he didn't want to skirmish. Daniel and his fellow troopers could only continue their probing and hope for contact.

Daniel got two letters in one week, one from Colleen and another from Summer. Both proved to be a study in contrasts.

Colleen's letter was full of references to sophomore life on campus. Her studies and extracurricular activities were filling up each week. She had become a columnist for the student newspaper and an editor for the yearbook. Her feedback from several query letters to two city newspapers gave her hope that she might have a shot at a paid internship there the next summer. She complained that the school dances were dull and weekends were full of studying, campus activities and the occasional return to Rochester to see her parents.

Daniel smiled at the soft blue stationary in his hand. He admired Colleen's perfect penmanship. Colleen's collegiate career was in full swing and she was doing well under pressure. He was envious of all her success … in a good way.

Daniel did notice that no mention was made of any other men in her life. Still, he had no idea if Colleen was abstaining from the single life or if she was just being kind not to bring up the subject. *Better that she didn't talk about the men,* Daniel thought, as he looked up at the Playboy centerfold pinned above his bunkmate's cot. He couldn't bear the thought of his old girlfriend with someone else in an intimate or even chaste existence.

Colleen ended her letter with a smiley face and the hopes that Daniel stayed safe while he was overseas. It was a nice, safe letter that gave no indication of her real feelings … if any were to be expressed. Daniel knew he could read into Colleen's letter whatever he wanted and he would probably be right.

Summer's letter, in contrast, was a full-blown expose on her Summer of Love. In January, 20,000 people had gathered in Golden Gate Park for the first Human Be-In. Summer called it a gathering of the tribes. She wrote that some of her friends went dressed as Indians, others as Afghan nomads and French peasants. Summer missed that first gathering but had participated in numerous other events in the park since then.

One time she wore her Indian sari. Other times she wore her paisley blouse or tie-dyed shirt - always with a long flowing cotton skirt and, of course, no underwear. Summer put a 'tee-hee' after that line. She had seen all of her favorite bands up close. The Grateful Dead, Big Brother and the Holding Company, Jefferson Airplane and Quicksilver Messenger Service, to name a few.

She and her friends rocked to the music, smoked a lot of dope and read poetry out loud. It was a huge gathering of like-minded people. And except for the growing legions of runaways and teenagers seeking their thrills away from home, Summer was content to spend her time doing not much of anything. At the same time, she was growing more concerned about the hardcore drugs on the street and the pushers who were selling all kinds of shit disguised as good weed.

She said she was moving from one crash pad to the next, always staying long enough to eke out an existence without work until her welcome had worn thin and she moved on to another place. Panhandling helped bring in a little cash but that was about all. Her job as a stringer for the Oracle hadn't panned out.

Daniel could read between the lines pretty easily. It wasn't a stretch to surmise that Summer still hadn't found herself or a real reason for taking a serious look into her future. Daniel knew it was something his friend just didn't want to face and Summer was determined to delay it as long as she could.

In short, Summer Blaze hadn't changed from the overweight, oversexed teenager who was still searching for some semblance of intimacy in her life. Daniel doubted that San Francisco would be the answer to the multiple problems facing his friend in the real world. Yet despite his misgivings, he did envy Summer for her freedom and her ability to throw herself totally into the creative maelstrom that was the Haight-Ashbury scene.

On the home front, politics and military policies were bouncing back and forth on the legitimacy of the war and the extent of America's involvement in Vietnam. The Johnson Administration and General Westmoreland had engaged in what many critics were calling a limited war. Translation: more 'search and destroy missions' instead of a concentrated attack on the north and the supply lines feeding Charlie in the south.

Daniel started life in the bush as a lowly grunt but through his actions in several ambushes and firefights, he'd been promoted to corporal and then squad leader. His leadership skills were evolving swiftly and Daniel was rapidly processing those survival skills necessary to keep himself and his men alive. Daniel was growing as a natural born leader and it was being noticed by the higher-ups.

Con Thien was Daniel's first taste of heavy combat. It was the first of several major battles where Daniel lost many friends but grew exponentially as a warrior and a military strategist.

Con Thien meant Hill of Angels in Vietnamese. It was a marine combat base located near the Vietnamese Demilitarized Zone close to the North Vietnam border. Before that, it had been a Special Forces camp. It was originally intended to be used as a base for preventing NVA (North Vietnamese Army) infiltration across the DMZ (Demilitarized Zone).

In late fall, Daniel's platoon, along with several others, were flown up to a base near the border in order to participate in select search and destroy missions. In addition, Daniel and his squad were assigned to interrogate prisoners captured from neighboring villages. The army was certain that most of the villagers were complicit in supplying the local VC with supplies and ammunition.

Daniel arrived in time for Operation Buffalo, where two companies began a sweep of the area north of Con Thien. It was a classic search and destroy mission meant to inflict as much damage as possible to enemy forces without suffering substantial casualties to themselves.

But as the infantrymen moved along route 561 in an area called the Marketplace, enemy fire inflicted severe casualties on one of the companies. Rumor had it that American journalists, unsympathetic to the war, had begun describing Con Thien as an American Dien Bien Phu. The growing dissension at home meant little to Daniel. His job was to stay alive and keep his men alive. What the politicians and longhairs back home thought wouldn't cover his ass once the bullets started flying.

Daniel's company was called up to reinforce the beleaguered soldiers who were taking fire from three directions. His column of troops pushed through a jungle clearing, traversed more open space and converged on a dirt path that approached the battlefield from the south. The troops walked abreast, edging the dirt path on either side. Tall elephant grass blanketed the area off to their left. Scrub brush and low-lying grasses bordered a ditch on their right. It was a rolling savanna of elephant grass with thick strands of trees - the perfect ambush terrain.

The air was still and hung heavy with the smell of wet grass and stifling humidity. In the far distance, the sound of mortars and light arms fire could be heard. The men were on edge, fingers on their rifle triggers. Their boots made a soft crunching sound as they marched along the dirt trail. The intensity of the radio chatter had died down. Quiet became their deadly companion.

The terrain began to change. Thick stalks of bamboo began to sprout up on either side of the trail. A slight breeze began moving the tall stalks, rubbing them against one another. The sound masked other sounds. Without the ability to hear unnatural sounds, Daniel and his men were at great risk of a surprise attack.

Daniel motioned the line to stop. Most of the soldiers crouched down; a few others just stood their ground and lit up.

An old staff sergeant standing next to Daniel filled his lower lip with an oversized pinch of Skoal. The sergeant squeezed his eyes, scanning the horizon. Daniel kept looking down the trail ahead.

Overhead, green fighter-bombers laden with brown bombs and white missiles streaked by on their way to the target drop.

"I heard they're dropping a lot of iron up north," the old sergeant said. "We may not get all the air support we need."

"At least for a while," Daniel commented.

"The OV-10s and Intruders are all north of here too. If it's raining too hard, they won't fly back here. They don't fly if they can't see."

Daniel nodded.

The sergeant pointed toward the west. The clear blue sky was being overcome by a large formation of steel gray clouds. The humidity was beginning to drop, a sure sign that thunderheads would appear soon on the horizon.

"We got, I figure, twenty, maybe thirty minutes before it hits us."

"We haven't got that far to go," Daniel said, waving his arm in the air for the column to start up again. He moved ahead of the mumbling old sergeant and closer to the head of the column. Two men were arguing up front.

One of them was a soldier they called Beatnik. He was eighteen and from New York City. He always had a shit-eating grin on his face. It was like he was on something or knew a secret no one else knew. Daniel liked the kid. He was a good soldier.

"You two…give it a rest," Daniel told the men. "Every swinging dick here is dependent on the both of you staying alert." The men stopped arguing and looked at Daniel.

The sergeant walked up behind Daniel.

"Beatnik, you're on point. You see any dinks, you grease the motherfuckers."

Beatnik turned to Daniel.

"We got your back," Daniel said softly, "now move out."

The kid started walking away.

"Watch yourself up there," Daniel cautioned the kid, "don't get distracted."

"Negative, that," Beatnik replied without turning around. He gripped his rifle higher and picked up his pace.

The bamboo stalks gradually gave way to more scrub brush and patches of elephant grass. The wind had begun to pick up again. Daniel kept scanning the waving grasses on either side of the trail. His finger ran slow methodical circles inside his trigger guard as he walked along. Sweat ran down his cheeks and settled in around his damp collar. Daniel knew the tranquil countryside could morph into a firestorm in less than a heartbeat.

Daniel was gradually closing the gap between himself and his point man when the first burst of machine gun fire erupted up ahead. Beatnik, not more than twenty yards away, flew backwards, arms outstretched. He landed flat on his back.

Daniel screamed out a command and threw himself forward onto the ground. Heavy machine gun fire began arching above his prone body. Return fire was sparse just behind his ear. It was obvious his troops couldn't see what they were firing at. Daniel wiggled his body to the side of the trail, rolled over several times, and landed in the muddy ditch that ran alongside the pathway. A quick glance up over the edge of the trail and Daniel could see a red blotch beginning to stain Beatnik's fatigues.

More gunfire erupted behind and to the side of Daniel, raking the scrub brush up ahead. Bent over and holding his helmet, Daniel scrambled down the ditch toward his fallen comrade. As he got closer, he could hear soft moaning coming from the wounded soldier.

"Stay still," Daniel screamed as he moved parallel to his point man. Daniel peeked over the edge of the ditch. Beatnik looked over at Daniel. His eyes were wide with terror. The red stain was growing on his chest.

"Lay still, man," Daniel shouted. "Don't move. Don't move."

Bullets relentlessly tore up the edge of the ditch, spraying dirt clumps and rock fragments into Daniel's face. He threw himself back against the opposite wall of the ditch and raised his head just above the edge again. He could see nothing. He ducked down and moved further down the ditch. He looked up again. Still nothing. He moved farther down into the ditch and something caught his eye at next glance. Not more than ten yards away was a slight rise in the ground. Daniel could make out several pistachio colored NVA helmets poking up behind the slope. It was a machine gun emplacement; one gunner and two feeders.

The enemy was well camouflaged. Daniel could barely see the emplacement because their khaki uniforms and hats blended in so well with the pale amber grass all around them. They each wore helmets with netting and grass stuck in them that looked like little trees.

The monotonous hours of training on the rifle range all came back to Daniel in an instant. He instinctively remembered the position of his weapon with its butt up against his cheek. His gun notch dropped down on the target. His finger was on the trigger, curling around the thin metal, softly squeezing back. The recoil slapped his cheek.

One shot off. A helmet flew into the air within a shroud of red.

Another deep breath. A second shot off. Another helmet exploded with brightly colored brain matter and metal fragments that showered up and over the rise.

The third NVA soldier stood up, fell to his knees then got up again. He was covered in blood. He started to turn around. Third shot off, a burst this time. His head and chest exploded simultaneously in a burst of red and black. The gun emplacement was quiet.

Daniel clawed his way up the side of the ditch and bending over, stumbled back to the fallen soldier. Beatnik still lay sprawled in the dirt. A pool of dark blood was still seeping from wounds in his neck and back. He was moaning softly. Daniel grabbed the boy's chest wrap, and crouching over to avoid getting hit, Daniel dragged him back to the ditch. Together they slid down the embankment and landed head first in the mud. A few scattered shots rang overhead - most likely snipers. Beatnik's helmet fell off and Daniel could see blood splattered inside. Daniel looked at Beatnik's chest. There were two small bullet holes in the fabric. He rolled him over and gasped at the gaping bloody wound in his back.

Daniel cradled the boy's head in his arms and laid beside him, talking softly to the youngster as other soldiers came up behind. He pressed his fist against the pulsating bloody hole. A medic closed in and began applying pressure to the boy's neck and back. But it was too late. The young soldier looked up at Daniel with empty eyes and went limp.

Later that night, back at base camp, Daniel sat in front of a small fire. He was lost to the world, his mind a million miles away. A sergeant came up and sat down beside him. They sat together and respected the silence. The non-com stretched his leg out and nudged some of the logs back into the center of the embers. He took off his helmet and scratched his thinning hair.

"You did well today, soldier. Seeing a man die is a horrible thing to experience. I wish I could say you get used to it but it never gets any easier. When it's our time to go, it's time to go, simple as that." He let the words sink in, "I'm putting you in for a field promotion to sergeant. It'll be temporary at first until the paperwork gets up to headquarters. You deserve it."

Daniel said nothing and nodded his head. He had nothing to say. He had felt a man die in his arms and he'd killed three other men in the same day. He was a killer. What would his girlfriend think of him? What did it matter? He'd done what he was trained to do. And probably saved other American lives in the process. That was all that mattered.

There was no way Colleen would be able to relate to killing three people in less than five seconds. Colleen's world was not his. Her life was not his. Her future was rapidly becoming something he could relate to less and less. They were becoming strangers. Whatever they might have had their freshman year was now done. Memories quickly became replaced by collegiate banners and bloody pith helmets.

Avoiding the Suits

Colleen's initial idea of tracking down Daniel's unit had now evolved into a full-blown obsession. Despite her continued misgivings about what the future might hold for the both of them; Colleen felt a deep-seated desire to find out what Daniel's unit was doing. Meeting Daniel's mother had only solidified Colleen's gut feeling that her old boyfriend wasn't about to shirk from his responsibilities in the military which meant, in turn, that he would probably be in the heat of battle.

Did Colleen still harbor feelings for Daniel that went beyond admiration? She wouldn't allow herself the option of exploring that question. This was a journalistic venture, nothing more, nothing less, Colleen told herself. It would help hone her investigative skills and help her become a better journalist.

The kind of military information Colleen was seeking was highly classified and extremely hard to find even for a seasoned journalist. How was she ever going to get that data? A trip to the St. Paul Pioneer Press was Colleen's first step on that journey. Her first stop was the desk of the news editor, Joe Ballantine; a quiet, almost demure man who stood out in the noisy, smoky news room.

Joe waved at Colleen as she first stepped into the organized chaos that defined the newsroom and started looking around. He motioned her toward a chair at the side of his desk and held up a coffee cup as she approached.

"How is my favorite summer reporter?" He asked as Colleen plopped herself in the chair and crossed her legs.

"Joe, it's nice of you to see me on such short notice. I've got a class early this afternoon so I can't stay long. I want to thank you again for the job last summer. It was great and I learned a lot. Really, it was a fantastic experience."

"You can probably come back next year if they still have the internship program and I think they will," Joe said finishing his third cup of java that morning.

"I would love to explore that option. I also want to see if I can expand my journalism skills in some other areas, too. But your job offer sounds intriguing too."

"Absolutely. You've got to find what's best for you and go for it."

"Joe … I have a favor to ask of you. I don't want you to get into any kind of trouble but I want to keep developing my skills as a reporter. It would mean the world to me if I could do a little research on Vietnam."

"Vietnam ... or somebody in particular in Vietnam?" Joe asked.

Colleen was stunned. She looked at the news editor and didn't know what to say.

"You want to track down your old boyfriend. Am I right?"

Colleen was stunned by her apparent transparency, and looked dumbfounded at the news editor who was giving her a broad grin right back. Joe started to laugh.

"How did you…"

"I'm still a damn good reporter despite this title. A good reporter does a lot of digging for a story. You mentioned that kid often enough for me to know that you two were once an item. It may have been a bit of a rocky road at times, but an item nevertheless. When you happened to mention that he'd quit school and got drafted, I figured you'd either forget about him or pretty soon you'd start wondering just what happened to him. Especially if he was shipped overseas like so many other draftees. Like to Southeast Asia." Joe looked at Colleen with pursed lips. "So how am I doing so far?"

Colleen returned his smile and said, "That's why you're a crack reporter and a news editor and I'm just a fledgling journalist looking for help. Can you help me?"

"Do you watch the news?"

"Sometimes. When I can get to the TV in the lobby."

"Well, start watching TV as often as you can. Walter Cronkite on CBS is one of the best. He's taken a personal interest in the war and does a damn good job of reporting about it. But that's just the start. Do you have access to any of the wire services; UPI or AP? … Probably not. Tell you what. We get a ton of wires every day. I've had my secretary keep anything related to Vietnam in a special file. They don't break them down by units or special areas but the information is all there. All you'd have to do is go through the wires and look for any reference to his unit or area where he might be stationed."

"Also, Neil Sheehan, who works for UPI, is one of the best. He's tough and thorough and truthful to the dime. Read anything and everything the man writes. If you want to know the truth about Vietnam and Southeast Asian politics, he's the man to trust. How he gets some of the stuff he reports past the censors I just don't know. But he does. The censors are going to cut out anything that might hurt or threaten national security. But a good investigative reporter knows how to read between the lines."

"That would be wonderful," Colleen began, but Joe was just getting started, his juices were starting to flow. He dug through his desk and came up with a handful of teletypes.

"We also get transcripts of press conferences that McNamara and other Department of Defense officials give on almost a daily basis. There might be tidbits of information there. You have to wade through a lot of bullshit and government rhetoric but there's sometimes a nugget of truth worth pursuing there." Joe reached down to a pile of smaller newspapers at the side of his desk. He brought up a tattered and torn newspaper. "And then there's one last place you can do your snooping," he said.

"I'm feeling a bit overwhelmed already."

"Stars and Stripes, the army's daily newspaper. We don't get those issues until they're probably two or three weeks old. Mind you, they're highly censored but if you can read between the lines, you can glean a lot of information on the conditions your soldier boy might be facing. If his unit gets into even a firefight, they might report it. Make no doubt, it'll be highly sanitized. Feeling *totally* overwhelmed yet?" he asked.

"Totally," Colleen said.

"Good. Welcome to the real world of investigative journalism. You'll learn more here than you will in all of your journalism classes combined at that fancy school of yours. You'll get your fingertips black with ink and learn the bad habit of drinking too much bad coffee. If you stick to it; if you've got the perseverance and the fortitude to keep digging deeper and deeper, you can find most of what you're looking for. Listen … if this doesn't work out between you and what's his name…"

"Daniel."

"Daniel, it is … even if you never see him again, you will be learning skills that you can use for the rest of your journalistic career. Not a bad tradeoff, if you ask me."

"I agree, Joe. I truly appreciate everything you're doing for me."

"I'm not doing a thing for you, kid. Just offering up some advice and a little access to hard work and some guaranteed disappointments along the way. I'll tell the boys that it's OK for you to hang around whenever you want. Just grab a desk someplace and go to it. We're open twenty-four seven. You need anything else? Bad coffee, perhaps?"

Colleen stood up and extended her hand. She shook it firmly then said, "I know how lucky I am and I…"

"Colleen? It is Colleen, isn't it?" Joe said standing up and starting to move toward the assignment desk. "Don't disappoint me, kid," he stopped and turned around, "Oh, one last piece of advice. If you run into anything that seems … doesn't make sense … anything classified - see me first."

"I don't understand."

"I don't want a lot of suits combing through my newsroom, that's all."

"Got it. I won't let you down."

"I know you won't, kid, I know it!" he answered and turned away.

Colleen grabbed the first bus that came along. It wasn't until she was halfway down West Seventh Street that she looked up at the bus route indicator to make sure she'd grabbed the right one back to school. She couldn't believe Joe had given her this opportunity. It would be a tough task digging through all that material, but Colleen was confident she could do it. Not only would she find out where Daniel's unit was; she hoped to cull more details about his daily life. She couldn't wait to share her news with Peggy.

Colleen's excitement was short-lived.

Peggy was waiting for her with news of her own. As Colleen climbed up the two flights of stairs to her dorm room, she could hear Peggy's voice calling out to her. Before she reached the second floor landing, Peggy saw her and ran down the hall, waving her hand in the air.

"Colleen, Colleen, we have to talk!" She grabbed Colleen by the hand and ushered her into their dorm room.

"What is it, Peggy?" Peggy pushed Colleen on her bed and sat down next to her. She inhaled deeply to catch her breath.

"I'm about to become engaged," Peggy said between gasps of air. "John and I are going to get engaged very soon. He promised me."

"John? That guy you just met a couple of weeks ago? You've got to be kidding. I mean you barely know him. And he doesn't even go to school here. Isn't he just out of the service?"

Undeterred by Colleen's hesitation, Peggy answered, "Yes, but that doesn't matter. He's going back to school soon. Besides, he's everything I've ever dreamed of in a man. I mean everything. He's just perfect." Peggy took another deep breath, "Aren't you happy for me?"

"Hold on, Peggy. I mean it's great news. But no man is perfect - not even your John." Colleen took Peggy by the shoulders and moved her face closer to Peggy's. "Don't you think you're pushing this just a little too fast? You've still got three years of school left. That's a long time to wait to get married."

"No, no, you don't understand," Peggy countered, standing up and beginning to pace the floor. "We're going to get married next summer and then I'll stay in school and John will work. When I graduate, he'll go back to school and I'll work to support the both of us."

"That's what you two have already decided?"

"Not quite," Peggy answered hesitantly. "We haven't exactly talked it all the way through. But I think he will agree to it. I think it will work. No, I will make it work. Colleen, I love him. I really do."

"Peggy, you don't know anything about him, really. I mean he could have girlfriends in every state. Maybe he's just playing around; do you really know him that well?"

"I know him well enough to know that he loves me and I love him."

"Have you two…"

"No! What would make you ask such a thing?"

"Peggy, be realistic for a moment. If you two are in love then I assume you're making out. At some point before next summer, either you or he is going to want to go all the way. And you know what would happen if you got pregnant. That would be the end of your college career. You can't let that happen. More importantly, you can't put yourself in such a compromising position. I would be very worried if I were you."

"Colleen, you're such a prude. Don't tell me you and Daniel didn't make out a lot. Because I know you two did."

"So."

"So he didn't touch you down there?"

"Peggy!"

"I'm just saying that you may still be a virgin technically but you've been tampered with too. So don't point your holy finger at me."

"That's all I'm saying," Colleen answered, shaking her head.

"I want you to meet him."

"Sure, sometime, I'm sure we'll…"

No, tonight! Some of his friends are having a party at a house they're renting. I want you to come and meet John. You'll see just what a great guy he is. Will you come?"

"Yes, Peggy, I'll come," Colleen answered reluctantly.

"OK, I've got to go and buy some things for the party. Don't be late … and be nice. John may be a little rough around the edges but he has a heart of gold. He's kind and sweet and … Oh, you'll see."

Peggy left the room and Colleen was left to ponder the strange juxtaposition of her seeking out information on Daniel and Peggy jumping at this premature chance to marry some guy. Two extremes they both suddenly found themselves facing.

The party was a bust. Few outsiders showed up and Colleen ended up with Peggy and her new boyfriend on the back porch during most of the evening. John seemed nice enough, Colleen thought, except that he drank a lot and smoked cigarettes. Peggy said he promised to quit smoking soon. But Colleen doubted he could by observing his chain-smoking that evening. At one point, Peggy left to go for more snacks and Colleen was left alone on the porch with John.

"I understand you just got out of the service?" she asked as he lit up another cigarette. "That you were in Vietnam for a while?"

"Yeah, I was."

"What was it like? I have a friend who is over there right now."

"Where's he stationed?"

"I don't know. I just have an APO address. I'd like to find out what's happening to him but it's difficult getting news about what's really happening over there."

"You know why that is, don't you?" John responded as he blew a perfect milky gray circle of smoke.

"No, why?"

"Because they're kicking the crap out of us, that's why. Is your friend regular infantry?"

"Yes."

"Then he's in a shitload of trouble. I know you don't want to hear that but it's the truth. They keep sending those poor slugs out on search and destroy missions. Night after night, going after Charlie. So unless he's a desk jockey, he's toting a gun and ducking Charlie's booby traps every night. You'll never get accurate casualty figures because commanders aren't allowed to give out accurate numbers. It would make the American public go nuts.. I hope you're not serious about this guy."

"Why do you say that?"

"Because, sorry to tell you this, but the chances of him coming home in one piece are pretty slim. He'll either come home in a body bag or so screwed up you'll never recognize him."

"You can't be serious!" Colleen asked in a shocked voice.

John stubbed out his cigarette butt and fished another white stick from his shirt pocket and lit up again. "Trust me, I not shitting you. It's a total clusterf… it's bad over there. Real bad."

Colleen stood up. "I have to go," she said suddenly and went back inside. She met Peggy who was just coming in the front door. "I have to go, Peggy. Thanks for inviting me. But I have lots of homework to do."

Peggy watched her leave and waved her off. Colleen walked at a brisk pace back to school. Her mind was swirling with images of Daniel in some battlefield, with soldiers dying all around him. Colleen was angry with John for making his comments. And even more upset at the images she couldn't shake from her head.

Maybe she was wrong to cling to this ridiculous notion that Daniel would come back a better man. He was thousands of miles away. She was in school. Even if he returned, Daniel would have to practically start all over again. She'd be long graduated before he even finished school.

And what if he didn't return? What if he was killed on the battlefield or taken captive? Or what if he survived the insanity of war only to come back a hollowed out shell of a man? What would she do then? Would she welcome him back as a friend? Could they still be friends if he came back a totally different person?

The idea began to creep into Colleen's mind that perhaps Peggy and her mother were right all along. They kept insisting that Colleen should drop Daniel right now. She should end their relationship before something happened to him. End it before she had to attend his funeral. Would she be better off never seeing him again? Would she be able to live with herself if she did write him a 'Dear John' letter and then she saw him on campus after that?

The thoughts kept swirling around in her brain, colliding with one another, canceling one another out, tossing her in a dozen different directions all at the same time. She would have to do something. As she began her research, Colleen would have to face the fact that she'd have to do something about their lingering relationship - before it was too late.

Summer of 1968

Vernacular Seduction

Sophomore year had been very good for Colleen. She'd done well in all of her journalism classes, garnering straight A's across the board. Her work as a researcher for the school newspaper had gotten the attention and praise from the administration. Copywriting for the yearbook had only strengthened her resolve to pursue writing as a fulltime career after school. All in all, things had gone very well for her on the academic front. Unfortunately, her dating life was another story.

It had been slim pickings in the men's department for most of the school year. There were a few repeat dates. But overall, Colleen found the men who called on her either too immature or too focused on things other than just having a good time. The Lake Minnetonka crowd had become almost passé in their continuing focus on partying and other narrow-minded carnal pursuits.

Peggy announced that she would be leaving for a job at a resort in Seattle right after school. Her aunt lived there and John promised to visit often. She told Colleen that it would be a chance for her to escape the restrictive supervision of her parents and be on her own for the first time.

The letters from Daniel had become more sporadic and less inclusive as time passed by. They only contained safe and innocuous comments that told Colleen nothing much of anything. She believed Daniel was trying to play it safe and reveal little about his own feelings or the conditions he was living under. The few times he might have tried to add something of relevance, it had been blacked out by the military censors.

Colleen was beginning to accept the fact that time and distance did make a big different in relationships. And as much as she wanted to continue their friendship, this lack of communication and intimacy was quickly diminishing any chance of that happening. In spite of this, at least once a week Colleen would trudge down to the six-story red brick building with the Dispatch-Pioneer Press neon sign out front. She would climb the three flights of stairs and find a corner in the newsroom where she could continue her research.

She knew that Daniel's unit was constantly on the move. Daniel himself had hinted about switching assignments and units but was never specific or detailed in his comments. Colleen knew there had been a lot of fighting in the province Daniel was operating in. She didn't know where he was located at any specific time. It was all after-the-fact information. As the school year dragged on, Colleen was becoming more and more discouraged in her research. She'd learned a lot about the war effort and the political maneuverings at the State Department level. It was becoming apparent that the peace movement at home was gaining momentum and protest marches were having an effect on people's attitudes towards the war.

Adding to the pressure of school classes and her research at the newspaper, Colleen's search for a summer job was intensifying. Near the end of the school year, an editor at the Saint Paul Shopping News, a tabloid next door to the Dispatch offices, offered her a summer job. But Colleen declined. She was determined to find something more challenging than selling want ads to grocery stores.

She always had the option of returning to the Dispatch-Pioneer Press but she was more intrigued with the idea of working for a smaller newspaper. She wanted someplace where she might get more varied assignments. One job ad in particular caught her attention.

It was with an alternative newspaper, just starting up, called the Twin City News. Initially it would be published biweekly. It would serve the entire Minneapolis-St. Paul metropolitan area. The plans were for it to offer feature news articles, film, theater and restaurant reviews and some music criticism. Its main selling point was a focus on investigative journalism. That sounded to Colleen like it was right up her alley.

Although it would be in a tabloid format initially, Garrison Buckley, its news editor, promised that the writing would be top-notch and thorough. He described it as a local youth-orientated newspaper that wouldn't be afraid to ruffle some political feathers and challenge the status quo.

Garrison Buckley had come from the east coast. His reputation preceded him, both the good and the bad. He was young. A local gossip columnist said in his mid-twenties. He'd proven himself at two other newspapers before being hired at Twin City News. He dressed right out of Playboy Magazine and led a lifestyle that could only be described as that of a globe-trotting sophisticate.

Local newspaper articles said Garrison was a dynamic leader who had attracted a very hip news crew and 'with it' young people on his previous assignments. His past newspapers were said to have the hardest working, hardest playing staff in town. He also had a reputation of being a ladies' man and a charmer.

Colleen's more experienced friends hinted that she might want to think twice about working for such a man if she wanted to keep her virginity intact. Colleen laughed off their comments and applied for the job anyway. She pulled out her simple black Valentino and dressed it up with a narrow silver belt and simple silver necklace. It worked like a charm.

She got the job after a brief interview with Garrison. She would begin work right after school ended.

As promised, Garrison was charming, brilliant, direct and on top of his game. It seemed as if the Twin City News was going to be everything he said it would be. Of all the new hires, Garrison seemed particularly interested in Colleen's desire to become a top flight journalist. He could help her, Garrison promised, if Colleen would take his advice and work harder than anyone else on staff. The hours would be tedious sometimes, he warned her. Weekends and evening would be considered part of a regular workday. If Colleen persisted and turned in good work, Garrison promised her his special attention and help.

The rest of the school year was a maze of endless classes, weekend assignments, a few sporting events and even fewer dates. Pickings from St. Paul's and the other private colleges provided a couple of weekend movies and pizza afterwards but little else. Peggy was so hopelessly wrapped up with John that she had few male contacts to pass on to Colleen.

The good news was that Colleen got a one bedroom apartment for the summer. It was in another red brick building on Grand Avenue and not far from her first apartment the summer before. It would provide her with plenty of time to work on her writing assignments and not be interrupted by socializing roommates.

If Colleen got a date and wanted her date over for a quiet evening, she could do so in the privacy of her own home. If Garrison Buckley wanted to work out of her place instead of the office Colleen fantasized, she'd welcome that too. Garrison would be a wonderful break from the collegiate material she had to choose from for dates thus far.

While everything in Colleen's life was coming together and pointing toward a wonderful summer, her relationship with Daniel grew more complicated. His letters were now so spread out that she'd go for months without word from him. The letters that did arrive had been heavily blacked out by army censors. The few sentences that she could read told her nothing about Daniel or any sense of his connection with the real world.

After Daniel's last blacked out letter arrived, Colleen skimmed over it once, crushed it in her hand and threw it on her bed. *Better to not write at all then to write such meaningless drivel!* Colleen felt guilty about feeling harshness toward his letters. Logic told her they would be censored. Daniel was probably in the field and couldn't write anyway. She was being unreasonable. She wasn't being a true friend. She hated herself for feeling the way she couldn't help but feel.

Daniel's ongoing absence had gradually worn away at her feelings for him. Colleen had her own life to lead. She had to focus on her career, her studies and her new job for the summer. Maybe, she dared ask herself, maybe it was time. The thought had occurred to her before - several times before. But Colleen had always dismissed it as something she would never do to someone in the service, especially not to a friend. Even as she went to retrieve the letter again to re-read it, Colleen didn't know how much longer she could continue this charade that they were still a couple.

It wasn't fair to Daniel. And it sure as heck wasn't fair to her. But a friend doesn't do that to a friend, Colleen reminded herself. She filed the letter away, along with all the others in her desk and forgot about it.

Garrison Buckley was everything his admirers claimed him to be - and more. He could charm new clients with his wit and exact sense of numbers. The investors gave him more and more free rein as the advertising dollars rolled in and the circulation numbers kept rising. Staffers loved him for his willingness to push the envelope in story content and a willingness to address what were previously taboo subjects like abortion and drug use. The job was becoming a perfect antidote to what ailed Colleen. It was the perfect job she had only dreamed about the year before.

Encouraged by his words of praise, Colleen even approached Garrison one day to talk about her research on Vietnam and her attempt to track down Daniel's unit. Buckley immediately dialed up a contact at the State Department to see if he could be of any help for Colleen. That left a lasting impression on her.

Rumors about Garrison's extracurricular activities with the ladies began to circulate almost immediately. Most of the comments were thirdhand whisperings from female staffers who knew someone who knew someone who had dated him. It was reported that he had a local lawyer on retainer just to handle complaints of his after-hours liaisons.

Despite some initial misgivings, Colleen found herself being drawn closer to the young dynamo as they spent more time together on various assignments. The job was everything Colleen had hoped for and more. Garrison Buckley was a genius at stirring up controversy and creating attention-grabbing stories from seemingly out of nowhere. He had Colleen writing more articles in a couple of weeks than she had completed during the entire summer at the Dispatch-Pioneer Press. He seemed to take a special interest in her work and complimented her often for her thoroughness and in-depth research. It wasn't long before they were going out for coffee to discuss newspaper work - and their personal lives.

By mid-summer, Garrison Buckley had taken Colleen under his wing completely. She would soon be a junior in college and was feeling very grown up. Garrison hinted at some part-time work during the school year and even larger assignments for the following summer. When Colleen commented about the boat shoe boys, Buckley could only laugh and remind her that she was far beyond those sophomoric trust fund babies and was becoming a real woman in her own way.

To show his belief in her, Garrison even gave Colleen an assignment to write the lead article for the next edition. Even the consistent rumors of Garrison 'spreading the wealth' (a euphemism for spreading his seed), wasn't enough to deter Colleen from pushing forward on that assignment and still date Buckley. She was feeling more and more confident about herself and her attractiveness to the opposite sex.

The dates increased with more frequency as Colleen kept turning in better articles. They would take long walks along the river boulevard. They attended openings at the Walker Art Center and the Guthrie Theater. Their kisses became more intense and Garrison even hinted at a weekend in Chicago several times. But Colleen always politely deferred and kept Garrison at bay with a laugh and her charm. He never pushed the issue beyond a casual comment or two.

At first Colleen felt uneasy dating Buckley with Daniel still in Vietnam, but her resolve to move on with her life was eating away those feelings of guilt each day. She continued writing to Daniel but never mentioned Garrison or much about her summer job.

On those occasions when Colleen did talk about Vietnam, Garrison was quick to point out the folly of that foreign intrusion into the lives of the South Vietnamese. He lamented the military's failure to quell NVA intrusions from the North. For centuries, other countries had tried to take over Vietnam and they had always failed.

One night, Colleen and Garrison were sitting in his new car at the monument parking lot, talking and making out. When Garrison's fingers reached the demarcation line between Colleen's legs she cut him off. They both leaned back in the front seat to catch their breath and let things cool off a bit.

Colleen absentmindedly brought up the subject of her friend in Vietnam again. As if on cue, Garrison launched into a catalogue of reasons why Vietnam was going to be a colossal failure of American policy.

This latest American involvement, he began, was nothing more than a political play. First initiated by President Eisenhower, then perpetuated by Kennedy, and lastly Johnson. All three of them were wrong. The French couldn't conquer the Vietnamese or the Chinese before them. Why would any American President think he could do what so many before him couldn't accomplish?

In Vietnam, their operations, their policies, even their procedures were misguided. Nothing much made sense over there. And to push their agenda forward, Garrison argued, they relied on the draft for their fuel to the fire. It was an archaic, unfair lottery that favored the rich over the poor.

"Did you know," Garrison began, "that the average age of a draftee today is nineteen? That's eight years younger than the soldiers who fought in World War II and Korea. Eight years!"

"I didn't know that," Colleen answered in surprise.

Garrison was on a roll. "You know most of those boys come from poor, working class homes or are minorities. If you're affluent or educated, you're home free. And it doesn't end there."

"What do you mean?" Colleen asked.

"Those poor Joes who have been drafted will be far behind their counterparts back in college if or when they ever return to the states. Statistically speaking, your friend Daniel will probably be among those who won't finish college after the service. He'll just end up taking some trade job after his discharge. That or worse; some low paying job that takes him nowhere fast."

"I don't think Daniel is like that. I think he will come back and finish college."

"Perhaps, perhaps not. But statistically speaking, the odds are against that ever happening. Sorry, but it's true."

"I don't think so," Colleen answered, looking out at the single monument light that was casting its elongated shadow across the hood of their car.

"You sound very fond of that guy," Garrison commented as he leaned in closer to Colleen.

"No, he's just a friend. Even though we haven't been corresponding much lately."

"By not much, what do you mean?" Garrison asked, placing his hand on Colleen's knee.

"I haven't gotten a letter from him for several months," Colleen answered, making no effort to remove Garrison's hand.

"And when he wrote last time, did he sound like he wanted to continue the relationship?"

"I don't know."

"Sure you do, Colleen. Now be honest," Garrison said inching closer to her.

Colleen moved back, indicating their making out was done for the evening.

Garrison smiled. Not willing to push the issue, he leaned back in his seat. He put his arm on the seat and let his hand rest on Colleen's shoulder.

"Be honest with him, and end it once and for all."

"I'm not sure..."

"Well, are you still fond of him?"

"No! ...I don't know ... I just don't know."

"You have to finalize it, Colleen. It isn't fair to lead him on. Believe me, if you're still sounding interested he's going to cling to that illusion. It'll be exaggerated in his mind and by the time he gets back, if he gets back, it will be blown way out of proportion." Garrison began rubbing Colleen's shoulder in a comforting manner. He leaned in closer again, dropping his voice as he spoke, "I know it sounds cruel but you're really doing him a favor in the long run. You're strong! You can do this. I'll help you craft the letter if you want me to."

"No, I can do it myself."

"Are you going to do it?"

"Yes, I..."

"Yes, I will do it? Or yes, but I'm still not sure? Which is it, Colleen?"

"I'll do it, Garrison. Now please take me home. I'm tired and I still have stuff to do. Please."

Single-Digit Midget

By the summer of '68, things were as crazy on the homefront as they were in Vietnam.

In April, Martin Luther King was gunned down in Memphis. Icons of the anti-war movement; Abbie Hoffman, Timothy Leary and Jerry Rubin were gearing up to bring a million flower guerrillas to disrupt the Democratic

National Convention in Chicago. The United States was becoming a polarized nation, torn apart by President Johnson's failed policy in Vietnam and simmering with racial tensions and violence at home.

The situation was no better abroad. University students in Paris battled police in the streets while protesting students were being gunned down in Mexico City. Reform-minded protesters were being crushed by Russian tanks in the Czech Republic. And the situation was even more absurd in Vietnam.

Vietnam was rife with dissention among the ranks of some enlisted men who questioned the direction of the war. Daniel kept an open mind and tried to go with the flow. One week he was an interpreter, the next he was point man leading his squad into the thick jungle on a search and destroy mission. There seemed neither rhyme nor reason for his assignments.

In a fit of melancholy and misguided patriotism, Daniel agreed to extend his tour of duty to stay with his men. Letters from Colleen had become fewer and far between. Daniel hadn't helped with that exchange by his even more infrequent letters home. His past life had become so irrelevant that Daniel didn't want to bother with it at all. His focus was now entirely on staying alive and keeping his men alive.

The in-country letter was waiting for Daniel when he came out of the bush after five straights days of light skirmishes and no confirmed kills. It was from Michael who was getting discharged from the army. He had left a phone number where Daniel could contact him before he shipped back to the states. They arranged to meet in Saigon as soon as Daniel could muster up a two-day pass.

Saigon had long been southern Indochina's social and cultural center. As a major commercial center, Saigon was booming during the war years.

Cars, trucks and motor scooters filled the wide boulevards and spilled over to narrow side streets. Diesel smoke filled the air and choked the blue sky overhead with a true purple haze.

Still, the scars of war were everywhere. Decades old bullet pockmarks still covered many building facades. Broken structures as far back as the Japanese and French occupation littered the urban landscape.

Daniel and Michael agreed to meet in Saigon's Old Town where a century of French influence had brought a plethora of old French colonial culture and architecture to the streets. Vendors crowded the sidewalks and pushed most pedestrian traffic out into the streets. Local inhabitants, vendors, soldiers and visiting businessmen dodged three-wheeled pedi-taxis and gas belching scooters that inched their way along the roadways.

Michael suggested they meet at a local bar where the scrip flowed freely and just about anything could be bought on the black market. Michael's choice of marijuana, Black Gold, was there. He said it was almost as good as Cambodian Red but not quite. Suzie Wong's was notorious for its open marketplace for goods stolen from the military bases outside of the city. The military had clamped down on the place in the past and closed it several times. But it kept reopening under a new name and it fit Michael's frame of mind.

It was just a short jeep ride out of Tan Son Nhut on relatively safe roads. Daniel met Michael there just as the evening sun was starting its decent over the rough and worn building landscape surrounding the bar.

Daniel pushed back the beaded curtain and stepped inside the dank gray room. There was a large bar area full of GIs and bar girls dancing. Behind the bar was a wide opening to a patio in back. Music blasted through speakers hung from the ceiling. Daniel pushed through the milling crowds of American and Asian bodies on the dance floor and went out to the patio.

Michael was in one corner of the patio, taking another belt of whiskey and fishing for a Pall Mall in his shirt pocket. As soon as he saw Daniel, he gave him a sloppy salute. Daniel returned it with a tap of his finger to his forehead.

"Thirty two and a wakeup!" Michael shouted at Daniel as he stumbled to his feet. Daniel waved at his friend and motioned him to sit back down. With the heavy traffic streaming by, the din was only marginally better inside the packed bar/whorehouse.

Daniel plopped himself down on a rickety wooden chair. Michael was beaming from ear to ear. His army uniform was unkempt and his shoes were dirty and unpolished. The short timer's shit-faced grin said it hardly mattered to him. Michael had a bottle of Carling Black Label waiting for Daniel.

"American beer, Michael, you're a genius. I've been drinking that Bier LaRue, rotten gook beer. Drink it warm and it'll blow your innards right out your ass."

Michael laughed and grabbed a second Black Label bottle. He promptly opened it and began chugging it down. When the bottle was half empty, he slammed it down on the table and stood up.

"Thirty-two more days and I'm outta this man's army," he announced in a loud bellowing voice. No one seemed to notice or care. Michael sat back down with a sheepish grin on his face. "Discharge, baby. I'll be a free man." He stood up again, did a little jig and collapsed back into his chair. "It's a duffle bag drag and a bowl of corn flakes," he said. "Isn't that what they call it when you get outta Dodge?"

"I wouldn't know," Daniel answered with a grin. "I'm staying put."

“You take their Green Bait”

“What? Re-enlist?” Daniel replied with a laugh. “No, I just extended my tour for another six months. That’s all.”

“Why on earth would you do that? Do you dig this shit?”

Daniel laughed. “Sometimes I think I distort my own reality.”

“What does that mean?”

“There was success. I could smell it in the air at boot camp. I wanted it - didn’t know how I was going to get it, but I knew I had to have it.”

“And get killed in the process.”

“Those are the rules of engagement.”

“You’re nuts. You know that, don’t you?”

Daniel smiled. “Price to be paid for the reward in the end.”

“What, killing gooks?”

“No.”

“No?”

“Becoming a man.”

“Did she have anything to do with it?”

“Who?”

“Yeah,” Michael laughed, “that’s what I thought.”

“Have another beer, my friend.”

“Jesus, man, give it up. Give her up.”

“Can’t … I’ve got to do this.”

“I don’t understand. You’re crazy. You really are.”

Daniel didn’t answer.

“Well, I’m done soldiering for Uncle Sam,” Michael said. “I shit you not. No more shithole hooch and bugs the size of a fist crawling across my belly. I’ve sucked dry air that was like Oklahoma dust and got drenched like I was under Niagara Falls.” Michael laughed and finished off his beer, “I’m a single digit midget.”

“I know, Michael, I’ve been there too, .Just had a change of heart. So what happened that you’re getting out early?”

“Nothin’, they’re just letting me go.”

“Bullshit, Michael, what did you do? Or what didn’t you do?”

“Did a little drugs. Got a little drunk. So Uncle Sam doesn’t want me fighting alongside those RA dicks. He thinks I might accidentally blow their asses away." Michael went for a swig of his beer, forgetting it was already empty. "Then the top sergeant found out what I meant when I kept telling him Buddha Understands and he really busted my chops."

"I don't understand, Michael."

"'Buddha Understands' in Vietnamese is pronounced, 'Phuc Hieuw.' Get it?"

"I got it, you dumb shit. What'd ya do that for?"

"He said I was a fuckin' hippie wing wiper and my friends were all undisciplined, lazy shitheads."

"Was he right? Did you get bad paper?"

"Fuck no!" Michael replied with a laugh. "Anyway it's not a Section Eight. No Article 15. So I'm not screwed if I want to get a job back home. Man, I just don't give a flying fuck anymore. I'd had it with having to break starch couple of times a week just cuz some sorry ass puke from HQ was coming down for another inspection. Then he tells us what a tough job they have in this man's army."

Daniel waved at the tiny waitress who was dressed in a very short white smock. "Four Black Labels," he shouted above the noise of the crowd and turned back to Michael. "So I heard your unit was in Operation Cedar Falls and Junction City?"

"Yeah, both of them … some heavy action there," Michael boasted. He reached into his shirt pocket for a cigarette. He stuck the butt in the corner of his mouth and flashed a match against it. The waitress came back with four more bottles of Falstaff beer instead. Michael immediately opened his bottle and chugged until it was nearly empty.

"Is that when you started drinking heavily?" Daniel asked.

"I always drank a lot, bro. You know that."

"I mean, when it became a problem."

"I keep having this nightmare, man."

"About what?"

"I wasted a guy once … a kid really."

"So?"

"We were out on patrol and we spotted a couple of trail runners up ahead. They saw us about the same time and took off running. My C.O. was right behind me screaming 'Burn his ass!' - so I just opened up on him and put a full magazine into his guts. I swear to God I could see daylight coming through his stomach before he dropped. That was some kind of bad shit."

"You gotta let it go, man."

"But the fucking nightmare won't go away, Daniel. It just won't go away."

"Michael, there's always collateral damage in war. It isn't fair. It isn't right. But it is."

"It was a kid, man. I wasted a goddamned kid and he wasn't even packing."

"Michael, I'm sorry. I truly am," Daniel said softly.

Silence fell between them as they finished their beers.

"You see any action?" Michael asked.

"Con Thien."

"I thought that was just gyrenes. Those leathernecks, the Devil Dogs!" Michael asked in an exaggerated tone of voice.

"We backed them up. They did most of the fighting. We did get into some heavy shit ourselves. That was the first time I killed a man … Three, in fact."

"Heavy shit, isn't it?" Michael said with a weak smile on his face.

"Tell me about it. I felt lower than whale shit."

"I suppose."

"I guess that was the first time I really understood the phrase that you can go from living to dying real fast in the Nam."

"You'll get used to it, bro. Either grease those motherfuckers first or they'll sneak up one night and cut your throat from ear to ear. Your pecker comes off next. Seriously, they'll do that to you."

"It's getting crazy here," Daniel said. "I'll give you that. Every swinging dick in charge has got an answer. But it's all asses and elbows and nobody really knows what the fuck is going on. Body count is all that means anything. Fresh recruits for graves registration on both sides of the playing field. And if a lot of innocents get greased in the process," he shook his head, "that's all part of the game. Fucking crazy is what it is."

"Amen to that!" Michael answered as he sucked deeply on his cigarette, letting the smoke dance out his mouth and nose. He became somber and reflective. "I agree. MACV doesn't seem to know what it's doing. I mean, one minute we've got clear priorities here and the next they're changing them all around. The only thing set in stone here are the grave markers."

He flipped his burnt stub out into the street and fished another cigarette out of his shirt. He raked a match against the wall and lit the cigarette in its middle. Without noticing his mistake, Michael continued, "There was a book circulating our camp by some frog named Bernard Fall. Book is called 'Street without Joy', all about the French campaign in Vietnam and their downfall here. Obviously nobody on our side read the damn book cuz we're all still here."

Daniel nodded. "Don't they say that truth is the first casualty of war? The army moves on half-truths, rumors and outright lies."

Daniel and Michael smiled at one another.

Changing the subject, Daniel asked, "So what are you going to do back stateside?"

Michael finished his beer, chewed the cap off another one and threw the empty into the street. He was nearly three sheets to the wind but his capacity was holding him steady and erect. "I might go to Frisco and look up Summer," he answered. "Sell a little dope on the side. Crash with a couple of old junkies I know who got out a couple of months ago."

"You could go back to Minnesota and enroll in school. Try to get a degree and get sober," Daniel said.

"I could … or not. So you're still writing to that old girlfriend of yours, what's her name?"

"Colleen, and you know her name. Yeah, I am; not much, but when I have a chance I'll send something off to her."

"She write you back?"

"Not often. But she's busy and I don't stay in any one place for long. They've got me moving from one unit to the next. Seems translators either get themselves shot or are sent back to Saigon to work in some air conditioned Quonset hut."

"So why not become a Saigon Cowboy?" Michael asked. "Kiss some shavetail's ass all day and get laid every night?"

"No way, man," Daniel answered. "There's no way in hell I could fiddle fuck my day away with some inbred ROTC ossifer telling me what to do. Not some dumb shit that's never humped his own load in the bush. Someone like that doesn't know jack shit what it's like out there." Daniel took a moment to finish his second beer, "I'll stay where I am. I'll take my chances with my Hog-60 and a few good men beside me."

Michael made quick work of yet another beer and leaned in closer to Daniel. "So were you one of those animals?"

"What?" Daniel asked, "A ranger? Nay."

"A green beanie?"

Daniel raised his middle finger to Michael. "Don't ever let one of those

Green Berets hear you say that because they will cut off your balls and make stew out of them."

"Seriously, Daniel. I did hear a rumor."

"So what's new about that?"

"I was talking to these Aussies in some dive bar in Saigon. We'd all gotten shit-faced drunk and they kinda let on that one of the guys in their unit was from Minnesota. He was their interpreter. Sounded just like you."

"SAS is among the best," Daniel answered with a smile then he shook his head. "But it was just that, long range reconnaissance patrol and studies and operations."

"Heard they were into some heavy shit."

"No comment."

Michael looked at Daniel with suspicion. He had doubt all over on his face, but Daniel wouldn't budge. Michael shrugged his shoulders and resumed the conversation. "They've got a low-key sense of humor, I'll tell you that. They can drink all night and go out on patrol the next morning; sober as shit."

"Can't say," Daniel answered.

"I also heard the Seventh Australian Royal Regiment really got into some heavy stuff not that long ago. Something about select elimination of target subjects. I heard they also had an American translator along with them in the bush."

"There were several GIs there," Daniel said simply.

"So you were with them?" Michael muttered as he sat up straight in his chair.

"No, man," Daniel answered with a laugh, "I'm just pulling your chain. I was made the offer but I declined - for now. I am taking a couple of correspondence courses. Takes forever by mail but the College of St. Paul will accept them. I checked."

Michael looked at Daniel. He knew Daniel was lying but he let it go. "You serious about going back to school when you get out?" he asked.

"Damn straight, I am!"

"Well good for you, bro," Michael said. "Think she'll be there for you?"

"Who knows. I think all that chanting about 'Jody getting in her blue jeans' really got to me. I have these weird dreams of her screwing other guys. Pretty upsetting."

"Them's called nightmares, my friend. They don't go away. Unless you're drunk. That helps."

Daniel got quiet. He just stared at Michael until his friend said, "What?"

"Nothing … I just realized you're the only true friend I've got in the whole world - man, I'm fucked!"

Michael thought he was going to bust a gut he laughed so hard. Daniel joined in the laughter and clinked his bottle against Michael's. They downed their beers and opened two more.

Daniel started to talk in a rapid fire manner. He began spilling his guts about the war, almost getting killed several times, losing friends in combat ,and his own numbness at killing other human beings.

Michael just listened and drank.

Hours later, Daniel felt drained and almost embarrassed at his rambling confessions. It was dark outside and the bar was crammed with loud drunken soldiers and sailors. Michael raised his hand for two cognacs.

They lit the surface of the drinks in the dim light of the bar and watched the deep blue flame atop the drink lick and curl the air. After a few seconds, they slowly and deliberately raised the flaming glasses and in one smooth movement drank the flaming liquid down and slammed the empty glasses back on the table. Lingering blue flame was still licking at the residual drops of liquor left.

"That, my friend, is an afterburner," Michael said. "I learned it from my ground crew buddies."

"Merry Christmas, Ho," Daniel chuckled.

"This war sucks," Michael said, "but you'll be home in no time and we can pick up where we left off. You'll see. It'll all work out for the best."

Daniel just shook his head. "I just feel as if she's slipping away from me. She's back in college, doing all that collegiate stuff and I'm knee deep in Southeast Asian shit. We're drifting apart, man… if she hasn't already gone her own separate way by now. I'll keep writing her and if she's around when I get back, that'll be great. If not, I don't know."

"That's your problem, Daniel."

"Which one?"

"You always want what you can't have. You've always been like that, even back in high school. I told you before to forget her. That woman's in a class of her own. And she's certainly out of your - *our* league." An evil grin came across Michael's face. "Bang another broad. Just to get your mind off her, that's what I'd do." He looked around and leaned in toward Daniel. "I can get you a little lady here. Sweet young thing. No diseases. She'll do anything you want. Lickety Split. I mean anything!

You interested in some Saigon Tea?"

"No, dickhead, I don't want to get laid," Daniel answered with a laugh. "Buy me another drink and let's fantasize about what it's like stateside right now." He waved for another round. "Right now, it's about eight in the morning. Triangle Bar opens in just three hours. We could be standing outside, waiting for Peter to show up and let us in early."

Michael smiled, his glassy eyes trying to focus on his friend across the table.

"It'd be cool inside," Daniel fantasized. "Dark and cool. The beer would be near frosty. Still 25 cents a schooner." He stopped and smiled at Michael. "That'll be you in less than a month, motherfucker."

"It will, goddamnit, it will! Outstanding!" he shouted into the air.

"Out-fucking-standing!" Daniel exclaimed.

They both laughed.

August 27th, Minnehaha Falls

The vision was so real that Colleen woke up with a cold chill shaking her body. Her nightgown was soaked in sweat. Her skin felt damp and clammy. She lay in her bed, staring up at the dark ceiling, sucking in air.

Just moments before Colleen had awakened from a dream. At least she thought it was a dream.

Colleen was in a dense jungle. It was dark and impenetrable. She saw Daniel up ahead of her. He was standing in a clearing alongside another soldier. They were firing their weapons, but she couldn't hear a thing. She saw smoke and muzzle flashes coming off their rifle barrels but still no sound.

Daniel was yelling something to the man next to him. The man suddenly clutched his side and dropped to the ground. Daniel turned to help him then looked back up. Suddenly everything around him erupted into a bright yellow sunburst. Daniel was engulfed by an explosion.

Colleen was transfixed, watching Daniel fly through the air, his uniform torn apart by the violent explosion. He landed on his back, his arms flailing out to his side. He was looking up with empty eyes. He was breathing heavily. There was blood all over his body. His lips were moving and he was trying to say something. It looked like he was calling out to someone.

The image faded to black and Colleen was left staring up at the ceiling, her body soaked with sweat and her panties plastered to her belly.

Colleen threw her body out of bed. She stumbled into the bathroom and closed the door. She sat on the stool and sobbed quietly in the darkness. Her damp curls of hair cascaded down around her face, enveloping her hands. A thousand thoughts raced through her head.

Was this a sign? Did Daniel just lose his life in Vietnam? Was Garrison right about Daniel never coming home again? Was it fair to Daniel to continue this illusion that he and Colleen could just pick up where they left off if he did come home? Wouldn't it be wiser just to end it right there and now as Garrison and Peggy and her parents had all urged her to do?

Colleen knew what she had to do. Even as the doubt kept pecking at her consciousness, Colleen had to write Daniel and end it once and for all.

The next morning, a long distance phone call to Peggy reconfirmed what Colleen already knew. Peggy was adamant that it was best for Colleen to end it right now. Peggy's relationship with John had hit a few rough spots but she had him within phone reach to iron out their misunderstandings. Colleen couldn't do that with Daniel. John had come out to visit her several times and the face-to-face contact had only resolved Peggy's determination to mend their differences and make their relationship work. Colleen had no such luxury.

Colleen decided to take a quick trip to Rochester to talk to her parents. Her mother sounded like she was reading from the same playbook as Peggy. Mary Rose repeated what Colleen's roommate had already said and took the additional tack of emphasizing Colleen's responsibility to her family in this matter. She told Colleen to move on, to forget about her freshman year romance and focus on her future instead.

Knowing her mother's preordained reaction, Colleen sought out her father's advice. Her father's response both surprised and confused Colleen.

"Sweetheart," Arthur Fitzpatrick said, "you have to go with your heart … but be realistic. This young man isn't one of us. I doubt it would have worked out anyway."

"What do you mean, Dad, he isn't one of us? What does that mean?"

"Oh, come on, Colleen, don't be naïve. Daniel is not one of us. You need to have higher standards than that. Don't shortchange yourself. It may sound a bit snotty but he isn't in our class."

"Oh, not you too, Dad."

"I beg your pardon."

"Dad, this has nothing to do with class."

"This has everything to do with class, Colleen."

"No, Dad. It doesn't!"

Arthur could feel the tension and anger growing in his daughter.

Colleen could feel her defensive posture taking hold, "What class is that?" She asked her father rapidly. "My parents are rich. But am I rich? No, I'm just a very privileged young woman who has had a lot of advantages over guys like Daniel."

"Colleen, let's not fight about this. You asked for my opinion and I'm giving it to you. That's all I can do. You're going to make the best decision that's right for you. I've got total confidence in your ability to see this whole thing through."

Colleen took a deep breath and spoke calmly. "Dad, I'm serious. What class are we talking about? Because like you've said in the past, you didn't start out that way. You married money."

"Now I don't think…"

"Come on, Dad, Mom's family is loaded and you had a lot of advantages when you married her. Now you're a doctor. But is that where you came from? No, it's not."

"I don't think that matters…"

"But don't you see, Daniel is just like you were back then. You were poor. Your family wasn't the best. And you pulled yourself up without anyone else's help. You did it by yourself. Just like Daniel is trying to do right now in Vietnam. I want to make something of myself too. Just like you did."

Colleen was on a roll. "You weren't privileged. He isn't privileged. You were ambitious. He is ambitious too. You're smart. He's smart too - except he doesn't know it…"

"Colleen! I get it! I really do get it. But nevertheless, you still have to reach deep within your heart and ask what is best for Daniel. If continuing this long distance relationship isn't being totally honest with him then you have to do the right thing and cut it off. It will be better for you and better for him in the long run so you can both get on with your lives."

Dr. Fitzpatrick smiled at his daughter and gave her a big hug. As he did, he realized just how grown up and mature his daughter had become. He couldn't help but wonder if Daniel had a lot to do with that.

When she got back to St. Paul, Colleen went directly to her apartment. The building was quiet. She closed her bedroom door and sat at her desk. She sat there for a long time, staring down at the baby blue stationary. She waited until her hands stopped shaking, and then began to compose her final letter to Daniel.

August 27th, 1968

Dear Daniel,

This is the hardest thing I've ever had to do in my life. After a lot of soul-searching it's something I feel I must do for both of us. It simply isn't fair to let you believe there is still something special between us when we both know there no longer is. I like you too much to let you live a lie.

We come from two entirely different worlds. While I knew that from the beginning, our differences only grew as we spent more time together. It was foolish of me to think that we could make our relationship work. We tried and we failed.

I don't want to feel like an imposter anymore. I need to move on with my life outside of this situation that has brought us both a lot of confusion, angst, and hurt.

I want to be totally honest with you, because I do treasure the times we spent together. Having you as my best friend was a wonderful experience freshmen year. I never understood your decision to quit school and join the service, but I respect you for it. I have tremendous admiration for your tenacity and ambition, both qualities I hope to achieve in myself eventually.

I know you will make something of yourself after the service. I just can't be there when you get out. You are a wonderful person. I know you will find someone to share your future with you. It just can't be me.

Colleen

At first she wanted to end the letter by writing, Love, Colleen. But she thought about it and instead simply wrote, Colleen.

She addressed the envelope and let it sit on the desk for a long time. She finally mustered up the strength to walk out of her apartment and slipped it in the mailbox outside.

That should have been the end of it. No more Daniel in her life. A freshman year well spent, but now just a memory quickly being crowded out with happy expectations for the future. Colleen felt a quiet sense of relief.

Several days went by before the guilt began to gnaw away at her. Colleen hadn't told anyone about the letter. There was no reason to let anyone know what she'd done. The letter had been written. It was over.

But was it?

Colleen began to feel that she had done something horribly wrong. Logically, writing that letter was the right thing to do. The people she loved and respected had all told her to do it. Colleen knew she wasn't in love with Daniel anymore. She couldn't imagine Daniel ever being a part of her family. There was no justifiable reason why ending their relationship wasn't the right thing to do.

So why did she feel so guilty?

Garrison's phone call that evening quickly brought Colleen out of her funk. He told Colleen that her article on draft deferments would be the lead article for the next edition of Twin City News. Her byline would be prominently displayed under the title. Garrison told her she'd proved herself as a writer and a journalist. It called for a celebration and he wouldn't take no for an answer. He'd pick her up that evening for dinner, champagne and a night out on the town. But dress casually he insisted, nothing fancy, just comfortable. He'd do the same.

It was a breath of fresh air to lighten Colleen's darkened mood. She quickly said yes and hoped the evening would be just the first step to putting her past behind her. She wanted to go back to living the life of a college junior who was dating an up-and-coming editor and had her future clearly laid out for her.

Maybe there's a future for me with Garrison Buckley, Colleen thought as she showered and then stood in front of her full-length mirror. She liked what she saw … so would any man. If it wasn't Garrison, there were lots of other guys out there who would fill the bill. Colleen was now free of her past and unencumbered by guilt. There were only great opportunities ahead and Colleen meant to take advantage of all of them.

As she was waiting for Garrison to show up, Colleen noticed the Galway shawl that Daniel had given her freshman year. She looked at it for a long time. It was still as beautiful as the day she unwrapped it before Daniel's beaming smile. Now it was a sad reminder of times past. She gathered it up and set it on her bed. She would have to return it to Daniel's mother. Colleen didn't need any reminder of Daniel in her life.

Garrison had a proof page of the article ready for Colleen to peruse when she slipped into his car that evening. She beamed from ear to ear. There was her name prominently displayed as promised, just below the title of her story. It was repeated on the inside page where the story began. Her first front page byline. It was a wonderful feeling.

Garrison patted her affectionately on her knee and said, "Good job, sweetheart," then laughed. Colleen joined him in laughing at that moniker. She could tell Garrison was very proud of her.

Although he wasn't a flashy dresser at work, that evening Garrison was wearing a pair of neatly pressed khaki trousers with a crisp white shirt and gold wrist chain. He smelled of expensive cologne or aftershave. It was intoxicating to Colleen. An older man interested in her, not just for her looks, but her journalistic skills as well. It was more than she could hope for.

Colleen opted for a free flowing skirt and peasant blouse. It was a mixture of casual, almost country flavor, with a hint of subtle sophistication thrown in. It was too warm for pantyhose so she just wore her favorite soft shoes and even dared to wear a pair of silk French panties. Her clothes were functional and yet very comfortable. Perfect for an evening of food and wine and great conversation.

As they drove down the Bloomington highway, Garrison kept up the conversation talking about the business and future feature articles he wanted to pursue. Although Colleen kept to her side in the front seat, she felt they were a couple connected by more than just an employer-employee relationship. It was a meeting of like minds on so many levels and a mutual respect for their own journalistic skills. She felt comfortable with Garrison and trusted his judgment in all things adult.

Garrison took Colleen to a very quiet French restaurant in the Hilton Hotel on the Bloomington strip. The building was nestled in the corner of two busy interchanges, yet the restaurant was quiet and very romantic. It was dark and cool inside and reeked of a quiet elegance as only the French can pull off. Colleen felt very mature and collected in the company of someone like Garrison.

Garrison was charming and complimentary and quite enthusiastic about Colleen's future with the newspaper. He talked about a position of feature writer for her when she graduated and another summer internship that next year. Colleen's future with Twin City News was secure as far as Buckley was concerned. He'd found a superb writer and he wasn't about to let her go to some other newspaper or magazine. It was an elixir to any doubts Colleen may have harbored about her own journalistic abilities.

After the waiter seated them in a small booth far away from the other patrons, Garrison leaned over the table and grasped Colleen's hands. He smiled broadly and said, "Congratulations again, Colleen, I feel quite fortunate to have someone as talented as you on my staff. And only a junior in college! I can't imagine where you will be in another five to ten years. Probably in New York working for Conde Nast or Hearst or some other global publishing powerhouse. Your future is quite unlimited, you know."

Colleen was embarrassed by his adulation and didn't know what to say. He released her hands and picked up the menu, which was written in French.

"Do you read French?" he asked Colleen.

"No."

"No matter, I'll pick out something for the both of us. You don't mind, do you?"

"No, of course not. I trust you implicitly."

"Now, be careful," Garrison said, laughing. "That could be dangerous."

Colleen laughed at his response.

Garrison insisted they start with fresh oysters flown in that morning from France.

After they were delivered to their table, Garrison picked up one and let it slide down his throat. "Here, try these," he said, slipping several on her large white plate. "These oysters are extraordinary! They're from a small seaside town in western France, a town called Marennes. Near the town are huge oyster beds, or parks, as the French call them."

"Have you ever been there, Garrison?"

"Oh yes, numerous times. I get my wine nearby whenever I'm overseas."

"Always on business?" Colleen asked, teasing him.

"No, I've been known to take friends along too. Have you ever been overseas, Colleen?"

"My parents took me to Europe right after high school graduation. I loved it. I can't wait to go back."

"Perhaps you can," Garrison said with a wink. "I go there quite often. I'd love some company the next time I go. Just a thought."

Colleen felt flushed and embarrassed at the direction their conversation was going. "Should we order some champagne?" she asked.

"Oh, not here. They're known for their wines instead. That's why I picked this place. Two of their best wines are a Chateau Cheval Blanc or a Chateau Ausone. They're both the best of the St. Emilion wines."

Garrison waved at the attentive waiter who was hovering in a corner. The waiter came over and Garrison ordered the wine in French. The waiter smiled, glanced at Colleen and retreated to the wine rack nearby. He came back shortly with a dusty bottle he wiped off as he approached the table.

Garrison took it out of his hand and showed the label to Colleen. He pointed to the writing just below the label. It read, Appellation St. Emilion Controlee. Garrison explained that that writing meant the French government guaranteed that this wine met or surpassed the minimum St. Emilion standards.

He handed the bottle back to the waiter who opened it and offered a small glass to Garrison. Garrison brought it up to his nose. He smelled it, swirling the liquid inside, smelled it again then pronounced it perfect. The waiter poured out the wine into Colleen's goblet then filled Garrison's glass.

"Did you know oysters are supposed to be an aphrodisiac?" Garrison asked her.

"I might recall some late night discussions around that subject matter our freshman year," Colleen answered. "Let me see, it went something like this. Aphrodite, the Greek goddess of love sprang forth from the sea out of an oyster shell. There she gave birth to Eros. Those pesky Greeks knew a good story when they made it up." Garrison joined her in laughing at the comment. "Then the Romans joined in with their own tales of love and sex and mounds of oysters at their banquets."

"Supposedly Casanova ate something like fifty raw oysters a day just to boost his libido," Garrison commented. "Where is that waiter when I need more oysters?" he laughed and touched Colleen's hand. He let his hand linger on hers until she moved to pick up her glass of wine.

"How many oysters have you had already today, Garrison?"

"Perhaps not enough," he answered as he winked at her again and picked up the menu.

The rest of the evening was filled with stimulating conversations about the latest showing at the Walker, a new play at the Guthrie and Colleen's upcoming junior year in college. Garrison was attentive, interested in what Colleen had to say and quick to embrace her hands several times. He kept filling her glass so it was never empty.

Colleen could feel herself getting more and more relaxed in the company of this charming, suave and sophisticated man. She wasn't sure if it was the wine or his charm. Since she was never much of a drinker, the wine was having its effect on her. Colleen could feel herself flush a couple of times when the conversation turned toward comments of sex and romance, but she was loving every minute of it; the wine, the meal, the conversation and the company of such a worldly man as Garrison Buckley.

Garrison was the first man who had paid Colleen so much attention. He was treating her like a real grown-up. Unlike Daniel, who was more of a friend than a lover, Garrison was showering her with platitudes she'd never heard before. She no longer felt like a college student. Instead, she felt mature and confident, ready to join the ranks of the hip urban adults who were seated all around the two of them.

Garrison was going on about his travels throughout Europe, the future direction for Twin City News and his excitement at meeting such an intelligent and beautiful woman like Colleen. She could feel herself flush again as he kept talking about her beauty and style.

Garrison leaned forward and said, “You mentioned champagne before. Do you enjoy it?”

“I’ve just had it a couple of times but yes I…”

“Did you know,” Garrison interrupted her, “that it has long been rumored that the saucer shaped Champagne glass called the coupe was modeled after the breasts of Marie Antoinette?”

Colleen felt a little uncomfortable with Garrison’s comment. But she also felt aroused by it.

“Another story is that a monk named Dom Perignon invented the drink. But, in fact, it was on the scene long before he took his vows. And the one about the bubbles in champagne getting you drunk faster turns out to be true. They did a test at the University of Surrey in Guildford and it was proven.”

By the end of their meal, the conversation had taken a decidedly different turn. Garrison had started talking about the French and their relaxed attitude toward sex. It was so different, he said, from the uptight and stodgy approach most Americans took. He admired the French for their casual, noncommittal approach to lovemaking and its release from the subconscious inhibitions that plagued most American women. He wished more American women felt that way too.

Colleen listened attentively. She was intrigued by the thought of casual sex with someone she didn’t necessarily love. It was so alien to how she had been raised and yet a titillating thought to ponder - casual sex just for the pleasure of it. *Is that what Garrison is hinting at*, Colleen wondered. She tried to dismiss the thoughts but the wine was having its effect on her. That and a sensation had begun below her belly and soon crept down between her legs. She began having images of her and Garrison in a sexual embrace. The tingling intensified and Colleen soon had to excuse herself to go to the bathroom. There she splashed cold water on her flushed face and took several deep breaths. When her composure returned she went back to their booth.

After Colleen assured Garrison that she felt fine, he kept on with his comments. He filled Colleen’s glass again over her objections and talked about his favorite wines. Out of the blue, he suggested they drive to

Minnehaha Falls. It was beautiful at night, her boss said. They could park by the falls and wander through the park. The spray and mist at night gave off an incandescent glitter above the falls. Colleen felt herself blushing but she quickly smiled and said yes, that would be wonderful.

"There's a new thing sweeping Europe right now. Quite intriguing," he dropped casually.

"What is it?"

Garrison just smiled back at Colleen silently.

"No, Garrison, I'm serious, what is it? I'm curious."

"The French and Spanish women are doing it. I think they're catching up to the Scandinavians…"

"Will you please tell me what you're talking about?" Colleen insisted.

"Well, if you insist. It's a new way of pleasuring yourself without using your hands. You remove your underwear and stand near a fountain or waterfalls where the spray comes off the splashing water and you let the mist tingle your extremities."

"Extremities?"

"That's why you take off your panties. For the sensation there," Garrison explained. His face wore an expression of curiosity. He was neither embarrassed nor ashamed to talk about sex in such a casual manner.

Colleen's mind was whirling with the images of women exposing themselves to the spray and mist. She was at once embarrassed and at the same time strangely intrigued by his comments. Colleen tried hard to keep her emotions in check, yet she couldn't help but become aroused by the images he was painting in her mind.

"And doing it in public makes it even more erotic," he said with a smile.

"Garrison, you're not serious!"

"Colleen, I'm not forcing you to do anything. I'm just telling you that if you want a very wonderful feeling, I know a way. I'm guessing this is one you've never had before. I'm not going to touch you. I'm just telling you that's what will happen if you do it."

"And that's what you want me to do at Minnehaha Falls?"

"No, forget it, Colleen," Garrison said defensively. He leaned back in his chair and took his napkin off his lap and set it on the table. "I shouldn't have brought it up. I don't want you to think badly of me. I was speaking out of turn. Just forget what I said."

"No, I'll do it," Colleen suddenly heard herself saying.

"You don't have to."

"Garrison, I said I'd try it. I'm not a child. I can take care of myself. No, I've never done something like that before. But I'm game."

"You'll love it," was all Garrison said with a smile. He got up. Colleen followed.

As they walked out into the parking lot holding hands, Colleen felt light-headed and a little woozy. Her speech wasn't slurred but she could feel herself floating on a soft fog. She slipped into the front seat and smiled at Garrison as he got in beside her.

Even in her heightened state of inebriation, Colleen felt she was still in control and therefore comfortable with this man who was so attentive to her. It would be a nice experience to see the falls at night with Garrison at her side.

Colleen slid across the front seat up next to Garrison. He put his hand on her knee again and she smiled at him. He put the car in gear and then slipped his hand between her legs but Colleen held firm. He laughed and slowly removed his hand and put it back on the steering wheel. Colleen almost felt disappointed.

They parked the car in a dark corner of the parking lot, far from the few other cars. Garrison leaned over and kissed Colleen gently. They held the kiss for a long time. He whispered in Colleen's ear to remove her panties before she got out. He got out of the car and stood in front, waiting for her.

Colleen sheepishly raised herself up just a little and slid her panties off. She put them under the front seat and got out of the car. Garrison took her hand and they walked hand in hand down the stone steps to the bottom of the falls.

Any feelings of guilt over her letter to Daniel had disappeared after the third glass of wine. Now as she walked down the stone steps, Colleen felt this was a new beginning for her. A new life unencumbered by her past relationship with Daniel. It was a good feeling. As was the chill of the swirling spray that began to creep up her bare legs.

No one else was around as they walked toward the metal railing that surrounded the crashing waters of the falls. Garrison pointed up at the water as it spilled over the edge of the falls and fell in torrents to the bottom. Looking up toward the top of the falls, Colleen could see through the water's clear transparency and the dark night illuminated behind it.

She found herself looking up and leaning backwards against Garrison's chest. He positioned his legs to support Colleen's weight propped against him and wrapped his arms around her. His hands found her breasts and cupped them gently. Colleen could feel her nipples growing hard. She felt warm and comfortable in Garrison's arms. She was in a near trancelike state. She could feel Garrison starting to get hard, creating a pressure against her spine.

The spray and mist swirled closer to them. Garrison began nuzzling her neck then leaned forward and kissed her; first on her cheek, then her lips - hard. Colleen hungrily returned his kiss. He began whispering in her ear about love and need and the two of them together. As he spoke in hushed tones, his arms dropped down to Colleen's stomach, then her thighs as he slowly began to raise her skirt. As he did so, the dampness brought a tingling sensation over her sex. He slipped his hand down and pressed harder as his fingers began to converge, and then touch, her coarse patch of hair.

Colleen let out a gasp. But the wine had numbed her senses and ability to react. It was an incredibly wonderful and sensual feeling. Colleen was totally aroused. She had never felt like that before. She let out another gasp as Garrison slowly slipped one finger into her, then another finger slid inside. He touched her spot and Colleen tensed up as a shudder exploded throughout her body. She could feel the warm moisture beginning to gather between the folds of her skin there.

"Let's go back to the car." Colleen didn't know what to say, how to react. He wrapped his arm around her waist and hurriedly turned her around. She let him lead her away from the falls and quickly up the stone stairs. He was rushing her back to the car.

When they got to the car, Garrison opened the passenger side door and practically pushed Colleen inside. He looked around quickly then climbed in himself. Colleen was sitting upright on the seat, still in a daze and feeling flushed. Garrison wrapped his arms around her, kissing her passionately. He pressed hard down on her lips as he moved her into a prone position.

His hands moved quickly. One grasped Colleen around her shoulder and laid her back down across the seat. The other pushed up her skirt and roughly spread her legs apart. It was awkward and cumbersome.

He moved on top of her, pressing his belly against her bare midriff. The hand, which had spread Colleen's legs, now dug into his unzipped pants. Moving his hips, Garrison began to penetrate Colleen.

During all of Garrison's awkward maneuvering, Colleen was only vaguely aware of what was going on. What was Garrison doing? She was on her back. Garrison was moving on top of her. He was pressing his lips against hers, pushing his tongue inside her mouth.

Suddenly Colleen felt a sharp pain between her legs. She let out a scream.

Garrison stopped in mid-motion, still inside her.

Colleen screamed again. "Get off of me," she shouted into his face.

Garrison quickly pulled out and off of her. He pushed himself up and rolled over to the driver's side, jamming his erect member back inside his pants.

"Oh, Christ," he exclaimed, "you're still a virgin?!"

"You bastard!" Colleen began to cry as she tugged at her skirt, which was bunched up around her stomach. The tears ran down her stained cheeks.

"Oh, God, don't cry. I didn't know. I just assumed… You're all right. I pulled out in time. God, my new upholstery."

"Fuck your upholstery, you son of a bitch!"

Colleen could feel warm liquid begin to pool between her legs and trickle down her thighs.

"There's nothing to worry about. Christ, girl, why didn't you tell me?" He looked angry and upset. "I don't date virgins," he said with disdain.

"You tried to rape me!"

"I did no such thing!"

"Take me home, now!" She reached down and scooped up her panties off the floor. She wrestled them back on and never once looked over at Garrison. He started the car and drove away.

"Look, Colleen, I'm sorry I yelled at you. I was just surprised. You're so worldly and sophisticated. I just thought … you know… I just thought you'd been with a man before. I had no idea."

"Just take me home," Colleen repeated.

As soon as Garrison pulled into her apartment parking lot, Colleen swung open her door and jumped out, slamming the door behind her. Garrison was long gone before she reached the front door.

As she walked through the front door, instead of feeling ashamed at what had just happened, Colleen felt anger. She was madder than she'd ever been in her life. But she also felt liberated, as if a huge weight of 'what if' had been lifted off her shoulders. She was free of fear, and shame, and guilt. She would never put herself in such a position ever again where she lost control. She would never be vulnerable like that again.

The next day Colleen turned in her resignation letter to the Twin City News.

As promised, that weekend Colleen went back to Rochester to see her parents before school started. It went fairly well. Colleen dodged the subject of boyfriends most of the time. It wasn't until she was about to leave that Colleen heard it again from her Mother about what a wonderful guy the editor must be and how wise Colleen was to have gotten out of her relationship with Daniel.

As Mary Rose went on about the benefits of having an older man as a boyfriend, Colleen bit her lip. She nodded approval of her mother's pontificating and smiled at her unwanted advice.

Her dad walked Colleen out to her car when she was leaving.

"Dad," Colleen began when she was out of earshot of her Mother. "Mom is really getting on my case about the editor. But I don't like him as much as I once did. No reason," Colleen lied. "It just didn't work out the way I thought it would."

"Dear, don't worry about it. Your Mother means well. She really does. But she isn't you. You have to decide for yourself who or what is best for you. If that fellow isn't the one, that's just fine. There will be other men in your life. There's no rush to get involved."

Colleen stood by her car door. She hesitated, took a deep breath, and then said, "Dad, I sent that Dear John letter to Daniel but I think I made a terrible mistake."

"Why? You said you wanted to end the relationship."

"I know I did, but I think I was wrong. I wasn't being true to myself. I listened to Peggy and mom. They got to me and I caved in."

"Why do you say that?" her father asked.

"Because I went with my head instead of my heart. Logic told me that while freshman year was great our relationship fell apart during last summer. I thought maybe we could patch things up sophomore year but he decided to drop out of school. He got drafted and that seemed to put the nail in the coffin of our relationship."

Mr. Fitzpatrick looked at his daughter. He wanted to say something but thought better of it.

"But, see dad, the essence of our relationship was our friendship. I lost track of that when I wrote the letter. A real friend doesn't treat another friend that way."

Colleen's father studied her. He smiled and put his hands on her shoulders.

"So what are you going to do about it?" he asked.

"I want to send Daniel another letter. I need to apologize for the first one and ask him if he'll still be my friend. I'll tell him that it won't be like it was before. Because I know we're now two very different people. I already told him that. I think he would understand what I'm trying to say to him."

"Sounds like a good idea, dear; as long as you don't lead him on. Remember he's under a tremendous amount of stress over there. He could easily misread your intentions. It can still be very dicey doing what you're suggesting."

"But I can't just let him get my Dear John letter and let that be the end of our friendship. If he decides he doesn't want to see me again, so be it! But at least I will have made an effort to reconnect with him."

"Colleen, you're going to do whatever you think you need to do. I support you one hundred percent. One hundred percent."

Colleen climbed into her car and started it up. Her father leaned into her window. He kissed her softly on her check. "I love you, sweetheart," he said. "And don't worry about your mother. She'll come around. I know her. She'll support whatever you decide to do."

Colleen drove off, feeling satisfied that her next letter would clarify her true feelings and let Daniel know she still wanted to be friends. She intended to write it just as soon as she got back to her apartment.

August 27th, A Shau Valley

Vietnam's Central Highlands was the scene of numerous battles and firefights between American and NVA forces. Part of the Annamite Chain of mountains, the highlands had an average width of 93 miles and could reach 5000 feet in height. The mountains there were heavily forested and extremely rugged. The VC and North Vietnamese Army owned the Highlands and meant to keep it that way.

Within the Central Highlands, the A Shau Valley was one of the principal entry points into the South off the Ho Chi Minh Trail, making it a strategic point of contact with the Viet Cong. It was Charlie's playground but the Americans intended to take it away.

The A Shau's dense triple canopy jungle and impenetrable mountainous terrain made clear contact with the enemy almost impossible. It had become a game of cat and mouse, hit and run ambushes and search and destroy missions. A regular army company would have a hard time finding the Viet Cong in such terrain. A smaller group would have a much better chance at success.

First Daniel and his men hitched a ride on a large Chinook transport helicopter which ferried them to the loading zone. There they boarded slicks for the ride to their drop-off zone. Daniel checked each man and his equipment as they loaded up. He hopped aboard and signaled the pilot for takeoff. A choking red cloud of dust enveloped the slicks as they strained toward liftoff.

Many of the ridges and hills in the A Shau were named for their height in meters. After setting up a fire support base on hill 484, one of the numerous indistinguishable mountaintops in the highlands, Daniel's reconnaissance unit prepared for its descent into the A Shau Valley. It was supposed to be a probing mission to search for and ascertain enemy concentration in the area.

The unit's objective was simple enough. Assess enemy strength, and if need be, engage and destroy as many of them as possible. The AO, area of operation, covered a large area within the A Shau, enough ground to keep Daniel's unit on the move for at least a week or more.

Three Hueys accompanied by two gunships left the mountaintop in the pre-dawn hours. Daniel had two squads of seasoned veterans with him and two non-Vietnamese highland tribesmen, the Montagnards. Called Yards by the Americans, these scouts, also affectionately known as the little people were superb bush fighters. The Yards would act as scouts and trail readers.

The flight took less than 10 minutes and they were soon beginning their descent into a deep green bowl surrounded by dense jungle on all four sides. On the horizon, the first few traces of light were beginning to differentiate the sky from jungle landscape below.

Daniel could see the orange glow of the rising sun off to his left and a smoggy gray darkness to his right. It would be dawn within minutes.

After landing quickly, the men lay dog, waiting in place in a security wheel formation to see if they'd been spotted. Above them, the gunships were at station, ready to swoop down to tear up the tree line if Charlie was spotted there.

Daniel and his men scanned the surrounding jungle tree line for more than ten minutes. Daniel radioed the helicopters overhead to move on. The LZ, landing zone, was secure. The air was still and quiet. Patches of wispy early morning ground fog rose lazily into the sky.

Daniel checked his weapon again and peered into the surrounding jungle. He wore a blue checked bandana around his neck and had a tiger claw attached to the bead chain of his dog tags. All of his senses were on high alert. At first glance, he looked like any other soldier. But his casual attire belied a battle hardened veteran, heavily armed and ready to kill at a moment's notice.

Veterans in the group had sensed a new attitude in Daniel even before this latest patrol. They saw it when he first took command of the group, briefing them on this particular mission. He was straightforward and to the point, firm about his rules in the bush and reaffirming in his conviction that they would come back alive if they followed directions.

The veterans knew from experience that soldiers would not always rally around the senior man in charge during a firefight gone badly. Instinctively the troops would gravitate toward the one person they believed would have the best chance of getting them out alive, regardless of his age or rank. Daniel was such a man.

It was more than just a kind of fearlessness or a willingness to do whatever was necessary to get the job done. More importantly, it was Daniel's refusal to put his men in harm's way unless he was at the helm. Daniel cared more for his men than most officers ever would. The men under his command understood that and respected him for it.

By the time he'd reached the A Shau for a second time, Daniel had matured far beyond his chronological years. He'd become a warrior, callused to the realities of battle each time one of his men died. Yet deep down, Daniel was still the same young kid grabbing at life experiences in the bush just as he had at the Triangle Bar and on Zack's front porch.

The men moved out as the first traces of early morning sunlight began to paint the pale sky gray. The air was still cool and bearable. A moment in time before the mist in the valley started to dissipate and heavy humidity began working its way up from the jungle floor. The two squads walked in silence in a single file line, saying very little to one another as, one by one, the jungle swallowed them up.

Going into the bush was where men died - on both sides of the battlefield. It was where Charlie hid and Daniel's men had to go to flush them out. They would go humping the boonies until contact was made and Charlie was eliminated.

It was also where GIs could die in a dozen different ways. There were punji stake traps to fall into, tin can grenades, spiked balls that flew out of the jungle if released by a trip wire, and hidden mines strategically placed just a foot fall away from a fallen log.

If the booby traps didn't do the trick, then snipers might pick off someone with only a faint pop somewhere in the distance. Or at a closer range, the Type 50 sub-machine gun or Type 56 assault rifle or AK-47 might wreck their havoc on their ranks. Each one of them was a lethal weapon at close and distant ranges. It made no difference if it was the VC or NVA that fought the Americans, either force was a killing machine to be reckoned with.

Normally the newest recruit would be the slack man, heading up the rear of the column. But Daniel knew that Charlie often waited for a patrol to pass by and then hit it from the rear. So he assigned one of the Yards back there. A good Yard could sense the presence of VC or NVA better than his men could.

The heat grew heavy and stifling. Daniel's jungle fatigues were soaked with sweat and spotted with patches down his back and arms. Most of the men wore t-shirts or nothing under their flak jackets. They wore floppy hats called boonies. Olive drab or black with strips of green to match their painted faces. No one carried their weapon slung over their shoulders. Every M-16 or M-60 light machine gun was ready.

Daniel carried a standard M-16 and wore a .45 automatic strapped to his hip. The handgun was powerful enough to take down any VC or penetrate several feet of enemy bunker if need be. It could tear a softball sized hole through soft tissue and go on for another hundred yards.

Daniel walked gingerly through the jungle, following closely behind the Yard point man. They both stopped frequently, listening to the jungle sounds, trying to feel out their surroundings with almost a sixth sense. The Yard never turned around. Instead he made motions with his hands.

The troops carried enough supplies for a week or more in the bush. Radio communication was limited and silence was the rule while traversing the narrow jungle trails. Smoking was forbidden. The alien smell of tobacco in the jungle would carry a long distance.

The first night brought little relief from the intense heat and invasive bugs. The two squads settled into their harbor site for a long and drawn out wait. They formed a tight back to back security circle around their bivouac site. By morning there had still been no sign of Charlie. But the men knew Charlie was out there. So were the NVA. All of them intent on finding and killing as many Americans as they could. Or die trying.

Long lines of biting red ants forced Daniel's group to move twice before they lost contact with the minuscule enemy. The two squads lay in their wagon wheel security position and waited.

Chow in the field was usually the same C-rations, zipped open with the little P-38 can openers most of the men wore on the dog tags around their necks. Once a day, every one of the team had to choke down their bitter, dime-sized yellow malaria pill. After the area was secured, Daniel would pinch off a small piece of C-4 plastic explosive from the emergency supply in his backpack. He used it to boil up a canteen cup of water for coffee. Like every veteran, Daniel understood that if used carefully, C-4 could bring water to a boil in thirty seconds. Used carelessly, it could blow off his arm.

They followed this pattern of marching during the day and bivouacking in a defensive line each night for almost five days straight. Still no sign of the NVA but both Daniel and the Yards knew the enemy was out there; unseen, unnoticed, but present nevertheless.

The routine was simple enough, walk slowly for several hundred yards and then stop to look and listen. Daniel scanned the terrain up ahead with his 7x50 binoculars. He could see the Yard point man moving cautiously through the tall elephant grass. No unnatural movement anywhere.

They'd covered most of their AO and were on a wide swing back to their LZ when things started to change.

First, the rains came just as the soldiers had set up their safe harbor site one night. They had just gotten their claymore mines in a defensive ring around their perimeter before the first big drops started to fall.

"Gawd!" Daniel exclaimed as he tried to wrap his poncho over a weak tree branch for a makeshift shelter. His second, nestled not far away, laughed. The heavy rain incessantly assaulted the men. The air was thick and dank and smelled of rotting vegetation and soggy ground cover. The men lay in red soil that stuck like glue to their rifle butts and boots.

"Where are you from, Daniel?" the old sergeant asked.

"Minnesota. You?"

"Galveston, Texas. Got me a fine piece of real estate down right on the beach. Hope to go back there and settle down once I retire."

"You…retire?"

The old sergeant laughed and dug his heels in closer out of the rain. It's gonna happen, Daniel…someday. What about you? Do you have anyone or anything to go back to?"

"I don't know, sarg," Daniel replied, "I really don't."

Silence fell between the men again.

The rains let up for a brief respite then came back with a vengeance. Monsoon rains ripped open the night sky and dumped sheet upon sheet of cold liquid down on the men. It turned the jungle floor into a series of small pools that filled every depression on the ground. Trickles of water became streams that wormed their way through their defense perimeter. Visibility was reduced to an arm's length or less. What ground cover that wasn't pooling or washing away became an ankle-deep sea of mud.

The men lay in a morass of mud and green, listening intently for any sign of the enemy. But the torrential rains drowned out any sounds other than branches cracking under the weight of the downpour. It was like sitting inside a washing machine, the turbulence drowning out any outside noises.

Gradually the rains began to subside and then fall away. When the rain stopped, all the men could hear was the sound of rain drops rolling off leaves and dripping to the ground. It slowly became very quiet except for the nocturnal animals that came out of their shelters to hunt.

Daniel looked up at the night sky which was beginning to fill with millions of tiny pinpricks of lights. He let himself think about Colleen half a world away. She was probably having lunch or starting her afternoon classes. She was safe and secure and slipping out of his life. Rain began tapping on his plastic once again and brought him back to reality. He started to pick away at the mud which coated the soles and porous green canvas sides of his boots.

"If those gooks get their shit together we might be in a world of hurt," his second commented. "They know this terrain better than those monkeys overhead. Command should have brought out more men."

"The Yards are good," Daniel whispered back. "So are the others. I'm not worried about them. But I agree it could be a bad scene tomorrow or the next day and we're going right into the middle of it. They're going to test our metal."

"I rest my case."

"Oh, come on, Top," Daniel replied. "That's why they pay us the big bucks."

"If that makes you feel any better you should believe it," his second shot back, "but I think you're just pissing into the wind."

They both laughed softly. "Trust me sergeant, only one of us is walking out of this gunfight alive and it won't be those dinks." The second nodded in agreement and pulled the plastic liner tighter up over his head.

The first beams of sunlight began to spear through the jungle canopy just as the rains started to subside. Within minutes, the mud had already begun drying up and turning to red clay. Soaked and miserable, Daniel's men moved themselves out into the pools of light so that sunlight could dry their clothes. They chewed down their C rations and began to move out once again.

The next day brought with it only more stifling heat and still no signs of enemy activity.

The troops moved slowly through the jungle, stopping often to get their bearings and to listen to the jungle sounds surrounding them. As long as the monkeys and birds were chattering overhead, ambush seemed unlikely.

By mid-morning their luck began to change. The scouts discovered a high-speed runner, a well used enemy trail. Boot prints were clearly visible in the caked mud as were the tire track marks of sandals worn by NVA soldiers. Two thin sets of bicycle tracks had hardened along the edge of the trail.

Following the trail, the Yard soon found fresh tracks in a clearing of elephant grass up ahead. It was a force of at least a dozen men, maybe more. They wore sandals and were traveling lightly - most likely VC on patrol and probably looking for Daniel's force.

Daniel signaled his men with a clenched fist held close to his face and index finger to his ear. Freeze and listen. Everyone froze in line. Slowly, Daniel sank to his knees. His men followed him down. He rested his weapon on his forearm for stability and listened for anything unusual.

Patches of sunlight were streaming down through the thick canopy overhead to the jungle floor. The chorus of jungle sounds roared unabated. Nothing seemed out of place and yet…

Daniel was nervous and getting more so by the moment. Nothing was wrong and that was precisely the problem. It was like Daniel and his men had stepped into a time warp, with everything around them frozen in place. The air was still and motionless. Double and triple canopy jungle made any movement difficult and very dangerous. The terrain was as thick as it was high.

Daniel didn't believe in a sixth sense but his gut told him something was wrong. He turned slowly to his second in command. "The man knows his stuff," he whispered, referring to the Yard scout. "But something tells me they're tailing us. They knew we'd find this trail. I want to set up a buttonhook."

The grizzly old veteran smiled. A buttonhook was a strategic movement if the squad thought it was being trailed by the enemy. You'd make a circle and come back to your own tracks. You waited in ambush for those enemy soldiers who were following you. First devised by the British against the Japanese in Burma in World War II, it was a proven technique in strategic combat planning.

Daniel's best guess was that the VC would return on that trail either that night or the next day. He quickly moved his two squads out in a fanning movement that took them off the trail, into the jungle and then back on either side of the runner. He had his men set up an ambush in the dense vegetation on either side of the trail. He moved the Yard far enough ahead that he could signal the squad if and when the VC returned. Then they waited.

Before leaving on their mission, Daniel had had his machine gunners switch their tracer rounds so that they were spaced three rounds apart instead of the normal five. In a firefight, the steady stream of tracer orange would belie the real amount of firepower coming from his group. It might give them the edge in case they ended up fighting an enemy force much larger than their own.

The two squads waited the entire evening but neither saw nor heard any sign of the enemy. Nor was there any letup in the heavy drone of insects or gnats that crawled into every exposed orifice of the men. By early dawn, Daniel and his men were sleep deprived and exhausted and still very tense. The night sounds began to fade away slowly and were replaced by the occasional calling of a black crow or other jungle bird.

Predawn was the ideal time for an enemy attack. The blanket chorus of night sounds was slowly beginning to give way to the calls of tropical birds and monkey's screeches high overhead. As the darkness of night slowly began to dissipate and its soft gray turned to green and black, the men grew ever more fidgety and uneasy.

There was an air of tension. Something was wrong, very wrong. The men could feel it in their guts. It pricked their skin and caused sweat to dampen their uniforms once again.

There was still no sign of the enemy. Daniel sent out the second Yard. He came back 10 minutes later with nothing to report.

Sweat droplets began to slowly run down Daniel's cheek and despite the growing heat, it felt almost chilly as they pooled around his neck. Heat and humidity were growing in intensity by the minute. Daniel feared prickly heat the most. It could cause severe scratching of the skin - a prelude to heat stroke or exhaustion.

Daniel looked at his second and shrugged his shoulders. There was value in fear, Daniel knew. It kept him on alert and stopped him from doing something stupid or hopefully, getting killed.

Charlie was still out there. Daniel knew it. The second knew it. The Yards knew it. But where and when they'd make contact no one could tell. Daniel nodded at his second. The old veteran motioned for the two squads to leave their ambush positions and gather on the trail again.

After they had spread out on the trail, Daniel silently signaled his unit to continue their search for the enemy.

Instinct had saved Daniel's life several times. Now his gut was telling him the enemy was near. Very close by. He and his men moved slowly along the jungle trail until it spilled out into a grassy opening. Overhead, the sun was just starting to rise in a bright yellow ball, crawling up into the pale blue sky. There was no wind. The trees and underbrush were still, almost dormant. A growing layer of heavy humidity was quickly replacing the early morning dew. Up ahead the jungle grew thick with its triple canopy.

It still didn't feel right to Daniel.

He held his men back of the clearing. His Yard had already crossed the opening and disappeared into the jungle beyond. With its triple canopy of towering trees and thick foliage, the jungle was a sooty green abyss that enveloped anything within several feet of entering it.

But Daniel hesitated, reluctant to take his men across the clearing unless he had a sign it was safe. They waited five minutes. Ten minutes. Then he heard something. The second heard it too and motioned for silence among the squads.

The first barely audible sound was a footfall, then boots on hard packed earth. Daniel knew immediately it had to be his scout. No VC or NVA would make so much noise. The Montagnard scout was racing toward his unit, with a purpose.

Within seconds, the scout came back running. He burst through the jungle clearing on the other side and moved quickly into the tall elephant grass. He stopped within clear view of Daniel. His fist went up against his face. His hand opened, spreading out five fingers then closed. He repeated the motion a second time. Ten fingers … then a third time, 15 fingers.

"Contact front," Daniel whispered to his second who quickly relayed the message down the column, freezing them in place.

Charlie was coming back along the trail up ahead. At least 15 enemy soldiers just minutes away. The Yard suddenly moved his hand from his mouth to his ear. He could hear something coming toward them from his right. It was two groups - one on the trail, and a second moving through the jungle. Both forces converging on that open area just across from Daniel's unit.

Immediately, Daniel ushered his men back into position. He had them set up their field of fire in a cross pattern. This half circle greatly expanded the kill zone until it covered the entire field, effectively eliminating any safe zone for the enemy. Anything or anyone caught in that pattern of cross fire would be hit from at least three different angles. The key to their success was total surprise and rapid fire. Laying down a killing blanket of bullets and explosions that would tear through the enemy column and lay waste to the VC. The kill zone was set.

Daniel's men settled into their firing positions and waited for Charlie to appear. Daniel cradled his M-16 in a firing position. He slowly turned the selector switch to full automatic, unsnapped his .45 from its hip holster, and waited. Tiny rivets of sweat began to bead across his forehead.

Next to him, the Yard smiled through his missing, tobacco stained teeth, black from betel nuts. "BooKoo VC," he whispered with a smile. It was all coming together. Daniel's gut instincts had saved him once again.

By now the colors of the rain forest were coming into full bloom. Rich greens and browns and blacks melted together in a tapestry that contrasted with the deep blue overhead. There was still no wind. Any movement by or near the opposite jungle clearing would be spotted immediately. Daniel took a deep breath, fighting back the feeling of stark terror which crept up his spine and rested in his shaking hands and clammy clothes.

Inexplicably, thoughts of Colleen began to creep into the back of his mind. Colleen on campus. He and Colleen making out. Colleen with someone else. Daniel blinked his eyes, focusing on the green jungle clearing across from him. He pushed the images of Colleen away. Christ, he thought, a distraction like that could get me killed in a heartbeat.

Still no sign of Charlie.

Suddenly, Daniel realized the jungle had grown very quiet. The sound of the birds and monkeys was muted, now far away. There were no sounds close by. Still unseen, the enemy had to be very close now.

They did not have to wait long for Charlie to appear. Within minutes of their repositioning, a slight movement on the edge of the jungle clearing caught Daniel's eye. It was there for a split second and then gone. Distant jungle sounds provided a monotonous drone. The sun beat overhead. The air was stifling and growing heavier by the moment.

Then the movement came back again. A slow motion smudge of black moving among the thick ruddy green surroundings. A mop of black hair slowly rose up among the green. A face appeared above the brush line. A second face appeared right next to it, also painted green black.

Two lead scouts, both dressed in black pajamas, stepped out into the edge of the clearing. Without looking at one another, they communicated by head nods and hand signals. No words were ever spoken. Both wore ChiCom chest pouch webbing that had smaller pouches designed to carry rifle rounds. Both carried PPSh sub machine guns at ready.

A typical VC squad was made up of three cells of three soldiers each, nine men or women total. These were scouts. But that still gave Daniel no indication if there were squads, platoons or a whole company of VC behind them. The scouts began to move toward the opening in the jungle.

Daniel watched them intensely for any sign that Charlie sensed an ambush. There were no signs his men had yet been detected. The VC were masters at the art of stealth movement. They seemed to float through the tall elephant grass as if it were soft carpeting. Their movements were fluid, carrying their weapons up high, ready to fire. Their eyes darted back and forth in a constant rapid motion.

Then, like the body of an elongated black snake, more men began to appear behind the two scouts, melting out of the jungle and into the clearing. More suddenly appeared off to the right just where the Yard had signaled they would be coming from.

The two lead scouts stopped for a moment, then fanned out and flowed through the grass until they were half way across the clearing. One signaled back to the jungle and the rest of the VC column slowly began winding its way into the grass. The black column flowed into the waist high grass and twisted from side to side as it wound its way through the clearing. By now the two scouts were across the grass and almost to the trail opening on the other side.

They reached the other side of the clearing and waited. The column of VC picked up its pace and moved quickly to cross the open space toward the shelter of the dense vegetation on the other side.

By then the Viet Cong were center mass. The entire column was fanned out in the elephant grass, exposed on three sides. They had moved directly into the killing zone.

The main body of VC was almost to the other side of the clearing when the first M-60 opened up and ripped into the lead scout. The first three rounds obliterated his face. The second three took his head clean off. Yet even as his headless torso slumped to the ground, the other scout could only swing around, firing wildly in all directions at an unseen enemy, before he was cut down.

Daniel's men opened up with volley after volley of withering point-blank machine gun and rifle fire. They heaved hand grenades into the packed ranks advancing against them.

Daniel could hear the woof of the M-79 grenade launcher, nicknamed the Blooper. Its first grenade exploded between three soldiers, tearing them into shreds of flying flesh mixed with metal fragments. A second M-60 opened up, amid a growing crescendo of M-16 rifle bursts filling the air with an ear-piercing assault of sound. In his peripheral vision, Daniel would see muzzle flashes all around him.

The din of battle was unbelievable. Machine gun and rifle fire along with grenade explosions reached a deafening crescendo. Men were screaming and shouting. The field of elephant grass was now blue with the haze of rifle fire and smoke from grenade explosions. The VC column broke rank and scattered, running back toward the surrounding jungle. Blood fountains burst from their black pajamas as round after round found its mark.

Several G.I.s stood up, firing their weapons from their hips as they sprayed the fleeing column of dying men. Daniel screamed for his men to get down but to no avail. Charlie still had fight in him and the VC responded back with their own fuselage of AK-47 and SKS Simonov carbines. One of the airborne soldiers got hit and flew back as his chest exploded in a sheet of red. Daniel crouched up on one leg, sweeping his M-16 back and forth across the grassy field.

Not more than ten yards away, Daniel saw four black shirts suddenly rise like quail out of the grass and sprint directly toward the tree line where he was standing. Daniel leapt up and planted his feet firmly in the soft ground. Methodically he began picking off the runners one by one.

The first caught a slug in his neck and pitched forward. A second had his hat blown off and with it half of his brain. Daniel automatically focused on a third sprinter. One snap shot and the man threw his arms in the air and pitched forward. Daniel focused on the last man running.

The soldier was almost to the brush when a bullet hit him in the back. He spun around, his hat flying away. Daniel aimed at the torso.

But as the hat flew off, a cascade of jet-black hair swirled around his face. Her face. She had a beautiful olive brown complexion that framed her frightened eyes. The teenager staggered as another bullet hit her full in the chest. She screamed in pain, clutching her blood wound. She stumbled backwards, looking up as if to heaven and fell to her knees. Her eyes were empty, life had left her body.

Daniel snap fired one shot and put a bullet center forehead.

The killing was almost done. Daniel blinked away the stinging acid cloud that still swirled around him. He focused on two more VC were running parallel to him. One clutched a long stemmed potato masher grenade. Daniel fired at the first man, hitting him in the chest. It exploded in a splash of red. The man stumbled backwards. Daniel focused on the second runner with the hand grenade. He fired once, hitting him in the belly. He fired again, hitting him in the torso this time. The man staggered forward then turned toward Daniel, grenade still in hand.

Suddenly the Yard next to Daniel screamed and fell to the ground, clutching his side. Daniel turned to help and as he did, he caught the blurry motion of something sailing through the air. It was arching up then falling toward him. A split second glance and Daniel was looking up at a brown circular tube twisting and turning as it descended down on him. He pitched forward, throwing his body over the Montagnard scout and tried to roll out of the way.

A deafening explosion momentarily obliterated his sight and hearing with a bright yellow red burst of light. A rush of warm air slammed into his body. Daniel could feel shrapnel from the grenade tearing through his torso. An enormous thunderclap smashed against his eardrums. Piercing, agonizing pain erupted inside his head. He could feel his clothing being ripped off his body. Blood began trickling out of both ears and he tasted dirt and other debris in his mouth. A sticky liquid began filling his throat, choking him. It felt like he was dying in slow motion.

There was no sound except the tremendous pounding against his eardrums.

The burning pain in his brain was almost unbearable. Everything went black. Daniel's body slumped to the ground. His face was planted in the dirt. A gasping breath only brought up dirt and leaves into his mouth. He instinctively coughed out blood and dirt and muck.

Then slowly his vision started coming back, unfocused and blurry. The shock wave was being replaced by darkness that slowly turned gray. He heard a buzzing sound, more like singing. Like the voices of angels singing down to him. Through the melting darkness, he saw a vision. It was like the image of someone hovering over him.

It was the figure of a woman - a woman like Colleen. It was Colleen standing over him. The darkness began to close in, washing over her image. Colleen was talking. Her lips were moving. She was trying to say something to Daniel. He tried to call out her name but she was moving away. She was leaving. Daniel lost consciousness.

The I Corp Hospital was a large complex within an even larger military base near the Laotian border. Daniel was flown there by medevac from his firebase. It took eight hours of surgery to repair his body from the shrapnel that had torn through it. The effects of the concussion lingered for over a week until his hearing came back and he realized he hadn't suffered any permanent damage. It took another four weeks before he was able to move about without great pain.

After the fourth week, Daniel's mail caught up with him. It was early evening and the ward was very quiet. A television was droning on in the background and a card game at the far end of the corridor was competing with it as a secondary sound blanket. A crotchety old female orderly brought in his stack of letters and dropped it on the table next to his bed. Daniel stirred from a fitful sleep and rolled over to one side. He stared at the small bundled pile for a long time before reaching out and laying it back on his belly.

Gingerly he untied the bundle and lifted up the first letter to read.

It was from the College of St. Paul informing Daniel that he could return to school after his discharge. The correspondence courses he'd been taking would all apply toward his credit requirements. All toll, he would be about a year or so behind his old classmates. Daniel didn't mind. He couldn't imagine there would be a lot of common interest between himself and those students once he returned to campus. Now he just had to get out of Vietnam alive so he could start school again. It wasn't a question of 'if' he returned but rather when he returned and finished college.

The Admissions Committee added a note that they were anxious to welcome all returning servicemen to their campus.

The next letter was from Daniel's mother. It was another one of her customarily short and vague communiqués. Work still stunk. She had a new boyfriend. This one was different from all the rest. She still didn't understand why Daniel dropped out of college. But since he did, he should consider staying in for 20 years or going to work for the Post Office. With both branches, Daniel could put in his 20 years and still be young enough to get a pension and another job. Double dipping would be heaven to someone like his mother.

Michael's was the third letter Daniel received that evening. It was confusing at best. His best friend was returning to the Twin Cities after giving San Francisco a go. The city by the bay hadn't worked out and Michael reluctantly was returning home. He had a couple of job leads but nothing concrete yet.

Twice Michael had been approached by men calling him a baby killer. At first he was confused by the accusations. The second time, he decked the caller and ran like hell from the fallen man's friends. Soldiers and sailors didn't dare hang out on Market Street after dark. San Francisco wasn't the welcoming place he'd expected it to be.

He told Daniel he might have a place by the time Daniel got out. If he did, Daniel could certainly crash with him for as long as he wanted to stay. That is, unless Michael moved to Chicago. Which was another possibility, he told Daniel.

Stuck beneath Michael's letter was another one. It was so thin Daniel had almost thrown it out with Michael's envelope. Despite being wafer thin and in a small envelope, Daniel immediately recognized the detailed penmanship of Colleen's handwriting.

Daniel quickly opened the letter. But there were no customary photos, no elongated descriptions of Colleen's current college activities. Instead it was a small handwritten note. The note started out 'Dear Daniel,' but it really read 'Dear John.'

Daniel read the note over and over again. He carefully scrutinized each line to make sure he wasn't misreading or misunderstanding its true meaning. But Colleen's well-crafted words were quite clear and succinct - painfully to the point.

Their relationship was over. Colleen was ending it with only a vague reference to the many changes they'd both gone through. She closed the letter without a clear reason for her actions or even an apology. Although Daniel knew in his heart of hearts that no explanation would ever suffice. And no apology was needed. Colleen did what she felt she had to do.

Daniel could feel a growing shortness of breath. His hands went numb and even under his bandaged chest he could feel his skin grow prickly and sticky. Sweat began to bead on his forehead, running down his nose and stinging his eyes. His blood turned to acid, coursing through his veins and burning a hole in his gut. And his heart was pounding so hard against his chest, Daniel felt like he was about to explode.

Daniel's mind was caught up in a whirlwind of jumbled thoughts, love scenes replayed and a hundred thousand what if's that had no answers.

The one thing, the one person, the one love that had held his life together through all this insanity of war was now gone. His reason for living had just slipped away. Colleen had rejected his sincere, honest efforts at love with a 'no thanks' to who he really was.

Yet in truth, Daniel knew their relationship had grown cancerous long before he'd left for the service. It began to wither away with Colleen's summer newspaper job and her time spent with the boat shoe boys. It only grew worse with Daniel's inability to let go when he couldn't accept Colleen dating other men. It grew hopeless when Daniel dropped out of school and got drafted.

It hadn't ended in one emotionally charged scene. Rather it had died in a hundred thousand fragments of estrangement; strained encounters and phone calls and long walks that had grown painfully quiet and uncommunicative. It had ended long before Daniel received that small little note card with a simple, "It just can't be me," at the end.

An hour passed, then two. The thoughts and scenes and fractured dialogue with Colleen slowly began to fade away. In their absence, Daniel's mind wandered back to the Triangle Bar and Zack's place. He thought about Rita, who had befriended him, and Zack's many comments about self-direction and following his heart. He caught himself smiling at the memories of those 'all-nighters' on Zack's porch with cheap Ripple wine and stale snacks. And his own growing appreciation for a world out there, ready for him to conquer.

After a long time of deep breathing and blinking away his tears, Daniel began to feel himself starting to relax. Strangely serene, he could feel a calmness wash over his body. The ache in his heart was slowly starting to subside.

It was done. Over. Finished. DOA. Colleen had moved on with her life. And now Daniel had to do the same.

And with that tiny note card came an end to the old Daniel; an end to that insecure fatherless beat down kid who had barely made it out of high school. The mediocre student who had to drop out of college. The love-starved kid who had grabbed too hard for the one thing that made him feel happy and safe and secure. And in the process had, once again, been abandoned by someone he desperately wanted to love. And be loved by.

The old Daniel was dead. He died on that operating table in a field hospital in Thua Thien Province near the Laotian border. And he was reborn again in a gray and dreary hospital ward that very afternoon.

And now Daniel had to move on. He had to focus on himself and stay alive; to live again as a new person. One who, if he survived the Nam, would return to school. He would graduate. He would be successful on his own, doing it his own way.

A noise caught Daniel's attention and he looked up. Several of the Philippine cleaning crew were coming through the ward, sweeping and mopping the floors. He brought the note card up in his hand and made a fist, crushing the stiff thick paper into a tiny ball. He squeezed it so hard his hand began to hurt. He dropped his arm and let the tiny ball of paper fall to the floor where a broom quickly caught it in one sweeping motion and it was gone.

Baby Makes Three

Peggy came back to town in late summer. She was there to pick up more clothes and move out of her parent's place permanently. They cried and tried to cajole her to stay but her mind was made up. Her parents, for as much as they pretended, could never have accepted their daughter with an illegitimate child in their home.

Peggy's pregnancy was a shock to everyone except her boyfriend. He'd skipped town a week before Peggy found out she was two months along. Perhaps it was past experience or some kind of male premonition that lead him to skip out on his roommates and head for the West Coast.

It was only after talking to his old roommates that Peggy found out her perfect boyfriend had, in fact, knocked up two other girls in just the last two years. Her judgment of him had been terribly misplaced. Now she was two months pregnant and unsure what to do with the rest of her life and that of her unborn child.

Colleen watched Peggy fidget in her chair as they sat in the coffee shop pondering Peggy's next move.

"My parents want me to give it up," Peggy said. "But I can't do that. I won't do that."

"Do you have any idea what you're going to do?" Colleen asked.

"I may move to Seattle. My grandmother lives there and she'll take me in.

She loves children and I could raise the child there with her. It'll just be the three of us."

"Is that realistic?" Colleen asked. "I mean what about school? What about the father? What if he comes back and you're not here?"

"Colleen, I don't care!" Peggy shot back. "I don't know if I will ever see him again. And I'm not sure if I care at this point. He lied to me. And he's done this to other girls." Peggy held back the tears, "I was so deceived by him. I was so stupid. How could I have believed all that crap he fed me about loving me and getting married?"

"Peggy, we all make mistakes. It could have happened to anyone. It could have happened to me."

"What, with Daniel?" Peggy said. "You two never did it. Did you, I mean?"

"No.

"Well, see then. It couldn't have happened to you," she stopped for a moment then asked. "So why didn't you two do it?"

"I don't know," Colleen answered. "I guess about the time we were getting really close, I got cold feet. I got my summer job and I was gone most of the time. He got mad when he couldn't see me so often. I started hanging out with those guys from Lake Minnetonka. Daniel dropped out of school and got drafted. That's the short of it."

"Better for you that you didn't….do it," Peggy said.

Peggy left the next day after Colleen helped her haul several boxes of clothes to the post office. Colleen drove her down to the Greyhound Bus Terminal in St. Paul. As they sat on a long wooden bench, they talked about their freshman year and the fun they both had back then.

"How is the job at the newspaper going?" Peggy asked.

"Fine," Colleen lied.

"Are you ready for next year?" Peggy asked. "I can't believe you'll be a junior already. It seems just like yesterday when we went to our first school dance. Remember, we met Daniel and Michael that first time."

"Oh, I remember," Colleen answered with a smile. "Now they're both in Vietnam and you're leaving too. I'm all alone now."

Just then the announcer called out the departure of Peggy's bus for points west. Peggy got up and Colleen gave her a long hug. "Please don't forget to write me," Colleen whispered in Peggy's ear. "Please let me know how you're doing and when the baby is born."

Peggy had tears in her eyes. "I will," she promised, as she reached for her traveling bag. Colleen walked her to the bus and waited until the bus pulled out with Peggy waving at her. She walked slowly back to her car and sat in the driver's seat for a long time.

Amazing how life can throw such twists and turns in one's life, she thought.

She had just broken up with Daniel, ending a relationship she could just as easily have tried to save. But she killed it instead. After the incident at Minnehaha Falls, she had lost faith in her judgment of men. Now Peggy was gone and with her all those wonderful memories of Colleen's first two years at college.

Now junior year was beckoning … without Peggy … without Daniel. And no more Garrison Buckley to plant lies in her willing ears. Colleen was on her own, devoid of close friends and companions. She was starting all over again.

Junior Year: 1968 - 1969

Apache Snow

On May 10th, 1969, while Colleen was enjoying a warm spring afternoon sunning herself by the campus pond, Daniel was among the hundreds of airborne troopers from the 101st who attacked NVA forces dug deep into the top of Ap Bia Mountain near the Laotian border.

Scattered among the mountain's rough terrain and ridgelines were hundreds of heavily armed North Vietnamese regulars. The hillside and ensuing battle later became known as Hamburger Hill, a meat grinder that chewed up the lives of 56 soldiers and wounded over 400 more. It would become Daniel's final descent into hell.

Daniel was nearing the end of his deployment in country. But as many veterans agreed, one year in Vietnam was like a jail sentence. Daniel only had a short time left before he shipped back to the states and his discharge was granted. Now as he jumped out of the slick and sprinted toward a wooded tree line, Daniel just hoped he'd make it through another firefight. And live long enough to return to civilian life.

About four miles from the LZ, the hueys and slicks had dropped down to treetop level to fly nap-of-the-earth on the final approach. The wind blasted Daniel's face as he hung out the side of the ship. Birds scattered as the helicopters roared along at 110 miles per hour just above their perches.

The plan was for a twenty minute artillery prep followed by thirty seconds of aerial rocket artillery then thirty seconds by the gunships. Daniel's unit got half of that. The air ships banked steeply away to take up an orbit nearby and wait for another strike order.

Daniel quickly sequestered his heavy weapons squad behind a low-lying ridge that ran parallel to the jungle tree line up ahead. His platoon hunched against the rotor blast as the slick lifted off. Overhead was abuzz with gunships and light observation choppers in slow orbit while lines of slicks brought in more troops. Daniel's platoon moved far enough away from the LZ that any enemy mortars would have to be redirected if Charlie wanted to harass them. He crunched down and waited for the lieutenant's next orders.

Christmas had been uneventful. It came and went along with the constant rains and high humidity that rotted anything left exposed to the blistering sun. Daniel no longer heard anything from his old pal, Michael. He had no idea if Michael had made it back to Minnesota or simply disappeared into the foggy mind warp of his old civilian lifestyle. And, of course, no more word from Colleen. Daniel hardly expected one. He could only assume his old girlfriend had simply moved on with her life.

There had been sporadic firefights in the past week but no casualties among his men. The knot in Daniel's stomach told him he might not be so lucky this time around. Rumors were rampant about a new NVA offensive somewhere in the Central Highlands. But such rumors had a tendency to come and go with little action to follow. Daniel was fast learning leadership skills, focused on keeping his men alive and their mission accomplished.

After that first firefight in the A Shau, Daniel had been given a permanent promotion to sergeant. He accepted it reluctantly. Daniel was more interested in the welfare of his men than three stripes on his shoulder. But his master sergeant wasn't about to give up that easily.

"Daniel, you've got what it takes to make it in this man's army. Ever thought about re-upping when the time comes?"

"Don't think so, Sarg. But thanks."

"Steady paycheck. Three meals a day, except here. Six hundred and change per month isn't bad. With hazardous duty pay and the overseas stipend, you could save enough for a house if you ever got married."

"No thanks, Sarg," Daniel replied. "I think I'll stick with my plans to go back to school and get a degree."

"Well, good for you, kid. I admire that in a man. Most college boys don't know shit. You just might be different."

"I'll take that as a compliment, Top."

"Take it any way you want," the crusty old soldier replied with a laugh.

In the end, Daniel realized that the military wasn't where he wanted to spend the rest of his life. While he was apprehensive about returning to college, he knew the GI Bill would help with his tuition. In all probability, he would go back to Minnesota to finish his degree, if he lived through the upcoming firefight.

It was called Operation Apache Snow; a combined 101st and ARVN operation consisting of ten battalions that would take Daniel and his unit back into the A Shau Valley. Previous sweeps of the valley in Operation Delaware and Operation Dewey Canyon had failed to keep the NVA and Charlie from operating there. Now Daniel and his men would try one more time to eliminate this continuing threat. The main objective of the offensive was Hill 937, a nondescript mountain bulge in a vast green carpet of jungle that defined the A Shau.

MAC-V Command had originated the offense in hopes of stopping the continuing movement of VC and NVA forces there.

After landing in LZ 2 without any opposition, Daniel had taken his fire team across a clearing, five hundred clicks away from the base of a mountain. Once there he spread them out along a small ridgeline. There was always the chance of well-concealed snipers on the other side waiting for them. The platoon hunkered down and waited for the order to advance.

Daniel was back in the A Shau one more time. An uneasy feeling nagged at Daniel as he crouched down, peering into the calm dimness of the jungle up ahead. All along the line, it was quiet but tense.

Daniel and his second-in-command moved cautiously up the ridge then down the other side. There was no movement in the jungle façade ahead of them. It was covered with a variety of trees and scrub brush. A heavily wooded draw ran up to the top and into the clouds. A few rock outcropping poked up through the thick vegetation along the mountain's baseline. Daniel was amazed at the beauty of the terrain all around him.

Daniel's body started to come down from the adrenaline rush of the landing. He turned to his second to say something when suddenly his foot stepped on a stick and cracked it in half. Daniel's mind snapped back to the present. He froze in place. If that stick had been a land mine, he wouldn't be back on campus ever again.

"Damn," he swore under his breath. *Keep your mind on the task ahead,* he thought. The second smiled at him. Daniel sheepishly smiled back. *Fucking lucky again.*

"Sergeant," a voice called out behind Daniel. Daniel turned to see his lieutenant standing behind him on the ridgeline. The young officer was motioning toward the jungle tree line. He pointed toward a narrow, barely defined trail that meandered its way through the elephant grass and scrub brush toward the base of the jungle facade.

"Sergeant, I'm going to follow that trail…scout it out. Have the men cover me."

"Sir, do you think that's wise? Let me send a point man up there."

"Negative, sergeant. This will just take a second," the officer stood up and looked down on Daniel, "and don't ever tell me what to do. Is that understood?"

"Roger that, sir," Daniel answered.

The officer pulled out his .45 and began walking up the trail. He would pause occasionally, scan the grass and brush on either side of the trail then continue on. Once he turned and waved at the men. Daniel returned his wave and sat back down.

“Guy’s fucking nuts,” Daniel said under his breath. The old veteran next to him just laughed and replied, “I heard he was a Pointer or just out of OCS.”

“Or worse,” Daniel interrupted him. “ROTC.”

They both laughed.

“Either way,” the veteran continued, “he doesn’t know what the fuck he’s doing. Sure as shit, he’s either going to get himself killed or take some of us down in the process. Dumb bastard.”

“Keep your eyes on the trail and up ahead of the lieutenant,” Daniel threw back at his squad, who by then had lined up belly-flat along the ridgeline.

The officer approached the end of the pathway. He turned and waved at Daniel then took another step forward.

A bright white flash preceded the dull thud by a microsecond. It sent the lieutenant’s body cartwheeling twice through the air, losing an arm and a leg in the process before landing it in a heap alongside the trail.

“Jesus H. Christ,” Daniel muttered.

“Ah, fuck!” was all the veteran could spit out.

Daniel started to get up but was hauled back down by his second.

“Not you,” the old trooper snarled. “I’m not gonna lose you, too.” He turned back to the squad behind him. “Malloy, Pellem, go check the lieutenant. If he’s dead, leave him be. We’re not going to haul his sorry ass back here. Medics can pick up the pieces.”

The two soldiers scrambled down the slope and through the grass alongside the trail. Once they got to the officer’s body, one of them bent over for a second. The other soldier turned back toward Daniel and ran his hand across his throat.

“Better get on the horn, Daniel,” the second said. “Tell headquarters.”

Daniel radioed headquarters. The line was rift with crackling sounds and scrambled voices. After what seemed an eternity, a voice came on the line.

“Major Maxwell,” Daniel said.

The line went dead again. Daniel waited. The second and other troops were staring at him. Occasionally one would glance over at the bloody heap in the grass in the distance. No one said a word.

“Maxwell,” a voice shouted at the other end of the line.

"Sir, this is 2nd platoon, third regiment, 506th…"

"Yes?"

"Sir, we just lost our lieutenant. He stepped on a mine…"

There was a momentary pause on the line.

"Who is the second in command?" the voice asked.

"Sir, that would be me, Sergeant Daniel…"

"We can't do a dust-off for the lieutenant now, it's too dangerous. Should have a medevac there by tonight. We'll get you a replacement for the lieutenant as soon as we can. As of now, you're in command."

"Sir?"

"Sergeant, did you lose your hearing? I said you're in charge. Now prepare your men to move out."

"Roger that, Sir. Understood," Daniel snapped back into the line.

"Good luck, son," then the line went dead.

Daniel looked at his second. The old man smiled at him, "You can do it, Daniel," the man said. "Now let's kick some gook ass."

Within minutes the order came down the line to move out.

Daniel set up several machine guns and grenadiers to cover their sweep as they advanced toward the tree line. He turned back and signaled his troops. "Saddle up," he said in a loud voice, "lock and load." He began moving his men out in their skirmish line. As he led his troops, Daniel looked up overhead. The sky was still full of circling gunships, bird dog observation planes and medevac ships.

A group of four new white recruits began talking as they got up and began tackling the ridgeline. "He's kinda young, isn't he?" the first kid said to his buddy next to him.

A grizzly old black veteran, up ahead of the four recruits, turned back to them. "Listen up, you crackers!" he snarled. "Pay attention to the man and do what he tells you to do. Daniel's got a good nose for trouble. This is a free fire zone. There are no friendlies here. You kill anything that moves. Remember your training and you may get out of this one alive."

Another one of the youngsters piped up, "Sarg, I heard scuttlebutt that he lost his girlfriend and went nuts."

The old soldier spat out his response, "Listen, you sorry ass bunch of numb nuts! Forget about what rumors you think you heard. Daniel's seen more action in the last six months than a Saigon tea girl on holiday. We may be looking at the bad end of a shit storm out here. So you just do as he says and you may save your sorry ass when hell comes a knocking."

Another veteran laughed at the recruits, "Welcome to Viet-fucking-Nam," he chuckled. Other soldiers around him laughed. The recruits grew quiet and sullen. They followed the old veteran over the ridgeline without saying another word.

Daniel's unit, the 1/506th Infantry, began its laborious trek toward the mountain baseline. After reaching the baseline, the unit began to move cautiously up the foothills after splitting up their forces into a three-pronged attack. Another ARVN unit was off to their right flank and the 3/187th Infantry off to their left flank.

The rucksack-laden soldiers moved slowly through the dense underbrush, crossing tall grasses of savanna-like plains, then quickly approached the steep, jungle-covered swelling of the mountain ahead.

The point man reported seeing shadowy clumps as they moved closer to the mountain base.

The cuts, draws and smaller hills were all perfect spots for the NVA to defend their mountain fortress. Enemy snipers could be hiding high in the canopies of the trees. The triple canopy jungle covered the mountainside in a blanket of green. It cast deep shadows everywhere. Contrasting dirty green shadows, with the piercing sunlight, streamed through the canopy overhead and made for an eerie setting.

Daniel's platoon soon found itself encountering small arms fire. These eventually subsided and Daniel and his men continued their arduous advance through the thick underbrush and entangling jungle vegetation. Point men up ahead reported no more signs of the enemy.

As the single line of men walked slowly through the ravines and draws, they kept encountering more and more spider holes and punji pits. They knew there might be booby traps anywhere on the trail. The platoon kept moving higher and higher, trying to re-establish contact with the enemy.

Near midday the platoon came upon a collection of abandoned bunkers, hootches and stores of food. The enemy fighting position was only the first of a string of interlocking, L-shaped, earthen bunkers dug deep into the hillside. They were meant to protect the narrow trail leading back up the hillside. The bunkers were six to seven feet long and dug four feet deep. They were nearly invisible to even the most watchful eye. Covered with a roof of logs and hard-packed dirt, the bunkers even had brush piled in front to conceal their positions. There was blue communications wire everywhere that the enemy hadn't even bothered to hide.

Over the entire NVA defensive line, a canopy of thick branches, vines, and foliage combined to form a nearly impenetrable forest arch, cutting off all observation from above. Air support would be difficult at best.

Overhead, Daniel could hear the whop-whop-whop of helicopter gunships through the foliage. They would be coming on station high overhead. With no targets to attack, the heavily armed choppers would circle above in high orbit holding patterns, ready to roll in if Daniel needed them.

Later that morning, a soldier walking point spotted and killed a trail watcher. If there was anyone else with the lone VC, he was immediately swallowed up by the jungle. Moving past the fallen body, the recon squad approached a small ridgeline but was soon driven back by snipers, small arms fire and RPG's, rocket propelled grenades.

Daniel moved his men back and set up a new perimeter defense line well below the ridgeline, but not far enough. A grenade arched up and came down in a clump of brush mid-point between both forces, then another, and yet a third. They exploded in loud geysers of dirt, debris and hot shrapnel.

"Out of range," someone commented behind him. But Daniel knew what was coming next.

Soon the distinct thump of enemy mortar rounds could be heard from up on the ridgeline and the explosions started. Whump! Whump! First mid-point where the grenades had just landed. Whump, whump - the mortar explosions began creeping down toward Daniel's front line.

"Shit," Daniel shouted. "Move the men back. We need air support. Now!" Daniel grabbed his phone as the column of men scrambled back down the hillside, searching for any depressions and hollowed out pieces of earth they could find. The mortar rounds came quickly downhill, ripping apart trees, brush and jungle foliage. The men hunkered down, squeezing their bodies into even the slightest depression in the earth. Daniel tossed a colored smoke grenade high into the air to mark his position.

Within seconds, Daniel and his men could hear the distinctive sound of the Cobra's twin rotor blades. With their rockets and machine guns, they were flying artillery. The first of three cobra helicopter gunships came screaming in at treetop level. The first gunship opened up with all of its miniguns, burning a wide strip of death and destruction up the hillside. The jungle foliage along the ridgeline was ripped apart by the gunship's miniguns and rockets. Red and green tracers arched overhead, tearing into the bunker fortifications there. Bright orange and yellow explosions sent plumps of dirt and debris and human remains high into the sky.

Daniel frantically waved his Sierra Loma; a strobe light used to identify his unit's position to the helicopters overhead. The last thing he wanted was to lose a man due to friendly fire. The light worked its magic and the gunships kept raking the hillside well above Daniel's defensive line.

After twenty minutes of numerous strafing runs, the helicopters called off their attack and started back to base. Daniel radioed in his thanks and moved his men forward once again.

The ridgeline was a pocked jumble of torn and twisted trees, gaping holes in the earth where bunkers used to be, and the remains of human bodies and equipment everywhere.

By late afternoon the area around the ridgeline had been secured and a wide defensive perimeter set up. As evening began to set in, the rich tapestry of jungle colors slowly gave way to the gray of night. Shadows began to grow out of the jungle and soon a blanket of black had engulfed the entire hillside.

Daniel and his men slept little that night, knowing that Charlie had to be within a hundred clicks of their forward line. The sweat of the day and the damp ground sent chills through Daniel's body. He pressed his arms around his waist to hold the heat but little remained in the chill of the night. He found himself moving constantly between foxholes to keep his men alert and to warm his shaking body. When he stopped, he could feel the closeness of death hovering over him and his men.

Even by the next morning, the presence of the Viet Cong could still be smelt and felt.

Daniel awoke with a start only to find himself watching a long brown rope sliding slowly along the ground several yards away. He peered intently at the rope as it curled and wove its way among the torn and twisted tree limbs scattered about.

"Jesus Christ," he snapped at his second. "That's a bamboo viper."

"Or a banded krait," his second offered.

"Tell the men to be careful," Daniel shot back. "The last thing I want is to lose a man to a damn snake bite." He shook his head. "What a crazy war. Fucking unbelievable!"

His second laughed and nodded his head, "Ain't that the truth," he said.

After a quick assessment of their situation, Daniel moved his men out again. So far they'd been lucky. Only a few men wounded, none killed thus far. But Daniel knew his odds in a firefight, any firefight, could go from hot to fatal in just seconds if they bumped heads with a superior force of VC or NVA.

The morning dragged on with no contact with the enemy. Noon was a ten minute rest in the shallow depression of yet another climbing ridgeline. Their point man was far enough ahead to prick the enemy lines if they were there. After scarfing down their C-rations, the troops moved out again.

The column hadn't gone several hundred clicks when the sound of gunfire erupted up ahead. It was the distinctive sound of AK-47 and Type-50 submachine gun fire. The column moved swiftly ahead. They hit a slow rise in the jungle floor and scrambled up its soft clay slopes. They saw the point man near the top, not more than 25 clicks away. He'd walked right up to a line of bunkers before the NVA had cut him down.

Daniel moved his men back down the slope about a dozen clicks and called in another air strike. He hunkered down behind a fallen tree and radioed in the coordinates. Sniper fire sporadically rung out overhead, pinging through the trees. His second scrambled back from his lead position.

"Can't see a damn thing," the old veteran announced. "There must be at least three if not more rows of bunkers dug into that slope up there." A bullet ricocheted off his helmet, sending him face first into the dirt. When he looked up, Daniel was still leaning back against the tree stump, with his radio to his ear. Daniel was smiling at him. Now was the time to pull the chain on everything Daniel could lay his hands on.

"We need to terminate those motherfuckers," the sergeant growled at Daniel.

Daniel laughed, "Yeah, with extreme prejudice. Tell the men the air jockeys are coming in less than a minute from now."

The second wriggled his way back down the hillside, shouting at the gathered men to seek shelter.

At first, they were just a small smudge against the horizon. The planes were leveled off and coming into the site on a ground-hugging path. They were coming in hot with their burners cooking. Both planes carried four CBU-52 canisters that would scatter 250 grapefruit-size bomblets over an area the size of a soccer field, each one detonating and sending shrapnel pellets from more than a half-mile at rifle bullet speed.

Then the planes were up on Daniel's radio frequency and ready to begin their bombing run. The radio crackled. The OV-10 observation plane radioed in that the first of three waves of attack aircraft were coming in wings level and cleared hot.

Their call sign was 'crow.'

Daniel shouted into his phone. "Targets are bunkers approximately fifty clicks north of our smoke. Crow, do you read."

"Roger that, targets in sight."

Daniel and his men wiggled their bodies as far into the dirt as they could. They twisted themselves into a fetal position and gripped their helmets. The sounds of the approaching jets got louder and louder.

Hell was about to rain on the mountainside.

Then the jets were over them and climbing quickly. Further up the slope, Daniel could hear the canisters erupting in mid-air. The exploding canisters were almost muted by the roar of the jets overhead and the sound of foliage and men being torn to shreds. The bombs obliterated the jungle slope with an ugly black and red firestorm of metal and shrapnel. One G.I. near the front line screamed in pain. *Collateral damage,* Daniel thought.

Soon two more Marine phantoms came in low, dropping napalm and 1000 pound bombs that shook the ground and shredded trees with the force of their explosions. Again, Daniel waved his Sierra Loma frantically in the air. Again, it worked.

Two more aircraft followed. The ground rumbled and shook as huge clouds of dirt and debris rained down the mountainside and over Daniel's prone men. It was like rolling thunder that sent shock waves slamming into the prone soldiers scattered on the hillside. They covered their ears against the deafening blasts that kept pounding against their steel helmets.

Overhead multiple silver canisters of napalm dropped from the phantom's belly and twisted and turned on their way down to earth. Blinding yellow fireballs splashed up against the mountainside and washed over the bunkers along the ridgeline. Even in the distance, amid the thundering explosions, Daniel and his men could hear the NVA screaming as they burnt to death.

Then as quickly as they had appeared on the horizon, the phantoms were gone and silence descended down the broken hillside.

Daniel waited until the smoke had cleared before cautiously moving his men out again.

Four rows of bunkers had been decimated by the phantom onslaught. Beyond the gaping holes in the earth, the burnt and splintered trees and piles of debris, Daniel and his men found heavy blood trails, shredded equipment everywhere, bits and pieces of hair and bone fragments scattered about. There were no intact bodies among the piles of dead VC and NVA.

Beyond the decimated bunkers, Daniel's men found a solid wall of jungle almost untouched by the carnage. They cautiously approached the wall of green and were soon engulfed in the dark jungle inside.

Another hundred clicks and sporadic sniper fire kept the men huddled over as they moved slowly through the thick vegetation and unsteady jungle floor.

This time they encountered Claymore mines set up in trees. One misstep would trip an almost invisible wire line that sent the Claymores swinging through the air and exploding above the advancing line of troops below. The platoon moved back and Daniel sent point men out to clear a path through the entanglement of cross wires and booby traps. Once they'd moved through the line of concealed Claymores, Daniel settled his men on yet another abandoned ridgeline.

Scouts went out and encountered no more enemy signs further ahead. After a brief rest in the hot midday sun, Daniel's unit moved out again. Soon the drizzle that had started minutes before erupted into a full-blown downpour, soaking the men and turning the soft ground to mud. Visibility was reduced to less than twenty meters. The advance slowed again as the men fought for footing on the slippery slopes.

The platoon spent the rest of that day and the next, moving slowly through the dense undergrowth as it inched its way up the mountainous slopes. North Vietnamese bunkers dotted the hillside, often cleverly concealed among fallen tree trunks and exposed boulders. So far, they'd all been abandoned. There was still no sign of the enemy.

By the third day it was obvious that Daniel's platoon had avoided a great deal of the heavy combat that other units were encountering. Nevertheless, sniper fire and the occasional RPG was slowing down his advancement through the jungle.

"If we go up on line, they'll probably fall back," the second advised Daniel, "they might leave a few behind in spider holes or up in the trees."

Daniel slowly shook his head, "I got a feeling about this one, Top. Something's coming down. Something heavy!"

Daniel's second perused the thick canvas of jungle brush and vegetation. "A little religious communication might not be a bad idea right about now," he said to Daniel with a smile.

Daniel nodded his understanding. "You do the praying for me, Sarg. Now let's move out." The Second motioned the line of soldiers behind them. The column moved forward.

Daniel led his group of soldiers through the thick brush. He flipped the selector switch to full automatic – time to rock and roll. He was carrying a pig, an M-60 machine gun known for its weight and heavy rate of fire, a very effective killing machine. Walking right behind Daniel were two soldiers with M-79 Bloopers, grenade launchers. As the trio cautiously slugged through the dense foliage, Daniel kept his ear trained for any sound that might indicate the enemy's presence. He pulled in the trigger slack on his weapon.

Daniel's mind was racing a million miles a second. It was processing the sounds, the smells and the tangled environment of the jungle all around them. His eyes darted back and forth, scanning the underbrush for any sign of disturbances that might indicate a booby trap or the presence of the enemy. His ears listened for any interruption in the melodic drone of insects, birds, monkeys or other jungle animals.

It was all so insane. This operatic dance they were performing with the enemy. Advance, shoot, kill, retreat and return again to repeat the same scenario again and again. Taking casualties was part of the equation. Losing lives was the price to be paid for lousy real estate that nobody really wanted in the first place.

They entered a small clearing. Up ahead there was a shallow ribbon of vegetation, hardly enough concealment for snipers or well-hidden bunkers. Behind the vegetation, strands of bamboo and scrub brush formed a solid muddy green background.

Yet something caught Daniel's attention. Unheard, unseen and yet felt in his gut. Something was amiss around them. Daniel dropped to his knees. The other two soldiers alongside him did the same. The platoon froze in their tracks, crouching down in the tall grass and brush. The blanket of sounds around the column was a constant. Nothing moved that should not have moved. Nothing sounded that shouldn't have sounded. Everything seemed perfectly normal in that claustrophobic theater they were stumbling through.

Daniel felt something in his bones and deep in his gut. He had an instinctive sixth sense borne out of numerous firefights and ambushes. He slowly stood up and turned to motion his men forward when the first burst of machine gun fire ripped through the vegetation and trees in front of him. The trees, the bushes and even the rocks seemed to explode with gunfire. Muzzle flashes sparkled amid the greenery. It was coming from three directions, spread out in front of them. Daniel's platoon had stepped into a deadly field of fire…a killing zone. It was a page out of Dante's Inferno.

The man to Daniel's left screamed and fell to the ground. He stumbled back to his feet and was hit again, this time in the chest. A shower of crimson sprayed blood over Daniel's face and body. Daniel threw himself forward, burying his chin in the grass. Machine gun slugs ripped the tops off the grasses just inches from his helmet. Several rounds tore through the rucksack on his back. The man to his right screamed, "Bunker," and motioned off to their left.

Small arms fire erupted alongside the unit. It sounded like popcorn to Daniel. Pop. Pop. Pop. Enemy machine guns competed with rifle fire to tear through his ranks of soldiers.

The enemy was boiling out of the trees and brush. Daniel could see the leaders blowing whistles and using hand signals. They were throwing ChiCom grenades ahead of their rush.

Ignoring the bullets zinging past his face, Daniel focused his heavy machine gun on a clump of brush and grass no more than fifty feet away.

Daniel could see and hear the enemy all around them. He knew he and his men could easily be cut off, surrounded, cut to pieces, and wiped out.

Daniel opened up on the green brown hump just below a strand of trees. A grenade launcher exploded next to Daniel's ear, sending a shock wave baffling his helmet. Another Blooper exploded in his other ear. A soldier next to him was struggling to load his weapon with a bloody arm. Daniel concentrated his stream of orange tracer fire on the bunker, ripping its well-concealed façade into a cascade of swirling tree branches, grass, dirt and human particles.

Another bunker opened up to their right in an attempt to catch Daniel's men in crossfire. "Two o'clock" Daniel screamed as he swung the barrel brace up and over to his right.

Between the two bunkers, Daniel could now see movement as NVA soldiers began pushing forward toward Daniel's column. "Sweep," he screamed above his own machine gun rant and the explosions of grenades just in front of them. He methodically began sweeping the area directly in front of himself with his M-60 as two more Bloopers followed suit with pinpoint accuracy.

In the smoke and haze and deafening din of battle, Daniel and his teammates became very effective killing machines, slaughtering the NVA as they emerged out of their underground bunkers and concealed trenches. Small figures, growing ever larger, started to materialize out of the jungle. Bunching up, they came running down the hillside.

"Tien-len. Tien-len."

The VC were screaming at Daniel's unit and firing their weapons as they rushed forward. But their high-pitched rants were muted by the crescendo of heavy machine gun and M-16 fire blasting through their ranks. Drab green and black bodies stumbled backwards or pitched over, showering blood into the air as they fell.

Daniel's body began to vibrate with the insanity of combat. It was a state of mind devoid of reason, fear or intimidation. It was a robotic, mechanical force of adrenaline that took over his mind and body. Grounded in instinct, hard core training and months in the bush, it propelled Daniel forward without hesitation. He walked forward, screaming at the top of his lungs, as he swept his machine gun fire back and forth into the oncoming VC ranks.

It was a slaughter of young men on both sides. The advancing NVA line kept getting thinner as a blanket of heavy fire depleted their ranks. The lead NVA soldiers slowed to aim their weapons and were cut down by heavy machine gun blasts that ripped through their column. Others turned to run and were torn in half by crossfire from the encircling 101st soldiers.

One soldier next to Daniel was hit and then another man went down. Daniel was alone, moving up the hillside, slapping a fresh ammo belt into his weapon as he walked along. It was an insane, exhilarating, mind-bending rush to spray his machine gun back and forth, cutting the enemy to pieces. He was oblivious to those other soldiers around him as he walked forward and fired at the same time. His mind had gone numb. It wasn't processing anything other than the stumbling, swaying targets that kept lining up in front of his white-hot gun barrel.

Daniel fired until his ammo belt ran out and he had to drop to his knees to reload. He swung a bandoleer off his chest and lined it up with his gun slot. Suddenly something exploded off to his left. Daniel felt himself being lifted off the ground and thrown to his side. He got back up, spitting the dirt and vegetation out of his mouth. His hands were shaking. He struggled to feed the ammo belt into the gun slot. His head was spinning, as his vision grew blurry. He fell down again, pitching forward into the dirt.

The baffling, ear-crushing sound of gunfire started to subside on both sides. The blanket of noise was replaced by a popping of selected gunfire as army marksmen began to pick off the staggering, struggling VC who were retreating back up the hillside. The swirling kaleidoscope of the fast moving battle had ended as quickly as it had begun.

Daniel lifted himself up on his knees, struggling to regain his footing in the loose soil. He braced himself on his machine gun and staggered to his feet. He stumbled forward and looked at the carnage all around him.

NVA bodies lay everywhere. Some were seemingly untouched by the gunfire that had pillaged their ranks. Others lay in pieces, their torn bodies scattered into trees and bushes. Their dark blood stained the ground and surrounding vegetation. Daniel ordered his own wounded to be taken back down the mountainside and then the rest of his platoon to set up a defensive perimeter in the now abandoned ridgeline. They would continue their assault tomorrow after another round of heavy air strikes softened the enemy positions up ahead.

"You OK?" his second asked as he walked up to Daniel sitting next to a shattered tree stump.

Daniel nodded and took a long drink from his battered canteen.

"We lost a bunch. Probably a dozen or more wounded. Other than that, we're pretty intact."

"There are more of them," Daniel began. "They'll be back tomorrow in force."

The second shook his shoulders, "So will we," he answered.

Daniel smiled and said nothing.

The next day of the assault began with an eerie silence on the mountainside. Daniel's platoon had only reached their halfway mark and command was anxious for his unit to move out. Phantoms swooped in a distance from the unit and began their systematic sweep of the hillside, dropping napalm and 500 pounders. The assault was far enough away that Daniel's men could sit up and watch the show as it reduced the green wall to shreds. After an hour of intensive bombing, the phantoms disappeared and the cobra gunships made one last sweep of the terrain ahead. It was time for Daniel's platoon to advance.

The call came over the radio set for Daniel's unit to move out shortly. Daniel stood up. His men followed. He signaled the scouts to move out and for his platoon to assemble for their march up the hillside. *I almost bought the farm the day before,* Daniel thought. *Maybe today will be my lucky day. Or not.*

A voice shouted out behind him, someplace further down the slope. Daniel turned and saw a lone soldier, frantically waving his arms. He was fast approaching his unit. Daniel watched as the soldier maneuvered his way among the rough-cut earth and thick ankle deep vegetation.

"I'm looking for the platoon leader," the runner yelled as he approached the unit.

Daniel waved the man over. "Lieutenant's not here," he said, "he's dead."

"Are you the non-com in charge of this sector?"

"Yeah, I am," Daniel answered.

"Then you're the man I'm supposed to find." The runner dropped down to his knees, to tie his shoelaces. "Sergeant," the man said looking up at Daniel, "I've got orders to bring you back to the CP. Pronto. We need to leave now."

"What are you talking about, corporal?" Daniel asked. "I can't just leave my men halfway up this mountain."

"Orders are orders, Sergeant. You need to accompany me back to base," the man repeated and took a long swig from his canteen, "I've got a slick a couple of hundred clicks down the mountain. They're waiting for us now."

"Shit," Daniel muttered as he waved over his second-in-command. "I won't be long," He told the man. "You've got the ball now. Be ready to move out when you get the orders. I'll be back as soon as I can." He motioned the runner and the two of them began their long sprint back down the hillside.

The CP was part of a larger base of operations located just a short distance from the base of Hill 937. As Daniel and the runner approached the base, the sound of Chinook transport helicopters with their heavy thump thump rotary movements filled the air. The pair passed through the first line of concertina wire and hastily built machine gun bunkers and fast approached the buried CP bunker.

Two sentries outside waved them through. Daniel followed the runner into the dimly lit headquarters. It was dark and cool inside with only bare light bulbs strung on wire overhead. The runner approached a Colonel and motioned Daniel to stand back. The two conversed for a brief moment and then the runner turned and walked away. He gave Daniel a quick glance, a slight smile and was out the bunker opening and gone.

The Colonel approached Daniel. Daniel snapped to attention as the senior officer walked up and stood in front of him.

"Relax soldier, your fighting days are over," he said to Daniel. "You're going to the land of the big PX."

Daniel's brow furrowed in a questioning stare. He absentmindedly pursed his lips and remained standing at attention. He had no idea what the man was talking about.

"You're going home, Sergeant," the Colonel said as he handed Daniel a roll of papers; his discharge papers.

Daniel took the paper roll in his hand and, without looking down at the papers, stared in disbelief at the Colonel. "I don't understand, Sir," he said. "I don't understand what you're saying."

"Your time's up! You'll be on the next Huey or Cobra out of here. Your papers have all been approved and signed. You'll be in Tan Son Nhut by tonight and back in the states within three days or less. You've got about three, maybe four weeks at Ford Ord and you'll be discharged from this man's army. Congratulations, son, you've served your country well."

"Sir, I can't leave my men," Daniel started to explain. "We still haven't taken 937. My men need me. We start our next assault this morning."

"You left your second-in-command in charge, right?"

"Yes, Sir, I did."

"Then he can do the job. I don't have time for arguing, Sergeant."

"But, Sir…"

"Listen son, I understand your desire to get back with your unit. I admire that. But if I don't have Lieutenant Colonel Honeycutt on my ass then it will be General Zais barking orders at me. I don't have time to discuss this with you."

"Yes, Sir, I understand," Daniel said reluctantly.

The colonel smiled for brief moment and said, "Your orders are quite clear. You will stand down effective immediately." He brought up his arm in a smart salute. "Dismissed!" he said then turned and walked away.

Daniel stood in place for a long time. It was all too sudden too soon. He hadn't planned nor even thought about his last day in country. Now Daniel was leaving without having a chance to say goodbye to his second or his men. He wanted to say something, to protest. But instead he just stood in place, numb to the organized chaos all around him.

Commanders and their subordinates moved around him, ignoring his stationary stance. Daniel walked back out into the bright sunlight of a new day.

Another Sergeant motioned him toward the landing pad where a Cobra gunship that was just beginning to start up its engine. "Son, this is your ticket home," the old Sergeant said, handing Daniel his walking papers and slapping him on his shoulder as Daniel turned toward the waiting bird.

Super-Charged Avanti

Fall that school year had been short-lived and pleasant enough. Without Peggy, Colleen elected to move into a single dorm room where she could focus on her studies without the drama of another roommate. She kept up her straight-A average and still found time for the many social activities on campus. It kept her busy but Colleen knew deep down there was still something missing in her life - connection with the opposite sex. Someone with whom she could share her thoughts and dreams and aspirations. Someone to replace the void that Daniel had left in her heart.

Her first letter of apology to Daniel had come back unopened. Two more subsequent letters suffered the same fate. Even a call to the DOD, Department of Defense, would only reveal their standard procedure for returned mail. Simply stated, if letters to Vietnam were returned unopened it could only be for two reasons; the recipient was deceased or out of the country.

Winter that year was long, harsh and brutal. Snow piled up into deep mounds that bordered the walkways on campus and made even a short dash between classrooms a challenge. Cold weather or not, the administration had set rules for their dress code and it was meant to be followed. Colleen knew that and still chose to circumvent the rule at times.

Instead of the usual winter attire for the women of Mother of the Lake, Colleen had her own dress style for the colder months. Since pants were strictly forbidden for women on campus, she decided that for a long walk or commute, she would wear woolen leggings or tights under her skirt - usually black for effect.

While the other women on campus would stick to their normal wardrobe of woolen skirts, long wraparound scarves, turtleneck cable sweaters, and cone caps; Colleen sought out clothes that were practical and yet still stylish.

Colleen didn't mind standing out. While it wasn't her primary motivation, she shunned the woolen plaid suits that were the rage of the day. She would stick with the basic utility wardrobe that fit her body type and her personality.

Reluctant though she might have been to admit it, Daniel's attitude toward fashion still had a major impact on her own personal style choices. She could afford the same long tailored coats from the Upper East Side New York fashion houses or Paris couture houses that some of her friends were wearing but it didn't fit her mindset or the practical side of her tastes in fashion.

Early spring brought little relief in the weather. The snow was gone but the April rains ran well into May and kept the air very chilly at night.

The night was particularly damp and chilly when Colleen was asked to run to the corner drugstore off campus for a friend's medicine. She snuck out the back door of Frazer Hall, wearing her tailored jeans, woolen boots, a Norwegian sweater and a long sheepskin coat. With her woolen hat tightly capped on her head, only her long auburn hair could give her away from the nun's ever-watchful eyes.

Since Colleen had dumped the editor, her dating life was sporadic at best. She had dated a few guys but nothing ever came of a second or third date. They were nice enough but none of them generated the same kind of excitement she'd felt with the editor when he first took her in his arms. Colleen was beginning to think the rest of her college career would find her unloved and unwanted.

She couldn't even rustle up a simple male friendship such as the one she'd had with Daniel. Her entanglement with romance seemed a lost cause until a red sports car came traveling down Cleveland Avenue in the waning light of that early spring Saturday night.

Bradley Godfrey Barrington III changed Colleen's life on the spot. He changed it all with his wit and charm and brand new red Avanti convertible.

Colleen was dodging puddles and covering her head from the light rain as she walked down the sidewalk. She never noticed the red car slow down just behind her and quickly pull up alongside of her. The electric passenger's side window rolled down and Bradley leaned over the front seat, looking up at Colleen. He gave her his best perfectly capped white teeth smile and said, "Hi, it's freezing out. Can I give you a lift back to campus?"

Colleen glanced over at the car and its driver but didn't slow her pace. "I don't even know you," Colleen said, surprised by the brashness of the young man. She kept walking and Bradley kept pacing her with his car. He leaned over even further, continuing to look out the window while he steered the sports car with one hand.

"I'm Bradley Barrington, your driver for the evening if you'll let me. Your name is Colleen. You go to Mother of the Lake and I go to St. Paul's. I saw your picture in the student newspaper. You write for the paper, right?"

"But how did you know it was me?" Colleen asked, pausing momentarily. "The light's so bad out here."

"OK, I have a confession to make," Bradley said as he stopped the car and leaned over to open the passenger side door. "I saw you coming out of that drugstore back there and I circled the block so I could catch up with you. Come on, it's freezing out here and my car is nice and warm."

Colleen smiled at the young man. She could see he was very handsome even in the dim light of the street lamps. Still she stood her ground. Colleen wasn't about to get into a car with a perfect stranger even this close to campus.

"How do I know you're not some dirty old man?" Colleen asked, turning her head in a questioning stare. She leaned over to look at Bradley even closer.

"You don't," Bradley replied with a wide smile. He pushed open the door even wider. "I could be a dirty young man instead." He patted the passenger seat with his gloved hand, "But come on, seriously, do I look like some dirty old man?"

"Looks can be deceiving," Colleen answered. "You could be in disguise." She stepped closer to the car. "My life might be in peril. What would I do then?"

"In that case, you just might be getting into a car with a dirty young man who is simply intent on not seeing you freeze your beautiful face in this harsh weather."

"Promise to behave yourself?" Colleen asked, stepping even closer to the open car door.

"If I want another date with you, why would I misbehave on our first date?" he asked.

Colleen slid into the front seat and quickly closed the door behind her. "How do you know there's going to be a second date, much less a first one?" She asked. Bradley laughed. "Because," he said, "I think you and I have a wonderful future ahead of us."

"Presumptuous, aren't you?"

Bradley shifted into gear and pulled away from the curb. He looked over and smiled at Colleen again. His white teeth seemed to shine despite the dim light inside the car. He flicked the heater to high and turned his soft romantic music down on the radio. He looked over at Colleen as he drove down the street. "I can take you straight back to your dorm or we can opt for a cup of coffee at the student center which I happen to know is still open until midnight. So what is it, a drop -off at your dorm or a cup of coffee and some pleasant conversation?"

Colleen had begun to warm up to the young man almost immediately. Bradley was definitely handsome, gracious and seemed very attentive to her needs. He had all the gentility of a southern gentleman no matter where he was from. Colleen could tell from his Burberry coat and sleek black leather gloves that he was a man of wealth, probably from his parents. He was certainly one of the moneyed elite on campus.

Colleen couldn't identify the cologne but it was intoxicating in the warm car. She was tempted to inch closer to Bradley just to get a better whiff of the aroma. But she thought that would be much too obvious for a first encounter. Bradley leaned over and turned up the radio. It was either an Andre Previn or some Henry Mancini song that was playing. Colleen almost felt like laughing at the man's attempt to set the atmosphere just right for romance.

"I suppose you think you're being very charming now?" Colleen said with a smile, cupping her hands under the dashboard heating vent. "You must be from the South, Atlanta maybe or perhaps, D.C. Which is it?"

"New York and Long Island," Bradley answered. "We have a couple of homes but I guess you could say the Barringtons are East Coast type of people. And you're from Rochester, Minnesota. Your dad is a physician at the Mayo clinic and your mom stays home. No brothers or sisters and you're very interested in journalism. You worked for the St. Paul Pioneer Press freshman year and then a smaller alternative newspaper last year."

"Now, Bradley, that is scary!" Colleen said. "You know too much about me. Are you stalking me?"

"Please just call me Brad, Colleen." He answered. "Let's just call it market research. I need to know my target audience as well as I can, before I present myself."

"Target audience?"

"OK, client. How is that?" Bradley responded.

"Better. At least, it sounds a little less formal. So you're a business major, I take it?"

"No, actually I'm pre-med," Bradley answered, "I'm going to be a doctor like your dad."

He parked the car near the front entrance and quickly got out to open Colleen's door. As Colleen got out of his car, he put his arm around her shoulder and said, "Come on, it's cold out here." He quickly moved the two of them up the front steps and into the student union. Colleen didn't resist as he kept his arm wrapped around her shoulder all the way into the building. It felt very nice. And secure.

For some reason even she didn't quite understand, Bradley's gesture was neither brash nor out of place. Colleen liked the idea that this young man wasn't afraid to take control and put his arms around her. Bradley seemed very confident and sure of himself. He liked what he saw and he had no hesitation to take command of the situation. He was forceful and direct. A man who knew what he wanted and wasn't afraid to go after it. So unlike any of the other men Colleen had known, including Daniel.

Bradley dropped his hand from Colleen's shoulder and gestured toward the coffee shop next to the student cafeteria. "We should be able to find a quiet spot in here," He said as he took hold of Colleen's gloved hand and ushered her into the sparsely populated room. They found a table in one corner and Bradley ordered two cappuccinos before they sat down.

They began talking about the trivial things that two people unfamiliar with one another might begin with. But Bradley was nothing if not blunt and to the point. "Enough of the small talk," he said suddenly during a lull in their conversation. "Let's talk about something interesting." And with that, they began an in-depth conversation about campus politics, the war in Vietnam and Bradley's own background.

He was old New York money. Their home in the Hamptons has been in the family since the turn of the century. The original structure had been torn down to the old oak studs, rebuilt and expanded upon until it was now larger than any of the other old money mansions that lined the east coast of the island.

Bradley's life was all planned out for him from summers working at his father's medical practice until his senior year to early admission into

Harvard Medical School. Winters were spent flying between New York and their ski chalet in Aspen, Colorado. He had already picked out a spot in the Hamptons, not far from his parents' home, for a home of his own. The brand new super-charged Avanti convertible was a gift from his parents to help get him through his two remaining years in college. Then it was back to New York and an endless array of art galas, theatrical openings, fundraising events and other must-attend social activities.

Colleen let him talk on for most of the evening. He was charming and attentive and seemed genuinely interested in what she had to say…when she could get a word in sideways. By the end of the evening when they got kicked out of the café at closing time, Colleen was truly smitten. Her love life had gone from barren desert to a flowering field full of wonderful possibilities within a couple of hours.

As they were wrapping up their evening, Bradley commented, "I couldn't help but notice the outfit you're wearing tonight," he said. "Kind of a hippie getup, isn't it?"

"It's functional," Colleen answered with a smile, "and warm."

"Don't get me wrong," Bradley said, "you still look beautiful in it. Stunning, in fact, but it takes guts to wear an outfit like that. And breaking the rules too."

"I got the idea from someone I used to know…a long time ago," was all Colleen would say.

The next few weeks were filled with one event after another, each picked by Bradley just for Colleen and her personal tastes. It worked like a charm. Bradley was nothing if not smooth in his choices. The Minneapolis Institute of Art. The Minnesota Opera. First run plays in the downtown Theater District. Private gallery showings in Uptown. Quiet dinners overlooking the Mississippi River in downtown St. Paul. Each date was a well-choreographed event designed for Colleen's enjoyment and pleasure. Bradley remained ever the gentleman and Colleen was beginning to feel more and more secure in the warm comfort of his strong arms.

Bradley was wealthy but not pretentious. He wasn't looking for a trophy wife but rather a partner to share his exciting life with him. He respected women and wasn't intimidated by their intelligence. There was no doubt in Colleen's mind that this young man would be a catch for any woman on campus. And here he was, sitting across from her right now, smiling at her and caressing her skin with his soft voice.

It was all coming together for Colleen.

Now, more than ever, she could focus on her college career. After graduation, the job prospects looked very promising. Her rocky relationship with Daniel was over. That freshman year romance was now just a part of her past. It had become just a distant memory as Colleen changed and matured and moved to this new and exciting next stage of her life.

Bradley was everything she'd ever wanted in a friend and companion. It was all so very perfect. More perfect than Colleen ever imagined it could be. Her life was back in order and nothing could stop her now.

Gung Ho

It was only by accident that Colleen happened to run into Michael that late spring afternoon. After dropping a friend off at the Highland Park library, Colleen was gassing up across from the Quick Mart. She glanced over her car and saw Daniel's old friend standing in front of the store.

Michael was wobbling back and forth, fumbling for a cigarette. He found one in his pocket, tried to light it and when that failed, he plopped himself down on the sidewalk curb. Colleen quickly gassed up, drove across the street and parked close by.

Michael never saw Colleen walk over and stand next to him. She leaned in a little closer to the disheveled young man. He was still fumbling with his cigarette.

"Michael, it's Colleen," she said, "how are you doing?"

Michael looked up at the gas pumps, his glassy eyes unfocused. He lit his cigarette and then refocused and looked back up at the woman standing over him.

"Hey, girl, how are you?" he answered. Colleen could smell the booze on his breath and saw that his hands were shaking.

"I'm fine, Michael," Colleen said. "Are you out of the service now?"

"Yeah, got a medical discharge from Uncle Sam," Michael answered. "Now he's paying me to get drunk and forget about his damn war over there." He took a long draw on the cigarette and slowly let it exhale out of his nose and mouth. He tried to stuff the cigarette pack in his shirt pocket but couldn't get it in. Colleen leaned over and slipped the pack inside the pocket for him.

"How did it go over there?" Colleen asked.

"Over where?" Michael answered back.

"Vietnam. How did it go for you over in Vietnam?"

"I'm here, aren't I?" Michael muttered back. He looked up at Colleen. His face was blank and revealed nothing.

"What did you do over there?" Colleen asked as she sat down on the curb next to him. "I mean, what was your job?"

"Staying alive," Michael answered. "Just like every other poor stiff." He searched in earnest for his next thought. "Point," he said then turned toward Colleen. "They put me on point near the end. Had me cutting trail a couple of dozen clicks ahead of everyone else. Know what the life expectancy of a point man is?"

Before Colleen could say anything, Michael resumed. "Even when I was short, they still put me out there. I ended up like everybody else. You just go numb. Frickin' nightmares every night. Point whispers."

"Point whispers," Colleen repeated. "I don't understand."

"Point whispers," Michael explained. "It's what you say to yourself when you're way out in front. You talk to yourself incessantly. You talk to temper the fear. You talk to distract yourself. You know that you're one footstep away from either getting blown to shit or cut in half by gook bullets…you…"

"Let's get you home," Colleen interrupted him in a soft voice. "I've got a car. Come on, I'll give you a ride." She stood up and offered her hand to Michael.

Michael waved her off then stumbled to his feet. He regained his balance and followed Colleen over to her Mustang. As he walked around the back of her car, a police car drove by. Michael lifted his hand and gave them 'the stick' as they passed by.

"Michael, get in!" Colleen snapped at him. "Don't do that!"

Michael climbed in and dropped into the front seat passenger side. "Nice wheels," he said, "You've done well for yourself, young lady. Your parents must have…."

"So, Michael, how long have you been out of the service?"

"Long enough to realize just how bad it is over there," Michael answered. He took another long drag on his cigarette then flicked it out the window. "I mean it's a real downer, man. Damn lucky I got out on my…Section Eight. Better to come home disgraced than in a body bag like a lot of my friends did."

Following Michael erratic directions, Colleen managed to find Michael's fourplex apartment building several blocks away. She parked in front and walked him to the front steps.

He stumbled up the steps and Colleen followed right behind, just in case Michael lost his balance and fell backwards. He fumbled with his key and opened the front door. He stepped inside and stood in the entryway. He was still wavering as he tried to steady his balance.

"Are you all right now?" Colleen asked, stepping closer.

"Yeah, hell, I'm fine," Michael answered, forcing out a smile. "Just a little tipsy from sitting in the sun too long and not getting enough sleep." He motioned toward his apartment door. "Want to come in for a brewski?" he asked.

"No, I really have to get back to campus," Colleen answered, moving back toward the stairway. She waved at Michael, threw him a smile and started down the front steps.

Michael gingerly walked to the end of the landing and looked down on Colleen. He spoke again slowly, "You'd be proud of him," he offered, "if you two were still an item."

The statement caught Colleen up short. She stopped on the bottom step and turned around. "What do you mean?" she asked.

"Daniel. He's doing what he set out to do. Going to make something of himself. Break out of the mold his old lady put him in at birth. He's done right well for himself over there, you know."

"I don't understand what you're talking about, Michael!" Colleen said, confused by Michael's rambling.

"You didn't hear? Hell, Daniel's got himself promoted. He's not a grunt anymore. Was field grade sergeant. Now it's a permanent promotion. The scuttlebutt is that he's getting himself into all kinds of covert ops and all that undercover shit. Heavy duty stuff for an enlisted man. They say confidence produces courage. Your boy, Daniel...he's got it in spades."

As Michael was rambling on, Colleen couldn't help but notice his quivering lips and at times, his thousand-yard stare. Michael was babbling on but he was emotionally empty. Colleen had no idea if he was telling the truth or just reminiscing about his military past that was checkered at best.

But what did that matter Colleen asked herself. It was all over between her and Daniel. She'd made an honest attempt to mend old fences with those follow-up letters. But that hadn't worked. Now she had a new boyfriend who was the perfect antidote for all the hurt and confusion that had defined her relationship with Daniel.

Let it go, her brain cautioned her. Let it go and walk away. Be done with it. Be done with him. Get on with your life. Just forget you ever saw

Michael today. He isn't a friend of yours. He's but a sad remnant of your freshman year. You've moved on from there. Turn around and walk away.

"Oh, come on in," Michael said, waving for Colleen to follow him inside. "I'll tell you all about your old boyfriend. He's really changed. For better or worse, he ain't the same."

Don't do it, Colleen's brain screamed at her. Don't continue this conversation. It will just stir up old memories. Old hurts. Forget about your past and move on with your life. Turn and walk away…right now.

Colleen looked up at the wavering young man motioning her to come inside. Colleen knew what she had to do. She knew the right thing to do.

But instead she started climbing back up the stairs.

"Just for a moment then," Colleen said and followed Michael down the dank musty hallway. Her nagging brain kept assaulting her conscience even as she walked inside Michael's dimly lit dump of an apartment.

As they entered his sparsely furnished living room, Colleen couldn't help but notice the smell. Marijuana or some other intoxicating substance, she thought. Then she saw a large banner nailed to the wall.

It was a brightly colored sheet, almost like a black velvet painting. It read: University of South Vietnam. The line below that read: College of Murder and Mayhem.

Michael began to laugh when he noticed Colleen staring at the sheet. "That says it all," he said, pointing toward the banner. "Murder and Mayhem was the order of the day. Our orders were very simple, to cause those Gooks as much pain and suffering as we possibly could." Michael shook his head at the absurdity of it all. "Dinks and Gooks, that's all it was. Just Dinks and Gooks. If a few civilians or water buffalo got greased along the way, that was just a part of the process. Crazy way to win a war." He stumbled into his tiny kitchen and opened the refrigerator. There were several six packs of beer and little else inside it. A box of Twenty Mule Team Borax was back in one corner.

Michael noticed Colleen staring into his fridge. "Know what that's for?" he asked her, pointing toward the Borax.

"Yes, I suppose it is used for…"

"No," he interrupted Colleen. "I heard that if you cook it, you can…"

"Michael, you can't be serious!"

Michael shrugged his shoulders and fished out a beer. "But that was all part of our everyday living. One day the monks were roasting themselves in protest of the war and the next day we'd be out in the bush making a goddamned meat grinder out of Charlie and the NVA. CYA, cover your ass became the order of the day, if you wanted to live another day … want a beer?"

"No."

"How about a Tab and some vodka?"

"No," Colleen said as she looked for a spot to sit down. There was a ratty cloth-covered high back chair across from an equally worn and tattered sofa. Colleen chose the chair and sat down, careful to check first for food and debris. She settled back into the chair and watched as Michael had plopped himself down on the sofa, slouching into one corner.

"See a church key anywhere?" Michael asked, looking around at the floor.

Colleen leaned over and picked up the bottle opener and tossed it to Michael.

The room was sparsely furnished with a dirty chair, a tattered sofa and a scratched, wobbly coffee table. A lava lamp competed for space with stacks of magazines and books on the tabletop. There was a ripped beanbag chair in one corner next to a bowl full of burnt incense sticks and cigarette butts.

The whole apartment smelled of stale cigarettes and liquor. The windows were shut and the tattered curtains were full of dust and cobwebs. A beaded curtain led to the bedroom. There were two posters on one wall. The other walls were bare and marked by peeling paint.

The first black and white poster showed three girls sitting on a sofa. It said: 'Girls Say Yes' above and below it: 'To Boys Who Say NO'. At the bottom of the poster it read: Proceeds from the sale of this poster go to the draft resistance. It brought a smile to Colleen's face.

The second poster looked at first like a child's drawing of a scarecrow. Only it wasn't a scarecrow but rather military gear propped up on a stick. The line above the military scarecrow read: What if they gave a war? Below the scarecrow it read: And nobody came. Colleen liked that poster too.

More magazines and comic books were stacked high up against the sofa. On top of one stack was a Zap Comix by R. Crumb. Leaning next to it was the Whole Earth Catalog. Next to that stack was a pile of Playboy magazines and next to that several Oz magazines.

Michael noticed Colleen staring down at the magazines.

"You read Oz?" he asked.

"No, can't say I have," Colleen answered him.

"It's got great articles by Clive James and Germaine Greer. You can take one if you want to," he said, pointing at the stack.

"Thanks, maybe some other time," Colleen answered with a smile.

As Michael started talking about the stupidity of war and the blind eye his government had turned to all the corruption there, Colleen noticed a stack of books on the coffee table. Most were library books with some paperbacks lying around the pile.

Colleen could read some of the titles clearly. 'In Cold Blood' by Truman Capote. 'The Medium Is the Message' by Marshall McLuhan. 'Death at an Early Age' by Jonathan Kozol and, 'Diary of a Mad Housewife' by Sue Kaufmann.

"That's an interesting collection of books you have there, Michael," Colleen commented.

Michael leaned forward to look down on the stack. He nodded in agreement, reached down, and from under some newspapers he pulled out a small paperback book.

"Got a good one last week," he said, holding up a tattered paperback. The cover was a dark blue with a large white circle 'O' on it. He smiled broadly.

"That's not what I think it is?" Colleen asked.

"The Story of O, yup, that's what it is. Ever heard of it?" he asked.

Colleen was astonished that Michael had gotten a hold of a book that was all but banned in the United States because of its graphic and detail descriptions of bondage and sexual depravity. She'd never seen the book herself but had heard about it from some of the girls in her dorm. Someone even tried to buy it at Shinders newsstand in downtown Minneapolis, but to no avail.

"What would possess you to read such a book?" she asked.

"Have you read Betty Friedan's 'The Feminine Mystique'?" he asked Colleen.

"Of course, I have," she answered, "I think all of my friends have read it."

"Well, this is just another approach to the same subject matter. When it comes to sex, the power rests with women. Women think they've got the power, you know, with their pu…"

"Yes, Michael, I get the picture," Colleen interjected quickly to change the subject, "You said Daniel got promoted over there? What else did you hear about him?" she asked.

Michael upended his beer, chugging half the bottle before he dropped it on his lap and answered, "We exchanged a couple of letters in country, then I saw him just before I shipped out," Michael said and smiled, "He's become one gung-ho mother.....son of a gun," he blurted out, then put the brakes to his mouth... "I heard second hand that he was part of a LRRP unit out of the 1st Cav or maybe it was with the Aussies, I'm not sure."

"Long Range Reconnaissance Patrol."

"Yeah, how'd you know that?"

"I've done a little research, that's all," Colleen answered. "Do you know anything else?"

"The LRRP's had these eight man teams. Two scouts and six soldiers. They're part of the Special Forces." Michael suddenly laughed out loud and belched, then took another long swig of his beer. "The NVA called them devils in green faces. Spooked the dinks pretty good the way our boys painted their faces green and black as well as all their exposed skin. They did look like the devil to those chinks."

"And SOG?"

"Studies and Observation Groups," Michael answered. "But Daniel only did a couple of those jaunts in the bush. Usually it was part of a LRRP Recon group."

"When they asked for volunteers, they always asked if the applicant was an orphan. Seriously, that's what they were looking for. Those dudes were a real crazy bunch of motherf... guys. Most of the time they were miserable but content. The causality rate was pretty high and you didn't want to get caught alive behind enemy lines. A lot of those guys carried a small pill with them. They weren't about to be captured alive if they could help it."

"Did Daniel have a pill?" Colleen asked.

"Probably," Michael answered. "They all did, I suppose."

"Why would he do such a thing? I mean put himself in such danger."

"Daniel's changed a lot since he's been in country," Michael began to explain. "I know all those pissant rules drove him crazy. He probably could have gotten stationed in Saigon if he had tried hard enough. But he couldn't stand what he called poodle officers. He said they were just politicians in uniform. He said he'd rather live out in Indian country rather than be with them. But he certainly respected the snake eaters. And soon he became one of them. He became a dog robber."

"A what?"

"Dog robber! Daniel became the go-to guy in his platoon. You know, locally available assets." Michael began to laugh, "Whatever it takes to get whatever you need. So you beg, borrow or steal whatever you need." Michael let out a loud belch. "So it wasn't much of a stretch that he would join an outfit like LRRP. He became their dog robber. He got whatever they needed to get their missions done."

Colleen shook her head in amazement. "Anything else besides rumors that you might have heard… that you can substantiate?" Colleen asked.

Michael stumbled to his feet and retreated to the refrigerator. This time he collected the entire six-pack of beer and returned with it to the sofa. He clutched the carton on his lap.

"The LRRP stuff I only heard about secondhand," Michael began, "But I do know that even though he wasn't RA, regular army, Daniel got himself assigned to a Special Forces unit. That one he told me about when we were in Saigon. Rumor was that the army was under a lot of pressure to increase their SOG units that were going into Laos and Cambodia.

"And if they got into trouble, then the QRF, Quick Reaction Force, would go in and get them out. They were all hot extractions, the worst kind. It's about as dangerous a job as you can get over there. I was told that Daniel always went in on the lead Huey. VC made the first extraction helicopters their favorite target. A pilot's life expectancy was less than a dozen missions. The extraction team….even less than that. Whenever one of those birds would land, Daniel was the first man out, guns blazing at gut level to set up a perimeter line of defense." Michael laughed as he chugged his beer. "Man, talk about stepping into the mouth of the dragon," he said. "His pucker factor must have been off the charts."

"I'm not even going to ask…" Colleen said.

"Pretty soon he became the go-to man to lead those extraction teams … fucking crazy … like he had a death wish." Michael swigged until the beer bottle was empty. He pursed his lips as he spoke, "The way Daniel talked about those ops, you'd think he didn't care if he got killed or not. He wasn't reckless but he sure had brass balls when the lead was flying."

"No more FNG. Daniel was the man," Michael said as he dropped the empty beer bottle over the end of the sofa.

"FNG?" Colleen asked.

Michael answered with a smirk. "FNG, Fucking New Guy. CYA, all the way."

"I got it!" Colleen said, "I got it," she took a moment to collect herself, "I understand the country has been divided into four corps tactical zones and Daniel was in the Central Highlands. At times in the A Shau Valley. Is that true?"

"Probably! I don't know exactly where he was operating out of," Michael answered, "but I do know he was assigned to the 101st Airborne for awhile as a translator because of his work with those SOG units. He also worked for the 1st Cav at one point," Michael finished his beer.

"If Daniel was in those Central Highlands of Vietnam, he'd be trying to win the hearts and minds of those people and, shit, they just wanted to be left alone. Westmoreland, old Westy, couldn't defeat the VC and NVA so General Abrams comes along with his Vietnamization of the war. Soldiering is a strange business."

"And you don't think it's working?" Colleen asked.

"Fu… hell no! Not at all," Michael answered. "They did it all wrong from the very beginning. It's a political war. Never was anything more than that! Body counts were a joke. The euphemism was, if it's dead, it's VC … but in reality, it didn't work that way. We were told; find them, fix them, kill them. In other words, search and destroy. It was supposed to be the cornerstone of our tactics in the Nam. But that's not working either."

He continued, "Daniel said it was very frustrating for him and his men. Despite the new approach, they were still searching for the enemy and would often get bloodied up pretty badly when they did. He said he missed the battle in the I Drang Valley with the First Cavalry Air Mobile Unit but a lot of his friends died there. Messed him up for a long time."

"Did he ever come close to getting killed himself?" Colleen asked with hesitation etched in her voice.

"There was really only one time when Daniel spilled his guts. We met back in Saigon when he told me much more than I really wanted to know. He said he may have missed that big one in the I Drang but there were a number of other firefights and skirmishes throughout the A Shau Valley. Everywhere he went it was a free fire zone. You just kill anything that moves. Just like this last one I heard about. The one they're calling Hamburger Hill. Hope to hell he wasn't in that one. A lot of good men died there."

"That was in the A Shau?" Colleen asked.

Michael seemed to sober up for a moment. "The A Shau Valley has got a fearsome reputation for some pretty fierce battles for both sides. Any soldier who served in the A Shau and survived was one tough son of a bitch. That would describe Daniel."

Michael got up to go over to the refrigerator. He'd already forgotten the four bottles still in the six-pack at his side. He turned back toward Colleen and said, "He'd talk about the times they'd have to gather up the wagons at night, send out listening posts and wait for the enemy to hit them. Couple of times they'd have a furious firefight and the next morning, the VC, Victor Charlie, had come back in the dead of night and picked up their dead and wounded. In the morning, not one of those motherfuckers could be found. Demoralizing as hell for the young recruits who weren't used to the insanity of war."

Michael opened the refrigerator door and dug out another beer. He opened the bottle and upended it until the bottle was half empty. He looked at Colleen with a dead calm in his eyes. "Yeah, Daniel almost bought the farm a couple of times. Had his helmet shot off several times. Took some shrapnel another time from a Gook grenade. Spent six weeks recovering from that incident. But he'd just rise up like a phoenix each time, hit the ground running and never slow down." Michael waited for a reaction but Colleen seemed frozen in place. "You wanted to know when he came the closest to being killed."

"Yes, do you know?" Colleen answered, trying hard to conceal the catch in her throat.

Michael's voice lowered and he spoke slowly, "Once in the Central Highlands….who knows exactly where," he began, "the closest Daniel ever came to being killed was on some small, miserable jungle hilltop. The OP was supposed to be just a listening and observation post. Nothing more than that. Their job was to collect as much Intel as they could, and then split. They were only supposed to be there for a couple of weeks. Hopefully, before Charlie got wind of what they were doing. But it didn't work out that way."

"What happened?" Colleen asked hesitantly.

"Daniel had a couple of squads, mostly fresh meat, new recruits as we used to call them, and some of the regular Vietnamese army to back them up. Oh, and a couple of the Montagnard, those mountain fighters. That was it. Daniel said it was ill conceived and poorly planned right from the start. Some shavetail lieutenant was supposed to lead the group but he got sick and stayed behind. Daniel was a non-com by then and he knew the rules of engagement, that is, whatever HQ decides you do, you do it. No questions asked. He knew what had to be done and he meant to do it…no matter the outcome."

Michael emptied the bottle and grabbed his third. He popped off the cap and took another swig. He slammed the bottle down and shook his head.

"The short of it is they nearly got overrun. Sappers crawled up the hill under the cover of a morning fog and blew through the concertina wire with their satchel demolition charges. Then more Gooks started lobbing grenades and RPGs into the lookout huts and trench lines. The Vietnamese regulars just ran like hell and Daniel was left with his scared young grunts and a couple of his Yards to defend the hill. It was a total cluster fuck."

"Daniel called in artillery but that was just a stay of execution if they couldn't stop the VC from overrunning their position. It got so bad he had to call in fire and brimstone; a Broken Arrow."

"I don't understand." Colleen said.

"He pulled the chain, calling in everything he could get his hands on. Artillery, aerial rocket artillery, and the phantoms."

Colleen just stared at Michael, frozen with fear at what Michael was going to say next.

"He called in the bombs on himself," Michael explained with a dazed look on his face. "The man had no choice. They were about to be overrun. If that happened, Daniel and his men would have all been slaughtered. So he called for air support and they dug in and waited for hell to come knocking on their doorstep."

He stared into Colleen's wide open eyes, "And it came with a fucking vengeance!"

"It did?" Colleen muttered in a soft voice.

"Those supersonic death machines, the F-4B Phantoms, only had a small hilltop to target so they zeroed in on it and let loose with every piece of ordinance they had. When the bombardment was over, half the damn mountaintop had been blown away, the enemy routed and Daniel's squad blown to pieces."

"How many of them survived?"

"No idea. But not many," Michael answered. "I never got a straight answer out of Daniel. He took it real hard. The few times I saw him after that incident, he'd never bring it up nor would he ever let me ask him any questions. It was a closed book."

Colleen was stunned.

"There was even talk of a battlefield commission," Michael said. "But Daniel just scoffed at the notion. He said one heroic deed doesn't make a man a hero. All too often it just defines a moment. He let it go at that and nothing more was ever said about it."

Colleen listened in stone silence. She hesitated to ask the question that suddenly seemed paramount on her mind. She didn't know why. It didn't make any sense considering their fractured past. But she felt she had to ask it nevertheless.

"Did he ever talk about me, Michael?"

"Yeah, all the time," Michael answered.

"Did he mention the letter I sent him?"

"No, what letter?"

"I messed up really badly," Colleen began speaking slowly as she tried to talk through the catch in her throat. She kept searching for the right words. "I got a lot of flak from my mother and my friend, Peggy and someone else to end it with Daniel. So I did. I sent him a Dear John letter."

"When did you send it?"

"About six or seven months ago."

"Shit."

"What?"

"That's about the time I heard Daniel was getting heavily involved in the program."

"I don't understand. What program?"

"…I heard Daniel was into some very heavy shit … stuff. Rumor has it that he was part of some Aussie covert operation that may have offed some of the bad guys. Hearts and minds, baby, hearts and minds. Cut out their hearts and they don't mind." Michael laughed and gulped down more beer.

"Oh, my God!" Colleen suddenly blurted out.

"What?"

"When I was working at the newspaper I'd occasionally come across some document that would reference covert operations in Vietnam. They would vaguely reference kidnapping and elimination of target suspects. But the reports were always very vague. And the other reporters were very quick to tell me to forget it if I didn't want a visit from the suits.

"Well," Michael began, quickly backing off the subject, "I don't know if that's true or not. The army lives on rumors and lies and flimsy intelligence, if you know what I mean," he raised his eyebrows as he grinned at Colleen.

You think because of my letter….?"

"Don't know," Michael answered with a shrug of his shoulders. "That letter must have killed him," he said out loud, not even realizing he was speaking.

"I know," Colleen said, a tremor in her voice. "Then I realized what a fool I'd been and I sent him another letter, saying I was sorry and that we should still remain friends."

"And?"

"It came back. So I sent a third letter but it came also back. I never heard back from Daniel so I assume he got my first letter but not those other two."

"That's probably because he was into his covert operations by then. The army wouldn't recognize that he existed at that point. Not if he was operating where he wasn't supposed to be. Their official line would be that he was missing in action with no record of his whereabouts."

Colleen fell silent. She was trying to process what might have gone through Daniel's mind when he got her first letter. What he was feeling now that he thought their relationship was completely over. Was he mad? Was he hurt and angry? Did he hate Colleen for doing that to him?

Michael paused, "Daniel shut down after that incident on the hilltop. And that is a very bad thing! Men like that can shut down but the images don't go away. They just ferment inside and some time, now or in the future, it could all come out. I've seen it drive men crazy. They'd either drink themselves to death or blow their brains out. They'll do anything to make the nightmares go away."

The room grew silent. Only the hum of the fan in the window cut the air. Michael leaned in close to Colleen. His eyes met hers and he shook his head, "You need to know. You need to understand," he began, "that shit changes a man…any man. It won't be the same Daniel that comes home…if he comes home at all. He'll be a changed person. For better or worse, he won't be the same."

"He was a good man," Colleen said.

"Is!" Michael corrected her. "He ain't dead yet."

"No! No!" Colleen said, embarrassed by her misstatement. "That's not what I meant, Michael. You know that!" she snapped back.

"I know, man. It's just too bad it didn't work out between you two. He once told me that you were the only girl….woman that he felt he could be himself with. No pretenses. No bullshit. Warts and all. And that you accepted him that way. At least at first you did."

"We all change, Michael. Time changes everything. I guess it wasn't meant to be, that's all."

"Well, it's still too bad."

"Do you know what his plans are….after the service?" Colleen asked.

"He told me that he was taking correspondence courses in his spare time. I guess he could return here, go to the U or go back to St. Paul's. Or he may stay on the coast and finish school out there. The last time I talked to him, he wasn't sure what he was going to do."

"But he is going back to college."

"Oh, trust me," Michael answered. "If he comes back in one piece or even a couple of pieces, Daniel's going to finish his education."

Michael finished his beer and stood up, "I think I need another drink and

I'm about out of booze." He started to ask Colleen something but he stopped in mid-sentence. "But you have to go," he began. "Daniel's OK for now. At least he was several months ago before I left the Nam."

Even in his half-drunk state, Michael could read Colleen's face. He stood close to the woman whose face registered sadness and fear.

"He's a fighter, that ex of yours. He'll make it. Whether he comes back here or not, I have no idea. But he'll come back a changed man. I hope for the better. Say a little prayer that he makes it through his tour." Michael started walking toward the door.

"I got to go," he said, "my friends at the Quick Mart are waiting. I may be moving soon. Got a house not far from here. Maybe."

Colleen followed Michael out of the building and watched him as he staggered down the sidewalk toward the Quick Mart. She sat in her car for a long time, staring out over the steering wheel at nothing. Her mind was a jumbled mess of conflicted thoughts and emotions.

Mid-Summer of 1969

Pirates of Haute Couture

Early August in New York City was boiling with temperatures hovering in the mid-90s.

Traffic clogged the streets in central Manhattan and the storefronts were packed tight with tourists and shoppers alike. The mighty Yankees were on a winning streak and the theaters were full every night. Now Colleen was venturing into Bradley Barrington's home turf for the very first time.

Vendors crowded the sidewalks on either side of the Plaza Hotel as Colleen stepped out of her cab and looked up at the towering monument to conspicuous consumption and the gathering spot of New York blueblood society, Bradley's kind of people.

She thought about one of her favorite authors, F. Scott Fitzgerald, who had lived in the Plaza while he embodied the Jazz Age in his writings and personal life. Her parents talked about one of their first dates in the Persian Room dancing to Duke Ellington's band. Bradley had bragged about the movies filmed there and the numerous movie stars his parents had introduced him to. For an entertainer to appear in the Persian Room, meant they were considered a headliner. It was the ultimate cabaret experience. The Room, along with the Plaza itself, embodied the magic that was New York City in the late fifties and early sixties. It was Bradley's world and one he intended to share with his girlfriend that weekend.

Now Colleen was staying at the Plaza just like New York royalty. It was almost too much for a young girl from the Midwest. Except with Bradley, it was all so very natural and normal. Colleen couldn't help but notice the attention passersby gave her as she began strolling up the steps toward the lobby.

The air conditioning in the lobby immediately swept over her, adding a sweet freshness to the air. Colleen walked up to the front desk and gave her name. A young man, probably interning from some Ivy League school, immediately recognized the name and as quickly slipped her a key and a small note. He snapped his fingers and a porter was suddenly by her side. The older gentleman grabbed Colleen's suitcase and nodding toward the elevator, he announced, "This way, if you please, Madam."

"Just a moment, please," Colleen said as she stepped aside to read the note. It was from Bradley.

It read: Welcome to New York, Darling. I have a full schedule of exciting events for us while we're in the city, then it's off to the Hamptons. Please forgive me for not having room for you at our place on the Upper East Side. Business demands have taken precedence over your visit and every room is taken. I hope the Plaza will be a suitable substitute.

It was signed, Love, Brad.

Colleen went into the elevator, smiling at the attendant there. Within seconds, she was being swept up to the penthouse suite. She felt like she was floating on air. The Plaza, the note from Bradley and the ambiance of New York City all made her feel like a queen. *Queen for the week,* she thought and smiled at her reflection in the elevator mirror.

She followed the porter to her room and was struck by the sheer opulence of the Presidential Suite. There were five bedrooms, five bathrooms, a living room the size of her home in Rochester and separate facilities for servants and catering staff. A huge colorful bouquet of fresh flowers, primarily roses, adorned the entryway. Another bouquet, strictly roses, was in her bedroom.

Colleen put her clothes in one of the three dressers in her room and lay on the bed. She gazed up at the ornate patterned ceiling and wanted to pinch herself. She was in the Plaza, the most famous hotel in all of New York City. And as she waited for her new boyfriend to call, Colleen still couldn't believe her good fortune to have met Bradley in the first place. *Quite unbelievable,* she thought. *What a strange, yet wonderful, turn of events from my placid and at times boring social life during sophomore and junior year.*

After a while, Colleen rolled over and grabbed the remote television controller. She turned on the large-screen color television console and began to watch some silly soap opera until Bradley called. He called within the hour. He was running late. Something about final preparations for an art gala that evening and other sundry tasks for his mother who was out of town. Bradley asked Colleen to go down to the bar and wait for him. He would be there within the hour.

As Colleen got up to change clothes, a knock on the door caught her attention. She opened the door to find a maid standing there.

"May I turn down your bed, Madam?" the maid asked quietly in broken English.

"Please give me just five minutes," Colleen answered. "Then I'll be gone and you can have the place entirely to yourself. Just five minutes, please.

Yet as the maid turned to go away, Colleen was struck by the fact that she seemed to resemble Daniel's mother at an earlier age. Colleen closed the door and went to her bedroom to change but the similarities stuck in her mind. Why would that thought bother her? She had no idea. But just the sight of that maid brought back memories of her two brief encounters with Daniel's mother. And she remembered how sad she felt thinking about Daniel growing up with such a woman.

Moving quickly to distract herself from any thoughts of Daniel, Colleen changed into a bright colorful spring dress and walked down the hall toward the elevator. She felt vibrant, alive and full of energy. The past four months had been a whirlwind of social and personal activities for her and Bradley. While they were still in school, the telephone grew hot with their phone calls back and forth almost every single day.

After school let out, Bradley had gone back to New York but returned on several occasions just to see Colleen for long weekends. They went to movies in downtown Minneapolis, the Guthrie Theater to see Shakespeare, the trendy Uptown neighborhood for quiet cocktails and then long walks along Mississippi River Boulevard in the twilight hours. It was utterly romantic, peaceful and filled Colleen with the promise of a future full of even more wonderful times.

Most evenings would find them back at Colleen's apartment where she would make coffee or a nightcap for Bradley and they'd sit on her sofa and just talk. Their lovemaking had been confined to passionate kissing, gentle foreplay but never to the point of carnal intrusion. The traumatic incident by Garrison had steeled Colleen's determination never to put herself in such a vulnerable position again. Peggy's pregnancy had sealed that decision for the time being.

Bradley demurred to Colleen's wishes but he made it clear that he'd much prefer to spend the night with her rather than to go back to his hotel for a cold shower. They both laughed. Colleen more so than Bradley.

The first thing Bradley did when he arrived at the Plaza bar was to apologize profusely for Colleen having to take a commercial flight to New York. He explained that the Barrington's corporate airplane was overseas on a business trip. It seemed the Six Day War the year before had disrupted logistics for many of his parent's factories in the Middle East. Bradley's father and several other board members were attending to business there right now.

"Bradley, don't worry about it," Colleen assured him as they sat in a secluded booth away from the early afternoon cocktail crowd. "The flight was fine. Minneapolis-St. Paul International wasn't that crowded and they served a wonderful meal on the flight. I'm just so excited to be in New York City with you. I get to see all the places you have talked about - and the Hamptons. I just can't wait."

"Let's go then," Bradley said. "I've got a limo waiting outside. We can go over to several shops on Fifth Avenue that I think you're going to love." He grabbed Colleen's hand and they were off.

The rest of that afternoon was spent browsing little boutiques on Fifth Avenue and several side streets, away from the mass of humanity crowding the major sidewalks. Bradley insisted on buying Colleen several fall dresses from top Paris designers, fashion accessories from Milan and shoes from Rome.

That evening they went to "Fiddler on the Roof" at the Imperial Theatre. Afterward, they enjoyed a cocktail in a small café that catered to actors and producers. Bradley, of course, knew most of the producers by name. As early investors, his parents had found a rich goldmine in backing select plays on Broadway. Bradley reaped the benefit of their investing acumen.

The next day was full of more shopping and some gallery explorations. Among the galleries they visited were several that explored the highly active and influential artistic psychedelic scene. Bradley took Colleen to a new spot called the Factory. It was the melting pot of an eclectic group of artists led by a young blond named Andy Warhol. Warhol and his cohorts were defining and creating Pop Art, a strange new mixture of everyday items shown in new and amazing ways. Colleen didn't quite understand the philosophy behind the art nor did Bradley, but they both enjoyed talking to the artists and browsing the galleries clustered around the Factory.

That evening they went to see "Hello, Dolly" at the St. James Theater. Again, Bradley knew just the spot for a cocktail beforehand and mingling with actors and producers from the show afterwards. Colleen was transfixed by the excitement and buzz of the crowded café. Afterwards, she and Bradley took a long walk along Battery Park as their limo followed behind them at a discrete distance.

Bradley pointed out the Statue of Liberty, Staten Island, the Ferry and the outlying boroughs. They stood by the windswept tip of Manhattan and held each other tightly as a strong breeze came off the Hudson River.

"Bradley," Colleen whispered in his ear, "this has been so wonderful. I feel so lucky to have met you this year."

Bradley tightened his squeeze on Colleen and replied, "Just think if you hadn't let me pick you up that cold Saturday night. We wouldn't be here on my home turf, previewing what's in store for us in the future."

Colleen looked up at Bradley and kissed him gently on his cheek, "I'm so lucky," she said in a soft voice.

Bradley brought his arms down and rested them on her buttocks. He squeezed them gently and pressed her body hard against his. Colleen could feel him starting to get aroused. For a moment, just a brief fleeting moment, she was tempted. It was all so right. All so perfect. There was no reason now to deny Bradley what he wanted. What she wanted. Colleen dropped her arms from around his neck and turned back toward the Statue.

"What's in store for tomorrow, darling?" she asked.

"Hair!"

"What?"

"A new play at the Biltmore," Bradley said, "It just opened. Tickets are impossible to get, but, of course, my parents were able to get us two front row seats. It's called, "Hair – The American Tribal Love Rock Musical." I think you're going to like it. The reviews have been outstanding." Bradley smiled slyly. "There's even nudity in the show."

Even before they got to the theater the next night, Colleen could sense the excitement in the air. She peered out their limousine to see a group of demonstrators in front of the theater. Bradley explained that they were from an art group called Black Mask. They were playing Neo-Dada noise music, which Colleen thought sounded like strange whistles and horns. Down the block there were even more demonstrations by another group who called themselves Situationists International. Bradley said their tack was to hand out flyers of art events to homeless people with the promise of free drinks at the events. Colleen laughed. Bradley didn't.

Bradley's limo maneuvered through the crowds that spilled out into the street and deposited them in a small alley adjacent to the theater. He took Colleen's hand and led her through the alley until they came to a small chipped metal door. Bradley pounded on the door until it slowly opened and an actor, dressed in full Indian garb, let them in.

Colleen found herself backstage amid a horde of milling actors, musicians, yelling stagehands and very worried producer types huddled in one corner. One of the producers waved at Bradley to come over. He and Colleen twisted and turned their way through the crowd until they got to the producer.

"Bradley, my man," the producer said, extending his hand. "Glad you could make it. You should have been here opening night. Unbelievable, simply unbelievable."

"And the nudity?" Bradley asked. "My Dad is concerned that it might affect ticket sales."

"Oh, it did!" laughed the producer. "Took them up through the stratosphere. We're projecting sold-out performances for the next six months. Listen, if all it takes is a couple of nude chicks to sell tickets, I say bring them on. Bring them on!" They both laughed. Bradley cupped Colleen's elbow and turned them both around. "See you after the show," he threw back at the man as he and Colleen went back to maneuvering their way through the backstage crowd and into the main theater.

"Bradley," Colleen asked, "shouldn't you have introduced me?"

"Why?" Bradley asked.

"Because it would have been the polite thing to do," Colleen answered.

"Colleen, darling," Bradley answered in a patronizing tone of voice. "My Dad is a major investor in this show. If he hadn't put up the money, we wouldn't be sitting here tonight. The man owes me. Simple as that."

"Owes your father, you mean." Colleen responded.

"Whatever!" Bradley said and let the conversation end there.

The show was a tremendous hit. Not exactly Colleen's cup of tea but entertaining enough. She was surprised but not particularly shocked at some of the songs like "Sodomy" and "Going Down." It was an expression of the times. Something that Daniel would have embraced had he been there. So starkly different from Colleen's upbringing and yet somehow intriguing to her inquisitive nature. Once again the thought that she and her old boyfriend actually shared some common interests amazed her. Even the nudity, which was explicit but somehow managed to be one small part of a group scene, didn't shock her. She found herself swaying in her chair as "Let the Sun Shine In" rocked the theater. Bradley sat still and just smiled at her gyrations.

During intermission, Bradley excused himself to talk to one of the producers. Colleen stood in the lobby, nursing a Dr. Pepper and perusing the crowds gathered there. An ever so slight smile crossed her lips. *This has got to be something like the gathering of the tribes,* she thought. The event that Daniel had once referenced about San Francisco a couple of years earlier.

Old patrons and young, three-piece suits and paisley shirts, all mixed and mingled together with flower children and beat poets. Plenty of hair, headbands, and enough exposed flesh to make most of the older audience members blush. One of the actors was carrying a piece of folk art called Ojo de Dios – "Eye of God", a yarn sculpture which was the universal talisman of good vibes.

Daniel would certainly be in his element here, Colleen thought. One crazy hodgepodge of colorful characters straight out of his fantasy world.

She overheard one of the actors talking about a new movie that had just come out called "Easy Rider," about two loners riding their motorcycles across country. "He's probably already seen it," she said out loud.

Another actor standing next to her turned and asked, "Who's already seen it?"

Colleen blushed. "Oh, just someone I used to know," she answered and quickly walked away, embarrassed.

Colleen let herself wonder, just for a second, where Daniel was at that very moment. Still alive? Still in Vietnam? Perhaps back in the states? She stopped herself thinking about him. It would do no good, she realized. She was in New York City with one of the most charming men she'd ever meet. He was showing her the time of her life. And her future with him looked beyond promising. Why waste time pondering a past that only brought confusion and often hurt feelings?

Bradley and Colleen were in New York for two more days of theater, shopping and river cruises followed by a quick weekend at his parent's estate on the sound in south Hampton.

Saturday was spent at the beach, sunbathing, making out and light reading. That evening they went into town and had dinner at an exclusive French restaurant that Bradley's parents had brought into town, then a major reception afterwards for four ministers from South Africa where the Barrington's had several factories.

Bradley's mother arrived back from Paris Sunday afternoon and summoned her son and his new girlfriend to meet her in her office.

Agnes Barrington II was the Grande Dame of the Hamptons. Seated behind her desk just off the main ballroom, Agnes greeted them with a slight wave of her hand. She pointed toward two elegant Regency chairs in front of her desk. Bradley took Colleen's hand and they both sat down. Agnes smiled, glanced down at the papers on her desk then looked up and said, "Hello, son, and this is….?"

"Colleen…mother," Bradley answered quickly. "Colleen Fitzpatrick. Remember this is the girl I met at school. The one who is going to be a journalist or a writer perhaps? She's already had some wonderful internships over the last couple of summers. Her father is a physician at Mayo in Rochester. And her mother is from here, out East. I think you're going to like her."

"Hello, Mrs. Barrington," Colleen said quickly. "It's a pleasure to meet you. Bradley has shown me such a wonderful time in New York."

Ignoring Colleen's comment, Mrs. Barrington began talking about her trip to Paris.

"I was visiting with the folks at Chanel," she began, directing her attention to Bradley. "They agreed with me that some strange things are going on in the fashion industry. And not for the better. Haute couture is becoming passé, we agreed. It was so easy before to know what was in and what was out. But that's all changing now. This so-called teenage fashion is really clashing with what we consider sophisticated dress." She glanced at Colleen's clothing for a moment then redirected her attention back to her son.

"It's just getting harder and harder to keep up with fashion now. I used to have Dior's people make some lovely things for me… St. Laurent after Dior died in '57. Now, good heavens, we have hippie dress, space fashion, mod jackets and who knows what else all clamoring for space on the runway."

As Mrs. Barrington rambled on about the difficulty of keeping up with fashion, Colleen just smiled. She suddenly felt acutely aware of her own outfit. So was Agnes.

"That's an interesting outfit you're wearing," Mrs. Barrington commented. "Is it something from Mary Quant or Barbara Hulanicki? You know, the new Biba line?"

"No, it's not," Colleen answered.

"Oh, I do hope it's not a knock off or an imitation," Agnes said with distain.

Colleen laughed and then realized that Agnes was dead serious and quickly lost her smile. "No, my girlfriends and I get our clothes from a new vintage clothing store. It's similar to another one in town called Ragstock. I just find pieces that I like. I mix and match them. I try to wear clothes that highlight my best features regardless of current trends. My girlfriends and I call ourselves the pirates of haute couture … and they have to be practical for Minnesota winters too."

"Ragstock?" Agnes replied, her face deadpan. "I don't understand."

"Mother, what Colleen is saying…"

"Bradley, please! Colleen can talk for herself."

"Mrs. Barrington," Colleen began, "I just….

"Agnes, dear. Please call me Agnes."

"Yes, Mrs. … Agnes. I don't have a favorite designer. I just go with whatever I like. Whatever suits my taste. When I saw 'Sabrina Fair' with Audrey Hepburn I was just blown away by the simplicity of her clothes. I did try the new Felicity green dress from Biba, but it wasn't really me."

"Blown away! I've never heard of such a thing," Agnes replied.

"Mother, Colleen's a very clever girl. Very inventive, not just in her clothing. I'm sure she would love what some of the new designers are doing for the spring collection this year."

Colleen just smiled at Bradley. He returned her smile with a certain air of smugness.

Agnes stood up. Bradley and Colleen quickly did the same.

"Bradley, the next time Colleen comes out, we should all fly to Paris so we can get her some really nice clothing. Perhaps from Yves Saint Laurent or Ungaro or even Rudi Gernreich? I mean if Audrey Hepburn can dress with Givenchy and Jackie O with Cassini, surely your new girlfriend can look as good as they do. Don't you think?"

Bradley nodded his approval and said, "That would be nice, mother."

Colleen just smiled.

Agnes turned to Colleen. "I'm sure you don't have those kinds of shops by your school in Minneapolis…"

"Actually my school is in St…"

"Please don't correct me, dear," Agnes answered with raised eyebrows.

Colleen smiled again and said nothing more.

Agnes turned to Bradley and said with a sweet smile, "You know, Bradley, Colleen is going to have to understand that your mother has only the best intentions for her. You understand that don't you, dear."

"Of course, mother," Bradley answered.

"I'm going to have to excuse you both now. I have to coordinate the reception tonight for the ambassador to Jordan. Colleen, will you be able to stay for the event? She asked.

"I'm sorry, no," Colleen answered. "I have to get back to Minnesota this evening. I have my job to go back to tomorrow morning."

"Well, if you become a part of this family, that won't be an issue. Bradley will be able to answer your every need. You won't have to work again. Not as long as you're a Barrington."

She stood up and extended her hand. Bradley quickly stood and standing between his mother and Colleen, he motioned his girlfriend. Colleen stood up, shook Agnes' limp hand and they left the room.

As soon as they left the room, Colleen loosened her hand from Bradley's grip. "Why did she act like she was my mother?" Colleen asked Bradley. "I do have my own mother, you know."

"I know that, Colleen," Bradley answered defensively. "But you have to understand that around here my mother rules. Back in New York, it's my dad. But here she is the queen. She sees herself as everybody's mother. Please just go along with it - to humor her."

Bradley wrapped his arm around Colleen. He gave her a hug and a quick peck on her cheek. "Come on," he said, "I've asked the captain to get our yacht ready for a quick cruise. We can go up the coast for a little ways. There's a sweet little bar I want to show you before we head back to the airport."

Homecoming Angst

Daniel reached the Twin Cities by late morning of the fifth day. After leaving San Francisco, he'd spent one night in Boulder and the rest of the trip in long forgotten motel rooms. His journey was almost over and Daniel was arriving in style … his style.

The Triumph Bonneville T120 was a 650 cc, twin cylinder, four stroke, mean ass street machine that could top out at 110 miles per hour. On the open road, it seemed to go twice that speed. Daniel's new bike was a gift to himself. Paid for by the money he had saved from his paychecks in Vietnam. Daniel intended to use the two-wheeled racing machine as his main source of transportation instead of a car. Somehow it seemed to fit the image Daniel had of himself as he began his life all over again.

He'd spent the previous night in a small town outside of Rochester, Minnesota. Daniel wasn't about to spend the night in the same town where Colleen might be home for the summer. The risk of accidentally running into her in a small town like Rochester was too great and something he wasn't ready to handle.

Yet, as he was cruising through Highland Park the next morning, Daniel made a split second decision to chance it after all. On more of a whim than for any other reason, Daniel swung off Cleveland Avenue and through a side entrance into Mother of the Lake College. Summer session was over and the campus was pretty empty. Clusters of nuns here and there were walking between buildings. Incoming freshmen with their parents were touring the campus grounds. Several couples, attached by arm or hand or hip, were sitting by the pond.

Daniel was wearing his leather jacket, California t-shirt, now dusty jeans and sunglasses. No one would recognize him from that same guy two years earlier. He hadn't shaved in a week. His hair was longer and he carried himself differently this time around. The veteran and ex-student was confident he could ride through campus and no one would know who he was. Anonymity made Daniel feel comfortable and protected from his past.

Daniel swung his motorcycle down a dirt path and ended up under a large shade tree that edged up to the pond. It was quiet and still with only the occasional butterfly darting between the cattails and flowers by the water's edge. He took off his helmet and thought about the numerous times he and Colleen had wandered down to the water's edge at night. They'd sit on the damp grass and talked for hours about anything or nothing in particular.

Voices cut into his mental meandering and Daniel turned to see a group of nuns approaching from the chapel that overlooked the pond. He put his helmet back on and rolled his bike down around the pond and back onto the blacktop that led toward the center of campus. He started up the Triumph and slowly rode around the cobblestone monument in front of the main building and started riding toward the dorms and another side entrance.

As Daniel rode through campus, he passed by the coffee shop where he and Colleen had spent a ton of time over bad coffee. He passed the cafeteria where the trio had gotten kicked out of a couple of times for laughing so loud they disturbed the other students. He passed by the dorm where he and Michael had dropped off Colleen and Peggy after their first unofficial date on the West Bank. He marveled at the sameness of it all. There was a new post office building and a new dorm being constructed. But all in all, it was the same campus he had been to many times before.

He first spotted them approaching out of the corner of his eye. A group of young women coming up fast on his left side. They'd just exited the Physical Education Building and would be in the crosswalk before he got there. They must have come from some kind of practice because they were all wearing short skirts or shorts. Several had tight t-shirts on.

Damn, he thought. *What have I been missing for two years? I'll bet Jody's been feasting on this campus.*

He could speed up and get through the crosswalk or stop and wait for them to pass by. He looked over at the group. He studied their faces, hoping and dreading the chance that she might be there. None had red hair. He slowed to a stop and waited, his eyes hidden behind dark aviator sunglasses.

They were chatting and only a couple of the girls glanced over at him as they passed by. One in particular gave him a second look. She was an attractive woman with dark hair and pronounced facial features, either of Middle Eastern descent or Jewish. She stood out from the other blonds and brown haired women around her. Her skirt seemed shorter than the other girls and she carried herself with confidence. It was as if she knew her looks and appearance was all she needed.

The young woman talked to her friends but blatantly eyed Daniel as the group passed by. A coquettish smile crossed her lips and her eyes opened a little wider. She was flirting with him alright; her eyes were sending messages that were unmistakable. *If I were alone with her,* he thought, *I would be the prey and not the pursuer.*

Hot damn, Daniel thought, *I have found Valhalla, and it is here.*

Then they were past, still chatting and laughing, and soon swallowed up by another group that joined them on the way to the student union. Daniel was left by the crosswalk, his feet straddling his bike and his mind marveling at the beauty of women and what he'd been missing for two grueling years.

And it wasn't her. He felt better about that. Stupid or not, he'd probably gone through the campus in hopes of seeing her again. Why? He had absolutely no idea, besides the fact that he was an idiot.

So what would I have done if I'd seen her? He asked himself. Say, hi, how have you been? Why'd you send me that Dear John letter a couple of days after I'd been nearly killed?

A loud car horn brought Daniel back to his senses and he dropped his clutch and roared off toward the side entrance to campus. As he rode down the side street to get back to Cleveland Avenue he realized it had been a stupid idea to go through campus like that. He felt embarrassed and angry that he still fantasized about Colleen after all this time. And he realized he had better get over it if he didn't want to go crazy this next year on campus.

Yet despite the misgivings of running into Colleen, Daniel still felt more confident on that campus than he had all freshman year. Mother of the Lake hadn't changed at all. It was the same nuns in uniform black and the same college girls scurrying from one class to the next. It was the same collegiate scenes played out on any campus, anywhere in the U.S. It hadn't changed at all but somehow it felt very different and Daniel wasn't sure why.

Summers of Past Regrets

Much like the college campus he'd just ridden through, Daniel's home hadn't changed at all in two years. His mother was still at work so Daniel busied himself making a sandwich and sitting on the front steps, watching the world go by.

When his mother did come home later that afternoon, her message was very clear. She never asked about his experiences overseas. Instead she said she expected Daniel to move back home and help make her mortgage payments. On weekends, her new boyfriend would be living with them. Daniel let her talk and when she was finished; he calmly informed her that he would only be home for a couple of days before he found other accommodations.

"No offense, Mom," he said. "But I need my own space now. I'm going to try to buy a house. Maybe something that I can fix up and use as a real estate investment."

"Where did you ever hear of such a thing?" His mother responded. "It took me years just to earn enough money for a down payment. And you expect to buy a house just like that? Who do you think you are, some goddamned banker or something?"

"Forget it," Daniel said standing up and starting to move away. "I've got some places to go. I'll be home later on tonight." Daniel was halfway down the front steps when his mother caught him up short.

"Are you going to see her now that you're back?" his mother asked.

"See who?" Daniel asked, turning around.

"That girl," his mother responded. "The one that you were dating before you went into the service. The rich one whose old man is a doctor."

"No," Daniel answered. "I'm not seeing her anymore."

"Well, good!" his mother said. "She wasn't your type anyway. She's not like us. She's not one of us."

"Jeez, mother. Don't start that again."

"Start what?" his mother asked. "I'm just saying…."

Daniel turned around to leave. "I said I wasn't seeing her anymore," he threw over his shoulder. "It's over, Mom. Done! Finished!"

"Girls like that," his mother began to lecture. "Girls like that never really fall in love. They just like the idea of being in love. They like having a man wrapped around their skinny little arms. Like a Sugar Daddy. Someone to pay the bills and take care of them. In the end, all a girl like that will do is break your heart. Mark my words. I've seen that type many times before. Back then we used to call a girl like that a heartbreaker. Or worse…"

Daniel spun around. He was pissed. "Enough with the lecture, Mom. I get the point you're trying to make."

"Are you sure?"

"Oh, for Christ's sake, Mom. I said I was over her. Let it go, OK? Just let it be!"

"You don't have to raise your voice with me, young man. I am your mother."

Daniel bit his tongue and said nothing. "I'll be home late," he said again, turning around. "I'll see you then."

His mother was still mumbling as Daniel threw his leg over the Triumph and roared away without even putting his helmet on. He rode to the library not far from campus and sat in the reading lounge for a long time.

While in the service, Daniel had started to think seriously about real estate and buying a house as an investment. Some friends had talked about getting a CD; a contract for deed, if a bank wouldn't lend him the money for a down payment. Daniel meant to follow up on that idea.

The information on real estate was sparse and not very helpful. He read both the Minneapolis and St. Paul newspapers. There were only a few homes for sale and all were being offered through realtors. The librarian said he'd have to go through a realtor if he wanted to see any of the official listings.

Daniel stayed in the library until it closed.

He went to Michael's last known address but his old friend had moved out recently. The new tenants had his forwarding address. They thought it was someplace by the University, in the Dinkytown neighborhood. Daniel rode over to the area, found the address but no one was home. The old dump of a house was dark and quiet. He checked the mailbox and there were several old envelopes addressed to Michael. They looked like bills. Same old Michael, Daniel thought as he climbed back on his bike. Nothing had changed with his old friend.

After that, Daniel rode around town until well past midnight. The lights were out in his house when he rode slowly through the alley and slipped his bike into the side door of the garage. He slept on the dirt floor of the garage that night and was gone before light broke the horizon the next morning. Worst-case scenario, he'd find a motel before he'd go back home again.

Huaraches on Campus

The next day, Daniel went back to the College of St. Paul for the first time in over two years. He was wearing his standard uniform of cargo shorts, a t-shirt that read San Francisco, Mexican huaraches and sunglasses. And yet strangely, he didn't feel out of place. Standard campus attire was now khaki pants and button down Oxford shirts with loafers. The few women on campus all wore dresses or a skirt and a blouse. The frat look had come to stay.

Daniel walked the grounds, quietly soaking in the old familiar sights and the few new things on campus. If anyone noticed his attire, they didn't react to it and he was alone in his own world.

The AKPsi fraternity had posted its signs up next to the Air Force ROTC signs. Intramural teams were advertising heavily again this year to fill in their respective ranks and a new series of Encyclical lectures from the Department of Christian Studies was being advertising on bright red sheets of paper inside the cafeteria. More signs for various clubs were posted on and around the main bulletin board. Nothing much had changed in anticipation for the incoming freshmen class in the next week.

Outside the entrance to the cafeteria, there was a large bulletin board with ads for homes for rent and roommates wanted. Daniel perused the ads carefully but saw nothing that interested him. The only homes listed were for rent. He walked back out into the bright late morning sunlight.

A monument was being erected to some long forgotten alumni donor of the field house. The campus theater had a new menu board in front and daily specials were posted on a new bulletin board outside the student union. Groups of freshmen were wandering the grounds with their attentive parents and a few professors were returning after summer hiatus.

Some things were the same, some weren't. Daniel felt like a total stranger on campus. He'd been warned it might happen. Army buddies had told him that the transition from military back to civilian life might be hard. Now he was beginning to understand their comments. The students seemed younger and more immature. Even the seniors seemed younger than he'd expected them to be. It was like he was experiencing campus life for the first time but from an entirely different perspective.

After wandering through several buildings and the campus quadrangle, Daniel ended up by the football stadium. He walked through an open iron gate and climbed several rows of bleachers to watch the team practicing. Before he could sit down, a voice called out.

"Daniel, that you? Hey man, how they hanging?"

Daniel turned and saw an old classmate, long since forgotten, ambling down the stairs. He was carrying a magazine in one hand and a coke in the other.

"That you, man?" the kid asked again, "where you been? I haven't seen you on campus for a long time." He sat down next to Daniel, dropping his Playboy magazine on the bench.

Daniel extended his hand and said, "I was in the service. I just got back a week or so ago. Going to come back here as a junior."

"The service, no shit. Were you in Vietnam?"

"Yeah, I was in Vietnam."

"See any action over there?"

"Yeah, I saw some action," Daniel said, offering no more information than that.

"Did you…"

"Don't ask!" Daniel said as he picked up the magazine to change the subject.

"Yeah, that's the latest issue, September. I just got it," the kid said as he pointed to the girl on the cover. "Is she something or what?" On the cover was a blond in pigtails hoisting up her t-shirt to reveal her splendid breasts. The playboy logo was written in white ink on her well-tanned belly.

Daniel smiled, "That is one fine looking woman," he said, "The stuff we had in the Nam was pretty tame compared to this. Good old U.S. of A. and freedom of the press." He gave the magazine back and looked out at the team. "Is the team any good this year?" he asked.

"Yeah, they could be contenders," the kid answered. "We've got a lot of returning juniors and seniors. I think the coaching staff has gotten better over the years, too. The conference has expanded so we're now playing a couple of teams from the Dakotas. Big farm boys on their lines. Should be one hell of a match up." He stood up, "Daniel, I've got to be going. Nice talking to you again. I'll see you around campus."

Daniel sat in place and extended his hand. "Good seeing you, man. Take care." The kid left and Daniel realized he still didn't remember the kid's name. A couple of the football players looked up at him and waved. Daniel returned their waves, wondering if they even knew who he was.

The overhead sun was beginning to warm the metal bleachers. Daniel peeled off his shirt and leaned back. How ironic, he thought as he looked up at the clear blue sky. Less than a month ago, he had been in Vietnam, peering up through the dense foliage of a jungle canopy. His only goal had been to stay alive and keep his men alive.

Now he was sitting in the football stadium, watching those young men argue about who would get drunk that evening. Or get laid that weekend. Those young men had totally different outlooks on life than his. And he was just starting the transition between the two worlds.

The warmth of the sun was beginning to bake Daniel's skin. It felt good. He spread his arms out and leaned back until he could feel the metal seat pressing into his skin. It felt comforting. He could feel himself drifting off to sleep. The distant sounds of the football players scrimmaging began to grow faint.

"Better put your shirt on!" a voice called out, accompanied by the sound of footsteps coming up the bleachers. Daniel opened his eyes. Consciousness returned quickly and he could hear the footsteps coming closer. He looked down the bleachers and saw a young woman fast approaching him.

She was wearing a pink cotton blouse, unbuttoned more than usual and a tan skirt, shorter than most. She had on dark sunglasses that concealed her eyes. Even at that distance, Daniel guessed it was an expensive outfit; if for no other reason than the gold jewelry that hung around her neck and wrist. She had dark hair and an olive complexion. Her skin was darker, perhaps Middle-Eastern or southern European. Or it was just a very good tan. It almost looked like the girl he'd seen that first day back in town when he had ridden through Mother of the Lake College and stopped for a group of girls to cross the street from the physical education building.

She smiled and walked up to Daniel, who by now was sitting back up on the seat. Her demeanor was perky and vivacious even before she got to Daniel. "I'm serious," she said, "They have new rules here."

"Now, why is that?" Daniel asked, making no attempt to put his shirt back on.

The girl sat down next to Daniel, then turned to face him. "Something to do with the nuns on campus during the summer. You don't want to get them all aroused."

"You've got to be kidding," Daniel said.

"I'm not kidding," the girl said. "I think the priests running this place are afraid the nuns might see some half naked guy like you and get all hot and bothered." She sat back and put her feet on the seat in front of theirs.

"Seriously?" Daniel asked.

"Yes, I'm serious," she answered, "They have that rule here. When I saw you, a half naked white guy, I assumed you didn't know the rules."

"A white guy?" Daniel smiled at the woman's statement.

"Yes, white," she responded, "Not your race, your skin. I assume you're not from around here. If you had been, you'd have a tan like everyone else. Not a farmer's tan."

"I was away for awhile. I just got back," Daniel said as he slipped his t-shirt back on.

"Where are you from?" The girl asked.

"Last stop was Fort Ord. Before that, Tan Son Nhut Air Base."

"You were in Vietnam?"

"I was."

"Still in the service?" she asked.

"Just got out," Daniel responded.

"Interesting!"

"You don't have a problem with servicemen?" Daniel asked, remembering the comments he'd heard about animosity regarding the service swirling through some campuses.

"Why should I? My father was a marine and proud of it."

"Do you go to Mother of the Lake?"

"I go to both schools."

"Are you taking classes here, too?" Daniel asked her.

"I take a few classes plus I volunteer at the bookstore. It's a good way to meet other students."

"Boys, you mean?" Daniel said, with a smile.

"Maybe, I'll quit now," the girl said, peering out from under her sunglasses.

"Don't quit because of me," Daniel said, laughing.

"What makes you think...?" she realized Daniel's joke and started laughing. "My name is Claudia Weinstein," she said. "What's yours?"

"Daniel."

"Daniel what?"

"Just Daniel."

"Well, OK, just Daniel," Claudia said. "Do you want to go out for a drink sometime? Or we could start out with coffee and advance to the harder stuff later on."

Daniel had noticed that Claudia's skirt had worked its way down her thighs. He leaned in toward her and said, "Before we schedule a coffee date, you may want to put your feet down. You're distracting the football players - and the coaches."

"What? No looky looky?" Claudia laughed.

"Don't!" Daniel said suddenly becoming very serious. "It doesn't become you."

"You don't know who I am, do you?" Claudia asked.

"No, should I?"

"Most other guys would love to date me because.....oh, nothing. You know what guys can be like."

"Maybe you're hanging around with the wrong kind of guys," Daniel offered.

"Maybe that's none of your business," Claudia shot back.

"Probably isn't," Daniel answered with a shrug of his shoulders.

"Even if you could be right," Claudia said, offering a slight smile to Daniel. "You could be a welcome change from the offerings around here - if you're not scared of a strong woman."

"Not in the least," Daniel answered. "I like a woman who is sure of herself."

"Good. Do you have a car?"

"No. A motorcycle," Daniel answered.

"Well, that won't work," Claudia said. "My dad would kill me if I rode on a motorcycle. He thinks only hoods and JDs ride motorcycles. We can use my car. I don't mind … you what; the bookstore opens in three days so students can buy their books for fall semester. I'll meet you there around nine and we can go out for coffee afterwards. How does that sound?"

"Like a date," Daniel said.

"Want to?"

"Sure," Daniel answered, "I'll see you there."

Shadowy Remains

Daniel went to the Triangle Bar later that afternoon. Almost immediately upon entering, he could feel a difference in the atmosphere. Nothing in the décor had changed. The patrons looked the same. It was probably the same old stale peanut shells on the floor. The music was current and the prices hadn't gotten any higher. But, somehow, it was a different place than before.

Daniel got a schooner of beer, intending to nurse it for a while. He bellied up to the bar and stared out at the glass mirror behind the bartender. As the hours passed by, he watched the patrons come and go. He saw the musicians changing their shifts. There were still a few people in the dark corner booths playing footsie under the table. He smiled at the bartenders who were hustling the college virgins trying to sneak into the bar for their first time.

So what was different at the Triangle Bar? Not the patrons. Not the music. Not the players in this continuing West Bank soap opera. Daniel realized all of the current and conscious things that made the Triangle Bar his old favorite haunt were still there. But he wasn't.

That naïve kid, desperately searching for something in his life, had found whatever it was he was searching for. And it was no longer at the Triangle Bar. That cauldron of information, guidance, and like-minded lost souls was no longer needed to shore up Daniel's self-confidence. He no longer needed the companionship of other seekers.

Daniel noticed another thing about the bar. He felt much older than the other patrons around him. Many were college seniors or dropouts who now espoused a hippie lifestyle but seemed to be faking it in their attire and attitude. Daniel used to feel much more comfortable around hippies, druggies and working class people like himself. But now Daniel could see that they hadn't changed at all.

Daniel asked the bartender about old Zack. He was told Zack hadn't been around the bar for quite some time. No one there seemed to know what had happened to him. Best try his house Daniel was advised. So Daniel slipped off his stool, upended the last of his beer and headed out the door to find his old prophet and mentor.

At a distance, Zack's house seemed the same. But once Daniel got closer, he could see things were amiss. The screens were gone from the front porch and there was a half-filled dumpster in the side yard. Through the open porch windows, Daniel could see there were no more hammocks hanging or assorted old furniture scattered about. On one side of the porch, the windows had been boarded up and sheetrock stacked up against the wall. The front door had no screen. Daniel's best guess was that the place was being remodeled.

He stood in front of the house for a long time, just staring at it.

"Hello," a young girl said, peering out the bottom half of the front porch door.

Daniel smiled back at the girl and gave her a wave. A man stepped onto the porch and came up behind the young girl. "Can I help you?" he asked through the broken screen door.

"I used to know the guy who lives here," Daniel answered. "Or perhaps used to live here?"

The man stepped out onto the front steps. "If you're looking for old Zack, you're out of luck. He's not here anymore. He left some time ago."

"Where did he go?" Daniel asked.

"Don't rightly know," the man answered. "You're younger than most of the guys who keep wandering back here."

Daniel laughed, "Yeah, I think I was the runt of Zack's litter."

The man laughed back and said, "It's hot out here. You want a beer?"

He motioned for Daniel to come forward and sit down on the front steps. "Molly," he said to the young girl, "get us two beers, would you please, sweetheart."

"Thanks!" Daniel said, stepping forward and dropping down on the steps besides the man.

"So Zack just sort of disappeared? Any idea what happened to him?" Daniel asked.

Before the man could answer Daniel, his daughter reappeared on the porch and passed two Carling Black Label beers through the front door. She also dropped a church key in her father's lap. The man opened both beers and handed one over to Daniel. "You wouldn't believe how many young folks, some hippies; some college students have been by here looking for that old man. Trust me, you're not the first and I suspect you won't be the last. He must have had quite a draw on young people here."

"He did," Daniel answered, without giving any other information.

"The place was empty for some time. We got it from the bank. So now we're in the process of doing some major remodeling. We'll either stay here or put it back on the market."

"Just turn it around like that?"

"You might call it that," the man responded.

"How did you get it from a bank?" Daniel asked.

"Whoever bought it from this Zack fellow couldn't make the payments so the bank took it back. I found out about it and offered to buy it from the bank."

Daniel nodded. *Just another piece of the whole real estate puzzle,* he thought. There was still a lot he had to learn.

"So you have no clue as to what might have happened to Zack?" Daniel asked.

The man took a long swig of his beer. He looked out at the traffic passing in front of the house. He turned to Daniel who was still nursing his beer. "There were rumors that he either went to the West Coast or he died. He or someone else sold the house. I heard that Zack was in poor health when he left. Maybe that's why so many people assume he headed west."

"But why west?" Daniel asked. "He was from the East Coast, and Europe before that."

"If you listen to some of the hippies who've been by here, they would tell you that Zack was going to the bohemian heaven here on earth."

"San Francisco!"

"Exactly!" the man responded with a smile. "Now whether that's true or not, I have no idea."

"He used to tell me that you can't go back," Daniel offered. "I'm beginning to find out that he was right. And I've only been back a couple of days."

"Back from where?"

"Vietnam."

"And it's changed since you've been back… Or perhaps you've changed and not your surroundings."

Daniel smiled at the man's intuitive comment. He nodded as he upended his beer. "I guess I must have had this fantasy of returning on my motorcycle and I'd be welcomed back with open arms. But, of course, that didn't happen."

The man nodded silently.

"I guess I thought I could rekindle some of those wonderful moments I had here on Zack's porch. But that's turned out to be a fantasy too. You really can't go back."

"Well, I can tell you this," the man offered. "Old Zack must have had some kind of spell over this place because I've gotten a steady stream of young people for the two weeks I've been working on this place. His spirit must have been a strong one. Perhaps it's still here lingering around someplace."

"Got to go," Daniel said suddenly, handing his beer bottle back to the man. "Thanks for the beer." He got up and walked to his motorcycle. As he swung his leg over the tank, he saw the man had moved back onto the porch. Wrapping his arm around his little girl, he walked back into the house - what used to be Zack's house.

As Daniel rode off, heading toward St. Paul, he had to smile at his discovery and the wisdom old Zack had laid on him more than two years before. He realized that his salon freshman summer was now a thing of the past. It was a place now shelved in his collective memory and a place he wasn't interested in returning to. It was only back there, sitting on Zackary's front porch steps just now, that Daniel realized what a wonderful gift that old man had given him.

Campus Queen

Colleen hadn't told a lot of people about her summer trip to the Big Apple. Nevertheless, word of her adventures there had spread quickly throughout the campus. By the time she was back and settled into her dorm room, a steady stream of curious classmates had already made the trek to get her first hand analysis of the trip. Colleen was both embarrassed and pleased at the attention she and her new boyfriend were generating among sometimes jealous friends and classmates.

Rumors aside, Colleen and Bradley had become unofficial campus royalty. Bradley's Avanti was often found parked in the lot behind her dorm until late in the evening. Their excursions to local hot spots and expensive restaurants were becoming the stuff of cafeteria gossip. Colleen could not have painted a more perfect picture for herself if she had wanted to. Her senior year would indeed be the stuff of dreams. She and Bradley were together almost every day. She had one more year in school, then a great job waiting after graduation. Does life get any better than this, Colleen asked herself. A broad smile was her answer.

That was until her perfect senior year was shattered by a casual comment from one unsuspecting classmate.

Colleen and the girl were in the dorm lounge. They were both soaking up the sun that was streaming in through the large windows there. Their conversation had lapsed but it didn't matter. Both were almost dosing off. Colleen had picked up an old copy of Vogue and was perusing its worn pages.

Suddenly, out of the blue, the other girl commented, "I saw your old boyfriend on the St. Paul campus." She said it matter-of-factly, almost as an afterthought.

Colleen's head shot up. She caught herself and went back to her magazine. "Daniel?" she kept her voice was calm and controlled. "When did you see him?"

"Yesterday," the girl answered as she busied herself picking at her nails. "I was crossing the quadrangle and saw this guy ahead of me. He looked something like Daniel." She glanced over at Colleen who was still holding her magazine in front of her face. "But he had on these cargo shorts, a t-shirt and silly looking sandals. His hair was long and hanging down over his ears. At first I thought it had to be someone new on campus because of his hippie look. But as I got closer, I saw it really was Daniel." She looked over at Colleen again who was now staring at her.

"Did you talk to him?" Colleen asked, trying hard to act and sound nonchalant.

"No!" the girl laughed. "By then I was at the student union. So I just went inside. But I stopped first on the steps to watch him go by. I couldn't believe it was really him. That wasn't the Daniel I remembered from freshman year."

Colleen's expression betrayed her. She looked at the other girl with puzzlement written all over her face. "Why?" she asked. "What do you mean?"

The other girl shrugged her shoulders. "Because there was something … I don't know … something strange … something very different about him."

"What do you mean…different?" Colleen's voice betrayed her again. She tried very hard to remain calm and collected. "How was he different?"

"It was his walk; almost a kind of swagger. Well, no, it wasn't a swagger," the girl corrected herself. "It was like he was projecting this attitude or something. He was looking around like he owned the place. His stance certainly stood out from the freshmen running around and the upper classmen just strolling across the quad."

"I don't understand?" Colleen responded.

"It was the way he carried himself - he was more sure of himself. You could see that in the way he was looking around; taking in everything without breaking his stride. I never saw anyone project such confidence just by his walk."

"Oh," Colleen threw out and went back to her magazine. The ploy worked. The other girl finished with her nails and stood up. She headed for the door. "Want anything at the cafeteria?" she asked Colleen as she stood in the doorway.

"No, thanks," Colleen answered without looking up. The girl left and the room grew very still. Down the hall, Colleen could hear other girls laughing and the sound of a basketball bouncing from one dorm room to the next. She stared at the bright window in front of her. But the knot remained in her stomach long after she got up and left the room to get some fresh air outside.

Dinkytown

Daniel came back looking for Michael later that evening and found him at home. The rundown structure, masquerading as a house, was set by the railroad yards that swept through the backend of town. Michael was renting the ground floor unit from some motorcycle hoods in exchange for marijuana and whatever booze that he could steal from the liquor store where he worked.

After an obligatory beer and joint on the front steps, Daniel and Michael meandered out of the house and sat on the back stoop facing the rail yards. They watched as the train cars were being switched back and forth. It was loud and noisy and the air was full of diesel fumes and clouds of blue hues. Michael lit up another joint and offered it to Daniel. Daniel declined and nursed his beer. Michael took a deep drag and slowly let the smoke curl out his nostrils.

"Have another brew, my friend," he said. "I get all I can carry with my five-finger discount." Michael laughed and used his teeth to pry the cap off another beer.

He started to ramble on about the new power brokers in Washington like Erlichman and Haldeman. And J. Edgar Hoover whom many people believed was accusing any citizen who expressed anti-war sentiments of being a Communist sympathizer and traitor. The FBI Chief was quoted as saying that hippies were just the same; long hair meant you were a commie, a drug addict and molested young women. Daniel let Michael ramble on and said nothing to his friend.

Michael lamented the fact that the Vietnamese people were not a threat to the United States or Europe. They weren't with the French. They weren't with the Americans. Yet, he said, to fulfill an old man's agenda, President Johnson was willing to let thousands of young men continue to die.

They finished off the six-pack of Bud and Michael chain-smoked.

Wanting to change the morose tone of their conversation, Daniel told Michael that he was taking up the guitar. His attempts at learning to play hadn't panned out in Vietnam but now that he was home, Daniel intended to give it another try. That gave Michael a loud laugh.

"Stick with school and get a real job. Playing guitar will get you nowhere!"

"Michael, it's a hobby," Daniel chided him, "like your recreational drugs - only safer."

"Well, if you're going back on campus, you'd better get a haircut," Michael warned him. "If you don't, you'll be considered a commie or a hippie or a pinko freak. You might even become a target for the super-patriots on campus. Those goddamned faggots who evaded the draft but still like to beat up hippies and longhairs."

When the beer had its desired effect and they'd both grown mellow and content in their broken down Adirondack chairs, Daniel began to talk.

He reminisced about the old times he and Michael shared back in high school. He talked about the mini road trips to Duluth and the many times they'd sat under the stars and smoked a little weed and fantasized about their future.

Daniel spoke briefly about Vietnam and some of the fine men he served with. He talked about being scared and pumped at the same time. When Michael asked about the A Shau Valley, all Daniel answered was, "Yeah, it was bad." He didn't say any more and Michael let it drop.

Even in his inebriated state, Michael could sense that Daniel was hesitant to ask about her. "So you gonna ask me about her or what?"

"Colleen?"

"Of course, Colleen, who the hell else would I be talking about?"

"Oh, screw her!" Daniel spat out.

Michael looked over at his friend who was still staring up into space. He smiled and said, "You don't mean that."

Daniel didn't respond.

"Do you?"

There was another long pause between them.

"Christ, I'm screwed," Daniel lamented in a soft voice.

"Love's a bitch."

"So," Daniel began, "have you seen her since I left?"

"Well, it's not good news. I ran into her this summer at the Quick Mart. She gave me a ride home and we talked a bit. I told her everything I knew about you which wasn't that much. She listened and asked a couple of questions," Daniel waited for what seemed like ages for Michael to continue. "I couldn't read her mind so I don't know if she was just curious or still interested. Sorry."

"No matter," Daniel said. "She's moved on with her life. So have I."

"Yeah," Michael answered. "We all make mistakes, Colleen was yours." He laughed, "But that's not all."

"What?"

"I heard she's got herself some rich East Coast boyfriend. Real Ivy Leaguer. Fancy clothes, bitchin sports car and he's already secured a slot at Harvard Medical School because of his parent's connections. He's rich, my man. His granddaddy started the family business and he's been sucking on that tit ever since. The word is that they'll probably be engaged by Christmas time and married right after graduation."

"And you heard all that from?"

"Can't remember. Some of the girls I hang out with," Michael answered. "I can't remember who said it."

"Oh, Michael, you were probably blitzed when you heard that."

"Could be! But I think that's what I heard," Michael said sheepishly. "That's not all."

Daniel said nothing.

"Before that I heard she was blowing some editor at the alternative city newspaper. A real rat fink. He was leaving a long gray rope on her cheeks," Michael laughed.

"Bullshit! Michael, you're demented."

"I'm just telling you what I heard, man," Michael shot back. "Don't get pissed at me if she kept her knees locked tight when she was with you."

"She's better than that!"

"Meaning what?"

"Colleen's not that kind of girl," Daniel said. "That's all. She's too classy."

"So how long has it been since you two saw one another?" Michael asked. "What, two years or more? Right? Things change, my friend. People change. That's more than enough time for folks to forget about one another. New people come into their lives."

"Michael, the great philosopher!"

"I'm just saying…."

"Besides," Daniel interjected, "I was just asking, that's all. I've already met someone who is different but nice and we seemed to hit it off right away. She's pretty hot. It's like she's got this sexuality thing going that oozes from her pores. Damn near incendiary. Different and kind of scary at the same time."

"Who's that?"

"I met her in the football stadium and we went out for coffee. She's got money by the way that she dresses but she's not snotty. Not too snotty anyway. She's pretty cool. Her name is Claudia..."

"Ha," Michael burst out laughing. "Claudia Weinstein - from Lake Minnetonka, am I right?"

"Yeah, that's her name...."

"Oh, man, she's a JAP," Michael said. "One hot tail I heard."

"What are you talking about?" Daniel said, "She's not a ...."

"Hell, man, Claudia is well known on both campuses. She's a Jewish American Princess, a JAP. Son, you just hit the mother lode. The girl's got a ton of money. A trust fund to die for. New big-ass Pontiac two-door hardtop. Her old man's got a yacht the size of Manhattan on Lake Minnetonka. Shit, she's got it all except a man in her life and between her legs. Looks like you may be her new man. Dude, you just scored a home run."

"Michael, you do have to cut back on that shit you're smoking, man. It's doing a number on your brain. Where do you hear all this stuff?"

"Listen, Mr. 'I Know Women,' you don't know this one very well. There are rumors about her that you wouldn't believe. I mean...."

A scowl appeared on Daniel's face.

Michael just shrugged his shoulders. "Well anyway, if Mad Mitch likes you, you could be in like Flynn for your career. The man's considered a genius on the street. He's a stockbroker in downtown Minneapolis. He runs one of the largest brokerage firms in town. Making millions ... billions of dollars a year. So what's a girl like Claudia doing with a gentile like you?"

"I don't know, Michael," Daniel answered smiling, "maybe she's desperate. Or maybe, just maybe she sees me for the handsome, intelligent ambitious young man that I am."

"Or maybe she's hoping you're long in the pants even if you're not black," Michael laughed.

Daniel stood up, shaking his head at Michael. "Good bye, my friend. You need to get sober. And stay that way."

"I'm just saying..."

"And if you don't get sober and stay that way, I'm going to drag your sorry ass to the V.A. and have them shit kick some sense back into you."

Michael stumbled to his feet and embraced Daniel. They hugged each other as only old soldiers could do. Daniel spoke to Michael with their faces only inches apart. “I mean it, dude. You need to get your shit together and soon or I’m taking you to the V.A., capische?”

“Yeah,” Michael answered reluctantly, “Capische.”

Senior Year: 1969-1970

'A Woman' Revisited

Daniel's new home was California-style bungalow situated on a quiet street about halfway between both campuses. It was in Mac-Groveland, a middle class neighborhood occupied mainly by older couples and a lot of young families. Tree-lined boulevards brought shade to the front yards where kids ran through sprinklers and neighbors gathered to share recipes and gossip.

The sad house was showing its age and a lot of neglect. Chipped and faded paint made it seem much older than it really was. The unkempt front yard matched the weeds and tall grasses bordering the house. A broken shutter lay on its side. The front porch had several missing screens that brought attention to their neglect. For the casual onlooker, it was a total wreck. For someone with Daniel's keen eye, it was a jewel in disguise.

Negotiations with the owner took all afternoon and a six pack of beer. But by early evening, Daniel had purchased the house on a CD, carried by the owner. The old man also agreed to pay all closing costs and do the title search. By the next morning, Daniel woke up in the shell of his new home, feeling more alive than he had in years.

By that afternoon there were two signs prominently displayed on bulletin boards at both campuses. Both read: 'Rooms available in quiet home. Art, design or architecture students preferred.' By the next morning, Daniel was waiting for his first potential renters to come knocking on his door.

They came in drips and drabs, a motley assortment of college students and a few dropouts trying to pass muster. Daniel wasn't impressed. None of them seemed suited for the kind of roommates Daniel had envisioned for his first home.

Three girls rode up in a battered late fifties Ford Fairlane. They piled out and approached Daniel with a collective wave and smile on each of their faces. *A possibility,* Daniel thought as they strolled up the sidewalk and deposited themselves around the front steps where Daniel was sitting.

They had their speech all planned but Daniel cut them short. He asked where they went to college. All three of them went to Mother of the Lake College. Each was a senior and wanted out of the dorms. Emily and Katie would room together. Sally was Emily's twin sister but she wanted her own room.

After showing them the house, Daniel sat on the porch as the three girls chatted amongst themselves on the curb. Within minutes they came back and announced that the house was perfect for them.

Daniel smiled a bit sheepishly and said. "That's great, girls, but there's just one problem."

"What's that?" They asked in unison.

"You probably noticed there wasn't any furniture inside. That's because I don't have any. So if you want to move in, you'll have to bring all your own furniture. Do you have stuff you can move from the dorm?"

"Oh, that's no problem," Emily nodded at Katie. "We both furnished our dorm rooms for the last three years. We're experts at finding good furniture, really cheap. Goodwill, Salvation Army, and a couple of thrift shops on University Avenue. If you pay, we'll furnish. How does that sound?" they asked Daniel.

"And if I paid you to help me paint the interior of the house, would that be something you'd consider?"

"When do we start?" all three answered in unison.

Standing up, Daniel announced. "It looks like I've got three new roommates. Come on in. I've got lemonade in the fridge and the porch chairs I sort of borrowed from my Mom's back deck." The girls followed Daniel into the porch, congratulating themselves on their great find.

Before school started, Daniel managed to get the front porch cleaned up, painted and its broken window screens repaired or replaced. The attic now housed his small twin bed, an end table and a dresser in one corner alcove. The kitchen cupboards were refinished and a new sink installed. The girls had set up their bedrooms, Emily and Katie in one and Sally in the second bedroom.

The house was slowly taking shape. In the basement, the old hot water boiler was tuned up and bled to find any leaks before winter set in. The decorating was almost complete and it was beginning to feel like home for Daniel…for the first time in his life.

One Saturday, after spending most of the day cleaning out his garage, Daniel saw in the newspaper that the Grandview Theater was doing a rerun of the French film classic A Man and A Woman. It was a one-time showing that evening.

He called Claudia and talked her into going. She wasn't really into foreign films but agreed to go only because Daniel insisted she would love it. Claudia hinted that she expected to be rewarded afterwards.

Claudia picked Daniel up in her mother's new BMW. The shiny black convertible would soon be replaced by a newer Thunderbird, Claudia explained, just as soon as her parents returned from Las Vegas. Daniel sank into the custom leather seats and leaned back. *Oh, the life of the wealthy, he* thought. He looked over at Claudia who returned his stare with a smile. Daniel knew exactly what she was expecting for dragging her to a film that had subtitles.

Even though he and Claudia had gone on several dates, their relationship was still slowly evolving. She was testing his virility on every date and he was challenging her intellectual capacity for entertainment beyond her normal activities. Daniel wanted to introduce Claudia to this part of his new life. His love of foreign films had grown exponentially during his time in the service. Now Daniel was anxious to return to one of his loves of that freshman summer. He hoped Claudia would become as enraptured with foreign films as he was.

Daniel couldn't help but reflect back to the first time he saw A Man and A Woman with Colleen two years earlier. She had been just as reluctant to go as Claudia was now. Daniel had already seen the film twice before talking Colleen into seeing it with him for a third time. He smiled as he thought about how he was struck by the many nuances of the film, its music, acting, storyline, French style and ambiance. He had been truly smitten by that film. And still was.

Claudia pulled into the parking lot and swore. The lot was full. Cars filled in every parking space and were even spilling out onto the side streets. Daniel calmed her down. He guided her to a small semi-secluded spot behind the paint store next door.

Climbing out of her car, Daniel assured Claudia it was safe to park there. "I know the owner," he said. "I should, after all the paint I've bought from him." Draping his arm around Claudia's shoulder, Daniel walked her to the theater around the corner. The Grandview was lit up with its Art Deco marquee and large lettering which read A Man and A Woman one showing only at 8 pm.

The crowd was sparse out on the sidewalk but packed inside the lobby.

"Edge toward the doors and I'll get us some popcorn," Daniel told Claudia after handing her the tickets. Claudia started to maneuver her way through the milling crowd. "Hurry," she cautioned him, "before all the seats are taken."

Daniel twisted and turned his way around the packed bodies until he found himself on the edge of the refreshment stand. Leaning over the warm glass, he ordered his popcorn. *This is just what I did back then too,* he thought. *I ordered Colleen's favorite flavored popcorn and had her grab our seats.*

The lobby hadn't changed its Art Deco interior since the theater was built in the late 40's. Daniel could sense that same old relaxed atmosphere there. He loved it. The place looked the same. It even smelled the same. He was beginning to feel just as he had two years earlier when he had gone there to see some of the French New Wave films. This time, the feeling was even better for Daniel.

The teen attendant gave Daniel his popcorn. Daniel turned to head for his seats.

As he started to turn around, Daniel stepped to within inches of Colleen's face. Their eyes widened and they both quickly stepped back, startled by their close encounter.

Daniel's mind suddenly shut down. It went blank. He couldn't hear a thing. There was an eerie buzzing sound even though the crowd was large and boisterous. Daniel stood frozen like a statue, mesmerized by this woman standing just a few feet away from him. Colleen was even more stunning than he had remembered her during all those dark days and nights back in Vietnam.

She was dressed in a tweed skirt and soft cream-colored sweater. It accented her high firm breasts and her auburn hair that swept down her shoulders. She had on light makeup that highlighted her deep blue eyes and welcoming smile. She also looked more mature and self-confident.

All those feelings that Daniel had buried two and a half years earlier came crashing back, cascading over his consciousness and hitting him like a sucker punch to the gut. He could see and feel her presence just inches away. He could smell her perfume and with it an instinctive urge to wrap his arms around her like before and hold her close.

Colleen was smiling at him. Strangely, she didn't seem surprised to see him there. Not even after all that time apart. There was some guy standing right behind her; probably her pre-med boyfriend.

Daniel was speechless and numb, still unable to respond when Colleen started to talk.

"Hello, Daniel, I heard you were back in town."

Daniel was gripped by emotions that held him like a vice. The knot in his stomach got tighter and tighter. Colleen was with someone else. She was now spoken for. It really was over between them.

"Hello, Colleen," was all that Daniel could stammer at that moment.

"When did you get back in town?"

"Late this summer," Daniel managed to get out.

"That's what I thought," Colleen said. She started to turn around, to introduce the guy behind her when Claudia walked up behind Daniel.

Claudia wrapped her arm around Daniel's arm. She threw a casual "Hi," toward Colleen and started to pull Daniel away. "Honey, we need to go," Claudia said, smiling back at Colleen with possessive eyes as if to say, "This is my man, stay away."

Claudia began to guide a reluctant Daniel toward the doors. As he started to walk away, Daniel glanced back and saw Colleen and her boyfriend hurriedly walking toward the front doors.

"Who was that?" Claudia asked as she and Daniel sat down in the theater.

"Just somebody I used to know … just an old acquaintance."

"She's beautiful," Claudia said, grabbing a handful of popcorn. "Were you two serious?"

"I was. She wasn't." Daniel answered with finality in his voice. "End of story."

"Are you sure?" Claudia asked as she passed the tub of popcorn back to Daniel.

"I'm sure!" Daniel said as he leaned over and kissed her. He put his hand on her knee. Claudia smiled back and wrapped her hand on top of Daniel's. She slowly guided it between her legs until she was squeezing it high up between her thighs.

Chance Encounter

Colleen was meandering down the hallway lost in her thoughts. The encounter with Daniel that evening had surprised, even shocked her. But she wasn't sure just why. Mrs. O'Reilly, the effervescent dorm mother, was talking to some other girls in an alcove by the bathrooms. Colleen stopped to eavesdrop for a moment.

As always, the girls' conversations consisted of the usual dilemmas: What to wear to the next dance? Who was really serious and would probably be engaged by year's end? Was the school really going to implement a J-term and what did it entail?

Colleen half-listened to the conversation and let her mind wander as the bantering went back and forth. The other girls started to disperse and Colleen was left standing across from Mrs. O'Reilly.

"Did you go to the movies?" She asked Colleen.

"We didn't stick around long enough to see it," Colleen explained. "I still have homework to do."

"Homework on a Saturday night. Isn't that a little unusual even for a straight A student such as yourself?"

"I have a lot of work to do," Colleen answered defensively. "Besides, I didn't want to see the film anyway. I'd already seen it years ago. I don't know why I went there in the first place."

Mrs. O'Reilly seemed perplexed by Colleen's answer. "So why would you want to see it for a second time?" she asked.

"A friend of mine talked me into seeing it back then. I thought I might experience it from a different perspective this time around … without him."

"But you said you didn't stay to see it?"

"No. Instead I ran into that old acquaintance at the theater; the same boy who took me to see the film in the first place."

"Did you talk to him?"

"No, I just said hi and left. He was with someone else."

Mrs. O'Reilly smiled, "I don't want to pry Colleen; but it sounds as if you almost expected to see him there, but when you did see him you didn't want to talk to him. Doesn't that sound a bit strange?"

Colleen answered defensively, "I know…I don't know why I did that. We just exchanged hellos and I decided to leave the theater instead of staying for the film. It was stirring up too many memories, I guess."

"I'm surprised you didn't at least want to talk to him if you hadn't seen him for such a long time."

"I couldn't," Colleen answered in a voice that suddenly dropped to almost a whisper.

"I don't understand," Mrs. O'Reilly said.

"It was his eyes."

"His eyes?"

Colleen looked at the dorm mother with perplexity written all over her face. "They were sad and empty…"

Mrs. O'Reilly waited for Colleen to continue, "…and he seemed so different."

"How was he different?"

"The last time I saw Daniel we were both kids. He's not a kid anymore."

"But Colleen, you've grown. You've matured."

"Not like him."

"I'm afraid I don't understand."

"He stood tall and confident like I've never seen him before. And yet he was distant …even as he stood just a few feet away from me." Colleen looked away for a moment, lost in thought. "It confused and even scared me a bit so I left right away. I suddenly had feelings I've never felt before with another person. It was very unsettling and uncomfortable."

A pensive look had invaded her eyes.

"Yes?" the dorm mother said.

Colleen forced out a weak smile, "And yet I felt strangely connected with him on some inexplicable level."

Mrs. O'Reilly smiled but said nothing.

"Does that make any sense?" Colleen asked.

"No," Mrs. O'Reilly answered. "But sometimes encounters like that don't make any sense at first. Not until you've had a chance to think about them and maybe mull over what those feelings were that you felt back then."

"But why would I bother?" Colleen asked herself out loud. "We're not even friends anymore."

"Why did you bring it up in the first place?"

"I don't really know," Colleen admitted.

Mrs. O'Reilly smiled at Colleen and gave her a quick hug. "Well, maybe," she began, "you should start there. Ask yourself why it's an issue…even though it really isn't."

Welcome Back to Campus

The Welcome Back to Campus weekend was an annual event jointly sponsored by the fraternities and sororities on both campuses. Working together, the various frat and sorority houses all sponsored their open houses on the same Saturday night in September.

This was hardly the kind of place Daniel expected to find himself several weeks into the fall semester. But it was an old high school buddy who had insisted Daniel should be at their house. He promised Daniel there would be no harassment, no questions about Vietnam and he reassured him that veterans were always welcome there.

At first, Daniel was reticent to attend. He had his studies. Work on the house was taking more time than he had anticipated and he frankly wasn't in the mood to mingle with most of the college crowd that would be there.

It was only after Michael's assurance that he would go along, that Daniel agreed to attend. Michael had chided him on that afternoon about forgetting his past and moving on with his life.

"Don't be a pussy, man," Michael hassled Daniel. "Colleen won't be there. It's not her scene. Besides, going to a couple of those parties will help get her off your mind. Meet some new chicks. Maybe you'll even get laid if you're lucky. Of course, don't let Claudia find out." Michael laughed at himself.

"Michael, I'm not looking to get laid," Daniel answered back, "and I'm not worried about what Claudia might say. She sees herself as above the frat and sorority crowd. I expect she'll either be at the racetrack or some club downtown."

But Daniel's friend just laughed and tossed another beer at him. They settled down into Michael's ratty torn chairs on his back steps, watching the trains roll down the tracks across the street.

Michael started babbling on about the obvious corrupt deals that Vice President Spiro Agnew was engaged in. He knew that because his friend in D.C. said it was the talk of the town. Daniel turned the conversation around to music. That seemed to get Michael off of the sad state of government affairs and on to something lighter. They drank beer all afternoon and by early evening Michael had gotten so whacked that he was in no shape to leave his chair.

So Daniel reluctantly went by himself. He was fairly confidant Colleen's new boyfriend wasn't a member of this particular fraternity so it was doubtful she would be there. With that self-assurance and liquor induced self-confidence, Daniel rode to the house and parked across the street.

Already there were scores of students passing in and out of the front door. Loud music blasted through the closed windows and several drunks were already being escorted out of the party. Once inside, he could feel the house was already cooking from so many bodies sandwiched in every room. They spilled out the back steps and onto the patio of the old Four Square.

Dress was casual with a leaning toward the standard khaki and madras shirts. Daniel mingled for a while, exchanging greetings with a couple of long forgotten acquaintances from high school.

He had a couple more beers but could never get into the partying scene. He enjoyed the music but the sophomoric antics of most of the students turned him off. The making out and assorted degrees of groping and foreplay seemed juvenile. What was once a sought-after refuge from the realities of college life was now just a sad joke.

Later that evening, after a couple more of hours of listening and watching, Daniel wandered upstairs. Word had come filtering down that the second floor was fairly quiet. When he crested the landing, Daniel could hear moans and giggling coming from several closed bedroom doors. The seduction phase of the party had begun.

Only the rooftop patio seemed relatively uninhabited. There were a few students making out on the chairs scattered about the blacktop roof. One drunk was asleep on the gravel, snoring loudly. Daniel settled in with several pledges on a broken down sofa back in one corner. A cooler was dragged out from behind the sofa. Beers were passed around.

The pledges wanted to talk war but Daniel politely deferred to other subjects like the Minnesota Vikings and their chances at the playoffs later in the fall. When one of the pledges insisted on talking to Daniel about his experiences in Vietnam, Daniel simply told the youngster that he'd killed a lot of people and sometimes he couldn't get a handle on his urge to kill again. His face was deadpan as he spoke and registered no emotion at all. That was enough to send the pledges scurrying back downstairs, among safer, saner people.

During the course of the evening, several women had come on to Daniel. Their message was straight and to the point. They loved military men and would be willing to show their undying patriotism if Daniel was interested. He smiled and said he wasn't.

One woman in particular had come back several times after finding Daniel alone on the rooftop. She made vague references to his relationship with Colleen and asked if they were an item again. Daniel assured her that they were not. And Claudia? Daniel answered that they were simply friends. That admission brought the girl's skirt up several inches higher and a very visible relaxation to her body. But it did her no good. Daniel wasn't interested. She left in a huff and eventually Daniel was left alone to gaze at the star-filled sky.

Finding the footprints of birds, Daniel smiled. That was his first date with Colleen - a lifetime away from this ratty old sofa on some fraternity rooftop.

Shit, how life gets confusing at times, he thought.

Daniel finished off the bottle and let the beer dribble out between his lips. He wiped his mouth and let out a loud belch. He laughed at himself; drunk again. *Seems to be a recurring theme with your sorry ass*, he thought.

Daniel looked up at the night sky again. The booze was working its magic. He could feel himself starting to drift off. His body went slack and a heaviness descended upon him.

But this time it was different.

> The air stunk with the smell of rotting vegetation. Daniel's ears were being bombarded by a crescendo of insects buzzing around his head. He could feel his clammy skin sticking to his shirtsleeves. He backhanded the sweat off his face but it kept coming. Humidity hung thick in the air, sucking the breath out of the small group of camouflaged men as they cautiously moved through the jungle
>
> There was a clearing ahead. Moonlight illuminated the village grounds that lay just beyond the elephant grass. Many of the Gooks had already scattered by the time Daniel and his team entered the compound. Like ghosts with cammie faces, they moved silently among the thatched huts until they found the right one. The villagers knew why Daniel and his Hawkeyes were there. The target was quickly found and dragged out of his hut.
>
> The dink was crying, his rail-thin body shaking uncontrollably. Even in the darkness, Daniel could see his yellow teeth chattering as he blubbered something in Vietnamese. A puddle formed at his feet. The old man was pissing in his pants.
>
> "Didi. Didi Mau," the village elder stuttered in fear.
>
> "Not likely, old man," said a black-faced devil standing next to Daniel.
>
> "Off him," another voice whispered into Daniel's ear.
>
> Daniel pressed the revolver barrel against the old man's temple.
>
> "Now!"
>
> Daniel hesitated.
>
> "Fuck, man. Remember what they did to Tennessee."
>
> One quick shot. A muffled crack in the still night air. The old man slumped over. A death card, the ace of spades, with a skull and crossbones in its center, was dropped on his bloody

forehead.

The group quickly left the compound. As they moved effortlessly through the tall grass and back into the enveloping jungle, the commander radioed back to base.

"Get Intruder One on the horn. Mission accomplished."

They were running back through the jungle. Twenty clicks to a rendezvous point and the team would be but a frightening memory to the villagers. Pickup at dawn and another successful mission completed. Another target was already scheduled for the day after tomorrow.

Daniel opened his eyes. He blinked away the salty sweat that had run down between his eyes and nose. He was alone on the rooftop, still sweating and feeling the chill of a nighttime breeze on his damp shirt. He was safe, except for his thoughts and those recurring dreams. The nightmare was gone.

Daniel was OK now. He shook his head and blinked his eyes. The thoughts had subsided. Usually they came in the middle of night. Not when he was awake. *Too much booze,* Daniel thought. Drunk or sober, he couldn't stop the images; those thoughts permeating his brain.

Beer bottles had piled up around his knees so Daniel nudged his leg up against the pile and pushed them alongside the sofa. As he did so, he noticed several people standing in the doorway. Two of them stepped out onto the patio. Even in the darkness, Daniel could make out the silhouettes of a man and a woman.

Daniel tried to focus on the newcomers but the darkness and his own intoxication prevented him from seeing clearly. He still couldn't get a stable picture of his new company. They stood just beyond the doorway, talking for a short while. The man turned and went back inside. The woman stood there briefly then began walking toward Daniel's sofa. He watched her approach, wondering if he was about to be accosted once again by another amorous sorority hound.

Colleen hadn't recognized Daniel when she first stepped out onto the rooftop patio. She had been downstairs for a long time but the blue haze and her blinking eyes pushed her and Bradley upstairs. Several of Brad's friends accompanied them to the rooftop patio.

Several gin and tonics and her own lack of sleep had combined to slow Colleen's reflexes and alertness. When Bradley and his friends insisted on going back downstairs to shoot some pool, Colleen excused herself to stay upstairs and get some fresh air. It was only then that she recognized the figure slumped back on the sofa. It was Daniel, obviously very intoxicated.

As she approached the sofa, Daniel looked up. He seemed to be staring at her, blinking his eyes as if to focus them. He straightened himself out, pretending to be sober or a poor semblance of it. He had a light growth of beard and longish hair. He wore old tattered blue jeans and black work boots. His plaid work shirt had seen better days. It was hardly the clothes someone would wear to a fraternity party if he intended to impress. *Obviously, Daniel didn't care what he looked like,* Colleen thought. Nothing had changed about him after all. The same old pretend hippie. *Poor Daniel,* she thought. It wasn't revulsion that Colleen felt but rather a profound sense of sadness for this man who had wanted so desperately to fit in and succeed in college.

Colleen sat down at the far end of the sofa. She turned to face Daniel on the other end. Her legs were properly locked together and her hands rested on her knees. Two thumbs held her skirt in place.

"How are you, Daniel?" she asked, trying hard to hide any tone in her voice.

The shock of seeing Colleen walking toward him had sobered Daniel up pretty quickly. While he couldn't control the amount of booze coursing through his body, Daniel could try to control what came out of his mouth. Slow and cautious was the name of the game. The less he said, Daniel reasoned, the less chance he'd have to make a fool of himself. He turned to face Colleen and managed to muster up a smile he hoped would pass for real.

"Good, I guess," he mumbled, trying to choose his words so he didn't sound like a complete idiot. His mind was spinning. *What the hell is she doing there? Why'd she have to show up now, after all this time?* She was talking but he wasn't hearing her.

Colleen talked about nothing in particular, anything safe that might help her slip into her real agenda. There were polite pleasantries about school starting again, Colleen's focus on her journalism classes and Peggy leaving school.

Daniel let her ramble on and didn't say a word. He faked his attentive look and worried that she might ask him a question or two. It was a safe, bland, empty conversation that held no meaning for either one of them. And they both knew it.

Just as Colleen was about to launch into a litany of more nervous chatter, Daniel cut her off.

"So was that your boyfriend?" he asked.

Colleen was taken aback for a moment. Daniel's voice was clear and resonated with control. He sounded perfectly sober. Perhaps she'd been wrong. Maybe he wasn't drunk but just lost in thought about something.

"Yes, that's Bradley," she answered. "He's a pre-med major. He's going to become a doctor."

"Nice."

Daniel's tone gave him away.

"You don't have to be sarcastic, Daniel," Colleen said.

"Colleen," Daniel came back quickly as he straightened himself up on the sofa. "I wasn't being sarcastic. I'm glad you've found someone nice." Daniel was now feeling a little more in control. He straightened himself up again until he was sitting upright on the worn sofa. "So does he take you to all those nice places that we never went to?"

"Like?"

"Oh, I don't know," Daniel answered with a smile. "We didn't go to a lot of nice places when we were dating."

"Yes, to answer your question. We do like to go to the Walker Art Center, the Minneapolis Institute of Art and the Guthrie for plays. Yes, we do a lot of that sort of thing."

"So, are you serious about this guy?"

"What do you mean, serious?"

"Oh, come on Colleen," Daniel shot back, "it's me. We can at least be civil to one another." Daniel was feeling a little more confident. His words didn't sound so slurred anymore. He thought his conversation had at least a faint resemblance of sobriety.

"I am being civil, Daniel. It's just that your question is rather personal."

"So, do I take that as an "I don't know?" Daniel felt he had her on the run.

"No, you can't take it that way," Colleen snapped back. "Yes, you could say we are an item. We've been dating for some time now and we really like one another. Brad is a wonderful guy and any girl would be thrilled to have him."

Daniel opened his mouth for a comeback. He could really nail her ass this time. As quickly as he opened his mouth for a retort, he shut it and said nothing. *Shit,* Daniel thought, *I almost blew it.*

"Thank you, Daniel. See, even if you're not sober, you still have a sense of decorum. I appreciate that."

Daniel tried to mentally regroup and try another approach. "Colleen, I think it's great that you've found someone. I am happy for you. Really."

"What about yourself? Are you serious about Claudia Weinstein?"

"Serious? No. We're just dating."

"That's not what I heard."

"Rumors, that's what you heard!" Daniel responded very quickly before he knew what he was saying.

Colleen leaned forward. Her eyes furrowed a bit and she asked softly, "Are you happy, Daniel? When we last saw one another before you left for the service, you were a pretty sad individual. Are you better now?"

For a moment, Daniel was taken aback by the sincerity of Colleen's question. He answered slowly, "Well, I'm back in school. I've got a house. I'm trying to use my creativity and eventually I'll decide what career track to follow." A smile came to his face, "Yeah, things are working out pretty well, you could say."

"You don't seem to have changed a lot," Colleen observed, looking at his outfit.

Daniel couldn't help but laugh, "You mean the same old beard, ratty clothes, beer in my hand and still looking like a hippie?"

Colleen was flustered. Daniel couldn't read her.

"I would hope it goes deeper than that, Daniel. I hope your gentleness and kindness have stayed the same. And your ambition," Colleen took a deep breath, "But I must warn you. Father Rollins won't tolerate your beard or scruffy looking clothes. He's a stickler for neatness and personal grooming. If you still want to dress like a hippie, you'll have to face the consequences."

"Thanks for the advice," Daniel answered in a monotone voice. "I've already met old chrome dome … again. The man is irrelevant."

"I'm serious, Daniel," Colleen stated emphatically. "When you're on his campus, you have to live by his rules." She hesitated to go the next step. "You once told me you didn't want to end up a drunk like your father."

"Meaning what?"

"I heard you were back hanging out at the Triangle Bar."

"Heard from whom?" Daniel asked defensively.

Before she could answer, Colleen saw Bradley suddenly appear in the doorway of the patio. Changing the subject, she stood up as Bradley started to approach them.

"I talked to Michael before school started," Colleen began. "He was in pretty rough shape. Have you seen him since you got back?"

"Yeah, a couple of times," Daniel answered, carefully getting to his feet and watching his balance as he did so. "I've talked to him about his problems. We're working on it."

Colleen started to turn toward Bradley. She lifted her hand to wave at him. She didn't see Daniel take a deep breath before he spoke.

"I thought I needed you in my life to make me whole," Daniel suddenly blurted out. "I don't need that from you anymore."

Colleen turned to face Daniel. Her mouth was open. She seemed confused.

"I had to lose you to find myself … Guess I should thank you for that."

Colleen was startled by Daniel's statement. His face was expressionless. Neither anger nor smugness was planted there. He'd made a statement of fact and he was done. Now he was just standing there, staring at her.

Bradley walked up to Colleen as Daniel gingerly extended his hand. They shook hands and Bradley put his arm around Colleen's shoulder. "We have to go," he said, "I've got some friends I want you to meet." He turned to Daniel. "Nice meeting you again," he said without meaning a word of it. Together he and Colleen turned and walked away, leaving Daniel to wobble back and forth on his unsteady feet.

Bradley's friends were nonexistent by the time he and Colleen got to the nearly deserted living room. Colleen presumed her boyfriend just wanted her back downstairs with his crowd.

"Get me a Seven-Up, will you, dear," Colleen said to Bradley. As Bradley exited the room, Colleen tried to understand what had just happened between her and Daniel.

Colleen had assumed that whenever she encountered Daniel for a second time she would be able to talk to him as she had before. She hoped it would be like freshman year when they would be very frank with one another about their deepest feelings. She thought she could engage in an honest conversation with Daniel and bring up the letter and her regrets about it.

Instead, she had just exchanged vapid, surface scratches of dialogue instead of any meaningful conversation. Daniel had been reserved, guarded and noncommittal. He wasn't opening up as he had in the past.

There seemed to be a wall built up around Daniel now. A facade Colleen couldn't see through and one he wasn't about to let down. That bothered Colleen. Not because Daniel was trying to hurt her feelings. This time he didn't seem to care…for her or anything else.

That man on the sofa was an enigma. It was not the same Daniel who'd left her two and a half years earlier. This was someone entirely different. Michael had been right. Daniel had changed. Whatever he and Colleen might have once had no longer existed. Not for him. And therefore, not for her.

Yet quite strangely, Colleen still felt a connection with Daniel. The words they had tossed back and forth meant little to nothing in terms of real emotions expressed. Yet his eyes, unfocused at times, still conveyed meaning to her.

His words said one thing. And yet, his eyes said something entirely different. Which was she to believe?

Colleen was sitting in a corner chair in the living room when she saw Daniel leave shortly afterwards. He stumbled out the front door, trying hard to hide his drunkenness. He never looked back.

A little while later, a girl walked up to Colleen as she stood on the curb waiting for Brad to get the car. The girl commented, "Same old Daniel except for the beard."

Colleen looked at the girl and answered, "No, he's changed."

"What do you mean?"

"I can see it in his eyes," Colleen answered.

"I don't understand," the girl said. "Besides he was drunk!"

Colleen turned and gave the girl a knowing, self-assured look and said, "That's because you don't know him the way I do … The way I used to."

As quickly, Colleen turned and slipped into Bradley's car and was gone.

Driven

Thanksgiving was always a very special time at the Fitzpatrick house. It was the perfect home setting for Colleen's mother, Mary Rose. The grand dame of Pill Hill loved that particular holiday and always over-decorated with festive flowers, pumpkins and colorful dried leaves. It was just a preamble to her over-the-top decorating the entire house for Christmas.

As Colleen entered the kitchen, her mother was hard at work, applying a dollop of whipping cream to each cut piece of pie. She glanced up from her work and said, "Colleen, you're late again. I thought you'd be home hours ago."

"Sorry, Mom," Colleen said as she dropped her overnight bag on a chair and walked up to the kitchen island. "I had to take Bradley to the airport. His parents were going to come out to get him but they decided to go to Bermuda instead."

"You should have brought him here," her mother answered, glancing up again from her pies. "We want to meet your young man. Why didn't you bring him home with you, darling?"

"Mom, I explained, he had to go home. Even though his parents are in Bermuda for the holidays, Bradley still has to attend a lot of company functions in the city and social gatherings on Long Island. It's his job to be stand-in for his parents or their firm whenever they're out of town. He's been doing that for years."

"Well, all the same, it would have been nice to meet him," her mother said as she scooped up two pieces of pie and handed them to Colleen. "Put them on the serving table and get washed up. We'll eat in just a couple of minutes as soon as your father gets home."

By the time Colleen had hauled her bag upstairs and freshened up, Arthur Fitzpatrick was home and sitting at the dinner table. Colleen gave him a quick kiss on the cheek and took her place at the table. Same place as always. Twenty years at the same table. Twenty years in the same chair.

"Darling, how is school coming along?" her father asked as he folded a napkin on his lap. He didn't look up at he started carving the turkey. Colleen looked over at him and smiled. Same ritual as always, she thought. Don't couples ever get tired of the same routines year in and year out? Apparently not, since her dad seemed happy in his cutting and slashing of the bird on the platter.

"It's going well, dad," Colleen answered him. "Not much longer and I'll be a college graduate and off to the real world of work. I can't wait. I've got several more interviews lined up. A couple of them look very promising."

Without looking up from his concentrated carving, Arthur Fitzpatrick said, "Your mother tells me that your friend, Bradley, won't be joining us. I guess I thought…."

"So did mom. Sorry to disappoint you too, dad, but he's back on the East Coast for the holidays."

"Mom said his parents usually come out to get him? Is that right?"

"Yes, they usually just fly out and pick him up."

"Couldn't he just fly back himself?"

"Dad," Colleen gave her father a disapproving look, "they have their own plane. They fly out to pick Bradley up so they can have some quality time before all of their social events back in New York. They did that when he was in boarding school in New Hampshire, too."

"Their own plane? They have their own airplane?" Mary Rose commented, shooting a look to her husband. Her father looked up at

Colleen for the first time since he started his carving. "Really?" he said.

"It's no big deal, mother. Believe me," Colleen began to explain. "I mean, he's not like most of those uber-rich kids on campus. Not at all. He's nice and kind and … he's just a nice guy."

"I agree with your mother," her father began. "We would have loved to have met him."

Colleen reached over and put her hand on her dad's arm. She gave him a reassuring smile. "You'll have your chance during parent's weekend," she said. "It isn't that far away now."

"So what else is happening on campus?" her father chimed in as he passed the heaping plate of carved turkey to Colleen.

"Oh, just the usual stuff," Colleen said as she put two pieces of turkey on her plate and passed the platter to her mother. "You know, fall festivals, soccer and lacrosse. We've had a number of really outstanding speakers at our all campus lectures."

Her parents were glancing up at Colleen as she spoke. But their real concentration was on the meal. That was typical of most holiday meals at the Fitzpatrick's home. *Now is as good a time as any,* Colleen thought. "I saw Daniel a couple of times this semester. You remember him. He was that boy I dated freshman year. He went into the service. He's back now at St. Paul's. He's changed a lot after being in Vietnam."

Stone-cold silence greeted her. Both parents slowly looked up at Colleen but didn't say a word. Her mother spoke up, "You're not seeing him anymore, are you?"

"No, mother! I'm not. I just said I saw him a couple of times…"

"Because you know, dear, now that you're with Bradley…"

"Mother, please!" Colleen answered. "I just ran into Daniel by accident a couple of times. That's all."

"Are you sure it was an accident?"

"Yes, mother, I'm sure!" Colleen answered, trying hard to control the tone of her voice. "Please, let's change the subject, can we?"

Arthur Fitzpatrick cleared his throat and spoke, "What your mother is trying to say, dear, is that we just want what's best for you. Bradley seems like a very nice young man. Good family. Solid credentials. Great future ahead of him. He would fit into this family very nicely."

Although she knew it was coming, Colleen was still having a hard time handling her parent's predictable reaction to any mention of Daniel. Their over-reaction was par for the course, but still irritating. But Colleen, as a product of Arthur Fitzpatrick, wasn't about to back down from a challenge.

"What does that mean, Dad?" Colleen asked in a monotone voice at first. "That Bradley's parents are rich? That he will be rich someday himself? That he's got good connections for business?" Colleen was on a roll and wasn't about to shut up this time around. "What does that have to do with love and family and lifelong commitment?"

"Colleen, please, your tone of voice!" her mother said.

Arthur Fitzpatrick had debated his daughter before; in high school and even before that in grade school, when his feisty little redhead wanted to make her point. He answered Colleen back in a calm, controlled voice.

"It certainly makes it easier to love someone who is financially secure, I can tell you that!" he said.

"Look, I like Bradley a lot. I really do. He may be more serious than I am right now, but I'm warming up to him. And yes, I could see myself being married to him … someday. But I have my career. I've already told you how important that is to me at this stage in my life. I'm in no hurry to get married, have kids and settle down."

"We just want you to be happy," Mary Rose said. "Bradley does make you happy, doesn't he?

"Yes, mother, he does. I like being with him," Colleen answered as she cut up a piece of her turkey. "OK, does that make you two happy?"

"Colleen, we're just thinking of…."

"But I have to tell you both that I really admire Daniel's ambition. He once told me that it was going to be harder for me to succeed than him because he was born poor and I was born rich. I never understood what he was saying until recently. I think I get it now."

"I don't understand," her mother began.

"I do," her father replied quickly. "The young man has a point. Poverty can power an enormous drive to succeed in some people. That's probably what happened to him. But I won't apologize for a moment for the opportunities we've been able to pass on to you. You're our daughter and we only want what's best for you."

"Dad, I'm not asking you to apologize for anything. Really, I know how lucky I am." Colleen calmly put her fork down. She focused on both parents, and then spoke with passion in her voice. "But I have to tell you both that Daniel isn't what you think he is. He's driven like no one else I've ever met before. He is going to make it - in a really big way. I just know he is!"

Mary Rose glanced over at her husband. She smiled weakly at Colleen,

"Please," she began, "pass the gravy and let's talk about something else."

Mid-Point Senior Year: 1969 - 1970

Runs with the Big Dogs

Several weeks after seeing Colleen at the frat house, Daniel was slumming with Michael at the Triangle Bar. It was well past noon on a Saturday and both men were sequestered in their favorite discussion corner. Sprawled in a tattered booth, Michael was expounding on his latest capitalistic venture. He was selling his blood and stealing money from apartment building laundry rooms.

Daniel just shook his head and frowned back at Michael, "You dumb shit; sooner or later you're going to get your ass caught and thrown in jail. Then what? Get a real job and stop this bullshitting around, man."

But Michael would have none of it. "I make good money," He argued. "The risks are minimal, man. I always case the place first. I wait until mid-afternoon when most of the tenants are at work. Hell, I won't be doing it much longer. Just long enough for me to get a grubstake in my next venture."

"What's next, ripping off paperboys or robbing little girls at their lemonade stand?" Daniel asked.

Michael smiled at his friend and upended yet another bottle of beer. "Getting my own place and getting a real job."

"Doing what?"

"Sales!"

"Sales?!" Daniel exclaimed. "Michael, you're an introvert. What the hell are you going to sell?"

"Used cars," Michael answered. "There's a car lot on University Avenue that just sells to the Negroes and Wetbacks. I can make good money selling junkers and slightly abused automobiles. Some of rods are even hot, but who gives a shit, they're too dumb to know."

Daniel got angry. He grabbed Michael's beer and held it to the table. "Man, grow up," he snarled, "you're sounding like a racist."

"I'm no racist," Michael answered defensively.

"You are when you talk like that." Daniel said. "Those Negros were our brothers back in the Nam. They were standing beside us when we were in the thick of it. Now they're back but they're still black. Don't be fucking with them." Daniel looked Michael straight in the eyes. "You're too smart to be talking stupid like that."

Michael shrugged his shoulders and stared down at his beer. "There is one other job I'd love to have."

"I'm afraid to ask," Daniel said.

"Being a bra fitter in a bra boutique," Michael chuckled with a smile.

"Now you have gone off the deep end."

"No, man, not at all," Michael responded with glee, "I'll be a mammary manipulator. A cans chorale. A jugs juggler. A nipple nudger. Guardian of the 'girls', that's what I'll be."

"Michael, get serious for a moment here."

"Listen, man, they have them all over France especially in Paris. I read about it in National Geographic; regular boutiques just for ladies trying to fit the perfect bra on less than perfect knockers. I'd start with Double D's for beginners. Once I've been able to corral those mothers, I'd move on to tamer ones.

"You're full of shit, my friend."

"And you're in one pissy mood. What's bugging you?"

"Nothing."

"Nothing, my ass! Listen Daniel, you're my counterbalance, my strain of sensibility, my conscious … sometimes. So what's bothering you, man? And be straight with me."

There was a long pause as Daniel struggled to find his words. He lowered his head. "I screwed up, man."

"What'd you do?" Michael asked.

"I was drunk and she was leaving…"

"She … she who?"

"Colleen."

"Shit, when'd you see her?" Michael asked.

"I was at the Phi Beta fraternity party….the one you crapped out on. I was pretty hammered and she came up on the roof and we talked."

"So?"

"We talked for a while and when she was about to leave, I just blurted out how I was feeling. How I felt about her dumping me."

"What'd she say?"

"Nothing, I just was blabbering on…."

"So what's the big deal?"

"I fucked up, man," Daniel said, shaking his head. "I shouldn't have said anything. I should have just let it go."

"What exactly did you tell her?" Michael asked.

"I can't remember … just that I didn't need her anymore."

"Well, you don't! Do you?"

"No."

"So, what's the big deal?"

"I shouldn't have said anything in the first place," Daniel answered in a soft voice, shaking his head. "I should have just let it go. But…"

"But what?"

"I can't get the damn broad outta my mind."

Michael shoved another bottle of beer toward Daniel who waved it away. Michael smiled at his dejected friend and upended the bottle himself. He finished the bottle and stood up.

"Got to go," he announced, "you staying?"

"Probably, no place else to go."

Michael smiled at his sad-faced friend and stumbled out the door.

Three fraternity brothers from the University of Minnesota were sitting up at the bar. They were staring intently in the back mirror that reflected Daniel and Michael in the corner. They silently watched Michael stagger out of the bar.

All three were huge men. Each was barrel-chested with thick arms and knots around their necks. They were battle-scarred veterans of Saturday afternoon collegiate turf wars - a quarterback's nightmare. They wore letter jackets, which were ablaze with athletic letters that announced their prowess in a multitude of sports.

"Are those the two?" one of them asked his companions. One of the other frat boys nodded. "Yeah, that's them. I've seen 'em in here before. Fat guy has got a big mouth. He likes to brag about his time over in Vietnam. The other one is quiet, doesn't say much. But look, he dresses like a goddamned hippie. They both look like a couple of pussies, if you ask me."

The bartender, who had been standing on the other side of the bar, moved closer to the three at the counter. He leaned in toward the fraternity boys and said, "If I were you guys, I'd cool it with all that macho talk about those two. I heard both of them were in Vietnam. The quiet one fought in the A Shau Valley, supposedly on Hamburger Hill. I heard he got chopped up real bad. Whether that's true or not, I wouldn't mess with them if I were you."

"Well, pops, you're not us, now are you?" one of the boys shot back at the old man. His companions laughed. The three narcissists went back to admiring themselves in the mirror. "Fucking commie hippies. What they both need is a good old fashioned ass-whooping."

The bartender stood his ground, resting his thick arms on the edge of the counter. He wrinkled his lips once and answered, "Word on the street is that the quiet one ran with the big dogs."

"Now, what the fuck is that supposed to mean, old man? Ran with what big dogs?"

"It means, pencil dick, that he was with some very mean hombres over in Vietnam. Back here, we'd consider them hardened criminals by their rap sheets. In the Nam, they were Special Ops. Guys like that are a time bomb. If you cross him, he just might go off and tear you a new asshole!" The bartender turned to walk away, shaking his head in disgust.

"I'm not afraid of any soldier boy," one of the frat boys bragged.

The bartender turned back to the frat boys and warned them again, "Take my advice, boys. Don't fuck with either one of them - especially the quiet one. I'm thinking there's still a lot of fight left in that old dog."

"What are you talking about? Just because that guy runs like a big dog?"

The bartender repeated, "You don't want to mess with him."

"What are you saying?" one asked, puffing out his chest, "That's bullshit."

The bartender came back closer to the trio. He leaned in again. "I've seen that kind before," he started to explain, "they come back from Vietnam all fucked up. They're wound up tighter than a 10-year-old pussy. You don't want to set him off. He could kill you in a second…and not even know he did it…or care for that matter. It's all instinct with that kind. I'm just giving you a little advice. If you want to go home to your mama in one piece, you best give him a lot of distance."

"OK, OK, we didn't mean anything," the leader of the group spoke up, "We're just having a little fun with you. Shit, we didn't mean anything. Let me buy you a drink and forget all our bullshit talk."

"No thanks," the bartender answered shaking his head and turning toward a new customer at the bar.

Above the Din

Around nine in the evening, Colleen and her partying girlfriends ended up on the West Bank near the University of Minnesota. Earlier that evening, it had started out simply as a birthday party for one of her dorm mates. It quickly escalated into a roving party from one dorm room to the next until it was suggested the girls hit a couple of bars in Highland Park.

They started at Tiffany's lounge. Soon one of the girls suggested they be even a little more daring and venture out into new territory. That translated into slumming at the gathering spot for hippies and other creatures of questionable habits; the West Bank.

The birthday girl told the group that if they were going to do that, they had to hit the Triangle Bar where all the freaks hung out. Since it was the first bar in the area to host live acts, the red brick building was always swarming with large crowds on weekends. They all laughed and agreed it was a great suggestion.

"I don't think that's such a good idea," Colleen offered without adding any explanation.

"Oh, come on," said birthday girl, "they've got live music. Maybe we can hear Willie Murphy or Spider John Koerner." "Yes, let's go," The others chimed in. The group moved toward the taxi stand. Colleen shrugged her shoulders and reluctantly followed along.

The Triangle parking lot was full. Cars and motorcycles filled the overflow gravel lot and alley behind the bar. Loud music could be heard blasting out of the front door and open windows. It sounded like a raucous party at full tilt inside. Several hippies, either drunk or stoned, were gathered around the front entrance trying to sell their wares to anyone who entered.

Colleen directed her friends inside and spotted an empty booth in one corner of the large room. They wove their way through the dance crowd and quickly piled into the booth and waved at the roving bartenders to order their drinks.

It was an electric crowd just as Daniel had once described the place several years before. Colorful hippies mingled with fraternity and sorority lookalikes. Nattily dressed businessmen were hustling the younger set from the University, male and female alike. A few suspicious-looking men lingered on the fringe of the dance floor, either undercover cops or lonely single men perusing their prey. No one seemed to notice who was coming in or going out of the front door. The bartenders were hustling drinks and schooners of beer were flowing freely from the taps. The band was on their obligatory break and now the Rolling Stones were screaming out of the ceiling speakers. It was a typical crazy weekend night at the Triangle Bar.

Even though simple conversations were almost impossible amid the loud din of the place, Colleen's friends did manage to keep up a steady litany of cutting remarks about the strange crowd surrounding them. Colleen had heard all those comments before. She'd grown tired of her trust fund friends looking down on everyone with their snide comments meant to degrade and mock those less affluent than them.

Colleen quickly grew irritated with their sophomoric naivety. This was a different group of people than her classmates but their differences also made them unique and interesting to watch. Colleen vaguely remembered a few of Daniel's comments about the Triangle Bar. *Maybe he's on to something*, she thought.

Their relationship that summer at that point had grown fragile at best. Colleen was dating other boys as she had said she would. Daniel was working his dead end job and pining over the loss of their intimacy. Theirs was just one of a million college romances that had hit the skids that summer and was slowly dying out.

"Colleen!" one of her girls shouted above the din of the room. "Didn't your old boyfriend used to hang out here?"

"I think so," Colleen lied. "He spent a lot of time on the West Bank. I suppose he could have hung out at this place, too."

"Whatever happened to him?"

Colleen shrugged her shoulders and turned back to watching the couples on the dance floor, ignoring her friends laughter and jokes about the crowd.

Was she subconsciously hoping to see Daniel again? Ridiculous, she thought. That was in the past. Her chance encounter with Daniel at the Grandview Theater had been an accident and the second meeting at the frat party was hardly planned. She wasn't about to go stalking an old boyfriend especially after she'd dumped him in Vietnam.

Colleen began to grow increasingly uncomfortable in Daniel's old stomping grounds. She didn't belong here. Perhaps, Lake Minnetonka wasn't her cup of tea but neither was the psychedelic mind-bending atmosphere of the West Bank. Colleen turned around to say something to her friends about leaving.

Suddenly out of the corner of her eye, she saw him.

He was sitting alone in a small booth, half hidden by the fast moving, swirling sea of humanity on the dance floor. Colleen looked again; wanting to make sure it wasn't her imagination that had brought her up short and caused her heart to start racing. She found herself taking quick, shallow breathes.

But it wasn't her imagination or her cocktail that brought up the mirage of the man her mind still couldn't shake. Daniel was in a corner booth with a bottle of beer in front of him. There were several more empties stacked up on the table. He was staring out at the dance floor but didn't seem focused on anything or anyone in particular.

Colleen's immediate reaction was one of dread. Daniel seemed to be drunk once again; a frightening pattern considering his family's history of alcoholism. She stared at him for a long time. No one else came to join him in the booth. He was alone and seemed wrapped in a blanket of loneliness.

Colleen was torn. *Should I go over and talk to him again? But for what purpose? To say what? To tell him that I'm disappointed to see him drunk again? Should I just let him be, drunk and alone in his booth?* The voices around her kept up a steady drumbeat of catty remarks and snide comments. Colleen ignored them all, focusing instead on the sad young man across the dance floor, seemingly lost.

Colleen knew that if she left with her friends and didn't say something to Daniel, she might never resolve her feelings of betrayal. A simple conversation might resolve those nagging feelings of guilt and let Colleen get on with her life. It couldn't hurt to talk to him one more time, she convinced herself.

She would do it, Colleen decided. She would go over and try to engage in a simple conversation and let Daniel know she was very sorry for her past actions. Simple, direct, and final. That's all it had to be. Colleen took a deep breath and started to slip out of the booth.

"I think I see someone I know," Colleen threw out as she stood up. Without looking back at her friends, she started across the dance floor. Several girls took fleeting notice, but swiftly went back to their cocktails and gossip.

Daniel was still staring out at the dancers, oblivious to all the commotion going on around him. She could see he was wearing denim jeans, a Norwegian Rolex sweater and boots. A navy pea coat lay slung over the end of his table. His eyes remained fixated into space.

Colleen eased her way around the gyrating, dancing bodies. Daniel turned slowly to see who was approaching his booth.

"Hello, Daniel," Colleen said, raising her voice above the din.

"Colleen!" his eyes followed her body sliding into his booth. "We meet again!" his voice dropped, "under less than auspicious circumstances."

Colleen tried to hide her look of disapproval. She tried not to count the beer bottles stacked up around Daniel.

"Welcome to my office," Daniel spread out his arms at the noisy surroundings. He gave a weak laugh and took a drink of beer.

"I hope not!" Colleen answered, a look of disapproval now firmly planted on her face.

"Oh, come on, Colleen, a libation or two doesn't hurt once in a while."

"You're drunk again, Daniel!"

"Are you out slumming with your friends?" Daniel shot back, his eyes now focused on his old girlfriend. "Want to see what the lowlifes are up to?"

"No, Daniel," Colleen responded by putting her hands on the table. "My friends wanted to come here and I agreed to tag along. It's not one of my favorite places to hang out. But I see you still like it here. And getting drunk - again! Remember what you told me about not wanting to end up like your father?"

"I remember."

"Well?"

A look of controlled anger crept across Daniel's face. He furrowed his eyes and leaned in toward Colleen. "You don't get to tell me that anymore, Colleen. No more homilies."

"Don't talk stupid, Daniel. I'm just concerned about your drinking."

"Not anymore! Besides, I've got a lot on my mind."

"Such as?"

"It appears some of your college friends don't approve of the fighting over in Vietnam. You know, those super-patriots with their college deferments. The draft dodgers, safely ensconced stateside, who scorned us soldiers when we're getting killed every day so you can plant your sweet tush in some bar and laugh at the rest of us. Viva La Resistance!" Daniel proclaimed as he raised his bottle of beer.

"If you're talking about some of those stupid fraternity boys, forget them!" Colleen said, "I don't feel that way. Nor do any of my friends. And if you're talking about America, love it or leave it. Forget that too! If those jerks knew what your unit went through, they wouldn't talk so stupid."

"How would you know what my unit went through?" Daniel started to ask.

“Is that your road attire?” Colleen quickly responded, pointing at Daniel’s pea coat.

Daniel glanced over at his coat. “Yeah, I call it bohemian chic,” He shot back with a laugh. “No, actually that’s all I’ve got. I haven’t bothered to buy any new clothes since I’ve been back.”

Daniel opened his mouth to say something when two bottles of beer came crashing down between them, startling both Daniel and Colleen. White foam gushed out of the bottles and onto their table. It was followed by a loud booming voice that cut through the din of the crowd. Daniel and Colleen both looked up at a bedraggled looking man, dressed in a white smock and white pants.

“Wild Man, how the hell are you?” Daniel shouted at the man towering over their table.

“Hey, G.B., I didn’t know you were back in town. How are you, man?” the stranger asked as he leaned his elbows on the edge of their table.

“G.B.?” Colleen said out loud, looking over at Daniel.

Daniel glanced over at her with a smile. “Long story,” he said, “I’ll tell you about it sometime.” He turned back to the man. “I’m great, Wild Man, what are you up to? Still teaching at the U hospital?” he asked.

“That and some other things,” Wild Man answered. He upended one of his bottles and gave out a loud belch. He looked over at Colleen who was staring at him.

“Who’s the chick, man? She’s bitchin.” he smiled at Colleen. “This your woman, G.B.?” he looked her over and gave her another bow.

For her part, Colleen just smiled back at the man and tilted her head a bit. “Just catching up on old times,” she said with a forced smile.

“This is an old friend of mine,” Daniel interjected. “This is Colleen, Wild Man. Say, whatever happened to old Zack? I was by his house a couple of weeks ago and he’s moved. Where’d he go?”

“Zack's gone, man. He’s long gone.”

“I know, Wild Man,” Daniel shouted back at the man swaying back and forth in front of him. “Where did he go? Do you know where he went?” If anyone should have known about the whereabouts of the old hippie, it would have been Wild Man.

“He’s gone with the wind, man. Gone like … just blowing in the wind.”

“So you don’t know either. Nobody seems to know what happened to him.”

Wild man shrugged his shoulders, smiled at Colleen and emptied his beer bottle with one long swig.

Daniel waved the inebriated man away, "Good seeing you, man. I'll look for you here again. Got to talk to my girl now."

Wild Man stuck out his wavering hand, still clutching the beer bottle. Daniel took hold of the bottle and shook it.

"Remember what I told you, G.B.?"

"About what?"

"Not going back. You can't go back again."

Daniel smiled broadly. "I did forget at first, Wild Man, but you're right. I understand what you guys were all telling me back at Zack's place. Yeah, I get it now."

Wild Man nodded at Colleen and staggered back onto the dance floor. He was quickly swallowed up by the milling, gyrating bodies. Colleen turned back to Daniel. "Now that's an interesting character … A friend from your past, I assume?"

Daniel explained, "I guess you could call my old friends here bar stool poets and whiskey whores. A real eccentric crowd but I loved each and every one of them…"

"Wild Man is a bit weirder than most," Daniel began again, "I think he may have fried his brains on drugs a long time ago. Supposedly he was a CIA agent at one time. He did tell some fascinating stories about his work in Southeast Asia. Whether they were true or not didn't really matter. We were either drunk or stoned most of time when he was telling us his tales."

"How did you meet him?"

Daniel smiled, "There was this old Eastern European bohemian I met here the summer after freshmen year. He had this very strange name none of us could pronounce. So we just called him Zack, short for Zackeri-something. He invited me over to his house one time and I just kept going back. It was my version of summer school."

"Summer school?"

"We'd hang out at Zack's house over on what we used to call Bleaker Street in honor of the same one in New York City. I have no idea what the real name of the street was. The old hippie had a couple of hammocks hanging on his porch and there was always a crowd there; an odd assortment of hippies, radicals, dropouts, and even the occasional professor. We'd drink cheap wine or beer and smoke a little weed - nothing serious. We'd stay up all night just talking." Daniel took another long swig of beer.

"He gave me a book to read that summer - 'The New Bohemia' about the East Village in New York. It really opened my eyes to what was going on all around me … It was at that point that I realized I was a mile wide in terms of interests but just an inch deep in terms of knowledge. I knew very little about a whole lot. Zack opened my eyes to a lot of new things I never knew existed."

Colleen was giving him a look Daniel couldn't decipher. "Ever try talking to a butterfly?" he asked whimsically.

Colleen spoke hesitantly, "Did you ever take…?"

Daniel laughed and smiled. "The serious stuff? Acid, no. That was done inside by the real speed freaks and junkies. I never got close to that shi … stuff. I saw what it was doing to some of those guys. I mean it was scary because they were space cadets twenty-four hours a day, seven days a week."

"So that's how you spent your summer before you enlisted."

"Got drafted," Daniel corrected her. "Yeah, I was traveling through a state of heightened consciousness … making up for the lapsed years of my life." *I like that*, he thought.

"What would you talk about all night?"

"Anything and everything," Daniel answered. "The bohemian culture and all kinds of radical ideas. Jack Kerouac's 'On the Road' and Ginsberg's 'Howl'. Did you know that Jack Kerouac never drove? He didn't know how to drive a car. He was a yarn-spinner and a rail-rider but never spent a minute behind the wheel himself. Isn't that interesting?"

Colleen shrugged her shoulders. "I guess," she said.

"We were like cultural pirates, taking what we wanted out of life and discarding the rest."

"A constant search for stimulation!" Colleen raised one eyebrow. "Like you were in a chrysalis, your inner world surrounded by a circle of so-called friends."

Daniel dismissed her comment. "We discussed the idea that most of us were trapped in a monolithic society that we couldn't escape from. The idea that there were no choices in life. We were living in fixed patterns and millions of people felt they had to follow that pattern. We talked about how the Beats came along and said no, you didn't have to follow that way of life. Zack espoused that kind of thing with the way he lived out his life. It was like we were all his 'Dharma Brats' and he was our parent."

Colleen sat silently, listening to Daniel talk in a way she'd never heard him talk before. He was more animated, more fired up, more energized than she'd ever seen him. Maybe it was the alcohol, she thought, or perhaps her old boyfriend had stumbled upon something that really affected him back then.

Could it be, she asked herself, that his fascination with hippies and beats and other esoteric mental meanderings had actually helped focus his attention on new kinds of literature that she had summarily dismissed as strange and foolish? And if so, had Daniel actually found new meaning and purpose in his life where none had existed before?

"We'd talk about poetry; the new stuff - and of course the old. There was some great work coming from the Wichita Vortex group out of Kansas. And the San Francisco scene with Plywell, the outlaw poet, and Richard Brautigan. Good stuff coming out of Paris too!"

Colleen didn't know what to say so she remained quiet.

"Have you ever read "Tell me lies about Vietnam," by Adrian Mitchell. He's the foremost poet of England's anti-bomb movement."

"No," was all Colleen could answer.

"We'd talk a lot about art. Especially the new art scene coming out of New York City, where Pop Art was becoming more and more popular by appropriating imagery and methods from print media. These guys are drawing from the stuff of everyday life. But the way they did it was unique and different. A guy named Warhol is using advertising and Lichtenstein is using comic books as art."

"Warhol?" Colleen said in surprise.

"Yeah," Daniel answered, surprised that Colleen would know the name.

"I'm impressed," Colleen said. "Tell me more."

"Are you really interested or just being polite?" Daniel asked.

"You know me better than that, Daniel," Colleen gave back, tilting her head and raising her eyebrows as she spoke.

Daniel laughed but got no response from Colleen. Her steel blue eyes became a very effective façade. "We'd get into all the great books and literature; the classics and poetry. We would talk all night and well into the next morning. Some of us would fall asleep for a couple of hours, wake up and join the conversation just as if we'd never left it."

"We'd play these great albums by Quicksilver Messenger Service and Big Brother and Jimi Hendrix. We'd get into jazz and funk and some Motown. The whole gamut of musical tastes. Just played them over and over again. All night long sometimes. We did that with Sgt. Pepper. Played it all night and tried to decipher the lyrics and what they really meant. It was magical."

"Rock and Roll? I'm not sure if I'd call that magical."

"It was to us!" Daniel leaned forward. "Did you know that Rock and Roll is really Negro slang for having sex?"

"No, Daniel. I didn't know that."

"Sorry," Daniel said, downing another swig of beer. "I was just messing with your mind."

Colleen tilted her head just a bit. She looked back at Daniel with her eyebrows furrowed. "No, Daniel, you weren't." she answered calmly.

Daniel stopped. He suddenly realized he was beginning to make a fool of himself. "Well, it was a different level of consciousness," he said, "I'll grant you that."

"And your long hair and ragged clothes?"

"A sign of the times, I suppose," Daniel answered. "I think the Beatles started it, but it became a sign of a person's political and social allegiance, and preference in music; for most of polite society, it was a sign of rebellion."

"So it fit you perfectly?"

"I guess," Daniel said with a smile.

"And it all started in this place?" Colleen asked.

Daniel smiled that familiar curl of his lips, bright white teeth and glint in his eyes. For a moment, just a moment, he seemed to be the same old Daniel she used to know.

"I found myself drawn to folk music because it had a language that was less polished and less slick than anything from Tin Pan Alley. They didn't try to pretty up their songs. Instead the music was more idiomatic, more democratic and much truer to the realities of life." A smile crossed his lips and disappeared just as quickly. "The realities of my life in particular," he hesitated, "as it was back then. It had a greater authenticity to it, more truth to it. I could relate to the music and the lyrics and the kind of people who were singing it or just drawn to it as I was. Same with the Beats."

"I'm sorry Daniel, but I still don't understand your fascination with the Beats."

"That's easy," Daniel answered. "The Beat Movement was intimately associated with the Folk Movement. Back in the late 50s and early 60s all over the Village…"

"The Village?"

Daniel stopped for a moment to look directly at Colleen. He answered slowly. "Greenwich Village, New York City."

Colleen nodded her understanding.

"All over the Village in coffee shops and small bars, you'd have a beat poet stand up and read several of his poems and folk singers would sing their works. And this was repeated over and over and over again. It was an economy of words in poems and song. But messages were presented and gotten across to the audience. They loved it."

Daniel was on a roll. "So with the Beats, you got free association, spontaneity and contempt for established popular culture. Hence the all-black outfits for the poets and folksy hardscrabble clothes for the folk singers. It was what the audience expected of their singers and poets."

Colleen slowly smiled at Daniel's enthusiasm. "An outlaw society that accepted you for what you were; good or bad, right or wrong, left or right-leaning," she commented without a hint of sarcasm in her voice. "So you found yourself immersed in beat poetry and folk music … and the intellectual musing of a bunch of misfits, cast-off students, drug-induced wild men and one father figure."

"You put it so nicely, Colleen. Cut to the core. A real economy of words. And, yes, that was my life. I could identify with what the Beats were talking about - same with the folk singers."

"What did Wild Man mean about going back?" Colleen asked. "And why did he call you G.B?"

"Nothing," Daniel said, shaking his head, "nothing important … G.B. means Gypsy Boy. It's an inside joke." He let his words hang in the air, offering no further explanation.

Colleen shook her head in amazement at Daniel's past behavior. "You never told me about this guy, Wild Man or Zack or going to his place that summer."

Daniel wrapped his hand around his beer and upended the bottle, finishing the little that was left. He pushed the bottle back to the edge of the table. He grew serious and leaned forward. He spoke softly but loud enough to be heard above the music and voices around them.

"Colleen, I tried to … many times! But you weren't listening," he searched her face for a reaction, "any time you heard me mention the Triangle Bar or anything hippie, you just zoned out."

"I probably did," the corner of her mouth wrinkled up. She was feeling very foolish and she didn't know why. "I guess I didn't understand just how important that was to you. I'm sorry. I should have been more sensitive." She gave a little shrug of her shoulders, suddenly feeling very dumb.

"Wild Man would talk about his trips through India and Southeast Asia and other places. I think it started up a little wanderlust in me. But more importantly, those guys taught me to believe in myself. That I didn't have to accept my status in society or my predetermined role in life."

"What my mother wanted from me was little to nothing. That became my self-fulfilling prophecy as I was growing up. But they taught me it didn't have to be that way. I didn't have to be a low achiever just because my mother thought I was. I could be anyone I wanted to be. I could become anything I wanted to become. I was my own master and not beholden to anyone else."

"We all felt like we were refugees from American culture. We were all trying to find our own answers in our own way." He reached for another beer, wrapping his hand around its stem. He paused to look at Colleen. Her facial expression was placid but he got the message. He opened his palm and slid his hand back in front of him.

"There were things going on all around us - and in the world. But I couldn't put my finger on it. It was this gnawing feeling that I was missing out on something. You could see it here in the bar. You could feel it."

"I'm afraid I don't understand, Daniel."

"You would watch someone come into the bar; a total stranger - somebody like Zack or Wild Man. And just by the way they looked around and the way they carried themselves, you knew that they were on to something. They knew something you didn't. They carried their attitude on their shoulders and in their eyes - by the way they walked. They had caught the vibe, the vision. They were with it, whatever 'it' was. That's what I wanted to be … to become."

Colleen was now listening with rapid attention, her eyes burrowing into Daniel, trying to penetrate those glassy eyes - his transfixed expression was revealing far too little for her needs.

"And did you?"

"That's why I let myself get drafted."

"To follow your gypsy muse?"

"Something like that."

"And what was your vision?"

"To find myself."

"Did you … find yourself?"

"Yeah, I think I did."

Colleen was amused and somewhat taken aback by Daniel's calm demeanor and matter of fact audacity. What happened to that shy, insecure young man she used to know? He certainly wasn't sitting across from her now. He had a presence about him that she could feel. It was strangely exciting and yet scary at the same time.

"See Colleen, while you were out sneaking dates with the boat shoe boys, I was hanging around with a bunch of old drugged up hippies getting an education in the ways of the world. Best learning I'd ever experienced. It was my tenth room."

Colleen looked at him with puzzlement written all over her face.

"'Tenth Room' … Virginia Woolf … oh, forget it."

"I wasn't sneaking out on dates," Colleen shot back.

"Forget it, it's the past. You had a right to do what you did. At that point, we were pretty much a couple in name only."

"You should have made other friends after Michael left."

"All along, I'd been looking for someone who might make a difference in my life. It wasn't my father. He was a void that wasn't missed. It wasn't my mother. She was too wrapped up in her own pathetic life to care about me. It wasn't my aunts or uncles."

Colleen grew tense. She would sense the anger welling up inside Daniel. His body had suddenly grown taut despite his inebriation. His hands were firmly planted on the table, bunched up into fists.

"So tell me, Colleen, what do you do when the people in your life who are supposed to make a difference when you're growing up, don't care about you? People who are supposed to love and support you? What happens when they don't give a damn because they're so wrapped up in their own self-centered lives?"

"I don't know, Daniel, maybe try to find other friends."

"And if that doesn't work? Where will you go?" Daniel asked, pushing her for an answer.

"Daniel, I don't know!" She was getting irritated at Daniel's accusatory tone. "I guess you just keep trying to find new friends - people who care about you."

"I thought I had when I met you."

"Daniel, please."

"Oh, forget it!"

"You need to let go."

"I have let go!"

"It doesn't sound like it."

"Don't flatter yourself."

"Don't be mean, Daniel."

Daniel reached over and upended his beer, forgetting that it was empty. When he put it down, Colleen was just staring at him. Her composure gave no indication if she was mad or angry or sad. Her placid expression told him nothing. When she spoke again, she began slowly and carefully.

"Daniel, you know you got very possessive. That's why I couldn't commit to you. And the more possessive you got, the more you turned me off and, in turn, turned me away. The more resentment I felt, the more I wanted to get away from you … even though I wanted to be with you at the same time."

Daniel didn't respond. She still couldn't read his expression.

"Can you understand now that you were stifling me? …That I couldn't let you hold me back any more."

"Oh, yeah, I do now," his stoic façade faded away, replaced by a knowing grin. "It was a very immature thing for me to do. Now I understand why I did it. Although, I certainly couldn't have seen it back then … I'm OK where I am in my life right now. I'm OK with myself. So I can look back and see the good and the bad, the right and the wrong. What worked and what didn't work between us."

Colleen was transfixed by Daniel's maturity and a candor utterly devoid of any guise.

"See, Colleen, I realize now that I was so in love with you that I was blinded by the reality of our situation and what was really going on between us. I'm sorry for that. I wish I could have started out as your friend, plain and simple." He stopped just to stare at the beautiful woman sitting across from him. "And then if it evolved into something else that would have been great. Instead, I fell head over heels in love with you right from the start - killing our friendship in the process."

Just as quickly as the smile appeared, it was gone and Daniel's face went pensive. He stared out, looking at nothing. His mind was a million miles away. Colleen said nothing. She just looked at him. Another smile broke his mask and he said. "There's a great book I read a while back. It's called 'The Fume of Poppies' by Jonathan Kozol. Ever read it?"

"No."

"It's us, Colleen … unrequited love and all that." Daniel grinned to himself. His body had grown more relaxed. A heavy burden had been lifted from his consciousness.

"So that's it. What I learned from yoga is that when you don't have something or you miss something, it's because you didn't own it in the first place. You don't own anything, much less another human being. I wanted it all to be so perfect between us, Colleen. But like Zack told me … well, Voltaire said it best, 'Perfect is the enemy of good.'"

Daniel's introspection shocked Colleen. Maybe it would be all right now, she thought. Maybe Daniel would be able to accept their past uncertainties and embrace a new life without her in it.

"I think I understand why you did it too," Colleen offered. "But I just wanted to make new friends - not just more boys in my life. I told you over and over to go out and make new friends yourself."

"And I did," Daniel said defensively.

"Of course, you did! Bohemians, beatniks and hippies of that ilk. Druggies, alcoholics and lost souls searching for a meaning to life. Hardly an auspicious start to finding your career or meaning in life."

"Well, Colleen, it worked for me!" Daniel answered, regaining his confidence again. "And I don't regret a single moment I spent with those people. They were my friends, even though they were probably as screwed up as I was. It didn't occur to me the extent of what I'd learned until I was sucking mud in a foxhole. That's when I realized what an incredible gift that summer had been for me."

Daniel leaned forward, closing the gap between his face and Colleen's. She started to lean back, afraid he was attempting to kiss her. She relaxed and let herself lean closer to Daniel.

"Face it, Colleen," Daniel said in a calm voice. "We were two very different people on two very different tracks in our lives. I wouldn't expect you to understand."

Colleen felt herself strangely transfixed and even more confused by the fleeting thought that she might still be attracted to this rough man sitting across from her. She felt herself being drawn to him. She wanted to feed on the energy pulsating from his every word.

Still, she found it hard to imagine that Daniel could find inspiration and contentment in such a dirty, chaotic place as the Triangle Bar. She still didn't completely understand his fascination with the hippies or other colorful characters who gathered there every day. But his enthusiasm for that summer was real and unapologetic. Colleen didn't understand but she accepted the fact that, once again, it just proved how very different she was from Daniel.

"Give me some credit, Daniel," Colleen responded, "I'm not stupid you know."

"Oh, come on, Colleen," Daniel answered. "I was a wannabe hippie, not a real one. I never espoused the true hippie lifestyle. I never got into their drug culture. The most I did was smoke some weed and have too much cheap wine. I never dropped any acid or popped pills. I was exploring my life in much the same way you were exploring yours during that period."

"Exactly! It's too bad we couldn't have talked about this at the time."

"It took time for me to figure it out myself while I was in Vietnam; which brings us back to your comment a moment ago."

"Which was?"

"You said you knew about my unit in Vietnam. How could you?"

Colleen started to explain her strategy for obtaining unclassified documents through her reporting job at the St. Paul newspapers. Without mentioning Garrison, Colleen talked about getting some help in finding the newspaper clippings from various sources. She would search out innocuous articles from the Armed Forces Network that gave her clues as to the whereabouts of Daniel's command.

Further research through foreign newspapers and magazine articles allowed her to track the political direction the country of Vietnam was taking. It was enough for her to make major assumptions about the direction of the war. It was a troubling account of a country in turmoil and sometimes chaos.

By perusing the articles for any mention of major or minor battles or skirmishes, Colleen had a pretty good idea of the intensity of conflict that Daniel's units were facing in Vietnam.

Daniel was impressed with Colleen's tenacity at collecting that information through regular army channels and other avenues not so official. He agreed that most of her information had been right on. She may have been off by several hundred miles but her investigation had pinpointed most of his unit's activities and the main areas of engagement with Charlie. Even if the reports she'd obtained were days or weeks old.

But as Colleen was talking, explaining in detail her journalistic endeavors, Daniel was beginning to realize more and more his level of intoxication. Her voice was fading in and out. He had trouble focusing on her and concentrating on what she was saying. The beers were beginning to take their toll. He had taken one too many long steps on a short pier.

In short, he was drunk and she was sober. Daniel was engaged in a conversation with a woman who had broken his heart and now wanted to talk about it. It was not the kind of situation Daniel wanted to find himself in. He was suddenly very cognizant of the advantage this woman held over him. He wasn't thinking clearly. And the last thing he wanted to do was to say something stupid, just as he had so often that last summer they were together. He felt vulnerable sitting across from this bright attractive woman.

But his lack of sobriety wasn't enough to stop him from asking the question that had plagued him for so long.

Colleen was babbling on, in a manner that would almost seem to indicate nervousness on her part. She was twisting and untwisting a paper napkin as she spoke.

"So why would you follow my unit like you did and then dump me? Why did you send me that Dear John letter?"

The question caught Colleen up short. She'd known it was coming for some time. It was a fact she couldn't deny. But now that the question had been asked, she was totally lacking a response.

"Daniel, that's something I've wanted to talk to you about," she stammered as she spoke. "That was a very confusing time for me. There was a lot going on in my life. Crazy and wonderful, yet scary. I was afraid..."

"So was I!"

"No, Daniel, hear me out….please," Colleen said. "I told you I knew our relationship was over at that point. It was time for both of us to move on. I didn't know what else to do. It seemed like the right thing to do at the time … to end it with a letter because I couldn't call you and I didn't know when, or if, you would be coming home again."

"So the Dear John letter. Just like that, quick and dirty."

"No, listen, I sent you another letter - and a third letter. I was trying to tell you I'd made a mistake. That I still wanted to be friends."

"Never got them!"

"I know," Colleen said, trying hard to regain her composure. "They were all returned."

"Doesn't matter," Daniel said, finishing off his beer. "The first one said it all."

"Don't! Please," Colleen said. "This is hard for me."

Daniel grew pensive. He looked directly into Colleen's eyes and spoke softly, "More than being hurt, I was disappointed in you." He let the words sink in. "You gave up on me, Colleen. Just like everyone else in my life. Friends don't give up on friends."

The words hit Colleen like a sucker punch. She took a deep breath and bit her lip. Tears began to well up in her eyes. She blinked them away and looked down so that Daniel wouldn't see her starting to cry. When she regained her composure, she looked up again.

The look on Daniel's face was a composite of anger, frustration and pity. Colleen could see the pain in his eyes. She started to say something more, to continue her apology. But Daniel held up his hand to silence her.

"No, please let me finish, Daniel, I need to get this out," Colleen said, almost pleading her case.

Just then one of the girls from Colleen's party came up to their table. "Colleen," she started to say.

"Not now, Patty!" Colleen snarled, still focusing all of her attention on Daniel.

Her friend started to say something else but Colleen held up her hand, eyes still locked on Daniel. She deeply searched Daniel's eyes as she spoke.

"Patty, I said…"

"I got it, Colleen, I got it!" the girl answered and turned away.

Daniel had grown silent and sullen. He let Colleen talk.

"I met your mom by accident one time while you were gone. We talked a bit. But, I think after that conversation I began to realize just how you felt about me. How you fell in love so quickly and so easily … and so hard. It was probably the first time you'd experienced love in your life."

"That would be my mother," Daniel said in a monotone voice. "People like my mother are stuck in their own generation."

"And what about your relatives, your aunts and uncles?"

Daniel took another gulp of beer. He got very serious, and agitated, "The best thing I can say about my relatives is that they're all dead!"

"Daniel, you don't mean that?"

"I do mean that!"

"And your father?"

"I just told you he was a non-entity in my life. He was marginally literate. His life was a waste of my time. Enough said about that!" Daniel answered. "I squandered a lot of those years being angry at my mother and father and feeling sorry for myself. But that was all bullshit! It was just self-pity. My growing up in that environment was neither good nor bad. It simply was." He looked at Colleen, trying to read her face. There was no reaction from her.

"My past doesn't define me…who I am or what I can become. So I'm looking…trying to accept my past for what it was…and my future for what it can be."

Colleen let it be. It was obvious that Daniel harbored deep feelings of anger toward his family. Colleen wasn't about to push him for further dialogue on the subject.

"I understand now why you were so possessive about our relationship and at the same time why I was feeling restricted and confined by it. We were coming from two entirely different places and colliding in the middle."

Daniel's expression revealed nothing. *Is he still so drunk that he didn't understand what I'm trying to tell him? Is he able to comprehend my anxiety over writing that letter and my honest motivation for doing so?*

"Do I make any sense, Daniel?"

Daniel focused his eyes back on Colleen. He leaned across the table, his hands nearly touching hers.

"You were right to dump me, Colleen. I understand that now."

"That's why I couldn't commit. The more possessive you got and tried to keep me, the more turned off I got. The more resentment I felt, the more I wanted to be away from you - even though I wanted to be with you at the same time. Can you understand that you were stifling me? To the point where I wouldn't….no, I couldn't let you hold me back any more."

"Colleen, I got it!"

Colleen was momentarily taken aback by Daniel's abrupt, forceful response. She feared another outburst that never came. "I sent you another letter saying I still wanted to be friends."

"Don't patronize me, Colleen. I heard you the first time. I said you were right to dump me when you did. My actions were very immature. I understand that now."

"So we can both just move on," Colleen said with a hint of finality in her voice. "We can forget about the past and focus on school and our future. Is that what you want?"

"Isn't that what you wanted?" Daniel asked.

"I'm just saying…"

"Enough, already," Daniel said, cutting her off. "You sound like a high school counselor." He started to slide out of the booth.

"I heard you're dating Claudia Weinstein," Colleen blurted, trying desperately to regain some communicative bond with Daniel.

The question took Daniel by surprise. "So?" he said, sitting back down in the booth.

"The rumor on campus is that you and Claudia are a pretty tight couple. Supposedly Claudia's been telling her girlfriends that she's going to have her dad help you get a job at his firm."

"That's news to me!"

"You do know her family is very wealthy? I heard they belong to the Minneapolis Club, the Lafayette Club on Lake Minnetonka, the Edina Country Club and Town and Country in St. Paul. Her father is reported to be one of the wealthiest businessmen in the Twin Cities."

"But who's counting?" Daniel shot back.

"She doesn't seem like your type, Daniel. That's all I'm saying."

Daniel leaned over, looking Colleen in her eyes. His stare was deep and penetrating. He was giving no quarter, "And what type would that be, Colleen, someone like you?"

"Don't be sarcastic; I wasn't trying to make anything of it. It was just an observation."

"We met my first day back on campus. We've been seeing each other on and off ever since. That's all there is to it. If she's been making something more of it you can chalk it up to her imagination."

Colleen was surprised at Daniel's candid admission. It was so different from the rumors running rampant on campus. "She could really be a big help to you," Colleen said, "if you wanted to get started in the brokerage business. That is your major isn't it, business?"

"I've got to go," Daniel said as he grabbed his coat and slid out of the booth, standing over Colleen. He struggled to put his coat on, growing increasingly irritated at one arm that wouldn't slide down his sleeve.

"Maybe we can talk about this when you're sober!" Colleen offered, looking up at Daniel.

"It's over, Colleen. We'll leave it at that," Daniel answered. With that, he turned and stumbled out the front door of the bar.

Colleen sat in the booth, frustrated and confused. She was unaware that the band had started up and the dance floor was again filling with people.

Patty came back over and slid into the booth. "You all right?" she asked.

Colleen quickly composed herself and smiled back at the girl. "I'm sorry," she explained, "I was into some heavy dialogue with an old acquaintance. I'm just trying to make sense of what he's become."

"And?"

"He's light years ahead of all of us."

"I don't understand."

"Neither do I!"

Dutch Uncle

Colleen went back to her dorm later that evening and encountered Mrs. O'Reilly in the lobby. The dorm mother was talking to a group of girls. They were all huddled in one corner away from the steady stream of foot traffic rushing in to beat the curfew. The topic of discussion was boyfriends; old ones, in particular.

Colleen sat for a while, listening to the comments, complaints and questions. She'd heard it all before, many times over; questions that had no answers and complaints about men that had no resolution. Colleen smiled and just let the other girls go on until gradually they ran out of complaints and began to drift back to their rooms.

Eventually it was just Mrs. O'Reilly and Colleen chuckling at the naiveté of freshmen and the wisdom of seniors - those girls in between were pretty much left to fend for themselves. But even as a senior, Colleen didn't count herself among the girls who had all the answers. She had far more questions than answers when it came to men.

"How was your evening, Colleen?" The dorm mother asked.

"Strange, to say the least," Colleen answered.

Mrs. O'Reilly raised an eyebrow, "And?"

"I ran into that same guy I saw at the Grandview Theater just before school started." Colleen began. "This time it was at the Triangle Bar over on West Bank. Ever hear of it?"

"Can't say I have," Mrs. O'Reilly answered. "I don't get out as much as I used to. I mostly just travel vicariously through the girls here. But you're not the first one I know that has crossed the river and entered hippie territory. What was it like?"

Colleen shook her head. "I guess, strange is the best way to describe it. It was pretty much as Daniel had talked about it; definitely a bohemian enclave for the strange and weird of heart."

"So, Daniel used to hang out there?"

"It turns out he did a lot of things I wasn't aware of," Colleen said. "Hanging out at the Triangle Bar was just one of them."

Colleen grew pensive. Mrs. O'Reilly let her sit quietly as she collected her thoughts. "...I had no idea that during that summer Daniel was really experimenting with so many different things," Colleen said.

The dorm mother's eyes widened, "I hope you don't mean drugs, my dear?"

"No, no. Nothing like that. He explained to me how he got into the whole hippie scene by talking to musicians, actors, intellectuals, writers and artists. He befriended a whole collection of far-out thinking, creative, crazy kind of people. While I was boating on Lake Minnetonka, Daniel was going to foreign films and staying up all night with those people."

"I have to admit, I was almost jealous of the passion he expressed tonight when he talked about that summer. I had no idea that was what he was doing. Whenever we'd get together, we'd just end up arguing about one stupid thing or another. It was very frustrating for both of us."

"So you argued a lot?"

"Not really argued, we just disagreed on a lot of different things. He would say things to me that other people wouldn't dare tell me. Like my hair was a mess or my skirt was too short or…"

"A Dutch Uncle."

"I don't understand."

"Someone who gives you honest feedback, telling you the tough love things you need to hear - like most married couples do."

"Exactly, yes! Yes, just like an old married couple. It used to drive me nuts. I'd get so mad at him sometimes."

"So he would tell you things that your so-called friends wouldn't tell you. Did he know you that well or was he just being bossy?"

"No, he wasn't being bossy," Colleen answered defensively. "I guess he just didn't want me to look bad…or stupid." Colleen was surprised at the words coming out of her mouth. "I guess….yes…. I guess he was doing it so I wouldn't make a fool of myself. I really hadn't thought of it that way before."

"Like an old married couple," Mrs. O'Reilly repeated with a smile.

Colleen hadn't thought of Daniel's comments in that light. A slight smile escaped her lips. Maybe Mrs. O'Reilly was on to something there.

"Well, did you at least have a nice conversation tonight?" Mrs. O'Reilly asked. "You know, catch up on old times?"

Colleen gave a loud sigh. "Unfortunately he was drunk again," she answered with a shrug of her shoulders, "just like he was at the fraternity party not long ago."

Mrs. O'Reilly gave Colleen a comforting look. "Perhaps it would be wise to talk to him again when he's sober and more coherent. Maybe then you can talk about old times."

Colleen shook her head, "Sorry, Mrs. O'Reilly, but I don't think Daniel wants to talk about old times with me. We broke up not long after he went into the service." She was afraid to say what was on her mind.

"That can be hard for both parties, my dear. But I'm sure it was for the best," the older woman commented. "You certainly seem very happy now with your life. You are happy now, aren't you?"

"I am," Colleen blurted out, "I really am."

"So what is the problem?"

Colleen hesitated trying to make sense of the jumbled feelings swirling through her brain. She spoke cautiously, "Frankly, Mrs. O'Reilly, I don't know why I can't get him out of my mind. On the surface, we're still so very different."

"Perhaps basic values and principles," Mrs. O'Reilly answered.

"I don't understand."

"You've told me enough about that young man that I can sense a driving determination on his part to succeed in school this time around. It sounds like he wants many of the same things you've talked about in your own career as a journalist," she smiled. "Maybe that's the connection between the two of you that you aren't seeing. Maybe you're drawn to him because he represents everything that you think is important in life."

"I don't know," Colleen answered with a shrug of her shoulders.

"Just the opinion of a casual observer," the dorm mother smiled.

"No, no. That is very helpful," Colleen said. "I suppose I could try to talk to him again. To explain why I broke up with him when he was in Vietnam. It seemed like the right thing to do, but now I'm not so sure. I need to get this feeling of guilt off my chest. That's why I tried to talk to him tonight. But it was frustrating because he was so different, so in control. He was more confident than I've ever seen him before, even if he was drunk."

Mrs. O'Reilly watched Colleen in silence, letting her ramble on.

"Daniel has followed his own muse. He's reinvented himself into someone I'd never recognize if I hadn't known him before. It's so very different from the man I used to know…"

"It seems to me that the only way to resolve this issue between the two of you is another conversation; one that takes place when he's sober and you can engage in a calm discussion and not let your feelings of guilt get the best of you. Do you think you can do that? Do you want to do that?"

"Yes! … No! … I don't know," Colleen blurted out again. She took a deep breath. "Yes, that's what I want to do. That's what I need to do."

"So there," Mrs. O'Reilly said, rising up off the sofa, "you've answered your own question. Find a time to talk to Daniel and just get your feelings out on the table. Let him know how you feel. If he's as smart as you say he is, he'll understand. He'll get it."

"Did I say he was smart?"

"No, you didn't have to. I can hear it in your voice."

Minneapolis Club

For 125 years, the venerable Minneapolis Club had stood as a stoic reminder of the strength and vitality of the Minnesota business community. Along with civic and community leaders, captains of industry plied their trade and made their contacts within its dark oak and mahogany restaurant and meeting rooms.

The red brick building was a second home for Mitchell Weinstein and his favorite spot for meeting new clients or prospective employees. He had his own private table in one corner of their large dining area and a select wait staff that knew his every whim and fancy.

It was Mitchell's arena of engagement where he made up his own rules of debate, negotiations and settling contracts. Over the years, he'd developed a subtle set of signals for the wait staff. He rewarded them handsomely for their efforts as long as they played by his rules. His guests seldom knew they were being played by a master manipulator and strategist.

Daniel walked in with Claudia and stopped for a moment at the doorway. He was amazed and intimidated by the sea of blue and black suits, mostly men, actively engaged in easy banter as well as serious conversations. The level of discussion was soft and yet constant with only the soft clinking of china to lay another blanket of sound over the room. No one bothered to look up from their intense discussions to notice the young couple standing in the doorway.

Daniel was wearing a dark blue blazer, gray slacks, a crisp white shirt and red tie. Most of it courtesy of Michael's long neglected clothes rack. His face was clean-shaven. His stance remained firm and erect. He looked like he belonged.

"I'm glad you shaved for me," Claudia said, whispering into Daniel's ear.

"Dear, this is a disguise," Daniel answered with a smile.

"I don't get it."

Daniel turned to Claudia, "This isn't my normal uniform. I shaved and got dressed up for your father. I need to make a good impression if he's going to let me date you, now don't I?"

Claudia reached out and took Daniel's hand. She gave it a tight squeeze and said. "I am a very lucky girl. And thanks for shaving. You're so handsome, you're making me nervous."

An older gentleman quickly approached Claudia and reached out to shake her hand. "Miss Weinstein, what a pleasure to see you here again," He said.

Claudia turned to shake his hand and just as quickly went back to perusing the room. "Fine, George, just fine," Claudia answered without bothering to look back at the man. "Is my dad….oh, I see him. Same old place. Thank you, George, that'll be all."

Claudia reached down and took Daniel's hand and led him toward his father's table in the back corner. She waved as she approached the table. It gave Daniel a chance to release his hand from hers. Daniel took a deep breath and walked up to Mitchell Weinstein just as the man was starting to stand up.

"Sir, my name is Daniel…"

Weinstein took his hand and grasped his other hand over the handshake. He smiled broadly at Daniel and shook his head. He pointed toward a chair across from his own. "Of course, son, my daughter has told me all about you. Please sit down." Mitchell turned to his daughter, "You sit here, dear." He pointed to a side chair.

The three sat down and immediately two wait staff appeared and began pouring water into their crystal goblets. Mitchell looked up and smiled at one of the staff and the two just as moved quickly from the table. The power broker's suit was an impeccable dark blue with faint pin stripes. He wore diamond cuff links and a gold silk tie. Every hair on his head was perfectly combed and in place. Daniel recognized it as the uniform of a man of immense power.

Weinstein leaned forward on the table, resting both elbows on the white linen tablecloth. "Claudia tells me you just got out of the service, son. What branch were you in?"

"Army, sir…."

"No, no," Mitchell interrupted, "you're out of the service now. No more 'sir' to me or anyone else - unless you're saying that in deference to my age. You aren't doing that, are you?"

Daniel smiled at Mitchell Weinstein and the man laughed.

"Good," he said.

"The army… Well, it's not the marines but it's the service."

"I take it you were a leatherneck?"

Mitchell looked at Daniel and immediately began to laugh a deep belly laugh that reverberated throughout the room. A few other diners looked up, saw it was Weinstein and went back to their own conversations.

"Good, Daniel, that was good. Yes, I was a leatherneck and damn proud of it."

"You should be sir…. Mr. Weinstein."

"Mitchell to you. My friends call me Mitchell; I'd like you to do the same."

Daniel glanced over at Claudia but could tell she'd been here many times before. She knew her place at her father's table. She quietly looked over the menu and let the men do the talking.

"What was your MOS?" Mitchell asked.

"Interpreter and I did some recon work."

"Recon," Mitchell said, shaking his head. "I worked intelligence with the British Royal Marine Commandos in Korea. They were a funny group, those Brits. We operated in a shadow war that was never recognized or ever made public. I guess some things are better left alone…even after the conflict ended."

Daniel smiled at Claudia's father. He nodded his understanding but didn't say anything.

"You know, son, it doesn't really matter where the conflict takes place, one war is really no different than the one that precedes it."

"That's probably true," Daniel replied.

"We had the Iron Triangle and the Yalu River."

Daniel smiled and answered, "We had our own Iron Triangle; called it Injun Country and the Ho Chi Mihn Trail. You're right. They were both staging areas and try as we might we couldn't knock them out."

"We had the ROK soldiers who were good sometimes and worthless other times."

"We had the ARVN," Daniel countered. "Ditto!"

"Medevac."

"Mash."

"Pork Chop Hill."

"Fire support base hill 931," Daniel said. "They called it Hamburger Hill."

"You were there...?" his eyes focused on Daniel. Daniel returned his stare but revealed nothing. Mitchell studied Daniel's non-reaction.

"I was." Daniel answered softly. He let the words linger between himself and Weinstein for a long time. Their eyes locked, communicating in a way that only two warriors who have faced death and destruction can.

Mitchell Weinstein regained his composure, "War's a bitch."

"Dad!"

"Sorry, dear, that's something between Daniel and me."

Daniel smiled, "Sweat and fear were cheap commodities in the Nam. We all carried them every day."

Mitchell Weinstein was warming up. He felt comfortable enough to begin his lecture. "I was in Korea for just over a year but it seemed like a lifetime," he said. "It was just as screwed up politically as this one is. Damn governments won't let the military do their job. Syngman Rhee had his politics and Truman had his own way of looking at things. If President Rhee had committed more ROK soldiers to the war right from the start, it might have ended differently than it did."

Daniel sat quietly and let the man ramble on.

"In the meantime, we've got young men, like you, getting killed for failed policies and civilian micromanagement."

"I'll admit that a lot of the decisions made over in the Nam didn't make sense," Daniel said. "But my men and I weren't fighting LBJ's war. I was fighting to stay alive and keep my men alive … My focus was on the next tree line and not how the broader war was going."

Mitchell Weinstein leaned back in his chair. He smiled at this young veteran sitting across from him. *Claudia has found a real man here,* he thought. Daniel understood the main tenants of war for any enlisted man. Stay alive and keep your buddies alive. Watch their back. They will watch yours. That hadn't changed in thousands of years of warfare.

"What Division were you in?" Daniel asked.

"First Marine Division," Mitchell answered.

"Were you at the Chosin Reservoir?" Daniel asked.

"I was, son," Weinstein immediately brought his body up straight and stiff. "I was one of the 'Chosin Few'." His eyes narrowed and he peered at this young man who knew his military history, a rarity among young people today.

“Is it true that the temperature was close to –40 below wind chill? That you were surrounded on all four sides? And that you had to fight your way back, all the time carrying the dead and wounded with you?”

“True as it can be. It meant we had no air support but we still kicked their yellow asses all the way back to the sea.” Mitchell’s eyes seemed to get teary all of a sudden.” I lost a lot of men in my platoon. We fought ten Chinese infantry divisions and we showed them what happens when you mess with a bunch of leathernecks … so how is it that someone your age knows so much about old military history?”

“We talked strategy a lot when I was assigned to the 101st. The Chosin Reservoir was one of our favorites.”

Mitchell Weinstein visibly relaxed and leaned back in his chair. He smiled at Daniel and nodded his head. “I’m impressed, son, I am very impressed,” he said.

Daniel suddenly smiled. Mitchell noticed it immediately and asked, “Yes?”

“We had a saying about Marines back in the Nam.”

“Which was?”

“USMC…Uncle Sam’s Misguided Children.”

Mitchell laughed so hard most of the tables around him looked up and stopped whatever conversation they were engaged in.

“Dad!” Claudia whispered to her father.

Mitchell ignored Claudia and leaned in closer to Daniel. “Got one better for you. Just heard it the other day. USMC…Unlimited Shit, Mass Confusion.”

Daniel joined Mitchell in a round of laughter.

“Daddy, can we talk about something else,” Claudia interrupted. “I’ve heard your war stories so often. Please, can we talk about your business and maybe let Daniel know what a great opportunity it might be for him.”

Mitchell smiled at his daughter and turned to Daniel, “I guess she’s right. I tend to get carried away when I reminisce about my time in the service.” He looked up for just a moment and the wait staff immediately came over and started to pass out menus. They placed three glasses on the table; a whiskey and soda for Mitchell, a glass of Chardonnay for Claudia and a coke for Daniel.

There is a fine line between being respectful and kissing ass. Daniel had learned those rules early on in his military career and it served him well with officers and non-coms alike. Now as Mitchell Weinstein began his spiel about Wall Street and his own brokerage firm, Daniel listened intently and kept his mouth shut.

The meal came and Mitchell showcased his familiar litany of the opportunities awaiting anyone smart enough to enter the brokerage business. Claudia had heard it all before dozens of times and so after the meal she excused herself with one word, library, and left the table. Weinstein watched her go and turned back to Daniel.

"I guess Claudia gets very bored when I talk business, but it's my life. It's done very well for her and her mother. Although I don't always feel appreciated for my hard work and effort."

"Women!" Daniel said, coaxing another loud laugh from Weinstein.

"So, you've got a year to go. What are your plans after graduation?"

"I don't know," Daniel answered. He was also feeling very relaxed with this titan of industry. Daniel admired this man's self-confidence and the knowledge that Mitchell Weinstein could command power and respect without any outward display of arrogance. *This broker might be a good role model for me,* he thought. And if something developed with Claudia, it would be a slam-dunk for a future in the brokerage business.

"I'm interested in real estate," Daniel said. "I bought a house not far from campus. And I've got it rented already. The tenants cover my mortgage payments and pay for upkeep. It works out well for all of us."

"Good for you. Good!" Mitchell said enthusiastically. "See, you already have a head for business. That kind of business savvy would show well in my line of work. You've got to know the tricks of your trade, know your customers, their wants and needs and be prepared to do whatever it takes to bring solutions to their problems. If they don't know what their problem is, you tell them and then offer real world solutions."

"Sounds intriguing, sir....sorry, it's a hard habit to break," Daniel said with a laugh.

"I'm a good teacher, son - one of the best. If you decide to enter my line of work, I could teach you everything you need to learn to become very successful. I'm talking six figures after a couple of years."

"Really?" Daniel said before he could stop himself.

"Absolutely," Mitchell responded. "I told you I only want winners on my team. Nothing less will do. My boys all make in the high six figures. Or else they don't work for me."

"I am impressed, I'll admit that," Daniel said shaking his head.

"One other thing, then I've got to go back to work."

Daniel waited.

Weinstein looked around the room and leaning forward, lowering his voice. He was almost whispering as he spoke. "Wall Street is changing. Not a lot of people are aware of it…or even care at this point. But it's changing and I mean to be at the cusp of that change. And I mean to make a lot of money on those changes."

"I'm sorry, but I don't understand," Daniel said.

"Of course, you don't!" Mitchell smiled. "Most of the folks in my own business don't see what's coming. But it's coming nevertheless."

Daniel gave Weinstein a look of confusion.

"Let me give you a little hint, and then we can talk about it more in the future if you think you're still interested. Sound fair?"

"Yes, sir, it does."

Mitchell glanced around as he spoke. "Wall Street is based on fixed commissions. Most of 'the street,' meaning New York Stock Exchange members, make a good living from their steady stream of brokerage commissions. Now, since the thirties, the SEC, the Securities and Exchange Commission, has allowed the NYSE to be self-regulating and really a closed self-aggrandizing system. It's for WASPS and the Irish primarily. Few if any Jews are allowed into the club. But that is all changing."

"How?"

"I won't go into details now, son, but if you're still interested the next time we meet, I can fill you in more on what I think is starting to happen."

"I'd like that, Mr. Weinstein," Daniel said, following Mitchell as the broker suddenly stood up.

"Now go find my daughter and continue to study hard," Mitchell said as he pointed Daniel toward the doorway to the dining hall. "I'm sure we'll be in touch. Maybe Claudia can bring you over to our house sometime. We can have a nice dinner and go out on the patio for drinks. I've got a great view of the lake and you can see my new boat. It's only a 40-footer but she's decked out to the nines. It's one of the perks in my business."

"A business expense," Daniel said as he shook the broker's hand.

Mitchell waved Daniel off as he started to walk away. "You're a fast learner, Daniel; I like that in a man. I like that a lot." He went down the stairs and out the front door in a flash.

Campus Soliloquy

Long Time Lost

The College of St. Paul student cafeteria was unusually busy for a late Friday afternoon. The tables were full of students visiting with one another, playing cards or concentrating on their course work. Colleen walked in and stood by the entry, away from the traffic flow milling in and out. She perused the room and the long lines at the cash register.

There was no sign of Daniel.

She walked next door to a small coffee shop that took the overflow from the cafeteria. There she saw Daniel sequestered a corner away from the other tables. At first she didn't recognize him. Instead of his usual attire of ragged jeans and flannel shirt, Daniel was sporting pressed jeans; a Creslan sports shirt and penny loafers. He looked strangely right in style with the Pendleton and Brooks Brothers dress shirts that surrounded him. His hair was neatly trimmed although he still sported his light beard.

Daniel was going over his class notes and working on a sandwich at the same time. He was engrossed in his studies and didn't even notice as tables around him changed occupants. Bent over, he was highlighting his book pages when Colleen quietly sat down in a chair directly across from him.

Colleen sat there for a moment or two, intently watching Daniel's focused attention on his work. She smiled at the way his finger slid down the pages which weren't highlighted, then went back and found something to highlight in almost every paragraph. She admired his concentration, which was so unlike him freshman year. His focus was intense. He didn't seem to hear anything or anyone around him.

Colleen cleared her throat and put a smile on her face. Daniel looked up to find her sitting directly across from him. Her hands were on her lap and she was smiling at him.

"Hello, Daniel. I'm glad I found you," she said in a soft voice.

Daniel straightened up, leaned his chair back up against the wall and slowly closed his book. His face was a well concealed mask that revealed nothing. He folded his arms across his chest and said nothing.

"I wanted to talk to you again now that you're … we're in a quiet place. Can we talk, please?"

"Oh, come on, Colleen," Daniel said as he let his chair fall forward with a loud thud. "We really don't have any more to talk about…now do we? I think we're pretty much talked out after the Triangle Bar. You had your say and I had mine. We agreed that freshman year was fun while it lasted but now we've both moved on." Daniel's expression began to crack but still revealed little. "That is what you said, isn't it? That you've moved on with your life and so should I."

Colleen pursed her lips, stalling for time as she collected her thoughts.

She answered slowly, measuring each word. "What I was trying to tell you that night, Daniel, is that I'm sorry for sending you that Dear John letter. I shouldn't have done it the way I did. I should have waited to talk to you in person. That's why I sent you a second and a third letter to say I was sorry and didn't want our friendship to end that way."

"Colleen, I heard you the first time. I wasn't so drunk that I didn't hear you say that you have a wonderful life and you want to move on. I got it."

"Daniel, you don't have to be curt."

"Colleen, what more do you want from me?" Daniel asked. His voice was controlled and measured yet his face remained a total blank. "You wanted to end our relationship and you did. You're sorry for the way you did it but it's done. Did I get that right?"

Colleen sat there, not saying a word. She felt her stomach growing knots but she could hardly lash out at Daniel for his anger at her actions. "I told you before … I told you that we were both at different places in our lives."

"Colleen, I got it! Really, I understand what you're saying," Daniel didn't want to say what was percolating in his mind. It was a minefield he didn't want to step into. But his gut told him he had to go for it. Daniel had to get it off his chest. So he took a deep breath and began, "You said you didn't mean for us to fall in love. Colleen, I have to be honest with you. I don't think you were really in love."

"What are you saying?" Colleen blurted out. "I most certainly was in love with you."

"There's an old gypsy expression that I never understood when I first heard it at Zack's place. But I get it now."

Colleen looked at him and said nothing.

"The expression goes like this, 'the first person to say I love you …

loses'," Daniel laughed, "I get it now. It's true."

"What's your point, Daniel?"

"That was my mistake," Daniel answered. "Besides, I think it's what you wanted to hear."

"What!"

"Colleen, I think you were in love with love. I think you liked the idea of being in love; the feeling, the excitement - the passion. That's what I think you felt. I'm not sure it was true love."

"But it was for you?" Colleen asked defensively.

"Yes, I believe so. Immature perhaps but love nevertheless."

"Bullshit!" Colleen snarled back at Daniel.

Daniel was startled. He'd never heard Colleen curse before. Irish was angry. Her face turned red and she leaned in toward Daniel.

"Don't tell me I wasn't in love, Daniel. Don't you ever do that to what we once had! It may have been an immature love. It may have been far-fetched to think it could work out considering our background and how we were both raised so differently. But don't you ever try to tell me that I didn't have strong feelings for you. Because I did, damn it, I did."

"Well, you're right about it being somewhat immature," Daniel offered up as a weak gesture to calm Colleen down.

"No, my love was mature. Yours was immature, you said so yourself," Colleen shot back.

Daniel visibly relaxed in his chair. He took a drink of coffee and set the cup down, looking back at Colleen. His face cracked. A slight smile slowly crossed his face. Old Colleen was back. The strong-willed independent beautiful redhead was her old self again. For a brief fleeting moment he was back there with her freshman year. They were together again. They were a couple before everything in his life went to hell in bits and pieces.

"You're right, Colleen," Daniel answered. "It was two freshmen in love. What more can I say? A lot of those issues we had seem pretty silly now. The whole money thing doesn't matter to me anymore. It was very intimidating, knowing how you were raised. But it doesn't matter anymore. I'm OK with rich people now."

"Is that because you're dating Claudia Weinstein now?"

"No," Daniel answered, "that has nothing to do with it."

"Strangely enough, Daniel, I believe you."

"After reflecting on everything I learned that summer on Zack's porch, I think I want my focus to be on personal growth and not some physical collection of material goods. That doesn't mean I won't have assets in my life. I just won't be collecting material things for the sake of having them. I want to appreciate life at its purest; the essence of what it means to be alive." He let his words hang there for the moment. "Does that make any sense?"

"It's never too late to become what you could have been," Colleen answered.

"Exactly!"

Colleen thought she would lighten the mood for the moment, trying to connect with Daniel's introspective mood. "So maybe you want to be a slacker," she said with a smile, "and live the life of a monk?"

"No, I want to eliminate unnecessary clutter in my life." Daniel answered as a wide grin grew on his face. "OK, yeah, I want to be a slacker, but a rich slacker."

"Aren't those contradictory stances?" Colleen asked.

"No," Daniel answered, "I don't think so. I think I can attain monetary success, have some nice things in my life but still concentrate on what's important to me. When I took away the equation of money for moneys' sake, things looked very different. I don't need material things to feel good about myself. Now does that make sense?"

"Very much so," Colleen answered. "I must say I'm impressed by your take on wealth. It's refreshingly different from what I'm used to. What a lot of people don't understand is that money doesn't equate with class. Someone can have a lot of money and still have little class. Someone can be poor and have a lot of class. They're not mutually exclusive."

"I hadn't thought of it that way," Daniel said, looking at her with raised eyebrows. "So there are people with class and then there's everybody else?" he smiled.

Colleen returned his smile. "Something like that. Is that philosophy something you learned from Zack, too?"

"It was," Daniel answered, "and from a little book called 'The Path of Prosperity' by James Allen, an Englishman. I think Zack was a disciple of his because he'd quote the guy all the time. The book is tiny, about thirty pages total. Zack gave me his old worn out copy and I've read it over and over again."

Colleen smiled at Daniel's intensity. His face was animated and his gestures growing as he moved his hands to emphasize his points. He was almost like a small child at Christmas time. She found it charming.

"What?" Daniel said, confused by the expression on Colleen's face.

"Nothing," she said. "Please, go on. It sounds fascinating."

"Allen's philosophy is simple enough. He believed that whatever difficulties or problems we're facing are the result of our previous thoughts and actions. For me, it was focusing on my screwed up mother and father and dysfunctional upbringing. Now I see those problems as a gift of sorts. At least they were an opportunity to change my focus from my past failure in college to my future. Hence, dropping out of school and joining the army. Allen also believed that if you can control your thoughts and emotions, you become the master of your own destiny. Aristotle said about the same thing, 'The hardest victory is the victory over self.'"

Colleen was amazed at the changes she was witnessing in Daniel … his intensity, his enthusiasm, and a sureness that seemed to emanate from his very soul. His intellectual growth and maturity were astounding.

"…Buddha also said all that we are is the result of what we have thought. It is founded on our thoughts. It is made up of our thoughts. Allen defined prosperity as having a good heart and becoming a person who is truly valuable to your fellow beings. I think I can do that with real estate. I think," Daniel chuckled, "so we'll see … we'll see."

"You do have very eclectic tastes, I'll grant you that," Colleen commented.

"Yeah, I'll admit it's a grab bag of varied interests but I think I can meld them into something that resembles work but is really play … at least that's my goal."

"So you're going to stay hungry and foolish," Colleen said with a laugh.

"Whole Earth Catalog!" Daniel replied with a knowing smile.

"See, I don't just read textbooks," Colleen said.

They both laughed and Colleen absentmindedly took one of his potato chips and flipped it in her mouth. "I'm sorry I never had you meet my parents," she said. "I think they might have liked you, especially my dad. He's kind of a philosopher, too."

"Meet your parents? I'm not so sure."

"Well," Colleen hesitated. "Perhaps not but we could have tried." She reached over and took another potato chip. It was an old habit she had picked up freshman year and it had quickly become a running joke between her and Daniel. He pushed his coffee cup toward her but she nodded no. "Remember what you told me about the old cliché, shirt-sleeves to shirtsleeves in three generations? Well it turns out that it is true. Statistically, it has been proven that after three generations, the wealth has been spent or dissipated."

"Do tell!" Daniel responded with a wide smile.

"In every culture around the world, there is the same proverb. In China it's called 'rice paddy to rice paddy.' In Ireland it's called 'clogs to clogs.' It means the first generation makes the money - that would be my mom's parents; the second generation preserves it - that would be my parents, and the third generation…"

"And you get to spend it all," Daniel interrupted with a laugh.

"I want to go back to what you said about me being 'in love with love.'"

"Forget it, Colleen," Daniel said with a shrug of his shoulders, "I was mad at you."

"And you're not mad now?"

"No, I'm not mad anymore."

"I wanted to tell you this so we could end our relationship on a good note. No hard feelings. I want to still be friends with you, Daniel."

"No hard feelings," Daniel said. "It was just brief moment in our lives. It wasn't going to last forever. I realize that now."

"I need to get this off my chest so I can proceed with my life without complications about our past. I'm not a bad person, Daniel. You need to understand that … I have a new man in my life and I don't want our past to come back to haunt me. Our relationship is a thing of the past and whether you think it was real or not, it is over and I want to move on."

"So move on! You don't need my permission to do that."

Colleen struggled with her feelings and how to express them to Daniel. "I thought you were going to die, Daniel, that's why I wrote that letter. I couldn't bear the thought of you dying out there on the battlefield. So I thought it would be easier for me if I ended our relationship before you died. So I wouldn't feel such guilt."

"Did it work?"

"No, it didn't. Not at all! I felt worse for doing it. I was a coward. There isn't a day that goes by that I don't regret what I did to you. It was wrong for me to break up with you that way. I should have had the courage to talk to you in person. That's why I sent those other…."

"Colleen, stop beating yourself up over this. It's done. It's over. You sent the letter and I didn't die. You've moved on with your life, and so have I."

"I need for you to understand that," Colleen said. "I can't go on without knowing that you will forgive me for doing that to you."

"We've both grown a lot," Daniel said in a soft voice. "I got really focused on my job after your letter. I guess in a way, your letter broke me down. The Nam built me back up. I did some things that could have gotten me killed but I got promoted instead. No real reason why I didn't buy the farm. Just lucky I guess."

"I would never have forgiven myself if that had happened," Colleen said.

Daniel finished his coffee. He pushed the sandwich and chips aside. He leaned toward Colleen, lowering his voice as he spoke.

"I had a kind of epiphany in the hospital ward after I was wounded and I got your letter. It was a crisis point that made me realize that I wanted to live and I had to do it on my own terms, without the confusion and hurt of knowing you to mess me up. So I resolved to do just that. To focus on *my* future - a future that didn't include you. Once I came to that resolution, it became much clearer for me. It gave me clarity and a purpose in living."

Colleen silently listened to Daniel's confession.

"And for what it's worth, I probably won't be going back to the Triangle Bar again. That phase of my life is pretty much over now. It was great while it lasted. But the allure and luster are gone. I'm in a different place now. I don't need it anymore."

Colleen said nothing. She just stared at the young man across from her. She studied the tautness of his cheek bones and the deep penetrating stare of his eyes. She could feel the energy pulsating from the intensity of his very presence. She also felt a strange calmness washing over her, warming her body, making her feel very relaxed in his presence. Colleen knew Daniel far too well. She knew there was more to his statement.

"What happened?" she asked softly.

"What do you mean?" Daniel asked.

Colleen pursed her lips. "You know what I mean," she said confidently.

Daniel smiled. "I woke up one morning and saw my father in the mirror," he calmly replied.

"What did you do?"

"I smashed the mirror with my fist - three stitches, nothing serious."

Daniel saw the slight curl of Colleen's lips. She knew she shouldn't be smiling but it didn't seem to matter. Not with Daniel. Not between the two of them. Not anymore. He knew it and she knew it.

At that moment, Colleen's emotions took her for a ride. They were back in freshman year. He was sitting on the bleacher where she saw him for the first time. "I noticed that you're dressed differently than the other times I've seen you." she said.

"It's my new authentic self - for now. I still have my old jeans in the closet for those times when…" he shrugged his shoulders, "when I'm in the mood."

Colleen smiled even more.

"Don't get me wrong, Colleen. Spending time at the Triangle Bar was a wonderful experience for me. And I don't regret a single minute I spent over at Zack's place with my friends there. What I missed the most that summer after freshman year was meaningful conversation."

"Oh, ouch!"

Daniel ignored her comment, "That's what I got at the Triangle Bar. I guess you could call it my salon."

"A salon," Colleen said, taking on a British accent. "A gathering of people of social or intellectual distinction…" she dropped the accent, "or in your case, an old-fashioned hippie pow-wow."

They both laughed out loud. "Which is really a French word that comes from the Italian 'salone'."

"Very good, Daniel!"

"It's time to put that part of me away and focus on the future," Daniel said. "My pseudo-hippie outfits were an allegiance to the hippie philosophy of freedom of expression. I wanted to be different, to prove something to myself and everyone else around me."

Colleen smiled with acknowledgment.

"I don't have to prove anything to anyone anymore."

"So you've moved on with your life."

Daniel looked at her. *Is she being sarcastic?* Before Daniel could answer his own question, Colleen spoke.

"Can I say I'm glad? Because I really am."

"It doesn't mean I won't have a beer once in a while."

"I know, I know! Is that what Wild Man was talking about when he said 'you can't go back again'?"

Daniel smiled at Colleen's perception. The woman didn't miss a thing. "It took a while for me to realize that it wasn't my surroundings that had changed. But it was me instead. Everything here is pretty much as it was two, three years ago. It's me that's changed."

"I realized that the moment I saw you at the Grandview Theater," Colleen said with a smile. "I saw it in your eyes, then again that night at the Triangle Bar and I knew I was right."

Daniel let the hint of a smile escape his lips but said nothing. "Yeah, I'm sorry about the Triangle Bar. I said what I had to say. And as best as I can remember I meant every word of it. But if I was rude, I apologize."

"You weren't rude, Daniel," Colleen answered with a smile.

"That period really did have an enormous influence on my life. The time spent on Zack's front porch, time spent at the Triangle Bar, talking to Zack and Wild Man and all the other crazies."

"I still don't quite understand it, Daniel," Colleen answered. "But I'll take your word for it."

Daniel laughed, "I had been a long time lost. But that was where I found myself or at least began to have a different image of myself."

"I think it's good that you found something that motivated you and gave you a reason to move ahead with your life."

"Yeah, now I think I've got focus and direction. I'm feeling much better about myself."

"Did Vietnam have a lot to do with that too?"

Daniel tensed up for a moment but relaxed again. "To a degree," he answered. "It was an awakening for me."

"It's probably none of my business, but Michael mentioned a program - he thought you might have been involved in some program..."

Daniel's stance changed instantly. His face went from a smile to a taut masking any emotion. His body turned rigid. Colleen could feel tension suddenly grip the two of them. It became deathly quiet in the room.

"Don't go there!" Daniel said in a soft voice as if he didn't want anyone around them to hear his statement.

"Daniel, I was just..."

"I don't talk about that ... not now - not ever!" Their eyes clashed in a stare down. Colleen blinked. She wanted to continue with her questions but Daniel's rock solid stare forbade her.

As Daniel began gathering his study material, Colleen noticed a small tattoo on the inside of his forearm. She reached over and gently touched it. He looked up at her. She wrapped her hand around his forearm and turned the tattoo toward herself. It was the Ace of Spades with a skull and crossbones inside the spade.

"What does it mean?" she asked in a hushed voice.

Daniel hesitated. He glanced down at his arm and back up into Colleen's eyes. "It's from my LRRP unit in Vietnam. Just something we all got after one particularly bad operation. It's in recognition of the Hill People of Laos that we helped that afternoon."

"Devils in green faces."

Daniel furrowed his brow but didn't say anything. She knew. How and why he didn't understand, but Colleen knew about LRRP. He noticed Colleen hadn't removed her hand from his forearm. She let her hand slide down his arm until her fingers were resting on top of his open palm. He looked up at Colleen's face. She had a smile on and her eyes were shining.

Colleen curled her fingers around his until they were intertwined. As she pressed her flesh to his, a surge of adrenaline rushed through her body. She felt his warmth, his pulse pounding blood against her fingertips. It was as if they were connected soul to soul. She felt an overwhelming sense of serenity.

…and vulnerability.

She wanted to press tighter, to clamp her fingers tightly into his. But she dared not. Their eyes locked on to one another's and wouldn't let go.

"We did have some fun times, Daniel," Colleen said, without removing her locked fingers.

"Heightened expectations on my part, I'm afraid," Daniel said, "immature thoughts that didn't match the reality of the times."

"There were some good times."

"And some bad."

"Let's just remember the good ones, OK?" Colleen said releasing her fingers from Daniels. "And don't forget to get a shave. Father Rollins is on the warpath again. He has the power to get you kicked out of school. Besides the fraternity boys here don't like hippies or soldiers strutting their stuff. You should just lay low."

"Thanks for the advice," Daniel answered, "but I'll handle it my way."

"Have you decided on a major yet?" Colleen asked.

"Yeah, I'm going to major in business with a minor in art and design."

"That's a curious choice."

"Not really," Daniel answered. "Business with a focus on real estate, plus Art and design to nurture my creative instincts."

Colleen started to push her chair back. She was more relaxed now than when she first entered the room. "I'm glad I found you and we could talk," she said. "And we can still be friends. I'd like to get to know you again."

"Colleen, I said it was over. Fin! I understand your actions now. I said I forgave you for the letter. But if 'it's over' … it's over. We can't go back to being friends again like nothing ever happened between us."

"Why not?"

“Because.”

“I don’t understand why we can’t be friends like before with you and I and Michael. Remember, we used to call ourselves the Gas House Gang?”

“If you don’t understand it, I can’t explain it to you,” Daniel answered bluntly. “You can’t have it both ways. I won’t pretend there wasn’t something very special between us at one time. But to be just friends now would diminish what we had. And I can’t…I won’t do that.”

Colleen could feel her emotions starting to well up inside. She blinked away a tear that was beginning its slow descent down her check. She backhanded the tear away. She got up and turned to walk away, but stopped in mid-step and turned back to Daniel.

“Alright, Daniel, if that’s the way you want it. I’ll still cherish those memories of freshman year … and leave it at that.”

She started walking toward the entrance of the coffee shop. Daniel watched her for a moment before going back to his studying.

Colleen got as far as the entryway when Claudia suddenly stepped out of nowhere right in front of her, effectively blocking her way. The woman seemed very angry, her piercing eyes cutting into Colleen.

“I see you were talking to Daniel again,” Claudia said.

“We were just talking,” Colleen replied flatly.

But Claudia wasn’t ready to accept that simple answer. “I can imagine you were just talking,” she snapped. “Don’t play me for a fool, girl. I know when a woman still has feelings for a man. Daniel and I are dating, as if you don’t know it. Back off if you know what’s good for you.”

Colleen sidestepped Claudia and took a step back. “Daniel and I were friends freshman year, that’s all. We haven’t spoken to each other for two years - since he went into the service. We were just catching up on old times.”

“You got my message, Red. Don’t forget it.”

Colleen folded her arms across her chest. “So tell me,” she challenged Claudia, “woman to woman, what makes you so enamored with someone like Daniel?”

Claudia put her hands on her hips. She pushed out her chest and stared at Colleen. “He’s unlike any man I’ve ever met. Nothing like the other men I used to date.”

Colleen nodded her understanding.

“He’s smart and clever and very creative.”

“I’ll grant you that,” Colleen said.

"He's very ambitious. Like my Dad."

"True!"

Claudia's voice rose in urgency. She was claiming her man. No bitch was going to take him away from her. She took a step toward Colleen, "Daniel likes me for whom I am. He's not impressed with my money. I even offered to buy him a car, but he refused. Of course, you and your Bradley wouldn't understand that."

"Who?" Colleen said, her face totally deadpan.

Claudia's eyes opened wide. Her checks went taut. "Screw you, bitch!" she snarled at Colleen, who by now was walking away.

Colleen walked out into the crowded hallway with a smile stretched ear to ear.

Last Chance

Daniel's luck ran out between his second and third cup of coffee. Normally he would have left the student coffee shop before first period classes piled in for a wake-up cup of Joe. Daniel knew Father James Rollins had a habit of slipping into the coffee shop through the kitchen entrance. The Dean of Students would parade past the rows of tables, looking for infractions to address and students to dress down. It was the Dean Rollin's way of keeping them on their toes and himself in charge. It was total bullshit as far as Daniel was concerned.

But Daniel had gotten so engrossed in his statistics assignment that he hardly noticed the café filling up with students. It was only when a hulking shadow crossed his table that Daniel looked up from his book. There, towering over his table was Father Rollins, his huge fists resting on the table's edge.

"Young man," he began, "you were told to shave. One chance to clean up your act or else. Nobody gets a free pass around here. Not even ex-servicemen."

Daniel looked up at the Dean of Students and said nothing. His face was expressionless. Deadpan would be the word. Daniel had learned that defensive posture back in basic training in order to cover his ass and give the D.I.s nothing to throw back at him.

"Well?" Father Rollins inquired, "what do you have to say for yourself?"

"Nothing really, Father. I don't think a clean shaven face is a prerequisite to a good education or a detriment to the learning process."

"Don't get smart with me, son! It'll only land you in more trouble than you're already in right now."

By now other students around Daniel's table had noticed Father Rollins and began poking their friends to watch the action. The fiery Dean of Students had a reputation for embarrassing and humiliating students at will, all a part of his reputation as the toughest man on campus. His cafeteria walkabouts were only a small part of his intimidation tours. Students not at the receiving end of his wrath loved to watch his victims squirm. Those who were caught were often afraid they'd pee in their pants at his voluminous rants.

"You call yourself a soldier?" Rollins began. "Son, you lack discipline and the ability to follow orders, both requirements for the CIB. How did you receive such a medal if you can't follow simple orders like shaving?"

Daniel didn't respond. His solid façade remained unbroken.

Father Rollins lowered his voice. He leaned in close to Daniel and said. "If you don't shave, you'll be suspended from classes for a minimum of six weeks. You can audit the classes or get a tutor but you won't be allowed back on campus during that period of time. Do you understand?"

Daniel nodded.

"Screw up again, bud, and you'll be in front of the disciplinary board in no time. You'd better shape up if you want any kind of leniency from the board. Now are you going to do it?"

"I still don't see…"

Father Rollins exploded. "I'll see to it that you bag drag out of here," he said, "and find someplace else to be a rebel. I'll have none of this nonsense on my campus. As an example for the rest of the students here, I'm going to report you to the school's disciplinary board. You will be ordered to stand in front of the board and explain your refusal to shave. We'll see how proudly you stand as a soldier!"

"Ex-soldier." Daniel answered, still giving Rollins his best deadpan look. "Now, if you're done, I have a class to attend." Daniel got up, took one last sip of coffee, and turned to walk away.

Father Rollins, hands on his hips, watched Daniel walk out of the room. The priest's mouth was open and slack. He'd never had a student respond to his warnings so calmly and emotionless. *This one would be different,* Rollins thought, and difficult. But he wasn't about to be bowled over by some 20-year-old hell-bent on making a mockery of his discipline on campus. He'd see to it that Daniel appeared before the board and he'd make sure that Daniel was off campus that same day. There was only one man ruling the campus and it was Father James Rollins.

Colleen's Baby

Peggy returned home with her new baby, Francesca. It would be a short visit beginning early Saturday morning. She was leaving Sunday night, probably never to return to Minnesota again.

Peggy's grandmother had insisted that Peggy show her parents the baby even if they were still in denial about Francesca's birth. "They have to face reality," her grandmother told Peggy. "My daughter has to recognize that she's a grandmother now whether she likes it or not. She has to meet Francesca even if it's only once in her life." Peggy reluctantly agreed to return to St. Paul and took the Greyhound bus the next day.

Peggy knew her homecoming would not be a welcoming affair. Her letters and phone calls to her parents had been sporadic at best. Now as she came into downtown St. Paul, she wished she'd never agreed to come in the first place. Peggy didn't want to spend any more time in her parent's hostile home environment than she had to.

As expected, Peggy's visit home was brief and painful. After less than a half-hour, she was out the back door with her baby and cabbing it to Colleen's dorm room. They met in the lobby and walked out toward the small pond in one corner of the campus. There they sat under a large oak tree and caught up on their lives.

Peggy told Colleen she was going to move to Seattle just as soon as she could. Her grandmother's home was welcoming but its small town atmosphere was something Peggy could never get used to. She was trying to build a new life for Francesca and herself. Nothing would get in the way of that. Not her parents. Not her old boyfriend. Nothing.

As soon as she could, Peggy intended to get an apartment and a job working someplace. Hopefully, the YWCA's daycare program would watch Francesca and Peggy could focus on earning enough to keep them both independent and free of parental intrusions.

"So what did you do this summer, Colleen?" Peggy asked. "Did you and Bradley go on any trips?"

"He did," Colleen answered with a shrug of her shoulders. "I stayed here and got a job with a small magazine in town. It wasn't as exciting as working for that tabloid or the St. Paul newspapers. But it was still good experience. I'd like to work for a bigger magazine after college if I could, but that will mean a move to New York where all the big publishing jobs are."

"What about Bradley?" Peggy asked. "What did he do this summer?"

Colleen looked at Peggy for a moment. She hesitated, choosing her words carefully.

"He was away for the summer, touring Europe mostly. His dad had him checking out several businesses his parents own over there."

"Behaving himself, I hope?" Peggy asked.

"They wanted him to go and have fun so he could settle down after college and focus on medical school and the family business after that." Colleen reflected back on that past summer. "We talked about it a little but Bradley said it was something he had to do. It was expected of him."

"But how did you feel about him being gone all summer?" Peggy asked. "You know he was probably fooling around over there. They all do that once they're in Europe."

"Peggy!"

"Well, don't you think?"

"Seriously, I don't know … no, I don't think so … I trust him, why shouldn't I? That's what his father did … travel, I mean. And his grandfather before that. It's kind of a family tradition."

"Sowing his wild oats. Isn't that what they used to call it?"

"Enough already! Can't we talk about something else? Like what your plans are for your future and the baby?"

"Stay with my grandmother for a little while. At least until I get on my feet financially," Peggy answered. "Once I move to Seattle, get a job. Maybe go back to school. Raise my baby the best way I can." She cuddled Francesca and rocked her back and forth on her lap. "Seriously, Colleen, are you going to marry Bradley?"

"Oh, probably," Colleen said without expressing any emotion. "But maybe not as soon as he would like. Bradley's been pushing us to get engaged soon and married right after graduation."

"What's wrong with that?" Peggy asked. "You can still work and be married, you know."

"He wants children sooner rather than later," Colleen answered. "I don't think I'm ready for that kind of commitment yet."

"It does change your life," Peggy said with a laugh. She hugged her baby tightly and kissed her on the check. "Believe me, your life is never the same after you have a baby."

"Here, let me hold her," Colleen said, extending her arms.

Peggy handed over Francesca who was starting to nod off to sleep. Colleen took the baby and held her close to her breast. The baby cooed and fell asleep. Colleen could feel her tiny heart beating against her chest. She could smell the baby powder Peggy had put on her tiny diaper. Colleen could feel Francesca's warmth and held her even closer.

It was a very strange and yet wonderful feeling. *Imagine,* Colleen thought, *me with my very own baby.* Someone she and her husband could raise together. *Her husband?* Could she see Bradley in that role? *Would he be a caring parent?* And what about … could she even imagine Daniel in that role? *Could he, would he, with his dysfunctional upbringing, be a caring father to our children?*

"You could have one of those by this time next year if you wanted to," Peggy interrupted Colleen's meandering thoughts. "Colleen's baby. What would you name it?"

"My own baby? I have no idea, and I'm not about to ponder that question right now."

"I love picking out baby names," Peggy said.

Colleen gazed down at the tiny infant cradled in her arms. "Francesca Theresa Scranton, what does life hold in store for you?" she whispered into the baby's ear. The baby breathed sweetly and softly.

"You could call her Franny, like in Fanny Hill."

"No!" Peggy shot back.

"Peggy, it's OK, I'm just kidding," Colleen said with a furrow of her brow. "Come on, you need to lighten up a bit."

"It's just that my parents get me so darn mad. They still can't accept the fact that I've had this baby and that I intend to keep it. In their eyes my life is ruined. My college career has ended and I'll probably be on welfare for the rest of my life," Peggy started to choke up, "They've given up on me, Colleen, they really have."

"Well, I haven't Peggy. You'll always be my friend. You and Francesca will always be welcome in my home wherever that may be. Always!"

"Getting back to Bradley…"

"Do we have to?" Colleen joked.

They both laughed, causing the baby to stir in her slumber.

Colleen tucked her legs under and became reflective as Francesca slept peacefully in her arms. "Seriously," she whispered, "I want to wait awhile…and not be in the family way right away."

"There's the pill, you know."

"Not if my parents have anything to do with it."

"You're kidding!"

"Not at all," Colleen answered. "They think only promiscuous girls are on the pill."

"So did you see anyone else while Bradley was gone?" Peggy asked. "I know you two are an item but you aren't attached at the hip yet."

"No!"

"What about Daniel?"

"No!"

"Haven't seen him at all?"

Colleen stared at her friend. She couldn't read Peggy's face. It was a mask painted with a pleasant grin. "So what have you heard, Miss Busybody?

"Just that you were seen with Daniel a couple of times. Once at a frat party, once at the Triangle Bar, and once at the coffee shop on campus. You see my dear, I have spies everywhere," she laughed. "Actually just a couple of nosey ex-classmates."

"But who's counting, right, Peggy?"

"Colleen, people talk! You know that," Peggy answered. "I don't care what you do with your life but I thought you two were through."

"We are!" Colleen insisted. "I just ran into him a couple of times by accident. Seriously! … Except that last time at the coffee shop. We had a good talk and formally ended our relationship there. I had a chance to tell him I was sorry I wrote that Dear John letter and he accepted my apology. End of story."

"For real?"

"Yes, Peggy, for real. We ended it as friends, but friends who won't see each other ever again."

"OK."

"Seriously, Peggy, why don't you believe me?" Colleen asked, irritated at Peggy's staid response to her explanation.

Peggy just smiled at Colleen and said nothing.

Biba on Parade

They were the elite from both campuses. The brightest, most academically gifted upperclassmen both schools had seen for a long time. And according to Colleen's boyfriend, Bradley, they were all the most likely to succeed in the real world.

Colleen was accepting of this crowd only because of the intellectual stimulation they offered her. Yet it was their lack of accountability that tempered her enthusiasm for continued friendship. Not one of them, men or women, had ever had to work hard for anything in their lives. With their storied pedigrees and family connections, they would probably never have financial stress in their lifetime either. They, along with a lot of help from their parents, had mapped out their future lives and it looked very bright for each and every one of them.

With Peggy now gone for good and Daniel all but a memory, Colleen found herself lacking close friendships that she could count on. Bradley's group was a poor substitute for real friends. But with one year left to go, Colleen was willing to forgo the search for better friends and force herself to accommodate this elite but snobbish crowd.

Bradley had rented a stretch limo for their grand entrance at the Town and Country Club. The limo was shiny black with chrome wheels and a sunroof. There were only three such vehicles in the entire Twin Cities. Leave it to Bradley to find the only one available for that night, Colleen thought. Her man was certainly one to get just what he wanted.

The men in the entourage were all wearing designer tuxedos; standard black with add-ons to match their personalities. Most of the young women had bought their dresses at Saks or Macy's in New York City or Chicago. A few had even flown to Paris for their purchases. There were gowns by Pierre Cardin, Andre Courreges, Givenchy, Yves Saint Laurent and Pucci.

For her part, Colleen had purchased a simple long black dress and altered it. In its original form with a plunging neckline, it was too risqué for her own taste. So Colleen raised the hemline and had a classmate sew in a fichu; a piece of silk lace between the deep V of the dress. It was simple yet elegant, another one of her own creations.

Not only did Bradley manage to come up with the longest, most elegant limousine for the evening, he even timed their arrival for maximum effect. It was just late enough to find most of the other students already congregated in the immense lobby or just entering the main ballroom.

Colleen wasn't comfortable with the showiness of it all. But this was Bradley's game and she wasn't about to embarrass him in his theatrics. A quick glance around the room and Colleen could tell they were definitely the best dressed ones there.

Yet, somehow, Colleen felt strangely uncomfortable standing by Bradley with his moneyed and privileged friends. Her dress matched that of the most expensive one there. Her makeup and hair were perfect. Yet, she didn't appreciate the ambiance her crowd was trying to create within their own sphere of influence. It was all show with very little substance.

Their group entered the ballroom with her and Bradley in the lead. They meandered through the rows of tables, acknowledging a few other couples, until Bradley found their assigned table. He quickly signaled his group to sit down as he looked around for the waiters.

Colleen looked around the room. He wasn't there. She breathed a sigh of relief. She could concentrate on her boyfriend without any distractions. The ballroom began to fill up quickly. Drinks were ordered and Bradley began to preside over his table, barking orders to the waiters and telling some jokes.

Colleen faked her smile at the others around her and absentmindedly ran her fingers over the dinner plate. She was already beginning to get bored with the pretense of meaningful conversation going on with her group. The men were all Bradley's handpicked fraternity buddies. Each came with their own wraparound date clinging to their every obnoxious word.

By now the room was nearly full. There were just a few tables left empty. Colleen could tell the band was winding down with its last song before the formal proceedings of the evening begin. Bradley was rambling on, eliciting loud laughter from his college cronies. Colleen took a deep breath and let out another sigh. *It's going to be a very long night,* she thought. If this was what Bradley's life was like back in New York City she would have to reevaluate just how excited she was to become a part of that elite group.

Colleen glanced at the entrance to the ballroom and over towards the band. Something caught her eye. She looked back at the entrance just in time to see Daniel enter the room.

Claudia was clutching his arm even though he seemed oblivious to her hanging there. They were leading the Lake Minnetonka old money crowd into the room.

When Colleen looked at their clothes she could not believe her eyes.

Every one of the women in Daniel's group was wearing something from Biba; the high fashion, low price point line of clothes aimed at teenagers. It was either an inside joke or a bold fashion statement on their part.

As the group walked in, it was like a sea of muddied color palettes of browns, sepia, gray and plum. Colleen guessed immediately that the couture collection was a deliberate attempt to be different from everyone else in the room. It had to have been Daniel's idea. There was no way Claudia Weinstein would have ever dared to wear such an inexpensive dress on her own. They were making a statement, a deliberate snub at the expensive dresses that Bradley's group was sporting.

He's done it again, Colleen thought as a smile stretched wide across her face. It was a bold statement of Daniel's independence, his own vision, his stand against the norm and the average. And fashion.

Claudia was wearing a pale blue (very) low cut, revealing cocktail dress. Colleen stared at her ample well-tanned breasts that were practically falling out. She looked around at the group laughing and having a good time. Most of the men were in tuxedos or suits. The other women were also in gowns or dresses that accented their cleavage and trim bodies. Their movements were exaggerated as if each was trying to out-maneuver the next. It was as if they were purposely mocking the sophisticated atmosphere that the Town and Country was trying to foster.

Rumors were flying about the magic couple, Daniel and Claudia. Claudia had been telling all her friends that her father would hire Daniel right after he graduated. Mitch would put him on the fast track at his firm, with a large salary and company car. No strings attached.

Colleen looked at Daniel and her smile grew even wider. Unlike the rest of his haute couture fashion crowd, Daniel was dressed in pressed blue jeans, an open necked blue shirt and a very expensive herringbone sport coat. Daniel was the only man not in a tuxedo or fancy suit.

Several of the other men were gathered around him. He was talking about something, holding all their attention. The women were talking and glancing over their shoulders at the rest of the room. All except for Claudia, who couldn't help but keep looking over at Daniel, trying to catch his attention. He was obviously the center of attention without even trying.

Colleen turned back to her table and softened her smile. Daniel was truly being just himself. He was wearing his own style. It was just like he had told her years earlier. Daniel had evolved into the kind of man he wanted to become; self-assured, confident, and emitting a quiet strength of personality and form.

Daniel led his group to a much larger table than Bradley's. It was almost directly across the dance floor from theirs. Claudia hung on him until he pried her hands off and dropped her into her chair. He sat down next to her and leaned back, placing his arm across the back of her chair. She kept looking over at him as she talked to some of the other women at her table.

Daniel smiled at his crowd but seemed to be focused someplace else.

Bradley was engaged in a heated discussion about economies at her table. Colleen smiled at the other women around her table but found herself being drawn back to Daniel's table, sneaking glances in that direction whenever she could.

Colleen couldn't help but notice how Claudia was pawing at him with her hand in his lap. Daniel didn't seem to resist her. But he wasn't being as affectionate back to her either. He was obviously comfortable with himself and his outfit. He stood out from that crowd and Colleen wasn't sure what he saw in Claudia other than the fact that she was very rich and influential.

The music began and Colleen grabbed Bradley and led him to the dance floor. She kept looking up at him and focused all her attention there. They danced, sneaking several kisses as they moved across the dance floor. Colleen forced herself not to look over at Daniel's table. One time she could sense that Claudia and Daniel were close by. But by deftly maneuvering Bradley away, she avoided any close contact with the other couple.

The avoidance only lasted part of the evening. Within the hour, Colleen found herself stealing more glances over in Daniel's direction just to see what he and Claudia were doing.

Claudia's party left the dance early that evening to head back to Lake Minnetonka and a large party there at one of the many mansions on the lake.

As the dance was winding down, Colleen and Bradley wandered out onto the balcony. The night air was brisk but not enough for Colleen to need her coat. They stood by the balcony railing and looked down on the others leaving early.

"Pretty neat evening, wasn't it?" Bradley commented.

"It was wonderful," Colleen agreed.

"Best that money can buy. First class all the way."

"Bradley, you don't wear class on your fingers or around your neck. Or have it because you have a limo bigger than anyone else."

Bradley looked at her in surprise.

He raised an eyebrow. "Oh, really? You don't seem to mind being showered with those little gifts of mine from de Givenchy or Chanel or Hermes. Don't tell me those little trinkets don't make you feel very special!"

"Bradley, those were thoughtful gifts but they didn't make me feel any different. That's not what I'm talking about. Class is internal. It's how you carry yourself and how you act and your value system."

"You've got to be kidding!" Bradley exclaimed. "My old girlfriends would have thought they'd died and gone to heaven if they had received just a fraction of the gifts I've given you. Those brands mean something to our kind. Class is class. You either have it or you don't. And my family has it in spades."

"I think you're wrong. Class is not something you can buy or inherit. A person can be poor and still have class. Wealth, genealogy and family lines don't necessarily determine if a person has it or not."

A scowl appeared on Bradley's face.

Colleen spoke without thinking. "Daniel said…" The words had barely slipped from her lips when Bradley was all over her.

"When did you see him?" Bradley demanded to know. "Are you seeing him behind my back?"

"No, Bradley," Colleen responded in a calm and reassuring voice. "I'm not seeing him or anyone else. I just happened to run into him at the Triangle Bar some time ago. It was strictly by accident."

"You never told me."

"There was nothing to tell. We met. We talked a little. End of conversation."

"At the Triangle Bar?"

"Yes."

"He was probably trolling for fresh meat from what I hear."

"What do you mean?"

"His living accommodations, Colleen."

"I heard he bought a house." Colleen said.

"No, he's got himself one hell of a bachelor pad I heard," Bradley responded with a chuckle.

"What do you mean?"

"His roommates, that's what."

"I don't understand. What are you trying to say?"

"Oh, Colleen, don't be so naïve! Your old beau has a two bedroom house and three hot chicks for roommates, that's what."

"I didn't hear that part but I'm sure there's no impropriety on Daniel's part."

"Yeah, right," Bradley laughed. "You're delusional if you believe that. Living with three women under the same roof. He probably goes hopping from one bedroom to the next."

"You wish!" Colleen blurted out.

"Are you jealous?" Bradley asked with a smirk.

"No!" Colleen snapped back.

"Colleen, he's trailer trash. Nothing more."

"Tell me about your summer," Colleen said, anxious to change the tone of their conversation.

Bradley looked over at Colleen, shrugged his shoulders and answered, "Nothing much to tell. We…"

"We?"

"Yes, we! You knew I wasn't traveling alone, Colleen."

"No, I didn't," Colleen answered glancing over at her boyfriend. "You said you had a lot of traveling to do. And you said you wouldn't be able to call often either."

"Is this what this is all about?" Bradley asked. "My not calling you while I was in Europe?"

"No!"

"Exactly what are you asking me, sweetheart?" Bradley asked, his voice hinting at condensation.

"Who were you traveling with?"

"Friends," he answered, "friends and business associates."

"Friends?"

"Yes, just some friends." Bradley turned to face Colleen who slowly turned toward him. "And I don't appreciate your tone of voice. I was with a group of friends from back east. We did a lot of touring. I visited my parent's plants in Ireland, Wales and on the continent. We went to the Mediterranean and rented a yacht for some deep sea fishing and cruising." He calmed down before he spoke. "We grabbed a private plane, flew to the Hamptons, spent some time there and I flew back here."

Colleen said nothing, waiting for Bradley to end the litany of his travels.

"Then I called you and wanted to come over…and make love, but you refused. Remember?"

"Don't!"

"Colleen, I was gone for the entire summer. I didn't call you - and I'm sorry for that. But it was mainly business and I couldn't let my parents down. One day all of those factories will be ours. I've got a responsibility to know what's going on there. If you're going to stick with me, those are some of the conditions. I thought that was understood?"

"Was it just guys with you?"

"Colleen, I won't have you make accusations like that."

"Well?"

"No!" Bradley answered with a cold snap. "There were several female executives on part of the trip - all managers; folks we met up with in England. Dad insisted part of his management team go on the tour of the plants with us; they all went back to the States - satisfied?"

"They didn't go to the Mediterranean with you?"

"No!"

Colleen could see that Bradley was upset and irritated with her. "Peggy just made mention of the fact that…."

"Peggy? What does she have to do with this?"

"Well, nothing, I guess. She was just saying…."

"Colleen you need to get better friends," Bradley threw back. "Besides, I thought you told me she got knocked up and moved out West?"

"She had a baby."

"Listen, Colleen," Bradley began, gathering Colleen up in his arms. "Nothing happened last summer. OK? Let's just focus on this last year and get on with our lives. Can we do that?"

Colleen looked into Bradley's penetrating eyes. He seemed so sincere that she felt badly that she'd pursued the subject as far as she had. If she were going to marry this man, she'd have to trust him implicitly. This would be a good first step for her.

"I'm sorry, Bradley. Really I am," Colleen said. "Yes, let's just focus on the rest of this school year and our future after that."

"Good," Bradley said with a smile. He put his hand up against the back of her thigh, cupping his fingers there until he could feel her panties. "Tonight?" he asked hopefully.

"No, silly boy, not tonight. It's, you know … that time of the month," she lied. Bradley followed with a much weaker chuckle and they went back for the last dance of the night.

Mother Hen

Something was amiss in Colleen's perfect world. The subtle feeling that things weren't just right tugged at her long after the Homecoming Dance and Parents Weekend was over. It wasn't just Bradley's obnoxious friends or his command performance every time he was in a group of any size. Colleen was slowly beginning to ponder whether something wasn't missing beyond their picture-perfect relationship.

Her head was telling her one thing but her heart kept sending out mixed messages. What Colleen couldn't figure out was whether the problem was with her boyfriend or herself? Whether her doubts were just a figment of her imagination or something more subtle? Whether her heart was filling her head with thoughts she couldn't grasp on a conscious level? Everything was so right with her life. Why would she have any lingering doubts about anything?

Talking to her parents would do no good. Neither one of them, but especially her mother, would want to question to validity of marriage to Bradley. He was everything they might wish for in a husband for Colleen. Even on a calm and rational level, Colleen couldn't really think of anything to criticize about Bradley. There was nothing conscious or subconscious that she could pin her muddled feelings on.

Some nights Colleen would toss and turn until she was exhausted by morning. Her roommate would ask her about those sleepless nights but Colleen just lied and said it was that "time of the month" or she had a headache from stress. The only common denominator Colleen could link to all the confusion swirling around in her head was Daniel. The mere mention of his name or the image of him made her increasingly uncomfortable and ill at ease. But why?

That weekend, Colleen went home for a brief stay. If she thought it would help her confusion, she was mistaken.

Mary Rose was of little help in the matter. While Arthur dismissed Colleen's concerns as simple nervousness about her pending finals, Colleen's mother argued with her.

"Bradley is a wonderful young man," she lectured Colleen. "He's perfect. Why aren't you able to see that? He's going to be a doctor and a large part of New York society. What woman wouldn't want to be a part of that? Why, at your age, I couldn't imagine a more perfect storybook ending to a stellar collegiate career. Have you ever looked at Town and Country magazine? That's the kind of life we're talking about."

Colleen winced at the words coming from her mother but Mary Rose didn't care. She wasn't about to let her only daughter just walk away from the chance of a lifetime. "You're always so happy when you're with Bradley," she reminded her daughter. "You're perfect together. Why, chances like this only come around once in a lifetime. If there are issues you're not sure about, they can always be worked out once you've settled down together."

"Mother, there's more to life than just money and status."

"True, dear," Mary Rose shot back, "but a real catch like Bradley is not someone you can dismiss as just another suitor. You have to give love a chance to grow and blossom. You'll find true love with him if you give it a chance. That's all I'm saying sweetheart, give him a chance."

"I am, Mother!" Colleen answered back. "I just have this gut feeling…."

"Feeling about what?"

"I don't know, Mother, I really don't know. It's just a feeling."

"That makes no sense whatsoever, Colleen. Now you're talking nonsense."

"Maybe, but the feeling is still there."

Mary Rose threw up her arms. "I don't know what to say, Colleen. Talk to your father and maybe he can talk some sense into you."

"I already did."

"And?"

"I have to go back to campus now," Colleen answered as she scooped up her book bag. She gave her mother a kiss and left before Mary Rose could take up her arguments again.

As Colleen's car pulled out of the driveway and disappeared down the road, her mother felt a sense of foreboding. Mary Rose walked back into the house and found her husband reading in the parlor. Arthur looked up briefly before going back to reading the Times. Mary Rose sat down next to him and said nothing. Arthur looked up and put his paper down.

"OK, Mary Rose," he asked. "What is it?"

"You know perfectly well what it is," Mary Rose began. "Your daughter, that's what. I just don't understand what's come over her. Why she can't see just how wonderful Bradley is for her."

"I've thought about that too," Arthur confessed. "My initial assumption is that she's just nervous about finals. But now I think it's bigger than that."

"Well, what, for heaven's sake? What is on that girl's mind?"

"Have you listened to her talk about Daniel?"

"Well, yes…. I suppose so….she's very defensive about the boy," Mary

Rose answered. "Why, I just don't know. He's certainly nothing like her other boyfriends. He's so different."

"Not as much as you might want to believe."

"What are you talking about, Arthur?"

"Like it or not," Arthur began to explain, "I think our daughter has found a kindred soul in Daniel."

"No!" Mary Rose shot back. "He's nothing like us…nothing. How could she possibly have anything in common with him?"

"From everything she's said about the boy, about Daniel, I think … or she thinks … they share the same kind of ambition and the same values - the same goals in life." Arthur smiled at his wife. "And, unfortunately for us, those goals don't always jive with what we think she ought to be doing with her life. Dear, we've raised a very strong, independent woman. One who isn't going to let outside influences affect or direct her life."

"But…"

"Colleen has become her own person, Mary Rose," Arthur countered. "And I'm not so sure that we would want anything else for her. I think we should be proud of how she's turned out. And I think we should support her in whatever choices she makes for her future."

Mary Rose looked at her husband, "I don't know," she answered. "I just don't know."

The lobby to the dorm was empty as Colleen walked in and absentmindedly threw her book bag on a lounge chair. She plopped down on the chair and laid her head back on the headrest. It was quiet and peaceful but would soon be filled with other girls returning from the long weekend. She closed her eyes. She could feel herself drifting off into a very peaceful resting place.

She wanted to try to process everything that was milling around in her brain. But instead her thoughts just kept bouncing back and forth between Bradley, Daniel, graduation and the many twists and turns her life was now taking.

"Hello, Colleen."

Colleen opened her eyes to see Mrs. O'Reilly standing in front of her. The dorm mother was smiling and holding her purse. Colleen moved her book bag out of the way. Mrs. O'Reilly sat down next to her and patted her knee. "How are you, dear?" she asked.

"I'm fine. I just got back from my parents place in Rochester."

"And how was your visit home this weekend?" Mrs. O'Reilly asked.

“Confusing!”

“Really? Why is that?”

Colleen hesitated to begin yet another conversation with Mrs. O’Reilly. But the dorm mother had always been so accommodating and understanding to Colleen. She felt safe talking to her about her feelings.

“I think I’m in love with the most perfect man,” Colleen began. “He loves me. He respects me. We have loads of fun together.”

“That all sounds wonderful.”

“It does sound that way, doesn’t it?” Colleen said with a hint of resignation in her voice.

“So what could be troubling about all of that?” Mrs. O’Reilly asked.

“I don’t honestly know. All of my life, I’ve been conditioned by my parents … really programmed by them to believe that I am somebody special and I deserve someone else just as special. My parents have told me that I deserve the very best and nothing less would be acceptable. It’s what is expected. All of my friends want me to marry someone like Bradley. I feel I have a responsibility to live up to people’s expectations of me.”

“No, that’s wrong,” Mrs. O’Reilly said, interrupting Colleen. “You have a responsibility to listen to your heart and not other people’s interpretation of your relationship with this Bradley person.”

“Maybe there’s something wrong with me, I don’t know,” Colleen said.

“There’s nothing wrong with you if you pay attention to your feelings. Not your head trying to make sense of what other people, including your parents, are trying to tell you.”

“What do you mean?” Colleen asked.

“Let me ask you one question,” Mrs. O’Reilly said. “Does your boyfriend, Bradley, make you feel truly happy?

Colleen was surprised by the question. “Why, yes, of course he does. I wouldn’t be with him unless he did. That’s a strange question.”

“I’m not so old that I’ve forgotten a young freshman girl in this same dorm four years ago. She was dating a sometimes-disheveled young man but a young man who made her feel very different from the high school boys she had been dating,” Mrs. O’Reilly looked at Colleen with a broad smile on her face.

Colleen smiled back.

“Yes, I remember those conversations,” she acknowledged.

“Granted, I thought you two were somewhat immature; he more so than you, but you were both pretty young."

"He's already admitted that he was very immature. But he's changed so much. You just wouldn't believe how much he has become a totally different person."

"I still remember how you talked about your feelings when you two were together. Do you remember that?"

"Oh, I remember," Colleen answered emphatically. "But it was a different kind of happy. It was unrestrained and spontaneous. We were open and painfully honest with one another. I sometimes think that's why we argued so much. I was really just being myself when I was with Daniel and didn't have to put on airs or try to impress anyone. I hadn't realized it at the time but a lot of his hippie philosophy must have rubbed off on me."

"Is he still like that now?" Mrs. O'Reilly asked.

Colleen shrugged her shoulders, "I've only talked to him a couple of times. But I can tell you one thing he has….."

"I'm listening."

Colleen looked up at her dorm mother. Mrs. O'Reilly's eyes were slits in a mask of serious concentration.

"Ambition!" Colleen punched the air with her words. "What Daniel has, that I admire the most, is his driving ambition. I've had the disadvantage, as strange as it may sound, of being born wealthy. Everything has been handed to me. I've led a very privileged life."

"Most of the girls on campus have," Mrs. O'Reilly answered with a smile.

"Exactly! Daniel was born hungry! I had to learn to be hungry. I had to work on my desire to succeed."

Mrs. O'Reilly just looked at Colleen, letting her spew forth her pent-up emotions. Colleen surprised herself at the words that came pouring forth.

"I've never met anyone as ambitious as Daniel. He's fiercely determined to be a success, no matter what. He won't let anything or anyone get in his way. He almost died in Vietnam, but he came back an entirely different person; stronger, focused, and so driven. If I had half the ambition of that man, I would be very proud of myself."

"Colleen, you are as ambitious as he is. Just in a different way," the dorm mother answered.

Colleen regained her composure.

"Might I venture a word here," Mrs. O'Reilly said. "The word is content."

"I don't understand?" Colleen said

"I think you do if you'll let yourself admit it."

"I still don't understand what you're trying to tell me, Mrs. O'Reilly."

The dorm mother smiled at Colleen. "Learn to accept your life as it is, not as you thought it should be or expected it to be. Be realistic and brutally honest with yourself. Listen to your heart more than your head."

Colleen listened intently.

"It seems to me that with Bradley your life is secure. It's content. No surprises. With Daniel, on the other hand, it's wide open. Anything can and might happen."

"I don't know," Colleen confessed. "I just don't know."

"And you might not for some time," Mrs. O'Reilly assured her. "Just take it slow. Listen to your heart. You'll make the right decision in the end. I'm confident of you, young lady. You will do the right thing."

Colleen went back to her room. She sat at her desk for a long time. Her roommate came in and started getting ready for bed. "I'm going to make a call," Colleen announced and walked out the door. She walked down the hall to the phone booth and called Bradley. He picked up on the second ring.

"Hi, Sweetheart," Colleen began, "I just wanted to say I had a wonderful time this last week with homecoming and the dance."

"Yeah, I did too."

"We're pretty lucky, you know; having met one another like that," Colleen paused for effect, "oh wait, you were stalking me, remember?"

"And you got into my car - with a perfect stranger, no less."

"That was my first mistake," Colleen said with a laugh.

"We are lucky. I'm so glad I met you like that. Now our future is pretty well laid out. I can't wait for graduation and moving on to the next phase of our lives. It's going to be so great."

"It will be great. Want to meet for coffee tomorrow morning? We can just talk some more."

"Love to, but I'm pretty bushed. Besides, there are some business dealings for my parents that I've got to tackle first thing in the morning … maybe some other time."

"That's OK, I understand. Business comes first."

"I'm glad you understand. And you better get used to it," Bradley cautioned her. "There'll be a lot more business dealings in my future. It's part of the package, I guess."

"I guess," Colleen responded. "Good night, dear, sleep tight." She hung up and went back to her room. The room was dark and her roommate was already in bed.

Colleen got undressed and laid in her bed, staring at the ceiling.

"Why'd you call your boyfriend so late at night?" her roommate asked.

"Oh, just to tell him I love him."

"But doesn't he already know that?"

"I just wanted to, that's all."

"As long as you're sure of yourself."

"Of course I am! What kind of question is that?" Colleen asked in a huff, sitting up in her bed.

Her roommate laughed. "It wasn't a question, Colleen. It was a statement. You sound very defensive."

"I'm not being defensive!"

"OK. Good night, then."

Colleen laid back and tried to think about Bradley. She stared up at the pale gray shadow that was on her ceiling. Slowly, she could feel herself drifting off to sleep. She imagined her wedding day with a flowing white dress and flowers and music and her proud parents looking on.

She imagined Bradley standing there waiting for her at the altar. She was walking down the church aisle on a white runner. Pachelbel was playing in the background. Eager eyes peered at her beautiful dress and her beaming smile. It was all so very perfect.

But as Colleen got closer, it was someone else standing next to the pastor. Someone with longish hair, dressed in blue jeans and a plaid shirt. He was smiling at her. Colleen blinked her eyes to change the image. She couldn't understand what had happened to Bradley.

Why was someone else standing there in his place?

She got closer to the altar. Her father was still there at her side. He hadn't slowed his pace. They got closer and she saw the stranger but couldn't recognize him. She saw his eyes peering at her. Their eyes locked on. Her breath got shorter. Her hand grew clammy clutching her father's hand. They stopped in front of the stranger. Her father drew her close and hugged her, then he held out her hand to the stranger. He smiled at Colleen.

Daniel took her hand in his and drew her up to the altar.

Colleen awoke in a cold sweat. It was much like the chill she felt when she dreamt of Daniel's death on the battlefield. She caught her breath and fell back on the bed. Her eyes fixed on the ceiling, searching for another image, but it remained gray and elusive.

CIB Material

Father Rollins was lying in wait for Daniel as he entered the Student Union Building after first period class. Before Daniel could react, Rollins confronted him in the hallway and blocked his entrance to the coffee shop. "Follow me," was all he said as he turned and marched away.

Daniel debated for a moment whether to follow the priest or not. He decided that ignoring that order would only hasten his academic demise before the disciplinary board.

They walked down the hallway to a door marked - Father James J. Rollins - Dean of Students. They went inside and passed a timid-looking secretary who barely glanced up before going back to her typing. The priest walked into his office and sat behind his desk, which was piled high with stacks of papers and books. He pointed to a chair in front of his desk and commanded Daniel to sit there.

"We need to talk, young man," he said as he sat down and proceeded to fish out a cigarette from his desk drawer. He lit up and drew in a deep breath before exhaling and putting the cigarette in an ashtray. He grabbed a small manila folder and opened it on his desk.

"When I was a chaplain during the Korean War, I encountered a lot of young men such as yourself. Brash kids really, full of themselves and hard to discipline. A lot of them got killed for just that very reason - their inability or unwillingness to follow orders." He looked Daniel straight in his eyes, "They just couldn't hack it. Do you understand?"

"Begging your pardon, Father, but this is different..."

"Do not interrupt me when I'm talking! Damn it, boy, don't you have any self-control?"

Daniel clenched his teeth and tightened his jaw. He took a very deep breath and leaned back in his chair. He let the priest ramble on.

"I've talked to you twice now about following the rules on campus. That means being clean shaven for you. I was hoping you would see the light and get some common sense. If you had shaved after our last meeting, I'm confident the disciplinary board would have gone easy on you. Probably just a warning, but obviously you chose to defy my order and not shave. So I've convened a formal hearing with the board for two weeks from today. Failure to appear before the board will mean immediate suspension of all classes until you do appear. Is that understood?"

"Buddha Understands."

"What?"

"Buddha Understands."

"What are you saying? Is that code for something?"

"Surely you're familiar with the Buddhist religion?"

"I'm Catholic, for God's sake. Why would I study other religions?"

Daniel kept his mouth shut. He stared at the priest.

"Well, is that understood?"

"Understood," Daniel said, trying hard to keep a smile from creeping across his face.

Father Rollins took another deep drag on his cigarette and twisting it between two fingers, he leaned in toward Daniel. "I don't understand you, son. A lot of vets that return from the service are still green as grass. But I've seen your 201 file. Your military record is outstanding. They don't give out the Combat Infantry Badge to anyone unless their action has been exemplary. I know you've seen a lot of combat. You were offered a battlefield commission. As an officer you could have gone all the way. So why would you come back to civilian life and decide that now you're going to start breaking all the rules? I just don't understand that!"

Daniel took a deep breath. "Father Rollins, I did my time…"

"I wouldn't call serving your country doing your..."

"I did my time!" Daniel repeated. "I gave it everything I had - and more. I saved lives … sometimes by breaking the rules. I did what I had to do to survive. I improvised when I had to..."

Father Rollins could see the determination in the young man's face. It was unlike anything he'd ever seen from another student being disciplined. This was no scared freshman or boisterous senior. The young man's intensity was growing with every word he chewed up and spat out.

"….I did my time with the First Air Cav and Special Ops. I've wasted dinks by the dozen. Hell was in session every time I went out on patrol. I did two tours in country; sucking mud on Hamburger Hill and watching snake and nape decimate a squad of gooks no more than ten clicks away from me. I prayed to my God when Spooky came overhead and hoped to hell he didn't cut me to ribbons instead of Charlie. I've identified my buddies by their body parts because the rest of them was scattered across some battlefield. I've cradled a dying kid in my arms, listening to him call out for his mother as he bled to death. And I couldn't do a goddamned thing to save him."

Daniel was finished. The good Reverend could do anything he wanted to do to him. He didn't much care anymore.

"So you see, Father Rollins, I've been to hell and back. Having to shave just to satisfy some archaic rule of yours isn't that much of a concern for me now." Daniel sucked in his breath as he growled out his final words. "So if you want to put me in a world of hurt, so be it. I learned three things in the Nam. Respect for myself. Respect for my unit. Respect for my enemy."

"Son, I am not…"

"See you at the board meeting," Daniel said as he stood up and walked out of the office.

Father Rollins watched Daniel go. Once again, the priest's mouth was open and slack. He couldn't believe what had just happened.

Later that evening, Claudia came over to pick up Daniel and go to a movie. Throughout most of the flick, Claudia put her hand over the slope of Daniel's thigh and began to massage him. Passionately kissing, Daniel let his hand slip under Claudia's dress and up her legs. Claudia caught her breath.

After the movie, Claudia insisted they drive down to the monument and park in one dark corner of the parking lot. There were just a few other cars parked in the lot. Claudia edged up closer to Daniel and began to nibble at his neck. She let her dress work its way up until most of her dark tan leg was exposed.

"My dad will get you off!" she told him when Daniel relayed what had happened in Father Rollin's office that morning.

"No thanks," Daniel answered as he wrapped his arms around her. "I'll handle this myself."

"But he's one of the largest donors the college has ever had. I know he can get you off."

"No, Claudia," Daniel said as he gently moved Claudia off of his neck. "This is my fight. And mine alone." Claudia smiled and said, 'OK." She went back to nuzzling the nape of his neck. Daniel began to feel himself getting aroused. He ran his hand down to her leg and began to softly caress her.

"Daniel, sweetheart, I need to ask you something," she said, "and please don't get mad at me."

"What?"

"My girlfriends keep telling me that they think you're still hot for her.

You know, that Colleen girl you were dating."

"Like I said before, get better friends."

Claudia put her hand over Daniel's crotch and began to massage him there. They began to kiss passionately. Daniel let his hand slip under Claudia's dress and up between her legs. Claudia caught her breath. She pulled her face away from Daniels, "Tell me you love me. Tell me."

"Claudia…"

"I love you, Daniel. I love you," Claudia whispered in his ear. With that, she wrapped her hand around him and began long, slow strokes.

As Daniel caressed Claudia, he could hear the labored release of her breath. Their mutual manipulation began to grow in speed and intensity. Their bodies were tight together, moving in a rapid frenzy. They came together almost in unison, gasping and breathless.

Afterwards, Claudia released herself from their tight grip and whispered into Daniel's ear, "I want to do it…all the way. I want it now."

Daniel kissed Claudia on her neck and answered, "Not tonight."

"Tomorrow night? Please, I want it so bad."

"Tell me more about your dad's business."

"Oh, you poop head," Claudia scolded Daniel as she nuzzled in closer to the nape of his neck. "OK, for now. But I still want to…"

"So what did he say about me working for him after graduation?"

Lost in the A Shau

Even though Peggy had been gone for several weeks, Colleen still couldn't get their last conversation out of her mind. Without meaning to, Peggy had challenged most of Colleen's safe, secure and confident assumptions about her and Daniel. And the conversation with Mrs. O'Reilly hadn't helped either. In fact, the Dorm Mother's comments had only stoked the fire, causing Colleen more confusion and uncertainty.

If the issues with Daniel were to be resolved, Colleen would have to face it head on. Once and for all, she had to know why she couldn't get Daniel off her mind.

The quadrangle at St. Paul's campus was relatively quiet and empty. There were only a few students coming and going out of the student union.

If Daniel was inside studying after his last class, he would probably be leaving shortly. Colleen sat and waited patiently. She didn't want to be seen with Daniel anyplace where a lot of people would see them together. She didn't need another confrontation with Claudia or for Bradley to hear rumors about her and Daniel.

The minutes dragged on. An hour passed. Colleen began to doubt her wisdom of waiting outside. Perhaps she should have gone inside. If Daniel was there, she could still talk to him even if the environment wasn't the best. If he wasn't inside, she'd just wasted an hour, feeling very stupid in the process. She began to get up. *He probably wasn't here in the first place*, she thought.

Just then she saw Daniel coming out of the library next door. He was by himself and walking at a brisk clip. Colleen got up and crossed the quadrangle at an angle, hoping to catch him before he got to his motorcycle.

When Colleen caught up to him, Daniel was almost to the parking lot. He was carrying a bunch of books cradled under one arm. She saw it was his beat up old books by Ferlinghetti, Kerouac and Ginsberg. Daniel had told her before that he liked their writing because it spoke to him of freedom and creativity. Daniel had always fantasized about being creative.

"Can we talk?" she asked as she fell into a stride that matched his clip.

Daniel looked over at Colleen but kept his brisk pace. Colleen had to force herself to walk even faster just to keep up with him. "Sure, I guess. But I thought we were officially done communicating with one another."

Colleen didn't answer. She just kept up with Daniel. As they approached Daniel's bike, Colleen spoke up again, "Just for a couple of minutes, Daniel, please."

Daniel stopped and turned to Colleen. He pointed toward a shade tree nestled on a slight crest overlooking the lot. "Over there," he said. They walked over to the tree and sat beneath the low hung branches. The air was still with no hint of a breeze. It was very quiet and secluded.

"I just wanted to tell you again how impressed I am with the depth to which you've gotten into this reading of yours. I really am."

Now that was a profoundly stupid way to start this conversation, she thought. *What the heck is wrong with me that I can't even talk in a rational manner to this guy? This is Daniel, for crying out loud!* She felt very uncomfortable sitting there across from her old boyfriend and she didn't know why.

Daniel just shrugged his shoulders. "Like I told you, it was really just a course in self education over at Zack's place. Front porch philosophy

101," he laughed and Colleen smiled at him.

"I saw Michael last spring. He told me all about your military valor and your battlefield promotion to sergeant. I had no idea you were in such heavy combat."

Daniel shrugged his shoulders again. "It was no big deal. My only goal was to stay alive and keep my men alive. No more than that."

"Michael hinted that you were involved in some dangerous operations and that you were almost killed in the Central Highlands."

"Michael drinks too much! And when he does, he gets to talking and makes stuff up."

"So those things never happened?" Colleen stumbled over her words.

"What did you want to talk about, Colleen?" Daniel grew restless.

"I don't know. I've been so confused lately. On one hand, everything seems to be falling into place; my graduation, meeting Bradley, and great prospects for a super job once I'm done with school. Everything is just perfect … on the surface."

"I agree, I think everything does seem to be coming together for you. You've worked hard and you'll probably get a great job. You've got a great future as a journalist and a writer. That's just what you've been striving for. I'm envious of you, and very proud."

"But…" Colleen began, caught up short by Daniel's compliment.

"But? But what? What's the problem?"

Colleen shook her head. "With Bradley, everything is so predetermined. It's preordained and there are never any surprises. Bradley doesn't like surprises, nor do his parents. He wants everything laid out for his future, so he knows just what his life will be like."

"Why are you telling me all this stuff about Bradley? That's the guy you love."

"I never said I loved him. I never said that."

"Well, are you 'in like' with him?"

"Don't be mean, Daniel. I'm very fond of Bradley. He seems perfect in every way except…."

"What do you mean except? Except you're talking to me about him. Obviously, there are some doubts on your mind."

"No, there's not."

"I think there is!" Daniel shot back.

Colleen got irritated, "There you go again, telling me what I think. Even my parents don't talk to me that way."

Daniel smiled, "You mean being honest with you? Yeah, sorry about that! I have this tendency to be honest with my friends even if it hurts them. I'd like to think I do it for their own good. But why do you want to talk to me about this? Why can't you talk to Bradley about your feelings?"

"Because he thinks I'm perfect. He has this image of a perfect woman to meet his perfect life's expectations."

"Nobody's perfect."

"Let's change the subject," Colleen was frustrated at herself for bringing up Bradley in the first place.

"You're the one doing all the talking, Colleen, so continue."

"I'm very worried about Michael. I've heard he's been drunk just about every time someone sees him now."

"I'm trying to get him help at the VA. But they aren't being very cooperative - and neither is Michael. It's an ongoing battle."

"Maybe if we all got together... Maybe we could hang out or do something - just like old times."

"No, that won't help."

"Why not?"

"Because we can't go back and replay the past. It's over and done with. Especially since Michael came back from Vietnam. I've already told you that we've all changed too much to play freshmen again."

"I just thought it might help."

"Is that why you stopped me, Colleen? To talk about Michael?"

"No. Not really."

"So?"

"I'm just very confused. I need a friend to talk to," Colleen hung her head.

"You have a friend. His name is Bradley Barrington!"

Colleen looked up at Daniel. He could see the moisture in her eyes. She was about to cry. "I need someone to talk to. I can't talk to my parents. And I don't feel I can talk to Bradley. Daniel, you're the only one I feel comfortable sharing my feelings with. Even after all this time and everything that has transpired between us. I still feel I can tell you almost anything. No," she corrected herself, "I can tell you anything."

"Tell me what?"

"Everything has come together for me, Daniel. If I get married to ... my life would be guaranteed. I would have anything and everything I've ever wanted."

"If you're asking me if you should marry Bradley Barrington, you have to make that decision yourself. You sure as heck don't need the advice of an ex-boyfriend to reach that conclusion."

"Daniel, I trust your opinion. Peggy's gone and I can't talk to my parents about this. I need a friend."

"Come on, Colleen, you're killing me here! Why are you doing this?"

"I can't explain it very well..."

"Colleen, I get it. You want to confide in me about your future with this other guy. And you're saying that you need me as a friend. Are you nuts? Don't you understand how much you hurt me when I got that letter? And the summer after freshman year, when I knew in my gut that we were through? I died a little bit every time I saw you. Now you want to confide in me as your best friend?"

"Daniel, I don't know where else to turn."

Daniel was dazed and confused. His mind was spinning in circles. His heart was pounding against his chest. Colleen wanted a friend. Daniel just wanted to bury his past and move on with his life. But Colleen wouldn't let go. And he couldn't … no, he wouldn't force the issue.

Colleen blinked her tears away. She had to face the truth as painful as it was. It had come to her gradually over the last several months. Now she had reality staring back at her. The realization that everything had changed just as Michael predicted it would.

Daniel had become just what he wished for back at the Triangle Bar. He was his own man now - not beholden to anyone, especially not an old girlfriend who had hurt him so deeply. She now knew in her heart that Daniel had finally moved on with his life, without her.

Just stand up, Colleen told herself. *Thank him for his time and leave. Just do it! Daniel can't help you anymore. He just doesn't care.*

She couldn't leave.

Colleen's feelings were not to be denied. She could feel it in her heart and in the blood that coursed through her veins. She felt her upset stomach punching at her insides. Her skin felt clammy. Yet even with the emotional roller coaster she was on, Colleen also felt an overwhelming urge to embrace Daniel and hold him close to her; to feel his warmth. She longed to smell his clothes and his body and somehow bring back freshman year all over again.

Slowly Colleen began to relax. A veil of serenity crept across her face. Her cheeks creased until she was visibly smiling at Daniel. He was perplexed at first. Colleen seemed to be back to her old self again. Her breathing had returned and with it, calmness. She began to lean over toward Daniel.

"Oh, God," Daniel muttered under his breath.

Colleen reached over and began to run her hand over his tattoo again. Daniel tensed up. He didn't move a muscle. Their eyes met and danced. Colleen began to slowly lean forward, inching closer to Daniel. He hesitated before taking a deep breath as he began to lean in closer to her in return.

Gradually they moved towards each other until their foreheads touched.

"We shouldn't," Daniel whispered. "We shouldn't be doing this."

"I know … I know."

Their noses slowly caressed one another. Their cheeks touched, pressing lightly against their skin. Their mouths brushed up against the other. Their lips found the safe refuge and held, pressing ever so gently together, just for a moment. With growing passion they embraced one another and kissed intensely. They clung to one another tightly. Their hands ran down each other's back and brought their bodies locked together.

All the pent-up emotions so long buried between the two of them exploded in a rush of hands on each other's bodies. Daniel's lips ran across Colleen's face, her cheek, her neck, and back to her waiting, anxious lips. Their breathing became rushed and almost gasping. Colleen could feel herself letting go. She wanted Daniel. She needed him. More than anything else she wanted to be a part of him. She wanted him inside her.

Suddenly, Daniel released himself from Colleen's grip and gently pushed her away. Colleen looked into his eyes. They were empty. She wanted to continue. She reached out to embrace him once again but Daniel started to get up.

"No, please stay!" she gasped, "We can just talk … please."

"I have feelings too, Colleen. I can't do this! It's tearing me up inside."

"Please," Colleen repeated. She held on to his arm, but he gently unwrapped her fingers, stood up, and turned to leave.

"Daniel, I have to know," she asked catching her breath. "Do you still have feelings for me?

Daniel turned back to Colleen with a mask of sadness like she'd never seen. "I told you before…"

"What?"

"I lost those in the A Shau."

Blind Before Her Eyes

Mary Fitzpatrick's visit wasn't entirely unexpected. She'd been after Colleen for several weeks to come home to Rochester so they could talk about Colleen's continuing relationship with Bradley. But Colleen's pending finals and outside assignments kept her on campus every weekend. Undaunted, Mary Rose announced that she would be up sometime soon to discuss the matter with her daughter.

So when Colleen's mother appeared in her dorm room one Saturday morning, Colleen wasn't entirely surprised. Not happy, but not really surprised. Mama bear wanted to protect her cub from making some bad decisions and she meant to do it face to face.

Mary Rose agreed to go down to the coffee shop so at least Colleen didn't have to worry about other classmates eavesdropping on what could be a very embarrassing conversation. They ordered their coffee and tea and Colleen put her back to the doorway, hoping that anyone who knew her wouldn't recognize her there.

"He loves you, dear. How can you be so blind as to not see that?" Mary Rose began. "He came down to see us last week."

"He did what?"

"He said he wanted to pop the question but you were hesitant. He didn't want to embarrass you or himself if he proposed at Christmas in front of his parents and you said no."

"Nice of him to talk to me about that. I think he's more worried about his own embarrassment than mine."

"Well, dear, I just think he's a little shy."

"Mother, Bradley Barrington is not shy! He is a lot of things, but he is definitely not shy. He knows what he wants and he'll do anything to get it. I can't believe he didn't talk to me about this. I don't believe him!"

"He said he did."

"Well," Colleen said, hesitating and stumbling over her words, "We talked … in general … I mean, I made it very clear that there were a few things I needed to clear up before…"

"Well, Colleen, I think that's what he took for your hesitancy. If you're not ready to commit…"

“I told both you and dad what my plans are … my goals for after college. What more do I have to say to get it through to you both that…”

”Lower your voice, young lady! We don’t want the entire cafeteria to hear us, now do we?”

Colleen regained her composure and took a long drink of coffee, “Mother, I told you and dad that there are some things I’ve got to iron out. I have a few things to clear up before I make such a huge commitment.”

“Colleen, we’re not stupid. We know you still haven’t gotten over that boy.”

“He has a name, mother!”

“Colleen, darling, you’re smart and ambitious and you’ve done everything right so far. You have a wonderful future ahead of you in journalism if that’s what you want to do. Don’t mess it up at this stage in your life. We don’t want to see you make a big mistake.”

Colleen said nothing. “We have empathy for Daniel but he’s at a different place in his life now - very different from yours. I’m sure things have been rough for him based on the little you’ve told us about him; with dropping out of school, getting drafted and ending up in Vietnam. But that’s really his problem. Not yours.”

“Mother, Daniel doesn’t need your pity,” Colleen answered. “Believe me. He’s become his own man now. He’s smart, articulate and very ambitious. He’s done more in the last two years to better himself than any man I know.”

But her mother wasn’t ready to give up that easily. “Colleen, you may think he’s becoming his own man but really…”

Colleen just stared at her mother.

“Besides, Daniel came from a very different background than you did. He is not of the same class as you. And yes, Colleen, we do have class in America and you are of the privileged class. I am not going to apologize for saying that. We only want what’s best for you. I’m afraid you’re simply enamored with him, dear.”

“No, mother!” Colleen snapped back, “He’s knowledgeable about the world and he has street smarts. I admire him for that. There’s a big difference.”

Colleen wasn’t in an argumentative mood but she couldn’t let it go. “I understand what you’re saying, mother. You and dad … dad especially … worked very hard for everything that you’ve both accomplished. I need to do the same. I need to make my own way in life. I cannot and I will not depend on you two for my future success. Whether I marry Bradley or someone else, I need to make that decision and I need you to trust me in making that decision."

"Bradley's perfect for you, Colleen. You do know that, don't you?"

"Mother, please! Bradley is a wonderful man. He's warm and caring and has always been a perfect gentleman toward me." Colleen was exasperated.

"So?" her mother asked. "You've seen how he dresses in those Catalina shirts and Savile Row suits. Now that's a sign of real refinement. His parents seem very nice, and it doesn't hurt that he comes from money … Oh, I know what you think about East Coast wealth but believe me, it doesn't hurt to know that you'll be well taken care of for the rest of your life. I should have been so lucky."

"Mother!"

"Oh, Colleen, don't get me wrong. Your father is a wonderful man and he's worked very hard to give us everything we have. But it would have been so much easier if he'd come from money as I did. Don't think badly of me for saying that. It's just the way it is!"

Colleen didn't want to argue any more with her mother. She took another drink of coffee and setting the cup down, she said, "Yes, mother, I agree, Bradley is perfect in every way. All I'm saying is that I need a little more time. That's all!"

"Well, don't take too long. A man like that won't wait around forever. This time next year, you could be on a Mediterranean cruise like he did last summer … as Mrs. Bradley Barrington."

"I don't know, mother, Bradley said it was all business on his last cruise. I'm not sure if he'd want to bring his old married wife along next time," Colleen laughed.

Mary Rose laughed along, "You might be right, dear; Bradley said he and his group had a great time except for the women who insisted on shopping in Naples and all those other ports during their Mediterranean cruise."

Colleen looked at her mother and didn't say a word.

Winter Break

In A New York Minute

Summit Avenue was ablaze with a range of vibrant fall hues. They washed the trees and boulevards in rich tones of red and yellow and brown. Leaves piled up on front lawns and blanketed the bushes and shrubs which lined many of the sidewalks along the avenue.

A light rain had begun to fall that late autumn morning, producing a clear reflective sheen on the Summit Avenue roadway. Colleen and Bradley were in the Avanti traveling down the thoroughfare on their way back to school. They'd just left a breakfast meeting at the University Club for one of Brad's student investment groups. Both sat quietly, lost in their own thoughts, as the rain kept tapping on the canvas car top.

Colleen was thinking about a journalism assignment coming due soon. Bradley was droning on about his father's latest acquisition in China. That, of course, meant another trip abroad for number one son. Colleen had heard it all before. She was beginning to accept the fact that Bradley's absence from their relationship was automatic whenever work called. She knew it was just part of the package her boyfriend whimsically referred to as their partnership.

Colleen closed her eyes. What was happening here, she asked herself. Everything was moving so quickly. Daniel's final exit from her life coincided with Bradley's continuing insistence on a firm commitment from her. Colleen's boyfriend even enlisted her mother's help for his cause. Colleen felt she was in a vice being squeezed from all directions. But why couldn't she just make a commitment to this wonderful man sitting next to her? What was she holding out for? None of it made any sense. Her head was competing against her heart to bring clarity to the situation but that only muddied the waters even more.

Colleen looked over at Brad and smiled. He smiled back and put his hand on her knee. He gently squeezed it. She was a total idiot not to love this guy with all her heart, Colleen told herself. There was something certifiably wrong with her. She just knew it.

She glanced out the windshield and her world suddenly got a lot more complicated.

Colleen was first to spot the young man walking on the sidewalk, his shoulders hunched up against the light drizzle. He had on a long duster, khaki pants and brown loafers. She never would have recognized him except for his stance which was straight and firm. He walked at a pace that was steady yet moving at a very brisk clip. His brown hair seemed matted down from the rain.

It was Daniel. She recognized the strength he seemed to carry with his very presence. The Avanti was fast approaching him. Within seconds, Bradley would drive by and on to school. Daniel was bent over in the rain. He would never see their car pass by. It would be over in a mere speck in time. Neither one would remember that day ever again. Colleen knew the right thing to do - the sane thing to do. *Why open up that wound again*, she asked herself. *Let it go.* Her mouth got ahead of her head and Colleen spoke out.

"Oh, there's my friend" she said, pointing out the window. "Pull over and let's give him a ride."

"Are you sure?" Bradley asked, skepticism rolling out with his words.

"Yes," Colleen answered firmly. "Please pull over."

The Avanti pulled alongside Daniel who gave the car a quick glance and kept walking. The electric car window slid down and Colleen stuck her head out. "Daniel, hi. We'll give you a ride to school."

Daniel stopped and looked over at the red convertible. He could see Colleen but not the driver. He hesitated, standing firm in the rain, blinking away the drops that were pelting him in the face.

"No, that's OK," he said, "thanks anyway."

"Daniel, get in, please."

"It's not that far to school..."

A voice began to speak behind Colleen. "He doesn't want to, Colleen, just let it..."

"Daniel, its pouring rain. Come on, don't be dumb."

"I'm not being dumb..."

"Daniel, get in," Colleen urged him. "You'll get the death of cold."

The voice started up again. "Colleen, he doesn't want to get in. Just let him…"

"Bradley!"

"I'm just saying…"

"Cool your jets, Brad" Colleen shot back. "He's my friend and he's getting a ride to school."

Daniel hesitated for a moment longer. Colleen swung open her car door. Raindrops began pelting her on her face. She pulled back her car seat so Daniel could climb in back. She looked up at Daniel again, blinking away the rain.

Daniel reluctantly stepped forward and climbed into the back seat of the sports car. His face was immediately washed with a wave of warm air from the car heater. It felt good on his chilled body. Bradley pulled out and quickly slipped the car into first gear. He glanced up at his rearview mirror and said nothing.

"Why are you walking to school?" Colleen asked as Daniel settled into the backseat. "What happened to your motorcycle?"

"It's in the shop," Daniel answered as he looked over the plush leather seats and ornate wood on the dashboard. The warmth inside the car felt good on his skin. Brad adjusted his rearview mirror so he could see Daniel better in the back seat. Colleen slid over, putting her back to the door and looked at Daniel. She threw a smile toward Bradley, then back at Daniel.

"What kind of bike do you ride?" Bradley asked.

"Triumph Bonneville T 120," Daniel answered.

"Twin cylinder?"

Daniel shook his head. "Six hundred and forty-nine CCs. Four stroke, twin engine. Air cooled. Four-speed, chain drive."

"Does it move?"

"Yeah, I can crank it up pretty fast on the straightaway," Daniel answered, "enough to get white line fever sometimes."

Bradley laughed. "Nice! I've got a Norton Atlas myself back home, and a BMW R69S - two sweet road machines. I got them both from the factory when I was in Europe last year. My uncle just bought me an original Hildebrand & Wolfmuller motorrad, totally restored. It's one of the first motorcycles ever built - know what that sucker is worth?"

Daniel glanced at Colleen but said nothing.

Bradley blathered on. "Triumph is a good bike but my friends tell me they take a lot of maintenance and upkeep. That true?"

"They do take a certain amount of hand-holding if you want them to run well."

"And they leak a lot."

"And they can sometimes run hot too," Daniel agreed, "I've straddled the red line couple of times before I got to water. The British make a good bike, but compared to the Japanese machines they've got way too many parts that can break down. The Japanese have got the right idea; keep it simple and easy to repair. It seems to be working out pretty well for them."

Bradley glanced in his rearview mirror and smiled back at Daniel. "I hear the Japanese are coming out with their own line of big bikes. My dad was in Japan not that long ago. He said both Honda and Kawasaki mean to take over the market for full sized motorcycles. Have you seen pictures of the CB750? It's the first four-cylinder Jap bike. It's fast as hell because it doesn't have the weight of your Triumph or those other European models."

"No, I haven't," Daniel answered. "I know they already have a line of bikes out - the smaller ones, not the big road bikes."

"Word is they'll be coming out next," Brad said. "The CB750 will be one of the first. Bitchin machine, man, just a real bitchin road bike.

"Paradigm, that's their secret."

"What do you mean?" Bradley asked.

"I mean the Japanese are savvy businessmen. They research a market to death, study the paradigms; people's assumptions, then they capitalize on the opportunities there by improving that product. They started with cars but now they're moving into electronics; radios and such. Watch them. Some day they just might take over our own American brand, Harley Davidson."

A song came on the radio. It was a brand new song by Credence Clearwater Revival called 'Fortunate Son'. The song was growing in volume. Bradley was still rambling on about the finance resources of the Harley Davidson Company.

Colleen was half-heartedly listening to Bradley and the song when one stanza caught her attention. She cocked her head toward the speaker, listening intently.

Yeah, some folks inherit star spangled eyes,
Ooh, they send you down to war, Lord,
And when you ask them, how much should we give,
Oh, they only answer, more, more, more, yoh,
It ain't me, it ain't me,
I ain't no millionaire's SON, NO
It ain't me, it ain't me,
I ain't no fortunate one, NO, NO

Daniel looked up at Colleen. She was mouthing something. He looked at her lips, studying them for a moment. She seemed to be mouthing the words 'That's you.' But it was only for a brief moment before she turned to look at Bradley. The song played on. When it ended, Colleen turned back to Daniel and smiled.

"How's your house coming along?" she asked Daniel, interrupting Bradley.

"It's a work in progress," Daniel answered, giving Colleen a smile as he spoke, "and I expect it will be for some time to come."

"Brad's into real estate too,"

Bradley smiled. "My dad and uncle have got a number of buildings on the Upper Eastside of Manhattan. They started buying them right after the war - before rent control. Now they're making out like bandits with that portfolio." Bradley glanced back at Daniel. A slight smirk crossed his face. "That's how they got me a place in the Hamptons right next to their compound … That's where Colleen and I will be spending the holidays, right dear?"

Colleen gave him a stern look but said nothing. She stole a glance back at Daniel.

Daniel smiled at Bradley's comment. Colleen's eyebrows furrowed up, expressing displeasure at her boyfriend's words. There was an awkward silence.

"I've talked to a number of people about real estate. It sounds like a good base to use to generate capitol for some other projects I've got in mind. I think there's a market for well-built multifamily buildings in the suburbs and some sections of the cities. It looks like a market ripe for innovation. If I can make my focus on providing a safe and comforting setting for folks, they'll be inclined to stay because they'll see it as their home, not necessarily just a place to stay."

"Forget about that, my friend," Bradley interrupted. "Focus your attention on the bottom line. That's where you'll make your money. Tenants come and tenants go. Keep your rents at their max. If folks don't like it, they can move." Bradley was on a roll. "If you want to make it in real estate, you have to build up your portfolio. That's the accumulation of assets that can grow in value for you. You need to be ruthless if you want the status, the power and the prestige of being one of the big players in the game. That's what my dad and uncle did. They're not the most liked players in New York but damn, they're respected."

"Respected or feared?" Daniel asked.

"Who cares?" Bradley replied with a laugh. "It's one in the same."

"Well, Bradley," Daniel replied. "I guess I have a different take on it." Daniel was calm and matter of fact. He stared at Colleen with a rigidity that spoke of self-confidence even as he spoke in a soft tone of voice.

Colleen looked at Bradley then back at Daniel. She didn't say anything. Daniel couldn't read her face until the wisp of a smile briefly appeared beneath her deep blue eyes then disappeared.

"It sounds like your grand plans would call for a large capital infusion. What are your sources of funding?" Bradley asked. "Don't forget, lenders are demanding even more skin in the game nowadays. Unless you're playing in the secondary markets or looking at Class B opportunities, you're going to find equity financing a tough way to go. Cap rates aren't getting any better."

"It's just talk right now. I'm still in the research stage. Once I've been able to determine the IRR on my proposed portfolio I can determine the next steps to take - sources of financing being one of those steps. Now whether that's a package with investors like a LLC, Sub-S or regular C Corp, I don't know at this point. And I've got to finish school first."

Colleen smiled at Daniel's answer but Bradley wasn't about to be upstaged by his girlfriend's old flame.

"I'm impressed that you've been studying the market like that," he said with a hint of sarcasm, "especially since you just got back into the states. It took me years just listening to my uncles to understand the nuances of the real estate business. You must be a quick study." He looked in the rearview mirror for a reaction from Daniel. He got none.

Colleen looked down Summit Avenue. "When is your first class," she asked Daniel without looking back at him.

"8:30 a.m. in the Science Building,"

The rain began to pick up, pummeling the windshield. Streams of water curved and twisted on the windshield and gathered along its edges.

Brad rambled on about his father's real estate holdings and the ongoing battle over rent control and property taxes. "Would I buy more buildings?" Bradley asked himself out loud. "In a New York minute," he answered himself, throwing a glance over at Colleen. She faked a smile in return and looked back at Daniel.

"…But the ROI would have to be attractive. I mean, you don't want to put money into a money pit. You know what I mean?"

Daniel just smiled at Bradley's babbling.

"Buy smart. Add value. Sell smart. That's what my uncles always told me," He said. "You add value by refurbishing your marketable space; redevelop what needs to be improved upon, move tenants if necessary. Hell, you can reschedule leases if that will help your bottom line. By improving the asset, you can improve your cap rate and ultimately your price. Some people may hold their properties. But I say, buy smart, fix it up and sell it for a nice profit. That's what my uncles do."

Daniel sat back, sizing up the Bradley and Colleen dynamic. He scoffed internally at the pompous drivel. Bradley was now rattling on about equity and appreciation. Colleen frowned to herself. She just knew what Daniel was thinking and she didn't appreciate it.

"Brad's going to Columbia for medical school. He's almost guaranteed residency at either Harvard or Mount Sinai. His parents are alumni. Isn't that neat?"

"That is nice."

Another song came on the radio and Bradley turned up the volume. It was the Kingston Trio singing 'Where have all the flowers gone?' Bradley turned to Colleen with a glance back at Daniel. "It's that hippie song." He looked in his rearview mirror and locked his eyes on Daniel. "You ever listen to those lyrics? ...About soldiers and graveyards?"

"I have."

"Colleen said you were in the service. You got drafted and did time in Vietnam?"

"That I did. Yeah, I did my time in the Nam."

"So what do you think about the war? I mean, what a waste of human capital and government resources to fight such a preposterous war!"

Daniel looked out the window. His face belied no emotion. He focused on the water beading on the side window. He was a million miles away from everyone and everything. He answered in a soft voice. "I wouldn't know. I was just doing my job, trying to stay alive. That's all."

He looked over at Colleen. Their eyes locked. She saw a vacancy there. Dark brown ovals that said nothing and yet told the depth of his feelings about the war. His stoicism revealed so much about the layers buried deep inside. Colleen knew him well enough that she could sense the bubbling open pit of an active volcano about to erupt.

He and Colleen were unmistakably communicating with their eyes and speaking volumes to one another. Colleen felt the same wonderful euphoria she felt whenever she was around Daniel. Something she never felt with Bradley.

"Let's change the subject, Brad. We don't want to talk about that. Daniel's back and he's safe now. That's all that counts."

The rain had slowed to a light drizzle by the time the Avanti pulled into the Science Building parking lot. It rolled up to the back entrance and stopped alongside the curb. Bradley turned in his seat and extended his arm back at Daniel.

"Good meeting you again," he lied. "Good luck with your studies - and your house."

Daniel shook Bradley's hand and started to climb out of the back seat. Colleen got out first and stood by the car door. Daniel climbed out and stood in front of her, inches away from her face.

"Thanks for the ride," he said, eyes still locked with hers.

"Oh, one other thing," Bradley said from the front seat. Daniel leaned back into the car.

"I heard some of the fraternity guys from my house might be gunning for you. It seems they're not too crazy about your stance on the war. Just a word of advice to stay clear of them. When they get bombed, they tend to do some stupid things. Hell, they're football players, whadya expect?" he laughed.

"Thanks for the warning," Daniel answered and stood up next to Colleen again. Their eyes met and locked onto one another. She seemed to be looking right through his eyes, into his soul, his consciousness, his inner most thoughts, trying to connect with them. She opened her mouth, trying to say something. She stopped and just smiled. "Stay dry," she said as she climbed back into the car.

Daniel stood there in the drizzle and mist as the Avanti rolled across the parking lot and back onto Summit Avenue.

"So what did you ever see in him?" Bradley asked as he turned back into the campus thoroughfare.

"What do you mean?" Colleen asked, hesitant to get into that conversation with her boyfriend.

"You said he was so immature as a freshman. He seems to have grown up a lot. What attracted you to him in the first place? No offense, but he hardly seems your type?"

"Who cares, Brad? That was a long time ago. I have you now. What more do you want?"

"You're right, Colleen, I'm a very lucky guy."

The Avanti rolled up to the quadrangle and Bradley turned to Colleen. "I'll be done around noon. Just pick me up back here by 12:15, Ok?"

Colleen slid over the front seat and shushed Brad out his side. "I'll be back," she said, giving him a quick kiss on the cheek as he exited the car. Before her boyfriend could turn and wave her off, Colleen had gunned the engine and swung around the quadrangle driveway. She gave him a quick wave and was moving quickly toward Summit Avenue and her own school.

As she drove down Cleveland Avenue toward Mother of the Lake, Colleen couldn't help but think about the look on Daniel's face when that second song came on the radio. He'd heard Brad's questions but his mind was a million miles away. Daniel was back in Vietnam. He was back in the middle of fighting and dying. Colleen feared Daniel was back to that moment when he first received her Dear John letter. The look Daniel had given her back in Bradley's car brought a crescendo of emotions that she didn't want to face with him ever again.

Cave Dog

After numerous phone calls to the Department of Defense, Daniel managed to get Michael back into a class to help him handle his post-combat stress. Michael's drinking was another issue and Daniel's buddy wasn't about to attempt two recoveries at the same time.

The first couple of classes went well enough for Michael. But by the third week, he'd grown irritable and disruptive in class. After a couple of warnings, he was thrown out and told to come back if, and when, he could control his temper. Michael stormed out of the building and swore he'd never go back again.

Daniel tried to talk to the doctors personally to get them to give Michael another chance. They agreed, but only under the condition that Michael cooperate fully with the instructor and not cause any further disruptions in class.

Daniel drove Michael to the Veterans Administration building and sat outside on a bench before class started. He began his lecture in a soft, controlled voice, gradually increased the tempo and tone as he got closer to his main point - Michael's cooperation in class.

"One more chance, dickhead, that's all they're giving you," Daniel said. "Don't fuck it up. Shut your mouth and let the instructor talk. Whether you think it's bullshit or not. Let the guy talk. Christ, they're all trained professionals. They've been teaching this stuff for years."

"They weren't there."

"Michael, you're wrong about that. If it wasn't Vietnam, it was Korea or World War II. They've all been there. They know what it's like. Just give them a chance."

Michael got up and stubbed out his cigarette under his shoe. He turned to Daniel who was looking up at him with a worried look. "I'll give them one more chance to make sense, bro. Otherwise, I'm outta here.....for good."

"And where will that leave you, smart guy?"

"Don't care."

"A drunk for the rest of your life or dead from drugs," Daniel said. "Not a lot of options for a junkie like you."

"Don't care."

"Why should I care, Michael, about your sorry ass?"

Michael sat back down next to Daniel. As he fought to catch his breath, he fumbled for another cigarette. His fingers were shaking as he connected a match to the white stick.

"Man, I'm sorry. I just don't know what to do. Fuck, man, I'm so screwed up. A total clusterfuck, that's what I am. A total clusterfuck."

"Michael, you're not. You may be a dumbass, but you're my friend and if you're not smart enough to get help, I'll be real disappointed in you. Can you do it for me, man? Just give it a chance. Can you do that? Can you be a cave dog?"

"What?

"Be tough. For me, Michael."

"Yeah, I guess. I guess I can do that."

"Good, do it." Daniel threw a light punch against Michael's shoulder. "Call me tonight or whenever - but let me know how it went, OK?"

"OK."

"Seriously, man!"

"I will, damnit, I will."

Tonka Chic

Throughout the 20th century, internationally famous industrialists, politicians and financiers had availed themselves of Trumpy yachts. The name was synonymous with cutting edge naval design wrapped around true craftsmanship and chic, opulent features.

Naturally, Mitchell Weinstein was the first in Minnesota and, in fact, the only man in the upper Midwest to have a Trumpy yacht. The boat's narrow beam and shallow design favored speed and maneuverability. Mitchell, the power broker, could cruise all over Lake Minnetonka for everyone to see.

Weinstein's particular Trumpy was a classic. Built in the late 40's, its frame was made of steam-bent oak and its hull was double-planked mahogany fastened with bronze screws. It was still emblazoned with the signature 'T' scrollwork, vertical Pullman windows and a counter stern with canvas awnings.

Claudia had convinced her dad to let her take the boat out one more time before it went into dry dock for the winter. He hired a crew so that his daughter could entertain her best friends one last time before winter set in.

The party started even before the boat left the dock. Several select fraternity and sorority houses piled on board and began partying. They filled up the expansive oak-lined stateroom and adjourning cabins. Deep brown leather seating and stainless steel fittings adorned every room. The drinks were freely flowing and the music was deafening.

Inside the stateroom, everyone had shed their winter coats and many were dancing with wild abandonment. The few souls who ventured outside would wander around the boat, briefly end up under the canvas-covered stern, then quickly come back inside to warm up.

Colleen and Bradley were the last couple to climb aboard before the yacht left its private dock near the Weinstein compound. Colleen had only reluctantly come along because Bradley had insisted it would help his future in business contacts and politics if he were seen with that crowd. Personally he didn't give a damn for most of the folks there. But it was important to be seen and heard among the yachting crowd. Colleen dreaded the thought of running into Daniel again when Bradley was so close by.

As soon as they entered the large stateroom, Colleen spotted Claudia entertaining a small group of friends at the far end of the room. She turned to Bradley, putting her back toward Claudia. But before she could begin talking to Bradley, a girl came up from behind and stood in between them.

"Isn't this just like yachting in the Hamptons?" she asked. "It's like the in thing to do, isn't it? I just love the idea of…"

"Believe me, Cheryl," Bradley interrupted her. "This isn't anything like the Hamptons. Not even close." He proceeded to explain that his parents, uncles and other relatives all had places in the Hamptons. This wasn't the same, he assured her. Colleen just stood and listened.

"Well, I heard they're all a bunch of snobs there anyway," Cheryl commented as she emptied her glass of wine with one long gulp.

Bradley was in his element, trading verbal fisticuffs with the uninitiated and uninformed. He loved it whenever he had an audience. He began his standard abbreviated history of the Hamptons. He went on to defend the Hamptons and claimed there was no snob factor in East Hampton. That was a rumor, he explained, that had been started by the people in South Hampton. "But those Southamptonites are just plain wrong," he said. "East Hampton is not as Palm Beach-ish as they would like you to believe."

Colleen spoke up. She couldn't hold her tongue any longer. "Bradley, I'm not impressed with the pretentiousness of either place, the Hamptons or Lake Minnetonka," she said.

Bradley jumped in quickly. "Colleen's just kidding," he assured Cheryl. "She's only been to the Hamptons once. I guess she considered her summer visit enough to make her an expert. But once we're married she'll be a true native in the Hamptons. She'll know of what she speaks."

Colleen let the statement go and listened to Bradley and Cheryl argue about the prestige of the Hamptons verses Lake Minnetonka. She absentmindedly looked about the room. People were clustered around the bar or mingling in small groups scattered about. Daniel was nowhere to be seen.

The Minnetonka princess regaled her society friends with her loud comments, which just brought a smile to Colleen's face. Colleen had heard all the wild and crazy stories of Claudia's hosting skills and her parties. The woman was always in control of her posse and this yachting group was no exception.

Bored with Bradley's lecturing stance, Colleen excused herself and grabbing her coat, she stepped outside the stateroom. There was a sharp chill in the fall air that slapped her face and immediately began to creep under her sweater neck. She tightened her coat collar and put on her leather gloves.

It was quiet and peaceful outside the stateroom. Only the dull thumping of the twin diesel engines competed with the waves slapping against the hull. Thick glass muted the loud party noises coming through the Pullman windows. Colleen turned up her collar and slowly started to meander back toward the stern of the boat. A light breeze swept alongside the boat as it passed multi-million dollar estates that dotted the shoreline.

As Colleen came around the side of the boat, she suddenly saw Daniel standing on the stern, staring down at the boat's wake.

Colleen hesitated for a moment. Daniel was alone, out of sight of Claudia and the others in the stateroom. Should Colleen turn around and walk back inside? Or dare another encounter with Daniel? She took a deep breath and walked back toward the stern.

Colleen slowly approached the back railing and stood next to Daniel. She said nothing at first but instead just stared out at the churning waters that bubbled up from behind the boat. Daniel glanced over at her then went back to looking out over the stern. There was no emotion registered on his face. Complete silence blanketed the space between them. It was only that initial glance that began their voiceless communication. Colleen removed her gloves and put them in her pocket.

She looked down at the railing where she'd placed her two hands. Daniel had also placed his hands on the railing. Their fingers were only inches apart. Then, almost in unison, as if they were part of a ballet performance, the two of them began to maneuver silently, without saying a word to one another or even looking over at the other person.

They each rested their elbows on the railing and leaned into it. Their elbows touched.

It was a silent ballet they knew all too well. A routine performed by two people so in sync, so connected by spirit that their movements were pure fluid motion. No one else standing close would have noticed it. Gradually, the two of them were tightly woven together, elbows and hips nudged tightly up against one another. Daniel glanced over at Colleen for a moment.

"How's the job hunt going?" Daniel asked her.

"Good."

"Good, as in I've got a job or I've got some good prospects?"

"I've got some good prospects. I'll find something, I'm sure of it," Colleen answered. "How's school coming along?"

"Good. Straight A's so far."

"How about your research on real estate? Have you thought any more about how or when you might be more involved, maybe start investing?"

"It's coming along," was all Daniel would say.

Silence slipped between them. Again, Colleen moved her hand until it was edged up alongside Daniel's hand. Skin touched skin. He didn't move his hand. She glanced over at him once again. He looked back at her. Their eyes locked in place for a moment but neither said a word. In unison they looked back out at the churning water beneath them.

Colleen looked over at Daniel. "People can make mistakes, you know."

Daniel studied the wake. "Where did that come from?"

"You said before that…"

Daniel glanced down at Colleen's hand. "You're right, everybody makes mistakes. Is that what we had, Colleen, a mistake?"

"That's not what I meant!"

"What *did* you mean?"

Colleen's composure changed. Her face softened. *What if we did have something ... but the timing was wrong?*

Daniel tried to read her eyes. He wasn't sure what Colleen was driving at.

"Perhaps we were in the wrong place in our lives for something meaningful to happen."

"Something meaningful did happen," Daniel countered. "At least for me, it did."

"No! No! That's not what I meant. What I meant to say was..."

"If you're asking if it's possible that our timing was off - I suppose. But why resurrect the past now? You're practically engaged."

Colleen stared out at the churning waters behind the boat.

"What's your point, Colleen?"

She engaged his eyes unflinchingly. "None of those are legitimate reasons to forget about the past or pretend that it didn't really happen. Just because two people aren't ready at one point in their lives for a commitment doesn't mean they might not be ready at some other point in their lives. Something could still be there if a person or persons were willing to give it a chance to blossom again."

"If there was something real back then?"

"You've already said there was something real."

"Colleen, you're talking in riddles. What are you trying to say? That we were in love? That we could rekindle those feelings again if we tried? I don't know! We're both in two different places now. We're very different people from what we were. I told you before … we can't go back to what we had. You can't recreate the past. We've both changed too much for that to happen."

"Daniel, what I'm trying to say is…"

Daniel cut her off as he started to step away. "If I were to fall in love again, it would be different."

"What do you mean?" Colleen took a step closer to him.

"I want to have love in my life again, but it would be a love without strings; a connection without conditions or apologies on my part. It would be a love between equals. It would be a partnership with someone who cared for me as much as I cared about her … and someone who accepted me for who I am, because that won't change. I want to begin with a friendship that burns so hot it blossoms into love and I don't want to be afraid to be the first one to say I love you."

"That's what I'm trying to say!" I know you've changed, and all for the better. You're a different person now and I think…"

"Colleen, there you are!" Colleen turned to see Bradley coming around the corner of the boat. A crowd of women were following him, laughing loudly and drinking their wine.

Bradley came up to Colleen and wrapped his arm around her shoulder. "Hey Daniel, how ya doing?" he laughed and began to turn Colleen away, "Time to go, sweetie. See ya, Daniel." Colleen looked back over her shoulder.

"Nice seeing you again, Colleen … Bradley."

"Yeah, see you around," Bradley threw out as he led Colleen back around the side of the boat.

The Trumpy came back to dock later that evening. The happy and inebriated crowd quickly dissipated into the evening chill and Daniel was left standing with Claudia on the dock. After the crew secured the boat, Claudia paid them off and began walking toward her car without saying a word. Daniel followed her. He could sense her anger that seemed to grow with each step she took.

The ride back from Lake Minnetonka was quiet; a seething silence that hinted of boiling emotions underneath. Claudia couldn't hold her feelings back any longer. As her car passed under the welcoming arches of Mother of the Lake College, Claudia told Daniel to pull over on the side of the road.

"We need to talk about this," She began. "I've been patient with you. A lot more than anyone else I've ever dated. But I'm not going to invest all this time and emotions in you if you aren't going to reciprocate. I need to know where this relationship is going, Daniel."

"Claudia..."

"I saw you talking to her again tonight, damn it," Claudia spat out. "I'm not stupid, you know. You don't think I can tell when a man is still in love with another woman. Well, I can. And it hurts, damn you, it hurts plenty."

"Claudia..."

"I gave you a chance..."

Daniel reached over and cupped his hand over Claudia's mouth. "Let me talk," he said. "Just let me have my say."

Claudia ripped Daniel's hand away. "Don't you shush me, Daniel. You're not my father. You're not half the man that he is."

"Will you let me talk?" Daniel asked, "Or do you just want to rant on without letting me get a word in?"

"So talk, Casanova!" Claudia said.

"When I first met you, Colleen was not in the picture. She'd broken up with me a long time ago when I was still in Vietnam."

"So?"

"I saw her a couple of times since."

"I know; I caught you two on campus. I even confronted her one time and told her to back off. Apparently, she didn't listen."

"I don't know where it's going with her. She has a boyfriend. She's supposed to be engaged soon. I don't know, Claudia, I really don't."

"You still love her, don't you?"

"I don't know."

"You're lying, you bastard!"

"I like you a lot, Claudia…"

"But?"

"But I can't give you what you want … what you need. I can't give you love that I don't have to give."

"You're a real son of a bitch, Daniel. You know that."

"I probably am, from your point of view. I can understand how you would feel that way."

"You're giving up a chance to be really successful. My dad could make you rich."

"Claudia, I like your father. He's a good man. But I'm not the one for you. I'm sure there's someone out there that is right for you. It's just not me. I like you a lot. I like being with you. But that's not the same as being in love. I have to be honest with you. I don't feel that commitment."

Claudia's anger boiled over. She pushed Daniel away. "Get out, Goddamned you." She pointed to the door. "Get out of my car!"

"I'm sorry Claudia. I do like you..."

"Go to hell, you bastard. You still love her. I know you do."

As Daniel stumbled out of her car, Claudia was still screaming and crying at him.

"Don't think about going to work in the stock market," she said, "because my dad will see to it that you never do. And forget about real estate because you'll never get a loan in this town either. Your future here is shit, Daniel. You fuck with me and I'll fuck you ten times over. I'm going to make your life a living hell, you son of a bitch. What do you think about that?"

"Move on with your life, Claudia," Daniel said, deadpan, "because I already have."

Daniel stood silently as Claudia screamed out at the top of her lungs and slammed her Pontiac into drive. The car vibrated violently, its back wheels spinning in a cloud of black smoke before racing away, laying black rubber streaks on the cobblestone pavement. Daniel waited until her car was just a speck in the distance. He stuck out his thumb and waited for a ride back to campus.

Was there anything else that could turn to shit in his life, Daniel wondered. Probably, he thought, but he'd have to face that when it happened.

Great White on a Seal Pup

The Triangle Bar was unusually quiet for a Thursday night. A few of the regulars were huddled over the pool table and several drunks were holding themselves up against the bar. The bartender was nursing their drinks and busying himself with restocking the liquor shelves behind the bar.

Daniel and Michael were back in their corner booth, talking about Michael's continuing headaches and sleepless nights. Michael had tried hard to convince his friend that he was making progress with the VA. But Daniel had his doubts.

"So, are classes going OK?" he asked Michael.

"Yeah."

Daniel studied his friend's placid demeanor. "Yeah, as in, I'm learning a lot about my problems. Or yeah, as in, I'm keeping my mouth shut and not causing problems in class."

"Both."

"You've got to keep going to class if you want them to fix what's wrong with you," Daniel urged his friend.

Michael wouldn't look at Daniel. He just kept tipping his beer bottle from one side to the other, almost knocking it over each time. Daniel pulled Michael's beer away from him. "Maybe you should go easy on this stuff for tonight," Daniel urged him. "Stay sober for tomorrow morning. I'll take you over there to talk to some other folks. What do you say? Is it a deal?"

Michael stared at Daniel for a while, then reached over and scooped his beer bottle back. He wrapped his hand around the bottle and held it tightly, continuing his stare back at Daniel.

"Well?"

"I guess," Michael said, still gripping his beer.

"Good," Daniel said. "I'll come by around nine and we can go there together. After your class, there are some tests you can take. It might help to figure out why your headaches won't go away. There's probably some medicine you can take too. Of course, you'll have to lay off the booze for a while. But you can do that."

"Speak for yourself!" Michael said with a weak smile. He released his grip on the beer bottle and went back to tipping it from one side to the other.

Neither Daniel nor Michael noticed the three fraternity boys approaching their booth.

"Well, look who's here," one of the seniors said as he slid a chair up facing their booth. He sat down. The other two stood behind him, like stone-faced bookends.

"Didi! Didi Mau!" Michael said, looking down.

"What did he just say?" The boy asked Daniel.

"He asked for you boys to move on - get out of here."

"That's what he said? In what language?"

"Vietnamese."

"Dinky Dau," Michael spouted out. "Dinky Dau."

"Now what did he say?"

"He's having a little trouble tonight, guys, give him some space. Just leave us alone."

"I asked, what did he say?" the boy in the chair demanded to know.

"Just let it be."

"Come on, let these pussies be. Let's go have a drink." The seated man stood up and stared down at Daniel and Michael. "Fuckin' doughboys! You think you're so goddamned macho. You're nothing but a piece of olive drab shit." The other two laughed.

Daniel ignored the comment and went back to drinking his beer. Michael followed suit.

They sat in silence for a long time. Daniel finished his beer and slid out of the booth. "Come on, Michael, Let's get out of here. There must be something to watch on TV. I'll crash at your place and we can go to the VA in the morning."

"Can't," Michael said.

"Can't what?"

Michael gave a weak smile and said, "I've got company tonight. You can pick me up in the morning."

"What company?"

"A girl. A real flower child, man. Bitchin hot!"

"Don't tell me she's got some stash for you, Michael, don't tell me that."

"No, no, man. No, she's just a friend. She wants to come over. Maybe I'll get lucky. She's doesn't do drugs. She's clean."

"Are you being straight with me, Michael?"

"Yeah, man, I am. I wouldn't lie to you, man."

"Come on, putz." Daniel wrapped his arm around Michael's shoulder and led him out of the bar.

The three frat boys watched Daniel and Michael leave. One by one they slid off their bar stools and turned to watch the two veterans stumble out the door. They looked at one another and smiled. One of them punched his fists together and puffed up his chest.

"You're taking your lives into your own hands," the bartender warned them.

"Shut the fuck up, old man - this won't take long."

"No it won't!" the bartender agreed.

The three fraternity boys followed Daniel out of the bar.

Daniel dropped Michael into the passenger seat of his car. Michael's head flopped back on the backrest. He was mumbling something, half asleep. Daniel closed the car door and turned to go around the car. One of the frat boys had approached Daniel from behind and now stood just inches away.

"Hey, soldier boy, let's see what you're made of," he said with a laugh as he pushed Daniel back up against the car.

Daniel slowly turned around and said in a very soft voice, "Don't do that again! I don't want to hurt you."

"What did the baby killer say?" Another frat boy asked.

The first guy glanced back at his companion and laughed. He turned back to Daniel, "Don't ever show up here again. We don't like fucking hippies and pussies in our place. You savvy?"

Michael started to stir. He was trying to say something. Daniel turned around and told him to stay in the car. He turned back to face the three men now crowding him.

"The head, man," Michael blurted out.

Daniel turned back to Michael.

Michael looked up at Daniel. His eyes were glassy and unfocused but his voice was very clear. "Cut off the head of the snake," he said to Daniel. "Cut it off!" Daniel nodded and turned back to the three menacing frat boys.

"Three seconds," he muttered, barely under his breath.

"What?"

"It would take about three seconds for me to drive my fist into your throat and collapse your air way. Or snap your neck. Or gouge your eyes out. Three seconds. Maybe less but I'm a little rusty. I haven't killed anybody in a couple of months. "

"You're full of shit," one of the boys said, swallowing hard as he spoke.

Daniel didn't say a word. He just stared at the three assailants. They stared back at him. It became a Mexican standoff. Two of the frat boys began circling around to flank either side of Daniel. He remained focused on the senior in front of him.

Daniel's body grew rigid. All his combat training was spilling back into his brain. His instincts were on heightened alert. He slowly moved his feet into a combat stance. The muscles on his forearms began to flex and grow solid, preparing for the blows to come. Daniel's mind was empty, save for the object in front of him. Now his target was twitching, visibly showing his nervousness. A slight bead of sweat appeared on the frat kid's forehead.

"Now I'm going to get into my car and leave," Daniel said, as he started to turn away. "And you're not going to do anything about it. We'll just forget tonight. And I won't have to kill you."

"He's bluffing, man," one of the three said, taking a step forward and blocking Daniel's way. "Yeah," another muttered, stepping up alongside the first. The first man, wearing his linebacker jersey, started punching his fists together again. “Pussies like you need to learn a lesson,” he said, letting a cruel smirk escape his lips.

“I warned you,” Daniel said softly, raising his finger toward the man. “Remember that tomorrow morning. That I warned you.” And with that statement; all the training, killings, terror and horror of the hill and the jungle came back into play. Daniel became the mad man he feared he might one day become again.

“Lose any buddies on blueberry h...?”

The words had barely left the man’s lips when Daniel’s brain spun through all the mental gyrations he had perfected in the Nam. His body was suddenly a study in fluid motion as Daniel ripped into the fat fraternity boy like a great white on a seal pup.

In less than a second, Daniel head butted the linebacker right between his eyes. He plowed his fist into the boy’s stomach even as blood exploded out of his nose. As the frat boy staggered back, gasping for air, Daniel hit him again with a savage upper cut. The powerful blow sent the football player sprawling backwards, spitting blood out in a crimson shower as he fell.

The second boy rushed forward, charging Daniel. Daniel took one, then two steps backwards. He stiffened one leg and drove his other foot deep into the frat boy’s testicles. As the frat boy stumbled forward, clutching his groin, Daniel punched him in the face with a fierce upper cut. The boy’s head snapped back. He gasped, coughing up blood and broken teeth before collapsing in a heap on the ground.

The third football player lunged toward Daniel, screaming at the top of his lungs. Daniel side-stepped the rush and grabbed the boy’s outstretched arm. Daniel yanked it behind his back and wrapped his own arm around the boy’s throat. He yanked back, sending the player falling backwards. He dropped onto the boy’s stomach and began punching him in the face, over and over again. All of his pent-up rage and anger exploded as Daniel kept pummeling the kid’s face until it was a bloody mess.

Suddenly, two arms came out of nowhere and wrapped themselves around Daniel. Before he could yank them off, a voice screamed into his ear. “Get off, Daniel; you’re killing him, man. Get off!”

Michael dragged Daniel off the bleeding, gasping boy. “Come on, man, we got to go.”

Daniel staggered to his feet. All three assailants were on the ground, moaning and coughing up blood. Daniel walked up to his first attacker and dropped down beside him. He leaned in close to the boy’s bloodied face and whispered.

"If I ever…ever…see you again, I will kill you. And your two buddies. I will snap your neck so fast you'll be dead in seconds. Do you understand?"

The fraternity boy looked up at Daniel with glassy, fear-driven eyes.

"Do you understand?" Daniel asked again, "do you?"

The boy nodded weakly, coughing up more blood and torn tissue. Daniel slowly got to his feet. The boy rolled to his side and curled into a fetal position.

Michael grabbed Daniel by his arm and began to drag him away. "Get in, man. Goddamned, let's get out of here."

As Daniel stumbled around to the driver's side of the car, he noticed the bartender standing in the doorway. He was looking at Daniel. The man's arm went up in a snap salute. Daniel stared at him for a moment then slipped into the car and quickly drove away.

"Can't do this anymore, man," Michael muttered. "Goddamned nightmares are gonna come back. I know they are. I can't do it."

"Michael, it'll be OK," Daniel tried to reassure him.

But Michael just kept mumbling over and over again.

Board of Inquiry

The Disciplinary Board at the College of St. Paul consisted of the Dean of Students, the Faculty President, several administrators, a couple of professors and the Student Council faculty representative. Proceedings were always held in private and the findings were never published or acknowledged. Students who were expelled from the college usually left quietly and their records were expunged. It was as if they had never attended St. Paul's in the first place.

The hearings were always held in the Administration Board Room just off of the Presidents' office. Daniel waited in the hallway before the appointed time, staring down at the dirty worn linoleum tiles. He was lost in thought. No one seemed to notice him sitting on the bench by himself. The Board Room was empty and only a few faculty and administrative staff passed by. Daniel had resigned himself to the fact that he would be leaving college that afternoon. But he'd held true to his beliefs and principles. Screw the rest of them.

As Daniel was going over his notes for a final argument against Father Rollins, two men approached him and stopped. Daniel ignored them, assuming they were there for the hearings.

Suddenly one of the men sat down next to him on the bench. The other man stood nearby, saying nothing. Daniel looked up. Both men were smiling at him. The first man extended his hand to Daniel. "My name is Jeff Winthrop. I'm the Chief Financial Officer here." He looked up at the other man. "This is Gordon Blankenship." He looked back at Daniel. "We have a couple of minutes before the hearing begins. Can we talk?"

"I guess," Daniel answered.

Blankenship pointed to an open door right behind their bench. "That room is empty," he said. "We can go in there." They moved into a small conference room.

As Daniel entered the small conference room, he noticed the walls were bare except for a small chalkboard at one end of the room. The three of them moved around the conference table. Winthrop turned around and closed the door. Blankenship sat down across from Daniel. Winthrop joined his partner facing Daniel. Winthrop laid down a manila folder and flipped it open. He glanced down at it for a second. "We have a proposition for you, Daniel. We feel there's a way to take care of this problem …situation and save face for everyone at the same time. Are you interested?"

Daniel nodded and said, "I'm listening."

Winthrop began to talk, "We've been advised by our legal council that we probably have a legitimate right to expel you from school since you clearly disobeyed our rules. No matter how archaic or outdated those rules might be."

Daniel said nothing.

"But legitimacy alone is no defense against bad publicity," Blankenship threw in, "if you know what I mean?"

Daniel still said nothing.

"This is a great school and we don't want anything to harm its reputation," Blankenship decreed.

"Here's the deal, Daniel," Winthrop began. "The College of St. Paul is a wonderful men's college. Has been since its inception and it's our goal to make sure it stays that way for many years to come. Those rules that have created this issue between yourself and the administration are outdated and need to change."

Blankenship piped up. "But any changes on campus can have their own repercussions."

"Exactly!" Winthrop agreed. "We need to settle this issue and make it go away. We can subtly address some changes to the dress code once things have settled down, like during summer break."

Daniel listened intently. He had no idea what was coming next. Winthrop looked over at Blankenship.

"Father Rollins is being transferred at the end of this school year. He doesn't know it yet but we've gotten confirmation that his Order will return him to their main campus out East once classes are over here. In other words, this is his last hurrah. He doesn't know it yet and he won't until just before school lets out."

"So if you would be willing to cooperate with us," Blankenship cut in. "We can all save face and this will be over. No expulsion. No punishment beyond you're having a clean-shaven face until school is over. There will be a new Dean of Students and I think...I know he will be more amenable to some changes around here."

"What do you say, Daniel?" Winthrop asked. "Can you see it in yourself to do this for the school? I won't bring up your military service but I checked with some friends at the DOD. We know you're rock solid and we were lucky to have you on our team in the Nam."

"You were there?"

"Unfortunately, no. I was in the forgotten war, Korea '51 and '52 as a combat engineer. I know what it's like, son. I've still got some army buddies who were on the ground about the same time you were. Within those circles, you've got quite a reputation. I know what we're asking of you, Daniel. Can you take one more order…for us?"

Daniel smiled at the man. He glanced over at Blankenship whose face was frozen, anxiously awaiting Daniel's reply. Daniel's hand went out toward Winthrop's. His arm was straight and rigid as iron. Both hands met in a tight clench. Daniel said nothing but looked directly at both men.

"Good! It's done," Winthrop said, as he leaned back in his chair, visibly relieved at Daniel's answer. Blankenship stood up beside Winthrop. He glanced over at his partner. Winthrop nodded at Daniel then motioned Blankenship to sit back down again.

"We follow Robert's Rules of Order in the proceedings," Winthrop began. "There will be a point in the proceedings when you are given one last chance to change your mind and agree to shave off your beard and keep it off while school is in session. That comes after Father Rollins makes his case against you. Either Winthrop or I will ask you if you have anything to say at that point. That's when you simply agree to shave. Any questions, Daniel?" Winthrop asked.

Daniel nodded no.

"Good," he said as he looked over at Blankenship. They smiled at one another then Winthrop turned back to Daniel. He smiled at Daniel with a look that was different than before, as if it were some kind of inside joke between him and his partner. Blankenship was smiling at Daniel the same way too.

Winthrop piped up, "We've got a couple of minutes until the hearing starts. Daniel, we have something else we'd like to talk to you about…"

Dark Cloud Lifted

The day after Daniel appeared before the Disciplinary Board, Michael hung himself. No note was left; no explanation for him ending it all - just the sour smell of urine that had pooled beneath his swinging feet. It was as if he were telling the world to piss off, one last time.

They found his body hanging on the back porch of his ramshackle old house. A passing train engineer had spotted the body early that morning and called the police. Daniel got the call that afternoon. He was at Michael's house 10 minutes later.

The house was eerily quiet with the roommates gone and the back porch scrubbed clean. Daniel sat on the steps, oblivious to the sounds of trains switching tracks and the blue cloud of diesel that hung in the air. He felt hollow and empty inside. Another friend was gone. Another veteran too fucked up to see the possibilities of rehab and redemption. Another part of Daniel that had abandoned him like his parents had a long time ago.

After a half-hour stupor, Daniel walked slowly over to his bike. He kick-started the Triumph and sat there for a long time, oblivious to the rumbling beneath his feet. He slowly slipped the bike into gear and rode away. He rode aimlessly through the city, out to the suburbs, and back again to his home. It was too late to call Michael's parents. That would have to wait until the next morning.

Michael's estranged parents were called the next morning and one of them left a message for Daniel with his roommates that afternoon. Michael was no longer their son, the voice told Sally. Michael's erratic behavior over the past few years had alienated him from everyone in his family. Neither mother nor father would be attending his funeral.

His parent's refusal to deal with the death of their long lost son didn't surprise Daniel. But it did leave him with a deep sadness. Even if Michael had totally screwed up his life, which he certainly had, he still deserved better than that from his parents.

Now it was up to Daniel to make the funeral arrangements by himself. He called Colleen and left a message with her roommate. The girl said she'd try to get a hold of Colleen but that Colleen was out East interviewing for a job. No one knew when she'd be back on campus.

Daniel paid for the service himself and based on one of their drunken conversations eons ago, he had Michael's body cremated.

There was a brief service at the cemetery with only Daniel and a few old high school classmates in attendance. Colleen still hadn't gotten back into town. Daniel watched the cemetery attendant place Michael's urn in a nondescript mausoleum built especially for cremated remains. Everyone else quickly dispersed and Daniel was left alone to face the small bronze plaque that covered the final resting place of his best friend.

Daniel sat in a corner by the brick structure for a long time, staring at the brass cover plate. The cemetery attendee left him alone with his friend. A few other folks arrived to visit their loved ones but Daniel didn't notice them come or go. He silently swore at Michael, telling his old friend what a dumbshit he was. How fucking stupid he was to do such a thing. How he'd become the total cluster fuck he always said he didn't want to become. A tear welled up and slowly ran down Daniel's cheek. He swallowed hard against the catch in his throat and slowly shook his head.

Daniel told Michael how much he loved him. How much he missed him and would for the rest of his life. He talked about losing Colleen. Summer was gone and he'd probably never see her again either. He lamented the loss of his three best friends in the whole world. Now they were all gone from Daniel's life. He was, once again, all alone.

Winter Respite

Colleen knew her life was about to change irrevocably in the very near future.

School was almost over. Just five brief months to go and Colleen would graduate. She already had three great job offers in the publishing industry. Three opportunities to use the skills she'd honed over the last several summers and during the school year. She would be able to call herself a professional journalist in the real world.

But there were still several unresolved issues she had to deal with. Issues that got even more complicated by Bradley's continuing insistence on seeing her every chance he had. Despite a hectic class schedule between the two of them, Bradley still made time for romantic dates nearly every weekend. He would buy out an entire restaurant just so they could dine alone. There were several quick trips to Chicago for opening night of some of the best plays from Broadway. If they stayed the weekend, it was always in a two bedroom suite on Colleen's insistence. Bradley demurred to her wishes but always under a lighthearted protest.

Bradley was open and upfront about what a marriage into the Barrington dynasty would mean for Colleen. He gave her every reason to believe that such a marriage would be a fairytale come true. Throughout her dormitory and on campus, the announcement of their engagement had become just a matter of time and formality. Everyone assumed they would be engaged over Christmas and married right after graduation.

Then there was the issue of Daniel.

Just the day before, Claudia had confronted Colleen as she was walking across the quadrangle the last day of class. The princess broke away from her posse and strolled up to Colleen and stood in her way. Claudia wore a mask of smugness and walked with the posture of a prizefighter. The dark-haired beauty stood erect and firm. She was back in charge and wanted to make sure that Daniel's bitch knew it.

"Hey, Red," she announced as she stood face to face with Colleen.

"Colleen Fitzpatrick is my name," Colleen threw back, standing her ground.

Claudia ignored the comment.

"Your war hero isn't so smug any more, is he?" She asked.

"What do you mean?"

"Daniel caved in, that's what I mean. All that bravado of his was just for show. When the chips were down, Daniel showed what he was really made of...a spineless piece of nothing, that's what."

"That's not how I heard it went," Colleen answered in a calm voice, returning Claudia's smirk with her own penetrating stance.

"You heard wrong, Red," Claudia snarled back at her.

Colleen smiled in return.

"He's such a loser anyway. I don't know what I saw in him in the first place. He'll never make it in this town. My dad will see to it that no employer gives him a job. Nobody screws around with me and gets away with it."

“Do you want to see the list?” Colleen asked.

“You bitch.”

“Why all the anger and hostility toward Daniel if you dumped him?” You got what you wanted. You won, Claudia.”

“Screw you!” Claudia turned and started to walk away, but stopped and swung around to face Colleen. “Oh, one more thing...”

“Claudia! You’ll get over it, really!”

Claudia’s face turned beet red. Her body stiffened and her fists clenched. The bitch didn’t care, she realized. Daniel was free again and his old flame didn’t care. That miserable son of a bitch threw away his chance of a lifetime with her for this redheaded piece of nothing standing in front of her. And the Mick didn’t even care!

“Oh, screw you, bitch!” was all she could come up with as she left in a huff.

When Colleen got back to the dorm to finish packing for home, there was a message that her mother had called. She grabbed the hall phone and called her back.

“When are you coming home?” Her mother asked.

“I have a couple of things I need to do first.” Colleen said.

“Are you coming home tonight?”

“I don’t know. It depends.”

“Depends on what?”

“It just depends! I’ll see you tonight or tomorrow,” Colleen answered in a calm reassuring tone of voice.

“OK, I love you, dear.”

“I love you too, mom.”

Colleen finished packing her bag and locked up her dorm room. She walked down the quiet hallway and into the lobby area. The lights on the Christmas tree had been turned off and the RA’s desk was empty. The holidays had officially begun. Mrs. O’Reilly was by the front door, ushering out one of the last girls to leave. She turned to Colleen with a bright smile on her face.

“Colleen, off for the holidays now?”

Colleen put her travel bag down. “I am, after I take care of a few things.”

A grin hit Mrs. O’Reilly’s face. She motioned for Colleen to step aside as a couple girls walked past. “I’ve heard several of the girl’s comment, between giggles, that you might be going out East during the holidays?"

"I do plan to go out East, too! Yes, Mrs. O'Reilly, your spies are correct."

The dorm mother waved at several girls who scurried by and motioned for Colleen to sit in one of the lounge chairs. "Can I assume, dear, that you've made up your mind about Bradley? I hope I'm not being too presumptuous to ask?"

Colleen shrugged her shoulders. "Life can get pretty complicated sometimes, don't you think?"

"You asked before if Bradley made me happy. Well, I thought about that a lot since we last talked. I thought about the times I've spent with him and all the wonderful things we've done. The experiences we've had together and the plans he's made for our future. Any girl would be very lucky to have a man like that for a husband."

"So you've decided?"

"The only constant between Daniel and me is uncertainty. It's just the opposite of Bradley. With Daniel, it's like living on the edge … I read somewhere that parents are usually the most important source of love and support in early childhood development. If someone doesn't have that love growing up, they often go looking for it without even knowing what they're looking for."

"And…" Mrs. O'Reilly added, "when they think they've found it, they tend to hold on for dear life."

"Exactly, I think that's what happened to Daniel and me."

"Could be."

"Bradley offers me a set future, a guaranteed easy life forever more. Security, kids, solid family structure, weekends in the Hamptons and vacations abroad - just what my parents would want for me. There's no question in my mind that's what everyone expects me to do. Everyone says Bradley and I are meant for one another."

Mrs. O'Reilly just sat and listened. She said nothing as Colleen went on.

"Life with Daniel, on the other hand, would be totally unpredictable. It would be like a journey that could end in uncertainty at any time. It would be so different from how I was raised and the expectations my parents have for me. It would certainly mean issues with my mother and her friends. It would be an entirely different lifestyle than with Bradley. The differences are about as clear and starkly different as they can be. And there would be no guarantees that a relationship with Daniel would even work out."

"So, is living on the edge bad?" Mrs. O'Reilly asked.

"No, not bad…just different. That's not the world I grew up in," Colleen answered.

Mrs. O'Reilly tried to offer reassurance that she understood the confusion Colleen was feeling. "My mother used to say to me; 'Bridget, you have to be careful not to fall in love when you're not ready for it.'"

Colleen moved uncomfortably in her chair. Intensity was written all over her face. "But when is the right time to fall in love?" Colleen asked. "You don't schedule it like orthopedic surgery. It's something that happens. And it happened to Daniel and me. Although I couldn't see it...I couldn't admit it at the time. But I don't' regret it for a single moment. It was wonderful… but we lost it." She looked past Mrs. O'Reilly, out at nothing for a moment, her eyes transfixed into space.

"Colleen," Mrs. O'Reilly answered. "There is no such thing as two people meant for one another. People enter into relationships when they're emotionally ready. Or they fall out of them for the same reason. It's all a matter of adjusting and adapting to the other person, accepting their faults and shortcomings and looking beyond that for the true connection with that person."

Colleen was at a loss. "Maybe that's what happened to you and Daniel. Neither one of you was ready...at that time."

Colleen shrugged her shoulders. "Now I have this wonderful opportunity to be with Bradley for the rest of my life," she said. "He's everything I ever thought I wanted in a man. He can offer me an exciting life. Aside from the material things, Bradley is a good man. He's a thoughtful person, a kind and considerate human being."

When Colleen was done, she looked up to see that Mrs. O'Reilly was still just smiling at her.

"Besides, I swore I'd never be vulnerable with a man again. Going back to Daniel would be taking all kinds of chances. It would be a tremendous risk. And I'm not a risk-taker."

Mrs. O'Reilly pointed her finger at Colleen. "Colleen, you are a risk-taker! You may not realize it yet but you are one of the biggest risk-takers I've ever met."

Colleen was astonished at her statement.

Mrs. O'Reilly's body moved in fluid motion, "You've never let your background distract you from the task ahead. I don't know of any other young woman who has pushed herself as hard as you have. You've earned a great education, had wonderful work experiences and endless possibilities for your future. You're focused and driven. You've matured into a strong vibrant woman."

Colleen didn't know where this was all leading.

"My blessed mother told me a long time ago," the dorm mother began, "that there are two kinds of love. Perhaps you might call them two levels of love. The first is what they call love at first sight. They see another person and they fall in love with their looks, their personality, their beliefs and many other wonderful attributes. Those are all good solid reasons to love someone else. And for many people, that kind of love can last a lifetime."

"What is the other kind of love?"

"The other kind of love is much deeper than the first. It's that intimate bond between two people who create a relationship based on mutual respect, admiration for the other person just as they are, not for what they hope to become or what society thinks they should be. It's an unspoken, special communication that two people have with one another where a simple glance between them can speak volumes."

"This second kind of love only grows over time. It's nurtured and challenged by the changes both individuals go through during different periods in their lives. And it's tested in a wide variety of ways. If both parties are willing to work at the difficult task of living with another person, they have a very good chance of attaining lasting love."

A smile began to grow on Colleen's face.

"Colleen, you've become your own person, beholden to no one. So I think the real question you have to ask yourself is how do you compare your relationship, your love for Bradley now, against the relationship you once had with Daniel?"

She leaned in closer to Colleen. Her voice dropped to almost a whisper. "Remember that the only way to achieve real intimacy with another person is to allow yourself to be open and vulnerable. Vulnerability can unlock emotions at the very deepest level. Taking a chance widens the scope of being alive."

"But..?" Colleen began and smiled back at her.

"Let's set aside this state of confusion you seem to be in." Mrs. O'Reilly said. "Is there something missing in your life? And how would you feel if it was still absent a year from now?

Colleen gave her a pensive look.

"Or try this. Is there someone you feel you could call at a moment's notice, for anything and they'd be there?"

"Oh, that's easy," Colleen answered.

"Perhaps you have your answer!" Mrs. O'Reilly said with a grin, "The only risk you'll ever regret … is the one you didn't take."

Colleen smiled at her.

"You know what you have to do."

"Yes, I think I do," Colleen answered.

A light snow had begun to fall as Colleen walked out of her dormitory. She tightened up the collar around her neck and dug her gloves out of her coat pocket. It was quiet and still on campus. Most of the dorms had emptied out earlier that evening. Now, as Colleen walked across campus toward the parking lot, she only passed a few stragglers who were hurrying to meet their parents or to catch a ride home.

The snow was everywhere; blanketing the entire campus with one long brush stroke of soft white. As she walked along, Colleen thought about all the times she'd spent passing through that area and never once stopped to look and appreciate the beauty all around her. She looked for a moment at the small chapel and its stone bell tower. She gazed over at the academic classroom buildings and the student center. The student commons was quiet; locked down for winter break.

Once she reached the center of campus, Colleen sat down on a small bench sheltered under a tall oak tree with its dull leaves still clinging to several branches. She thought about the times she and Bradley had walked through the center, debating where to go next so that they didn't have to go back to the dorm before curfew. She thought about the times Daniel had walked her to her dorm after her last period class. Both men had been a major part of her life on campus.

The serenity of that winter's evening was beginning to have an almost hypnotic effect on Colleen. She forgot the nip in the air and the light coating of white gathering on her lap. Her mind was a million miles away; bouncing from one school incident to the next. Four years of the good, the bad and the wonderful. Four years had quickly come to an end; the closing of one chapter of her life and the unfolding of another had begun.

Colleen watched the snow falling on the stone and brick structures around her and thought about the snowball fights she and Daniel and Michael had there. She thought about the first time Daniel kissed her under a single lamp light that first fall on campus.

So why didn't it end freshman year like so many other first time love affairs, Colleen asked herself. Why couldn't she get that man out of her mind? What was it that kept her reminiscing about their first encounter, their arguments, their awkward attempts at lovemaking and their glances at one another that spoke volumes no one else could see or feel?

Colleen thought about her first impressions of Garrison Buckley and how that all ended on the front seat of his car. She had never reported the sexual assault nor did she ever tell anyone. Not even her parents. She was ashamed of herself for falling for that guy; and even worse, putting herself in such a vulnerable situation.

She thought about all the advice her parents had given her over those last four years. She knew what their expectations were for her. Colleen understood their fear that she would marry someone beneath her station in life - or worse yet, someone beneath her intellectual prowess. Colleen didn't want to disappoint them.

She thought about Peggy now back in Seattle, facing an uncertain future for herself and her baby.

She thought about her many conversations with Mrs. O'Reilly. The dorm mother had heard it all before. She could see through the complexities of first love. She could bring her homespun wisdom and common sense approach to any romantic challenge. She had given Colleen some very good advice.

Each and every one of Colleen's friends and her parents had an opinion. They may have been at odds on occasion, but in each case the message was clear - Colleen had to make the right decision, and they knew what that decision had to be.

But what was it that her heart was trying to tell her? What was it that even a focused analysis of her feelings toward both men still couldn't decipher? Where was the logic in all of this? On a cursory level it made no sense whatsoever. So why couldn't she let go? Forget about her past and move on to the continuity that marrying Bradley would provide?

Unresolved Differences

Christmas was always the toughest time of the year for Daniel. His mother was usually on a date Christmas Eve or just out partying. He would either stay home alone or find some other lost soul like Summer or Michael and go out drinking with them. It was usually a sad and lonely time he'd just as soon forget.

In Vietnam, he had his buddies to keep him distracted. They'd either ignore Christmas or fake a reason to celebrate it with cheap beer or local hooch. It was less painful that way, pretending there was no one back home who cared anyway. Any diversion was better than the reality of their situation in the bush and their limited prospects for coming home alive.

But this time back in St. Paul it was a different story for Daniel. There were no army buddies to keep him distracted. There would no more booze to numb the pain he felt at the thought of Colleen becoming engaged soon.

He'd been dreading the holidays. For a brief moment there was the fleeting thought of a trip to visit Summer. But Daniel realized just as quickly that it was really just a silly diversion that wouldn't have helped anyway. So Daniel decided to spend the holidays working on his house and prepping for next semester's classes.

Daniel's roommates had all left for home right after Christmas break started. Emily and Katie were the first to go, leaving that morning for Chicago and separate homes for Christmas. They planned to meet up right after the New Year for a short vacation to Florida without their parent's knowledge. That would be their J-term.

Sally left right after lunch, hugging Daniel and catching her ride back up to Duluth for Christmas on the North Shore. She promised to call but probably wouldn't once all her relatives came into town. She tended to get caught up in the holiday's festivities.

It had been a remarkable first semester back at school. Things were starting to fall into place and Daniel's future looked promising. But with the good inevitably came the painful; Fractured dialogue with Colleen, her engagement to Bradley, Michael's death and Claudia's vengeful stance on their breakup.

Michael was gone, burnt up by the insanity of the Vietnam War and his own inability to adjust to civilian life. Daniel had tried to save him. He'd taken on the caretaker role to help his friend but instead had buried him just before the first snow started falling. Daniel visited the mausoleum every week. But it never got any easier reflecting back on a young life so sadly wasted and Daniel's own failure to save him.

Claudia had a new boyfriend. Her badmouthing of Daniel had lasted for almost a month. Until her new boyfriend's stamina and her own carnal satisfaction distracted her enough to forget about Daniel. Any notion that he might get a job in the financial services industry was over. If Daniel were to be successful, it would probably have to be with his own business.

Although the disciplinary hearing was over, Daniel knew that Father Rollins would still be gunning for him. Even though Daniel had shaved off his beard, the priest still scrutinized his every movement. The Dean of Students would be looking for anything else he could pin on Daniel for an infraction of student rules. Daniel had to follow the straight and narrow until spring semester ended and Rollins was gone. His sponsors wanted it that way and Daniel meant to keep his word.

So this holiday, Daniel planned to spend part of Christmas Day at his mother's place even though her new boyfriend would be there. A couple of hours were probably all he'd be able to stomach. He'd continue his work on the house and its multiple projects that were always present. That would keep him busy until Christmas break was over and he could return to school.

He had Friday night and Saturday to kill before Christmas Day. So that Friday night, he found himself in his favorite old high-back chair, taking in the flames flickering in his fireplace. It was good, this old house of his. He was comfortable with his friends living there and the knowledge that it was a first step toward a career in real estate.

Back in Vietnam, on one of his sporadic trips to Saigon, Daniel had picked up a cheap, second hand guitar. He'd begun practicing when the mood struck him. Although he wasn't very good, a newer guitar back in Minnesota had rekindled his interest in trying to create something out of the old wooden string box.

After a light dinner and a glass of mineral water, Daniel retired to his living room. He thought he'd try practicing again. His fingers were strumming the cords and he was humming one of his favorite songs by Tom Rush, "The Circle Game."

He glanced out the front living room windows and in the glow of the streetlight, he could see snow was lightly falling. It was quiet and peaceful outside. Before the snow, the ground had been a dirty brown. Now with the snowfall, it was a soft warm white. The temperature was steadily dropping. It was a good night to be inside by a warm fire and the comfort of home.

Many of his neighbors were either at holiday activities or off to church. It was typical of his Minnesota neighborhood just before Christmas. Daniel would spend it alone - again. He was alright with that. His vision was clear and focused. He would be successful. Even without Colleen in his life, he would go on.

The thought of seeing Colleen again after she was engaged was something Daniel refused to consider. He tried hard to push it out of his mind. Better to ignore reality than face the pain it would certainly cause him.

Daniel raised his voice, forcing out the words even though they hurt. Following tradition, Daniel had changed some of the words to the song just as folksingers had been doing for hundreds of years. He began to sing:

Yesterday
A child went out to wander
And caught a dragonfly inside a jar
And fearful when the skies were full of thunder
And tearful at the ending of the day

And the seasons go round and round
Painted ponies go up and down
We're captured on a carousel of time
We can't turn, we can only look
Behind from where we came
And go round and round
In the circle game

His fingers pressed down harder, strumming against the cords. Perhaps, he thought, if his words got louder a new melody might burst forth from the old wooden box. But one cord seemed out of tune, out of place from the sounds he'd just created. He realized it wasn't the cord. It was the front doorbell ringing.

Someone was at his front door.

Daniel got up and walked to the front door. He peered out onto the front porch. Through the darkness, he could see the shape of someone standing on the front steps. The person was bundled up with a scarf over their head. It was a woman, looking down and rubbing her gloved hands to keep them warm; probably a solicitor, or maybe someone from the neighborhood. He opened the door and walked into the cold porch. His feet made a crunching sound as he crossed the cold wooden flooring. He looked carefully through the front door window down at his visitor. The woman looked up at Daniel and smiled at him.

It was Colleen.

She was standing there in the falling snow, brushing the flakes off her coat that had turned her shoulders white. Daniel looked down at her, momentarily stunned.

"Well, Daniel, are you going to invite me in or am I going to freeze my tush out here in the snow?"

"Sorry, please come in," Daniel stammered, quickly opening the door for her.

Colleen stepped inside the front porch. She pulled off her scarf and brushed the snow from her shoulders and arms.

"I'm so sorry about Michael," she began. "I was out of town when you called. By the time I got back, it was too late. I felt badly but I didn't know what else I could do. I should have called you. I'm sorry."

"No big deal," Daniel began with a shrug of his shoulders. "I mean it was a shock … actually it wasn't really. Michael was in a really bad way … I guess … but I never expected him to…"

Colleen suddenly stepped up to Daniel and wrapped her arms around his neck. She held him tightly. "I'm so sorry I wasn't there for you," she whispered in his ear.

Daniel was taken aback by Colleen's actions but he reluctantly brought his arms up and wrapped them around her. He held her tightly, burying his face in her soft hair. They held each other tightly, oblivious to the cold and the awkwardness of the situation. Daniel released his grip on Colleen, not sure what to say next.

"Still working on your house?" Colleen asked, blinking her eyes to clear away the tears. She looked at the summer porch furniture stacked up in one corner. She moved her hand out front and handed a small wrapped gift to Daniel. "Here, this is just a little something for Christmas."

"I didn't expect…"

"Daniel, it's still cold out here. Can we move inside," Colleen took a step toward the front door. Daniel moved quickly to open the door for her. "How is the place shaping up?"

"It's still a work in progress."

She laughed, "So this is your bachelor pad?"

"Aren't you supposed to be on the east coast?"

Colleen started to take off her coat. Daniel grabbed it off her shoulders. As he did so, Daniel caught a whiff of her perfume. It was intoxicating and made his legs go weak. Colleen was wearing a tweed skirt and soft cream-colored cashmere sweater. Daniel could feel the sweat start to collect on his forehead as he put her coat in the front hall closet.

Colleen looked around and was amazed. The living room was simply, yet very tastefully, decorated. It had been dressed in soft muted tones of brown and white. The walls were an off-white that provided a perfect background for the paintings on the walls and a decorative flower arrangement in one corner of the room. It looked like something out of a model showroom.

"Who decorated this place for you?"

"My girls."

"Girls? Isn't that a little demeaning to women?"

"That's what they call themselves, so that's what I call them."

"Well, they've done a fabulous job of decorating. It's tasteful, yet understated."

"I just told them to study the craftsman style and add their own modern day approach to it. I said I wasn't interested in chasing the latest trend. Just invest in some nice, perhaps classic pieces and build the rooms around those foundation pieces. So that's what they did."

"But where did they get such an eclectic collection of furniture?" Colleen asked. "They all seem to fit so perfectly together."

"Oh, they're all art students. I gave them an allowance. First they went downtown to Donaldson's, The Golden Rule and the Emporium. But everything there was way too expensive, so they started hitting estate sales, garage sales and even the thrift stores along University Avenue. We'd grab Michael's car and run from one sale to the next. It took us awhile to collect all this stuff, but it worked."

"You mean this is all used furniture?"

"Gently used furniture," Daniel corrected her with a smile. "Every stick of it."

"This is not what I expected. Either you or your roommates have very good taste."

Daniel laughed. "I think it's a combination of their interior design skills and my pocketbook."

Colleen noticed the one wall that was covered with bookshelves and piled with books.

"Yours?"

"Mostly; the girls have got some, but it's mostly my stuff."

"Well, I'm very impressed. So how many roommates do you have?"

"Three."

"All girls I suppose?"

"Yes."

"Are you sleeping with any of them?" she asked with a glint in her eye.

"All of them!" Daniel answered with a smile.

"Liar!" Colleen cajoled. She turned to look down the hallway and spotted the Galway shawl draped across the back of one chair. It was the same one Daniel had given her freshman year that she'd returned to his mother - after the letter.

"I'd like to see the rest of the house. Can you give me a tour?" she asked, without commenting on the shawl. "I like the layout of your house. It seems to be very functional."

"It is. It's got good bones."

"Good bones … I see you're learning the jargon."

Daniel took her down the hall to the first bedroom. "This is Emily and Kate's room."

The room was sparsely furnished with a single bed and two pillows. There were two desks nestled up against one wall. A dresser sat along the other wall. Beautiful color prints decorated the opposite wall. There were none of the accoutrements one would expect from a girl's dorm room. It was tastefully yet functionally laid out.

"But there's only one bed," Colleen said. She turned back to Daniel who said nothing but just smiled. Then it struck her. "O….K, next room," Colleen said, turning away from Daniel. "You never cease to amaze me," she said, shaking her head.

They moved on to Sally's bedroom. The bed was piled high with dolls and stuffed animals. There was a single bed in one corner and a chest of drawers across from it. A large desk occupied one corner of the room. On the walls were posters of Bob Dylan, Jefferson Airplane and Janice Joplin.

"What's her story?"

"This is Sally's room. She's a good kid with a heart of gold. We all treat her like our kid sister. As it turns out, she was looking for a big brother, so it all worked out well."

"So you're the big brother?"

"I guess."

They walked through the rest of the house. "So where do you sleep? I only see two bedrooms."

"In the attic. They turned it into living quarters for me. They said it's my New York loft. It works out well. I've got my bed, desk and dresser up there. It's enough room. I spend a lot of time at the campus library so I don't mind the close quarters.

"Just enough room for you?"

"Just for me!"

Daniel led Colleen back to the living room. She sat down on his brown cloth sofa, sinking into one side. She wiggled herself into the corner to get comfortable and started to look around.

"Would you like a drink?"

"Oh, anything would be fine. I might even try some hard stuff if you have any - to take off the chill."

Daniel got a mineral water for himself and a small glass of Smirnoff for Colleen. He raked over the smoldering logs in the fireplace and threw in several more logs on the small flickering flames that were just starting to reappear again. Colleen sat back on the sofa, feeling very relaxed and comfortable. Daniel sat across from her in the high-backed chair.

Daniel proceeded to open his gift. He looked up at Colleen and smiled.

It was a small polished silver bird, a phoenix. Just like the one that Colleen had given him the day before he shipped out.

"It's just like the one you gave me..."

"I know. I see you have a fireplace just like you wanted."

"Thanks for the gift. That was really thoughtful of you. Yeah the fireplace was an added bonus to this place."

Colleen adjusted her skirt, getting more comfortable as the minutes passed by. "You really have become a phoenix, you know. You've changed so much."

"I'm sorry, I didn't buy you anything."

"That's OK, Daniel."

"I mean I had no idea."

"Men can be so dense sometimes. Don't worry about it."

"Sometimes we're slow - OK, most of the time."

Daniel got up and placed the phoenix on the oak mantel over the fireplace. "Here's the perfect place for it. I like your outfit. It's very attractive on you. It fits your shape and your color. Is that a designer label?"

"No, it's my own creation. I call it a combination of snobby Pill Hill and West Bank retro. No sense in following fashion trends when you can make your own style, you know."

Daniel gave her a knowing smile.

The room grew quieter than either of them was willing to tolerate

"You have a very a nice place here, Daniel."

"Yeah, it's my home."

"It's the home you never had."

"You know me too well."

"I know."

They both laughed, then fell silent. They knew the formalities were over. Both waited for the other to begin. They danced with their eyes until Colleen laughed out loud again.

Daniel smiled. "You know, I have to ask you…"

"I know. I know," she took a sip of her drink and set it back down on the end table. Absentmindedly, her lips began to purse and her body got fidgety. She knew the conversation was about to get very serious. And she had no idea what the outcome might be…or where it might lead.

"I thought you'd be on the east coast by now."

"There were some things I needed to tell you, Daniel. But first; I heard about this real estate deal I thought you should know about." She raised her hand to ward off an immediate response from Daniel. "It might be too early in your career to act on it, but Bradley said it's one of those rare opportunities that doesn't come around too often in the business."

"I'm listening."

"It's in the Highland Park neighborhood, not that far from here. The neighborhood is stable. I've driven through there a number of times since it's so close to campus."

"I know that area pretty well."

"I heard that there are three fourplex buildings that might be for sale. The owners are an elderly couple that live in one of the units right now. Most of the apartments are in good shape, but a couple of them need some work done. Not much, just enough to get them back up to code. It's near public transportation and lots of shopping in Highland Village. It's not that far from the river boulevard. It's mainly two bedrooms with one single in each building."

Daniel listened intently.

"Bradley's friend, who is majoring in real estate, said it's his understanding that the owners - the elderly couple - might be willing to carry the buildings on a Contract for Deed. There's nothing in writing so far. I guess you could say it's pure speculation at this point."

Colleen expected a reaction from Daniel. To her surprise, she got none. His face showed neither acceptance nor rejection of her proposal. "Daniel, this might be a very good way for you to get started in real estate with a manageable amount of risk. If you lived in one of those units, you could homestead one of those buildings starting next year. Maybe you could rent this place out or just let your roommates stay here in your absence?"

A smile crept onto Daniel's face. He seemed strangely complacent. "I'm surprised that you would go through so much research for me, Colleen. I know we talked about real estate briefly..."

"Daniel, I can read you like a book. I know when you're focused on something. If you're interested and you think there's a way you could swing this deal, you'd better move on it soon. I understand there's another company bidding on it. It's a new company in town called B.A.I. They're very aggressive. I heard they've put together a very attractive management package and I think they have a very good chance at..."

"Why are you telling me all this?"

"Because you said you were interested in real estate and I thought you might like…"

"Broken Arrow Investments," Daniel said calmly, as he leaned back in his chair.

"What?"

"That's what B.A.I. stands for. Broken Arrow Investments."

"How do you know…?" Colleen detected just the slightest curl of his lip. Silence fell between them. The curl blossomed into a smirk, then a full toothy smile.

"Oh, my god! I don't believe it. Daniel, that's you! Broken Arrow Investments is *you*!"

Daniel added a raised brow to the gleaming smile.

"But how? Was it Claudia's dad? His money?"

"Hardly. She's moved on with her life."

"But how?"

"I have a group of investors backing me. Several board members approached me before the disciplinary hearing. They were looking for someone to manage their investments in real estate. They've formed an LLC and hired me on as their manager. They're just passive investors. I get to do all the work for my part of the equity."

Colleen was visibly impressed and couldn't hide the look on her face. "But that's not why you delayed your trip out East - to tell me about a couple of buildings for sale."

"No. That was just an aside. I like being around you. You should know that by now. I never have to be anyone but myself when I'm around you. You make me feel safe and secure … even if you're so darn unpredictable sometimes. That part about you hasn't changed since freshman year."

"Unlike your boyfriend?"

"Yes, unlike most of the people in my life, including Bradley," Colleen took another sip of her Smirnoff and set the glass down. "It's like it was when we first met. And yet it's nothing like that at all. I think we've both changed a lot. I know you have. And we're both a lot more mature."

Colleen got serious, "Daniel, I think we're far more like one another than either one of us is willing to admit. We both have the same values and principles. We're both willing to work very hard for what we want."

Daniel gave her a look. "Colleen, I told you before we can't go back to just being friends. This is what happens when you talk that way."

"I know that! I said I understood. I'm just here to talk to you. We don't have to be intimate friends just to talk to one another."

"It helps!"

She ignored his comment.

"I thought you were going out East with your premed boyfriend. Why are you here with me?"

"I'm still going, but I'm not going to miss Christmas with my parents. I'll fly back East the next day."

"To see Bradley?"

"He'll still be home the day after Christmas. He's going to Europe with a couple of his buddies."

"Not with you?"

"No."

"Why not?"

"Because I have a new job. It starts part-time right after the holidays. Full-time when I graduate."

Daniel didn't respond. Colleen waited for the question. Finally she said, "Aren't you going to ask me where I got a job?"

Daniel took a long swig of water. He took a deep breath. Now things were getting even more complicated. "I assume some place like New York or Philly or Boston."

Colleen shook her head. "No, downtown Minneapolis. It's with a new magazine just starting up. It's called Minnesota Weekend. It'll be an entertainment piece with some serious articles. I'm starting as a junior writer but if I prove myself I've been promised I can move up very quickly into management and still continue to write."

"Why here?"

"Because it was the right fit. There are a lot of chances for advancement. I think it's the right opportunity for me at this stage in my life."

"Is that the only reason?"

"And…"

"And?"

"And I didn't want to leave the Twin Cities."

"What about your boyfriend?"

"Bradley deserves someone who truly loves him. He's a great guy…" Colleen looked deeply into Daniel's eyes. "But I don't see my future with him."

"Are you sure you know what you're doing?"

"No!" Colleen answered emphatically, "not in the least. It's been tearing at my insides for a long time. Most other women would have jumped at the chance I've been given..."

"So?"

"So, it doesn't feel right. That's all I can tell you. It doesn't feel right in my heart."

"Is that why you came here? To tell me you're staying in the cities and you broke up with your boyfriend?"

"That and something else."

"Like what?"

"You've changed so much since freshman year. I need to know what happened to you while you were gone for those two-and–a-half years."

"I learned to like myself. Simple as that."

"But there has to be more! Like Vietnam? Maybe that program…?"

Daniel tensed up. He shifted his weight in his chair and crossed his legs. Then he uncrossed them again. "No! I told you before. I don't want talk about that. Not now! Not ever!"

Colleen's eyes opened just a little wider. Her voice dropped and she said, "Daniel, this is me you're talking to. You can tell me anything … just like I can tell you anything. That's the bond we have together. We don't have that with anyone else. Just you and I."

"I haven't really talked to anyone about Vietnam, not even Michael when he was alive. Why should I talk about it now?"

"Because, Daniel, I want … I need to know. I heard about your fight with those frat boys awhile back. You almost killed them. Michael said he'd heard you were on some very dangerous missions in Vietnam. I think it's eating you up inside. You have to talk about it with someone."

"No, I don't think so."

But Colleen wasn't about to give up so easily. "You need to let it go."

"There's nothing to talk about."

"Please, I need to know what it was like; what it did to you. What happened to you over there? You're a completely changed person and I have to know why."

Daniel pondered his answer. He spoke slowly and deliberately. "I made it through. For that I am grateful. I guess I was just lucky. A lot of my buddies weren't."

"But not entirely. It's still on your mind. Please, talk to me."

"Why? Are you suddenly feeling guilty?"

The look on Colleen's face was sudden and direct. She turned pale. Her lips began to quiver as if she was about to cry. The hurt feelings radiated off her face. Daniel could see her fingers clutching at her skirt. He felt like a total shit.

Daniel shot to his feet and went over to the sofa. He sat down next to Colleen and put his hand on her knee, "I'm sorry. That was totally uncalled for. I'm sorry."

"I probably deserved it," Colleen said, wiping a tear off her cheek.

"No, you didn't," Daniel put his other hand on her shoulder and drew her closer. "I said I was sorry. I mean it, Colleen, I'm very sorry I said it."

"Colleen looked at Daniel and put her hand over his. Their fingers locked together, holding on tightly. She locked eyes with Daniel.

"So if I don't talk, you won't let up, will you?" Daniel asked as he drew his arm away from her shoulder.

Colleen shifted her weight so she was facing Daniel. She placed her hands over his. "I haven't stopped thinking about you since I first saw you again at the Grandview Theater. I wanted to forget about you. I wanted to go on with my life - to have the perfect life with Bradley. But that wasn't being true to myself. That wasn't being honest. I was trying not to listen to my heart but I couldn't stop. I can't get you out of my mind, Daniel. I think about you all the time. I worry about you."

Daniel felt amazing holding her now, after all this time.

"I can't imagine my life without you in it Daniel." She looked over at the glowing embers. "I need you in my life, Daniel … and I think you need me in yours."

She leaned against Daniel, her back on his chest. They looked at the flickering fire. "Maybe it'll help if you don't have to look at me," Colleen said. She nestled back tightly against Daniel. Her hands rested over Daniel's arms that had now encircled her, crossing over her breasts. Colleen put her hands over his, pressing them tightly against her chest. She could feel her nipples growing hard, but it didn't matter. She wasn't aroused. Instead she felt a deep sense of serenity. This was right. She and Daniel talking about their feelings, revealing truths about themselves.

Being vulnerable with one another.

Napalm Flashbacks

For the next several hours, Daniel rambled on about Vietnam. He had begun to study the country and it's storied history even before he shipped out from Fort Ord. Instructors had hammered home the fact that only by understanding the country could they truly grasp the magnitude of their mission over there. But through his own studies, Daniel had come to a far different conclusion than what the army had tried to foist on him.

Colleen tentatively interrupted Daniel, "Michael said you were involved in some special operations."

"I told you before," Daniel answered in a calm tone of voice, "Michael did a lot of drinking. And when he was drunk, he did a lot of talking. It didn't mean much of anything."

"Daniel."

"What?"

"Talk to me! Is that what your tattoo is really about? I mean was it really about the Hill People of Laos?"

He took a deep breath. "We helped them a lot. That part was true. The tattoo is called the Ace of Death. The symbol is considered bad luck in Vietnam."

"Was it bad luck?"

"It was for the bad guys, but not for the Hawkeyes!"

"Hawkeyes?"

"The Hawkeyes were teams of assassins."

"I don't understand."

Daniel clawed for the right words. "Let's just say it was an eradication program. We were saving American lives."

"We … you mean you … assassinations?" Colleen asked even as she could feel Daniel's body suddenly tense up. She squeezed his hand and began to stroke it gently with her fingertips. She waited for him to speak. Daniel's heart was beating against her back. She held his arms tightly against her chest and waited.

"I was pretty messed up," he said softly.

"But you're not any more. You're no more flawed than I am or anyone else for that matter."

"I did things in the Nam I could never have done back here."

"You were a different person in Vietnam. But you're back now and I love the person you've become. You don't have to tell me anymore."

"No, I do. I have to get it off my chest." He tried futilely to explain the blood on his hands. "You turn off your head and your heart. It just becomes rote behavior and you go numb. You're trained to do what you have to do. You don't think it through. You just do it! You don't dwell on what might happen to you. Dying was just a part of living over there. Only if it comes, you hope it's quick and clean. That's how they trained me. I became a very effective killing machine. Killing another human being isn't hard. It's living with it afterwards that is tough. It didn't bother me…until…I got out. That's when the nightmares would come…when I realized what I had done."

"Daniel, please stop! Don't do this to yourself."

"But I volunteered. I knew what the program was about. I knew what I would have to do. I willingly did it. I did my job. And I did it well."

"That is the cruelty of war. It's different now. You're not there anymore."

Daniel dismissed her plea, "If you had found one of your buddies skewered on a bed of bamboo stakes you wouldn't have a problem eliminating the head of the snake." Daniel's voice was barely audible. "Cut off the head … the body just goes in circles. That's what we were doing."

Colleen was stunned.

Daniel's eyes went vacant. "A couple of them yelled and screamed and begged us not to kill them. But we knew what would happen if we let them live..."

"Daniel, I'm sorry. You don't have to talk about it anymore. Please don't do this to yourself. Just let it be."

"No, Colleen. I need to do this … I joined the grave dancers. At that point, I didn't much give a…"

Colleen flinched in his arms. He grew quiet. When he spoke again it was in a much softer voice. "Sorry," he said.

"I don't understand."

"Bad joke, but it seemed to make sense at the time."

"I still don't get it."

"Grave dancers..."

"I get that part, but why would you think so morbidly? It sounds so fatalistic."

"To help us forget about the reality of our situation, that's why; to laugh at the danger and say we were going to dance on their graves - before they spat on ours. It's all part of the inexplicable insanity of war, because there is no explanation for what men do in combat."

"Michael said you were on Hamburger Hill?"

"Michael talked too..."

"Don't, Daniel. He's gone."

Daniel held his tongue. Colleen could feel his body slowly begin to lose its rigidity. He was growing less tense. His fingers intertwined with hers and gently began caressing her fingers.

"I was there at the beginning," Daniel started to explain. "But I got called back to base and was shipped off to the states. Forty-eight hours from Vietnam mud to the Oakland Induction Center. I missed most of the action. What a waste. We covered all that geography for what? It wasn't worth it. Not one damn life was lost there for any good purpose."

"But you survived, Daniel. You made it. You didn't lose your life there or later like Michael did back here in the states."

Daniel's mood grew pensive and somber. His voice dropped and he barely talked in a whisper, "When I think about the Nam," he began, "I only see a country in ashes. A country burnt out. A people burnt out. Soldiers like me and my buddies all burnt out. A hollow shell of what we once were before the killing and dying and hurting. For everyone involved. One gigantic hellhole. Not worth a good goddamned…"

"Did you always feel that way?" Colleen asked.

"Not at the beginning. But that was probably more a matter of being young and naïve and eager for battle. But after awhile it all went bad. I could see it in the eyes of those villagers every time we were on a search and destroy mission."

"What do you mean?"

"They wouldn't look us straight in the eyes. They'd look down and never look up. They'd just nod if we asked them a question. They all knew the VC or NVA had spies everywhere. If those villagers talked to us, even seemed to talk to us, they'd be suspect. And they might disappear in the middle of the night. Poor bastards were caught in the middle. They were stuck between gung-ho GIs intent on avenging their buddy's deaths and the VC who were looking for anyone to call a friend of the Americans."

Colleen's fingers found a rhythm as she gently stroked Daniel. "I lost a lot of good men over there - none of them friends. A man stops making friends after a while. It's just too hard to keep losing your buddies day after day. One second the point man is walking ahead of you. The next moment he's on the ground covered with blood and screaming for you to save his life. You pack the wounds with gauze wondering if the next bullet is for you. At times, I'd have to push my knuckles deep into someone's flesh just to stop the bleeding. Sometimes it worked. Sometimes it didn't."

Daniel grew quiet. Colleen could feel his heart beating against her back. His warm hands still wrapped around her, pressing against her breasts. It felt warm and wonderful and very secure.

"You don't have to talk about it anymore. We can get through this together."

"We?"

"Yes, we. I'm not going to let you go ever again."

Daniel remained in place, still holding on tightly to Colleen. He leaned forward and gently placed his chin on her shoulder. He smelled her hair and the faint whiff of perfume on her neck. It was intoxicating.

"I used to talk to you in my head all the time Colleen, even when it was going badly between us. It made me think about a lot of things. Thoughts I had buried away and tried to forget back while I was in basic, even AIT and after I landed in country … Then when I got your letter … I died. Right there on that smelly old hospital cot someplace in Thua Thien Province. Nothing seemed to matter after that. So I became determined to be the best damn soldier the army ever had. Or die trying. Didn't make much of a difference to me because I had nothing to live for anyway."

Colleen caught her breath. She held on tightly to Daniel.

"But after I cursed you out and said horrible things about you, I realized that you were right to get on with your life. That made me determined to make something of my life after I got back home. I looked around and recognized I was homesick for someplace to call home, even if you weren't going to be a part of my life."

"And you did."

Daniel could feel Colleen's body tense up. He brushed her hair back and nestled his cheek against hers. She turned her head until it was resting up alongside Daniel's, cheek-to-cheek. "It's done," he whispered in her ear.

They sat on the sofa watching the embers slowly turn to grayish lumps and start to die out. Daniel leaned back on the sofa, still clutching Colleen. She turned halfway around to glance back at him. She leaned forward and released his hands from her chest. She moved around so she was facing him. Her face was serious and somber. It was a look of concern and trepidation at what she was about to say.

"I did something really stupid that I've never told anyone about. Not Bradley. Not my parents. Not Peggy. No one. I couldn't tell anyone … except you. I need to tell you."

"You slept with someone."

"No. Yes … No, it wasn't like that."

"Colleen, you either did or you didn't."

"He tried to..."

"Jeez, Colleen, what happened?"

"I thought you and I were through. I thought I was in love with him and it seemed just right but…"

Daniel looked at Colleen's concerned expression. "You don't have to do this. I don't need to know. It won't make any difference as to how I feel about you, you must know that."

"I need to tell you. I need to do this for me."

"But why? Is your honesty supposed to make me feel good? It hurts just to think about another guy touching you."

"But he didn't do it; I mean he tried but…" She put her head in her hands and started to cry. Daniel wrapped his arms around her and cradled her.

"It didn't mean anything, Daniel," Colleen choked on her words. "I was ashamed of myself for what I'd done. I'd lost control. I wasn't myself. I knew you'd be ashamed of me too if you knew what happened."

"Hurt, not ashamed," Daniel said calmly.

"I never told anyone else. I can't tell anyone but you. I only trust you."

They held each other tightly for a long time. "I want to dance," she suddenly said, standing up. She grabbed Daniel's hand and brought him to his feet, "What records do you have?"

Daniel walked over to a small console next to the fireplace. He pulled out a stack of 45s and some albums. "These belong to the girls but I have no idea what's here." Colleen walked over and began thumbing through the stack. She found a record and pulled it out.

She dropped the record along with several other 45s onto the turntable and turned on the phonograph player. The first song was 'When a Man Loves a Woman' by Percy Sledge. She put her arms around Daniel's neck as the song started. She kissed Daniel gently, but with purpose. "Remember, this was our song," she whispered in his ear.

They danced through the first song, and then the rest of the stack until the last song started to repeat itself. They kept dancing, as if in a trance. Their surroundings were lost in a blur of slow caresses; pressing their bodies as close to one another as the laws of physics would allow.

"Daniel."

"Yes?"

"I want to go to the attic and look for the footprints of birds when the sun comes up."

"Are you sure?"

"More sure than I've ever been about anything in my life."

Daniel looked into Colleen's eyes and saw the brightness of her soul. He knew this time it was right.

A New Dawn

Sunlight was peeking through the small window in Daniel's attic bedroom. It splashed down the side of the wall and spread out across two figures still huddled together beneath a thick comforter. The naked bodies began to stir and untangle themselves from one another.

Daniel looked over at Colleen's auburn hair that had spilled down across her soft cheekbones and closed eyelids. He took one hand and gently pushed the hair away from her eyes. She started to stir then slipped back into sleep.

Daniel rolled onto his back and looked up at the ceiling, pondering the confusing yet wonderful events of the night before. He noticed how the sunlight was coloring his bead board walls with strange patterns of yellow and white. He could feel the warmth of the sunlight on the blanket and across his arm.

Colleen started to stir once again. This time she moaned something softly and wrinkled her nose. She nuzzled her face up against Daniel's shoulder and laid her cheek on his skin. One eye opened, closed, and moments later opened again. She raised her head ever so slightly, saw Daniel, and smiled. "I love waking up next to you," she whispered in his ear.

Daniel ran his hand against her side and across her back, then down her spine coming to a rest upon her thigh. Colleen stroked his chest with her fingers.

Their eyes sparkled back and forth, as they basked in the afterglow for what seemed like ages. Colleen rolled over onto her back, breaking their gaze.

"I knew you were going to make it, Daniel. I saw it in your eyes the first time we met at the Grandview. Then again when we talked at that frat party. You were the same old Daniel and yet you had changed so much."

"Well, you saw something I didn't, at least not at first. I just saw myself back on campus, trying to figure out why it hadn't changed and yet why I felt so different."

"I knew when we first met at that freshman dance that you had ambition. You just needed something to get you going."

"You mean Vietnam?"

"For you it was Vietnam," she said, still looking up at the ceiling. "For me it was that summer on the newspaper. We both had different motivators to drive us. So now we're well on our way and we're both going to be very successful."

"You sound sure about that."

Colleen raised herself up on one elbow. "I didn't always think that of you. Not when you went all hippie on me and dropped out of school. But now I understand what you did and why you did it. I'm sorry I doubted you."

Daniel reached up and brushed his hand against her breast. Colleen closed her eyes and let out a sigh. His fingers moved slowly over her breast. He slid his hand down her stomach. She opened her eyes and smiled at Daniel.

"You've done a lot of apologizing lately," Daniel whispered.

"I must be honest."

"That's what I love about you, Colleen, you're always honest."

"Love?"

"What?" Daniel said, looking over at her with a soft expression on his face.

"You said you loved that about me."

"I do…love that about you."

"Do you love *me*, Daniel?"

"Colleen, come on."

"No, don't Colleen me, just answer the question."

"Of course I love you! So much it hurts just to think about - but you already knew the answer. Why did you have to ask?"

"Because I wanted to hear it from you. I needed to hear it from you."

"It hurt like hell to be so close to you and think about you with someone else. I've always loved you, and I never stopped loving you - not for a heartbeat … ever."

"I know."

"Then why bring it up?"

Colleen brought one leg up and over Daniel's legs and leaned over him. "I knew you loved me but I was confused about my own feelings. I realize now that I've always loved you too."

"Always loved me?" He brushed her hair away from her face and placed his hand on her cheek. "You had a strange way of showing it sometimes."

Colleen kissed his hand. "Not at first. It was 'like' at first. I grew to love you; less impulsively than you did, but it's love nevertheless."

"Questioning it all the time…"

"Not all the time… I'm here in your bed, aren't I?"

Daniel playfully, then passionately, kissed Colleen repeatedly as he ran his hand down the curve of her back. Breaking the embrace, he put his hands behind his head and lay back, taking in all her beauty as she spoke again.

"There was always something between us… Even in the worst of times, there was something that neither one of us could let go. I know it's a bad cliché, but you're my soulmate Daniel. We were meant to be together. It took a lot to admit to myself that you were the only one that truly loved me for me."

"I can't imagine spending the rest of my life without you, Daniel. I hope my parents can grow to like you, maybe even love you as I do - but they *will* accept you if they want to keep me in their lives. I want to be your wife, your lover, your partner, your champion, and the mother of your children. I'm no longer afraid to want what my heart has always wanted … to be with you forever."

Daniel brought her to his chest and whispered, "Forever."

ABOUT THE AUTHOR

Denis LaComb is a storyteller.

Dissatisfied with a single title such as novelist, screenwriter, or playwright; Denis decided that the most apt description of his work would simply be: Storytelling.

Regardless of genre, the essence of Denis' work is storytelling in its purest form. While the characters may change and the story may vary, at the core of all of Denis' work is a story to be told. That story that might involve mystery, passion, conflict, or the intricacies of relationships.

The catalyst for Denis to begin writing full time was a decision to wind down his video production business. With the threat of retirement looming in his future, Denis went back to work on a Western novel he'd written forty years earlier. The original Western project became Apache Death Wind.

Denis has completed three more novels and four screenplays. He has also decided to take some of the made-up tales he'd created for his grandchildren and turn them into picture books. Denis is also writing scripts for television movies and has completed several plays, which he is shopping around for the proper venue.

Denis and his wife Sharon divide their time between Minnesota and Southern California; with long layovers in Colorado, where three of their grandchildren live.

Connect with Denis online

www.DenisJLaComb.com
www.LoveInTheAShau.com

Facebook
www.facebook.com/denisjlacombofficial

Blog
denisjlacomb.blogspot.com

Twitter
@AuthorDLaComb

Other Titles by Denis J. LaComb

Apache Death Wind (Jeb Burns Series, Volume I)

Other Projects in Development by Denis J. LaComb

Debris
Follow the Cobbler
Volume II of the Jeb Burns Series
Trans Con
Wake: The Musical
Sweet Pea & The Gang
Untitled Western Novel

www.ingramcontent.com/pod-product-compliance
Lightning Source LLC
Chambersburg PA
CBHW070759180626
46818CB00001B/16

* 9 7 8 0 9 8 8 4 2 0 3 4 2 *